THE
MUSIC
STALKER

BRUCE J. BERGER

Black Rose Writing | Texas

First printing

ISBN: 978-1-68433-791-0
PUBLISHED BY BLACK ROSE WRITING
www.blackrosewriting.com

Printed in the United States of America
Suggested Retail Price (SRP) $20.95

The Music Stalker is printed in Calluna

*As a planet-friendly publisher, Black Rose Writing does its best to eliminate unnecessary waste to reduce paper usage and energy costs, while never compromising the reading experience. As a result, the final word count vs. page count may not meet common expectations.

PRAISE FOR

THE MUSIC STALKER

"A captivating family portrait with an enigmatic piano prodigy at its center, Bruce Berger's THE MUSIC STALKER sings. In arresting prose, Berger offers searing meditations on music and mental health, spirituality and Jewish identity, passion and anguish and fear—leaving the reader gasping for breath."

–**Patricia Park,** author of *Re Jane*

"Descriptions of Kayla's responses to her music, as well as her audiences', were right on track, especially the sense of transport, the departure from her physical surroundings, that she experienced when she played, not just performing in front of an audience, but even in solitary practice by herself."

–**Don Greenfield,** Ph.D., Musicology, Princeton University.

ALSO BY BRUCE J. BERGER

THE FLIGHT OF THE VEIL

Winner — Illumination Bronze Award in General Fiction

"A well-crafted tale about trauma and miracles."
-Kirkus Reviews

"In the intelligent historical novel *The Flight of the Veil*, a psychiatrist returns to places that were treacherous in his childhood, reconciling internal contradictions."
-Clarion Reviews

"Berger has created a compelling Everyman who must wrestle with grand theological questions: In times of great calamity,
why does God save only some?"
-Stephanie Grant, author of *Map of Ireland* and *The Passion of Alice*

"The text skirts between fantastic realism, real realism, and a protagonist who has not taught himself how to go entirely insane..."
-Carolivia Herron, author of *Thereafter Johnnie*

"Provocative character discussions span a variety of topics, including religion, mental health, and family and romantic love, achieving an enlightening balance between logic and emotion. ... Illustrative language is used to render the Greek landscape in gorgeous terms. An intelligent historical novel ..."
-Foreword Reviews

"At its heart, *THE FLIGHT OF THE VEIL* is a mystery novel – the mystery of faith and the illogical presence of hope in the midst of tremendous suffering – and the ultimate connection of all the dots is satisfying, both in plot and theme; it lives up to its opening quote by Elie Wiesel, "Because I remember, I despair. Because I remember, I have the duty to reject despair. I remember the killers, I remember the victims, even as I struggle to invent a thousand and one reasons to hope." ... With deft, vivid prose, Bruce J. Berger's *THE FLIGHT OF THE VEIL* takes the reader on the searing and inspiring journey of Nicky Covo, a man who thinks he has buried his World War II memories, only to have them demand his attention again with news of a possible modern-day miracle."
-IndieReader Reviews

FOR MARTY AND JEAN

THE
MUSIC
STALKER

"I will incline my ear to a parable; I will solve my riddle upon the harp."
–Psalm 49, Verse 5

"My essence wasn't hidden from You when You formed it; rather,
You saw my essence, *Hashem*, with Your own eyes,
as it was written in Your book."
–Psalm 139, Verses 15-16

PROLOGUE

West Caldwell, New Jersey, March 1999

Kayla Covo emerges from her bedroom at six, listens for sounds that might indicate an intruder, and, hearing none, sighs with relief and offers up a quick prayer of thanks to *Hashem*. She dresses modestly in a long black skirt and long-sleeved grey blouse buttoned all the way up. Her dark brown hair, once kept long to emphasize her femininity, is now short, falling to just touch her pale white neck. She wears under her blouse a small Star of David necklace given to her when she was a child, a remembrance of the mother whose instability Kayla has inherited. No one but her ever sees it now.

She makes her way downstairs to make breakfast. In minutes, she sets Jackie's eggs and toast on a plate, knocks on his door to wake him, and slips out of the house to drive to the morning service. The men at *Chabad* don't count her as one of the *minyan*, the ten needed for communal prayers, but she doesn't care. A few will occasionally greet her with a vague smile and wish her good day, but she's ignored by the rest. They feel she's out of place, she knows, inhibiting them by her presence, yet she's compelled to be there at a quarter to seven every weekday morning, and she'll often return for the evening service. Her hands shake from the medicine, but not so much she can't drive to West Orange or hold the prayer book when she gets there. She sometimes stops at intersections when she has the right of way, pulling over to check the traffic behind her for anyone who might be following. She takes twenty minutes to get to *Chabad* when the trip should take only ten.

By the time she returns, Jackie's already off to school. She makes sure that he's taken his clarinet with him, hoping to avoid chasing the school bus again because he's forgotten. He's good at the clarinet, good enough to be a file leader in the band next year, but he's not particularly musical. Kayla's not worried, though. Music has been her life, but it doesn't have to be Jackie's. Yet, she forced him to study piano a year before allowing him to switch to the clarinet at age six. The music instruction she's insisted upon will help Jackie, whatever career he pursues. She thinks a lot about Jackie's path through life, how he views being black and Jewish as paving his way to a good college and beyond. She concedes to herself that he's casual in his studies and could do better, because he's smart. All he needs is focus and motivation.

Kayla changes into a blue sweat suit, dons her Brooklyn Dodgers cap, and goes for a long walk around the hilly, wooded neighborhood. Her doctor tells her she needs the exercise to avoid gaining weight, so she manages at least a couple of miles every day. She varies her route, associating each street with the different bird songs she can distinguish. She's constantly turning over the sounds in her brain and imagining new melodies for violin and cello based on what she hears. Music fills her mind even while she sleeps, and she often wakes in the middle of a violin sonata thrumming through her head, her arm muscles twitching as she plays the complicated piano part. It might be Beethoven; it might be something she's composed in her dreams. If it's new, she'll turn on her bedside lamp and jot notes on the staff paper she keeps at hand.

When she returns to the house, Kayla sits at the Steinway she's played all her life. She might amuse herself with a Chopin waltz or struggle through his B-Minor Scherzo, cringing occasionally if she fails to corral into coherence the blizzard of notes. She's long past the point where she can perform publicly. Although she remembers the excitement and happiness of her brief career and from time to time looks through her scrapbooks—she would never wear such revealing clothes now—she does not resent the way things turned out.

Her brother Max, who often explains how the law is a demanding mistress, gets home from the city late, even on most Fridays. The three of them share their *Shabbat* dinner when he arrives. She wishes Max would try to be observant and serve as a Jewish male role model for Jackie, but

Max is just not that kind of person. For him, religion is little more than a charade and a waste of time, but he cares for her enough to keep their house kosher and to be mindful of not turning on the television in the family room on *Shabbat.*

Jackie's still undecided on religion, she knows, but walks with her to *shul* on *Shabbat* and says his prayers dutifully. He, too, draws stares from the more traditional *Chabad* members, but they're always polite. Jackie's status as a Jew makes him a bit of a mystery to his black friends, a situation Jackie enjoys. He's invited quite a few to *Shabbat* dinner over the years.

Whenever Max gets back from the city, unless it's Friday, he'll often come to where Kayla sits at the table in her small bedroom, absorbed in her composing. He'll often kiss her on top of her head, putting his hands on her shoulders briefly, gently squeezing hello. She'll smile and ask how his day went. He'll occasionally remark upon her work: the notes, the tempo markings, the dynamics, the harmonic modulations, whatever strikes him. He knows a lot about music, too, and she values his suggestions.

From time to time, she plays for him. When the two of them are focused on the Steinway, Jackie shrugs his shoulders and puts on his headphones so he doesn't have to hear. If it's not a Sousa march or a jazzy band arrangement of "Memory" from *Cats,* then he's not interested.

Kayla's friends at the Bellington School of Music help her get her musical creations out to the performers who love them. Her old piano instructor is now an *emeritus* professor and looks after her musical reputation as if he still feels guilty for how things ended. Occasionally, Max and Kayla attend a Sunday matinee in New York at Bellington or Carnegie Recital Hall to hear one of her compositions – a cello sonata or a string quartet, perhaps – played by the world's best musicians. She's cautious as they take their seats, always in the last row, so she can monitor the entire audience and be close to the exit in case she has to run.

When the audiences love her music and heartily applaud, as they always do, Kayla's warm smile returns. Max sees her smile, pleased.

No one recognizes her.

CHAPTER 1

Dear Joseph and Rosina,

This will certainly be a long letter, long overdue, and it's a letter I have to write, but it's one I might not send. Why bother sending something your mother will shred if she gets her hands on it before you even see it? And if you did read it? You might just laugh and throw it in the trash.

You're not bad kids, not at all, but you've been brainwashed. Sadly, I would add, and there's little I can do about it. I stand where millions of fathers have stood before, separated from meaningful contact with their children because ...? Because being a father means little in our society, especially little when judges have to decide custody disputes.

You'll be thirteen this summer, the first time you're required, based on the present court order, to visit me in New Jersey. And yes, I know you hate this idea, screwing up whatever other plans you might've made, but it's only for three goddam weeks in June. Your mother has told you that you have to visit – which she must do unless she wants to go back to court and revisit the whole unpleasant thing – so that's that.

So this letter is the story of my family or, more precisely, the story of your Aunt Kayla, whom of course I live with. And it's the story of your grandfather, Nicky Covo, and your cousin, Jackie, whom you'll also spend time with. And it's the story of Adel Covo, your grandmother, long deceased, whom I know you don't recall.

When you come, keep an open mind about our living arrangements and try to see why things came to be this way. You can snigger behind my back, that's what teenagers do, but in the long run, because I want our relationship to improve, these are things I think you should know.

Keep reading.

CHAPTER 2

Adel Covo doesn't need to set an alarm, because the whispers that only she can hear begin by four in the morning and slowly but surely burn away the fog of sleep. And if, by chance, she's managed to fight off the voices, Nicky wakes her when his alarm goes off. He never gets out of their bed without turning to kiss her, murmur her name, his arms not quite able to circle her large body.

If she were a helium balloon, she'd float to the ceiling and easily pull him up with her, his weight insufficient to keep them on the bed. If there were no ceiling, if there were no house surrounding them, they'd both float lazily into the sky, to be caught by the strong sea breeze and pushed farther into Brooklyn. Their bedroom window faces a broad expanse of grey choppy water, the bay that separates Sea Gate from Staten Island two miles distant. While her husband showers, she lies in the depression her body has made, looking with great longing at the sea gulls, their loud squeals resonating, proclaiming their freedom. They speak a language she understands. She yearns to be part of their flock, to be untethered from the leaden earth, but instead she must listen for her kids.

She recalls fondly the times when she herself could fly, years before she knew Nicky. She'd start early in the morning by soaring out the window of her house in Borough Park, rise above the treetops, and watch the other birds hunt insects and worms. Always hungry, she could not force herself to eat the buzzing, hopping, and slithering meals the other birds loved. Instead, she'd scavenge around the benches of Prospect Park for crusts of bread, for bits of popcorn, for anything a human hand once held. But often, hungry or not, she'd fly east later in the day to land on the right centerfield wall of Ebbets Field, just over the red Bulova sign, and take in the afternoon game. No one missed her at home in the afternoons. Her father was at work, and there was no more bitch of a mother to worry about. Adel had chased her away, trying to kill her with a kitchen knife. Whenever Adel thought about her these days, it was with the sense of good riddance to bad rubbish.

Ebbets Field was where she'd wished she could've lived her entire life. On so many afternoons, Adel could mark the flight of the ball sailing over her head into the bleachers as it rocketed off Duke Snider's bat. Duke had been such a classy, graceful player until he hurt his knee. And more than once she flapped her wings to fly out of the way when Duke reached over the wall to snag what otherwise would have been a home run. And she watched with glee as Gil Hodges dove for a backhand stop of a scalding liner into the hole. And so many times she'd fly to the top of the Dodgers' dugout when they won and chirp her joy.

But her true love was Jackie Robinson, for whom she would've readily given her life. He heard and understood her bird songs. He tickled her heart and always made her feel good about herself. He talked to her in a voice only she could hear and told her repeatedly of his love. He wanted to marry her. Adel's happiness was never greater than when Jackie stole a base and she knew he'd done so just for her. He was hers and hers only.

Soaring unfettered in the air above Brooklyn was a charm of her existence that had stopped forever when she'd been put on Thorazine – brain cleanser, she calls it – and the drug ended her ability to hear Jackie's soothing voice. Losing the good voices and being bound forever into her own heavy, disgusting body were the price she had to pay for getting closer to a normal life, for the ability to work responsibly at a steady job, to have a boyfriend, who became a lover, who became her husband, and who became her partner in creating a family. She can't fly anymore, not when she's a mother of two small, darling kids, not when she's devoted her life to making a home for Nicky. But the bad voices often return, most often at times of stress, most often when she's forgotten – or maybe willfully failed – to take her medicine. The voices remind her she's a horrible person, a good-for-nothing cunt; sometimes they tell her to kill, who or what she's never entirely sure. Maybe just kill the people who look at her funny. Maybe just kill the crybabies.

When she finally gets out of bed, the first thing she's supposed to do is reach for her pills. She's been told again and again that she must take her brain cleanser, that it must be her daily routine, and she tries hard to remember, but sometimes Nicky must force her. Was it Nicky who first put her on Thorazine? She's not sure anymore.

On November 22, 1966, a Tuesday, Adel Covo steps out of her blue robe and into the shower, making sure not to look at herself in the mirror. Despite all the walking she does for exercise and for running errands, fat keeps spreading. She knows it's the pills. Why Nicky keeps telling her she's beautiful she's never understood, but has come to accept. Why he kept asking her out, refusing to take no for an answer, until she laughed and said yes, is something else she's never fathomed, but is immensely grateful just the same, because love had come after she'd long accepted she was destined to live her life alone.

They usually save sex for Friday nights and Sunday mornings, and when it's not their time to be together Adel still thinks a lot about sex. She still lusts after Nicky, five years of marriage not changing how he makes her feel. When he touches her, her body is consumed by firestorm, an inferno over which she has no control. He's tall and skinny, but sinewy; his touch is strong and determined. Ounce for ounce, she's never known anyone else with as much drive. Nicky's love manages to push away the demons from her mind, from the moments of anticipation, their murmured beginnings, through climax and the gradual slowing of their heartbeats. His handsome, dark complexion stands in stark contrast to Adel's pasty white look. They're so different, she doesn't see why they match up so well, but she knows she's the luckiest nut case in the world.

He was the one who wanted children and who convinced her to go along with the plan even though she wasn't sure. She worried she might hurt her children the way the bitch hurt her; even more, she worried she might kill her children the way she almost killed the bitch and would have succeeded had not her intended victim locked herself in a bathroom. But Adel had been desperate to do whatever she could to make Nicky happy, to make him want to stay forever, and she wanted him to have a chance to be a loving, good dad, like her own dad had been to her. Then Max arrived

– what a horrible day! Their baby had to be named Max after Nicky's father, and she'd gone along with the demand. It occurred to Adel too late that she might've named the baby Nate, after her own dad.

As she uses a blue towel to dry, she hears Max bang toys together in his room, happily talking to himself, and she hears Kayla gurgling in her crib. Adel throws on her robe and rushes out to start the kids' day. Kayla first. She's surprised to find Nicky in Kayla's room already, playing with her and talking to her quietly in Ladino, Nicky's first language. He leans over her crib and brings his head just above Kayla's face. Adel thinks once again how much Kayla takes after Nicky, particularly in the eyes, with their tantalizing mix of hazel and grey. Kayla's hair, just starting to come in, will be very dark brown too.

"What're you saying?"

"I was just telling her what a beautiful little girl she is. And how she reminds me of Kal." He'd picked their daughter's name too, in memory of his young sister, six years old when packed into a railroad car with a one-way ticket to Auschwitz.

"You need to say that in English. She should be hearing English." Adel tries to sound annoyed but she doesn't really mind Nicky using Ladino with the kids. When they get to school, Spanish will be a breeze.

Nicky laughs. "Don't worry, she'll be as fluent in English as we are. More fluent than me. Do you mind changing her? I need to get to work."

Kayla's lying on her back in a grey sleeping suit and does indeed need diaper attention. Adel wonders for a second why Nicky didn't do it himself, then sees, of course; Nicky is already dressed in his suit. Changing diapers is mostly a mother's job, anyway. She lifts the six-month-old infant out of the crib, places her on a changing table, and thinks she's as cute as Myrtle, the doll Adel loved as a child. She feels sad for a second that Kayla looks so much like Nicky. It was fine Max looked like his father. That was to be expected because he was a boy, but Adel had imagined a girl would look more like her, but better, slenderer, with straighter and more manageable hair, more alert, more intelligent.

Then Adel's throat tightens as if she were being throttled, and she places one hand on Kayla's head, pressing it firmly down, and the other hand she places on Kayla's feet, pressing them as well. A surge of anger courses through her. Kayla looks up, aware of the sudden change in her mother's aura, and a twinge of fear can be seen in her eyes. Adel sees before her, not Kayla, but Myrtle. She grits her teeth as dizziness passes through her. She grabs the table for support, letting go of Kayla. As Kayla's wide-open eyes are focused on Adel, she cries and struggles to regain Adel's touch.

Adel forces herself to take a few deep breaths as she leans on the changing table, hoping not to collapse. The baby is Kayla, not Myrtle. Adel's dimly aware she mustn't let Kayla fall. Slowly, Adel begins to sing softly, calms down, and her dizziness fades. It's a tune she's heard recently on the radio, from a Broadway show. Music is one of the things, in addition to sex, that help keep her in the real world. In a minute, she's got her bearings and gets back to the business of changing a diaper. Kayla's crying subsides.

Adel has forgotten her anger. She has forgotten what dizzied her in the first place.

CHAPTER 3

It seems right to begin my story with Kayla's Town Hall recital, although this is far from a chronological presentation. I'll explain later what led up to this, as well as what followed, but here we must start if the story's going to make sense.

Your Aunt Kayla was a piano prodigy of the highest degree. The term is thrown around way too much to describe any child who displays virtuosity on a musical instrument at an early age. Most of those deemed "prodigy" are talented, yes, but don't really have the inner drive to propel them to greatness. Years pass, they may study their instrument with dedication, but almost inevitably their talent no longer seems extraordinary, and few can pursue music as a career. Kayla was one of the very few who deserved the term "prodigy."

So. Town Hall. A budding pianist's debut there is more important than everything that came before put together. Kayla was thirteen – getting close to fourteen – when she brightened that stage and, kids, let me assure you that "brightened" is a gross understatement.

The publicity was phenomenal, with feature articles appearing in the main New York papers in the days leading up to the event. The family had been instructed by Herr Lindorf – Kayla's teacher at Bellington – to refuse all requests for interviews of Kayla, because, he said in his heavy German accent, it would make the intrigue much greater when Kayla did perform. But Lindorf himself, if not the entire Bellington hierarchy, gave a lot of information to the media and passed out copies of the professional photographs Bellington had made. The shots selected for the campaign portrayed Kayla as a little girl, making her look perhaps only nine. She'd been posed in frilly costumes, which I knew Kayla hated. They'd stood her next to a grand piano, which looked large enough to engulf her. The articles stressed that Kayla Covo's first full-length recital would be a miracle coming to fruition.

If the publicity bothered Kayla, she didn't let on. It bothered everyone else in our family, though. Dad grumbled that he didn't see why his little girl had to be plastered on posters at the entrance to the subway and likened the Bellington publicity to Nazi propaganda. Mom worried Kayla would be overwhelmed by all the attention. My own unhappiness stemmed from the realization that my influence in Kayla's life was waning quickly, but my concern was more than outweighed by excitement and anticipation. I couldn't wait for my sister to show the world what an outstanding pianist she was.

All Kayla would say is "I've got much more practice to do so everything is perfect."

She spoke of perfection often, and, if there's such a thing as perfection in music, then Kayla came as close to it as a human being can come. From the moment your Aunt Kayla walked on stage to warm applause, she held the audience in her hand and never let go. Her smile said it all. She loved being in front of the hundreds of people lucky enough to attend and exuded an air of extreme confidence, nothing feigned. She knew her power and her abilities. After a modest bow, she took her seat at the Steinway, placed her hands in her lap, and looked down, her gaze beneath the keyboard. All accomplished pianists pause to gather their thoughts before beginning, but Kayla had the habit of stretching the silence almost beyond endurance. While we waited at Town Hall, not a cough could be heard. Then Kayla started to play, and the wait had been well worth it.

We sat on the right side of the audience, to have the best view of Kayla's face. From her look, we knew she'd transported herself well beyond the recital hall into a realm only she could occupy. I'd seen that look many times, a look I interpreted as complete oneness with the music. I'd often asked her to explain where she'd been in those moments, and she could never really say, but it was always clear she'd been *in* the music and part of the music at the same time. The Pathetique that day sang through the hall, beautiful in its simplicity, the first movement pushed by an unstoppable, frenetic energy, the *cantabile* blossoming into an opera, and the third movement attacked with precision and passion. (I don't even know if you ever listen to classical music or know what I'm talking about. You should bone up on this before you get here. Beethoven. Look it up.) At its end, the audience sat for a second as if wanting more, before applause and cheers rang through the hall. Rightfully pleased with her effort, Kayla smiled and bowed, breathing in the love of the audience. More than anything else, she lived for that love.

Then came an even more stunning performance, her rendition of the Appassionata, an unusual sonata to be paired with the Pathetique. Kayla had explained to me that Lindorf wanted her to show off her abilities – she was too modest to use the word genius – on two, not one, Beethoven sonatas. The effect was amazing, the Appassionata accentuating the incongruence between Kayla's slight form and her strength. The piano thundered, every note struck with authority. One couldn't help but wonder how her thin limbs could harness such force. One couldn't help but marvel at how this wisp of a girl possessed the bravado to brilliantly drive through such a difficult piece.

The rest of the recital continued in that vein. For the second half, she'd chosen three works by Chopin – the Grand Valse Brilliant, the G-sharp Minor Etude, and the B-Minor Scherzo – and three Scriabin preludes. Each piece revealed a new side of Kayla, a unique musical sensibility, a polished talent that could hardly be believed in one so young. It seemed the audience's love for her grew throughout the afternoon. Of course, the audience demanded an encore, and she played Ravel's *Jeux d'eau*, a mysterious, complex, and flashy piece, which she completed to yet another standing ovation. Twice Kayla took her bows, left the stage, and had to return because the audience was not satisfied, demanding more. I confess I was among those screaming for yet another encore, even though I had no idea what she might play. I didn't think she'd been working on another encore.

Finally, Kayla sat again at the Steinway, turned to the audience, and spoke as loudly as she could in her little voice. "Thank you so much. I'm so happy to be playing for you this afternoon. I'll finish my recital with a Chopin Mazurka, Opus 17, Number 4." I hadn't heard her play it for years.

It was such a contrast with the Ravel; the Mazurka was a sad, soft, voice of tragedy crying out for solace, a plea for compassion. As its final F-major chord faded away, Kayla sat still, lifting her left hand from the piano with agonizing slowness, and the audience erupted for the final time. Kayla bowed and smiled to the audience once more, but I could see tears in her beautiful hazel-grey eyes, as if she'd just had a heart-to-heart meeting with a dying Chopin.

As soon as we were able to work our way backstage, we encountered the throng of journalists who'd been promised a short question-and-answer session. A small dais had been set up, and Kayla sat in a folding chair, still clutching the roses given to her after the Ravel. Opal, the hired-gun photographer, roamed around taking shots with her Nikon. Reporters shouted questions at Kayla, who sat quietly, not answering, her eyes wiped clear of tears, until the program manager picked one journalist, asked for a question, and then the fun began. Amazingly, after so many years, I can still hear this conversation in my head. That's how focused I was on every detail.

"Ms. Covo, how ..."

"Oh, just call me Kayla."

"Okay, Kayla. How do you explain your great mastery of the piano at such a young age?"

"I love to play, and I practice a lot."

"How long do you practice?"

"Maybe ten hours? Well, on some days, if I'm not feeling well, I will practice only six."

"You don't tire of practicing?" She thought for a moment, probably wondering how anyone could ask such a question. But she'd been coached by Lindorf to consider every question seriously and to answer seriously. "No, never. I love to practice."

"What's next in your career?"

She searched the room for Lindorf, spotted him nearby, smiling broadly at her. He was almost floating off the floor with pride in his very special student, but he wouldn't answer for her, motioning for her to continue. "I want to learn more pieces and learn to play better the ones I already know."

"Did you know the Mazurka was in the Ingmar Bergman movie, *Cries and Whispers*, that came out a few years ago?"

"No. I don't go to the movies." She flashed her smile.

"What do you do for fun when you're not playing the piano?"

"That is my fun!"

CHAPTER 4

Despite his slender build, Nicky eats a large breakfast, which he prepares for himself. That he's not starving in a frigid hut on top of a mountain in central Greece is a fact for which he is eternally grateful, and he still eats to fill the emptiness left over from the hunger of decades past. He remembers all too well how three days might pass without food, the only nourishment coming from melted snow. He scrambles three Grade A eggs with chopped onion; he meticulously butters his toast; he pours boiling water to drip through the ground coffee beans. It takes time – it would be much easier to pour himself a bowl of Cheerios – but he deserves to eat properly. Every mouthful is a luxury, something he never wants to take for granted. While he goes through his ritual, he hears Adel dealing with the kids.

They're happy sounds. On most days, Adel sings to their children, often a tune from Broadway, sometimes her version of a Beatles hit. This particular morning she's singing "The Impossible Dream," although Nicky thinks she's not quite got the lyrics right. He loves her voice, though, which carries with it a tinge of amazement and laughter. Her voice causes a tingling sensation behind his knees. He hums along as he reads in the New York Times about the third anniversary of Kennedy's assassination. Bad stuff, to have to remember that awful day, but the worst for Nicky and Adel was that the tragedy occurred just as Max was born. Nicky was holding his son for the first time when they heard the gasps of incredulity, the crying and shouts, people running back and forth just outside Adel's hospital room. He had handed Max back to Adel and walked out to listen to a radio at the nurses' station, turned up loud enough so everyone on the floor could catch the horrible news.

As Nicky absorbs himself in reading, Adel's voice fades. Done with breakfast, he folds the *Times* and is about to look for Adel to say goodbye when she comes into the room, holding Kayla. Kayla seems quite happy and is wearing the newborn baby outfit that Nicky's old friends from New Jersey sent after Kayla's birth, the pink pants with brown polka-dots and the pink "Daddy's Girl" shirt. It's Nicky's favorite outfit for Kayla. He reaches to take Kayla into his arms while Adel warms Kayla's bottle. Kayla, quiet a moment earlier, whimpers. Nicky tries to amuse her by swinging her in gentle arcs, but her crying increases.

"Look. As soon as I take her, she's unhappy. Must not like me." One can hear the last vestige of his Greek accent, the slightest guttural h.

"She's only hungry. It's a sin to let your child go hungry, you know. Here, give her back to me." Adel retrieves their daughter and tickles her nose, but the crying doesn't stop until Adel gives Kayla a bottle.

"Where's Max? Does he remember it's his birthday?"

"Playing with toys and didn't want to come down. Probably not."

He laughs and kisses her, Kayla between them. He caresses Adel's breast, lets his hand fondle her until he feels her nipple stiffen, then pulls away, grabs his briefcase, and leaves. In his powder blue Mercury, Nicky makes his way out of Sea Gate, through Coney Island, and turns north toward the heart of Brooklyn. As he drives, his thoughts turn to the patients he's about to see.

First comes Ezra, the fourteen-year-old who tried to burn down his family's house, not once, but twice, brought in by his uncle with whom he now lives. Next comes Adrienne, the thirty-five-year-old housewife depressed because she's bored with her life. Finally, the morning ends with Lyle, the catatonic elderly man whose devoted daughter brings him in every other week for what's a fruitless effort to get him to talk. He thinks about each patient, can see their faces, feel their need. They come or are brought to him to have a chance at normalcy and happiness. He works hard to build trust, to get his patients to feel more comfortable with him and with themselves, to get them finally to open up about their problems. He works hard to know what drugs to try. He feels he's as devoted to his patients as a doctor can be. His father – Dr. Max Covo, Salonika's leading neurologist before he was murdered at Auschwitz – would've been proud.

Nicky's office is modestly furnished, but organized to convey knowledge and calmness, as if his patients were entering a library whose every book was in its proper place and whose quiet could settle one's soul. He spends a lot of time adjusting the books on their shelves, making sure the cleaning crew has reached every corner of every surface. He encourages his patients to pace around, look at things, pick them up, if that motivates them to talk. He's spent a lot of time selecting framed artwork – reproductions are all he can afford when he starts his practice – with the purpose of making patients relax: a basket of garden vegetables, a river, a barn, a covered New England bridge.

Nicky opens a file on his desk, thinking to review his prior meeting with Ezra, but his glance falls on a photograph of his and Adel's wedding and he picks up the frame. Despite the photographer's instructions, Adel hadn't looked at the camera, but kept her glance up toward Nicky, a dreamy look on her face. Her right arm circled Nicky's waist and Nicky's left arm surrounded as much of her as possible. She'd needed help finding a suitable dress because the only clothes she'd owned were jeans and sweat suits, but one of her co-workers at Norm's Diner had stepped in to help, and together they'd found a stylish blue dress in the required plus-plus size.

Nicky tries to remember how he'd felt that day. Despite his joy at marrying Adel, despite the presence of his *ersatz* family and their friends at the Brooklyn courthouse, he recalls the gnawing emptiness he fought to hide, the same emptiness he fights to hide every day, the feeling he's an impostor, the guilt always threatening to overwhelm him.

He sighs, puts down the photograph, and the pathetic boy shows up in a few minutes. The boy is painfully thin, as if he's starving himself. His face is acne-ridden, his hair is long, unwashed, and scraggly. He ignores Nicky, sitting across from Nicky's desk, playing with a toy Mercury space capsule. Nicky glances at his notes, but doesn't need to. He knows by heart the sad history of acting out against his immediate family with increasing violence. How Ezra, then thirteen, started a newspapers-and-gasoline bonfire in the basement of his house in a pique of anger and ran without warning anyone. Only raw luck contrived to allow his parents and younger brother to escape. The Juvenile Court could've committed Ezra to a state institution for delinquents, but his uncle intervened, offering to make a home for the troubled boy. So Ezra was granted probation on the condition he undergo psychiatric treatment weekly. Ezra had become Nicky's patient – a charity case – only a month earlier.

"You're thinking you'd like to go up into space, too, aren't you?"

Ezra glances up for a second, a surprised, concerned, guilty look, as if he's just discovering he's not alone. As if he's been caught masturbating. Then, he looks back at his toy, reaches through the capsule's open hatch, and pulls out the plastic astronaut. He says nothing.

"Think you could live in a small place like that for days on end?" Anything to get him talking, Nicky thinks. Use what's available. Let the patient lead. All the maxims pounded into him during his residency jump around in his brain. Nicky is unperturbed and patient. He will work like this for years with any patient who keeps returning. He never lets a patient get the better of him.

"If you went to the moon, like President Kennedy promised we'd go someday, do you think you'd miss your family?"

"I hate my family!" Ezra cries out, loud enough to be heard by Nicky's receptionist. "They're pigs!" He tosses the toy on Nicky's desk and glares at Nicky. Good, Nicky thinks. Engagement. Now, time to provoke even more.

"Your father's a smart man, isn't he? Teaches math, right?"

"So what? You think that makes him good?" Ezra's eyes blaze with hatred. Ezra is telling him without words that the hatred of son for father lies at the center of his aberrant behavior.

"Your mother took good care of you and Alan, right?"

"You're trying to get me talk, but it ain't gonna happen, doc."

"Dr. Covo, if you don't mind."

"I do fucking mind."

Nicky lets that sit for a beat. Not good to rush a response here. He wants Ezra's profanity to linger in the air for a bit. He wants Ezra to hear his own voice. A minute passes, then two. Nicky remains silent, using the pressure of the silence to force Ezra to speak again, and the technique works like it has always worked.

"Did you hear what I said? I said I fucking will call you whatever I fucking want, *Doc.*"

Nicky suppresses a smile. Dead serious now. "You must hate doctors as well as your family, right? I bet your mother never took you to see a good doctor, though. She must've found the cheapest one in Sheepshead Bay."

"You don't know shit about doctors, *Doc*."

"My father was a doctor."

"Yeah, well good for him. Good for both of you. So what's he do now? Play golf?"

Another moment of silence. The anger tells Nicky that Ezra has been abused by his father. In what way, he cannot know at this point, but anger like this at his father – at fathers in general – doesn't arise without a good reason. The uncle hasn't provided any useful information, but, in time, Ezra himself will. Of that, Nicky is confident.

"My father can't play golf, Ezra. He was murdered."

The boy glances at Nicky with uncertainty, for a second letting down his guard and showing a glimpse of the fear lying under the mask, a fear unveiled because of Nicky's use of "murder." It's as if Ezra can sense danger waiting at the door of Nicky's office, a power ready to stalk the boy as soon as he leaves. But Ezra shrugs, feigning lack of concern. "People get murdered." No big deal.

"You like fire, don't you?"

"You know what I did, *Doc*. Stupid question."

"Fire destroys evidence, doesn't it?"

"I don't fucking know what you're talking about."

"Fire destroys everything around it, everything it can, right? You destroyed your family's house. But what were you really trying to wipe out, Ezra?"

"Wouldn't you like to know?"

Nicky senses what Ezra is going through, having to defend himself to an adult, when adults – particularly his father – have been his enemy all his fourteen years. Nicky assumes that he reminds Ezra in some way of his father, which would explain Ezra's resistance, but in the long run that connection can be used, can lead to quicker healing. He feels the boy's pain as he feels the pain of all of his patients, but children are the most difficult. Nicky deems himself responsible for them, as if he had to be the good parent whom the disturbed child deserved but never enjoyed. If he fails to help them, he can spiral into depression himself.

"Here's the thing about fire, Ezra. It never completely destroys. It changes things, but never solves the problems it's supposed to solve. Whatever those problems are will still be there after the fire dies out."

"Shut up, *Doc.*"

"You wanted to burn your house down, and you did. But you're not happy at all, are you?"

"Fuck off."

•   •   •   •   •

Adrienne is next. Before her marriage, she'd worked hard at poetry and had published two well-received books. She'd involved herself in local charities and activities at her church. It all seemed to fall apart after her wedding, almost instantaneously, if one would take her at her word. Yet she wouldn't point to any specific failure or misdeed of her husband, whom she claimed was ideal in every way. Yes, she still loved him, she thought, but her love didn't seem to energize her. She couldn't write a line of poetry, and she stopped being involved in church activities. She'd even stopped seeing her friends. Now, it appeared, her main activity was drinking. For reasons neither she nor Nicky can fathom, she appears to have given up on life. Nicky feels he's all that stands between her and a plunge into deeper depression. He desperately wants to help her.

He's enrolled her in a zimeldine trial, but after a month he sees no appreciable improvement. He wonders now whether to take her off the drug, keep going with it, or add a second antidepressant. Taking her off zimeldine or adding another drug would void her participation in the trial, but that's of no importance to Nicky compared to Adrienne's welfare.

She enters his office and slams the door. "This is the last visit, Dr. Covo, let me tell you right now. I don't need to see you anymore." Despite her threat to stop treatment, Nicky is encouraged because Adrienne shows more emotion than he's ever seen. She sits across from Nicky and crosses her legs, displaying a considerable amount of thigh. Nicky notes that she seems better dressed than usual. She's never worn a skirt to his office before, nor put on makeup, and the dark circles under her eyes have faded. She's getting more sleep. He notices her eyes are light blue, reminding him of a young girl he knew once in Athens.

"You don't have to be here, Adrienne, but I suggest you stick with therapy for a while. We've not gotten close yet to why you're so depressed, why you've lost interest in sex and in life generally."

"No, and that's why I think we should stop. We're not making progress."

"Therapy can take a long time."

She continues as if she's not heard his comment. "And the drugs you're giving me aren't doing anything either." She uncrosses her legs, reaches into her purse, pulls out a lipstick, and paints the dark red around her mouth.

"I wouldn't be too sure that the therapy isn't helping. You don't think you feel even a tiny bit more like your old self? You look better."

Adrienne ignores him, finishes with her lipstick, then blots the excess with a tissue. When she's done, she smiles at him. "Better, you say. Do you think I'm attractive, Dr. Covo?"

He's used to female patients flirting with him or pretending to. It's part of the business of being a psychiatrist to ignore all that, redirect the patient, and get on with therapy.

"How's the alcohol use?"

"I've cut back."

"Good. Tell me about cutting back."

She thinks about this request for a long while. Nicky patiently tries to read her mind. He perceives she's in a state of conflict about therapy. Only part of her wants the whole process to be over. He deduces that, if she'd really wanted to stop, she'd have cancelled, and her improved appearance also suggests she's trying to engage him rather than cut him off.

"The booze wasn't doing me any good. You warned me. You told me alcohol would make everything worse, and you were right."

"So coming here is helping you. You've just proved it yourself. That's why you should continue. I call that a good prognostic sign, heeding what I said."

"But there's another problem, now. It's Ted. He's much less patient with me. He keeps pressing me to fuck him, to get over whatever's bothering me, but I still don't feel like it, and don't know if I ever will." Nicky jots a note on his pad: "fuck." It's the first time Adrienne has used profanity.

"But you love him, you've told me many times."

"That doesn't mean I can stand for him to touch me. It's like two completely different things. I feel a visceral need to push him away. I can't explain it better than that. What should I do?"

"For now, it sounds like you're doing what you need to do if you're not ready sexually. Push him away. Gently, of course."

"But how much longer can this go on? How can I be a wife to a man when I have no interest in fucking?"

"As I've said, it's not likely to be a permanent loss of interest. You're young." He means her hormones will inevitably kindle her desire again, but he's not sure she gets his meaning.

"Do you think I'm attractive?"

"It's not the job of a doctor, to think that or to think the opposite."

"So you won't answer me." She pouts. Now he knows she's toying with him. It's her way of turning the session away from what's really bothering her. He contemplates once again recommending that she see a marriage counselor with her husband.

"Do you want to talk about why you're depressed?"

"I wish I knew. Just bored. We've gone over this a million times. It's all useless." She sniffles, as if trying to hold back tears. "Did you ever think about killing yourself, Dr. Covo?"

• • • • •

When Nicky next enters the waiting room, he sees that Laura – Lyle's daughter – is alone. He wonders for a second whether Lyle's in the restroom, but the concerned look on Laura's face tells him that something's not right.

"Where's your father?"

"He wouldn't budge from his bed. I didn't know whether to call you or what, so I ..." She looks around with uncertainty, as if lost in a deep fog. She's never been there without Lyle.

"Well, come in."

It's been a troublesome case. Nothing seems organically wrong with the patient, who after all is only sixty-eight. A widower for five years, he'd gone through the normal grieving process, had continued to work as an architect for two years, and in retirement had improved his tennis game. Then, without explanation, he'd stopped talking to his daughters, sons-in-law, and grandchildren, barely responded to questions, dropped all hobbies, and spent untold hours lying on his bed, staring at the ceiling. He's been referred to Nicky as a likely depressive, but none of the drugs Nicky uses has any beneficial effect, nor have Nicky's efforts at talk therapy. He gets only one-word responses, with no affect.

"So tell me what happened this morning when you went to get him," Nicky says, now perched on the edge of his chair.

"I honked, as usual, but Dad didn't come out. Then I parked, went in, and found him sitting on his bed in his underwear. I said, Dad! It's time to go see Dr. Covo, and he said no, not again, and that was it. I said, well, you're gonna catch cold if sit here all day in no clothes and he said no, go away, so then I came by myself. I left him there in his undies for God's sake. Tossed his robe at him, but he wouldn't put it on."

"I won't bill you for today. You can go back right now and check on him. Maybe he needs you to make him a cup of tea."

She ignored his suggestion. "What can I do for him I haven't already done, Dr. Covo? How long do I have to keep trying to take care of him, when he's little better than a vegetable? When there's no there there?"

"There's no easy answer, Laura. You can't force him here if he doesn't want to come and, honestly, our sessions so far haven't been helpful. Maybe this is a problem psychiatry can't solve." He hates to hear himself say that, but it has to be said now. "Have you talked to your sister lately? She lives in Chicago, right?"

"Jane's got her hands full with the boys, she's busy at the paper, and she's not going to help with Dad, so there's no point."

He considers this, relates it to his own life's experience. Siblings not wanting to help each other in the care of a parent? It was unheard of in the community in which he grew up, where family always stuck together, regardless of circumstances. For an instant he envisions himself as a doddering old fool confined to a wheelchair, wearing diapers, and sees both Max and Kayla standing near, eager to help.

"Still, unless you've talked to Jane, told her what's going on, and asked her for assistance, you don't know what she'd say, do you?"

"Maybe not."

"A change of scenery might do him good, you know. Take him to Chicago for a week, maybe two. Let him visit with your sister."

Even as he makes the suggestion, he doubts its wisdom. Changing the scenery, as he puts it, usually doesn't work with someone chronically depressed. But he's compelled as a doctor to try; offering ideas based on nothing more than gut instinct is the best he can do.

Before Laura gets up to leave, Nicky's mind drifts back to Adrienne, the flirting, her new look, and her question about suicide. Then he again hears Ezra's rage, even as he's seeing Laura out the door. He feels the absurd difficulty of being a parent. Then he thinks once more of Adrienne, this time envisioning her legs and imagining what must be the feel of her sensuous mouth.

CHAPTER 5

Music has been one of Kayla's earliest memories, the soothing sound of Mommy's nursery songs before she's put down for the night, the calming lullabies. When the nightmares intrude, as they often do, and she wakes screaming in unfathomable fear, it's usually Mommy's songs that divert her thoughts from the approaching monsters. "I've got a loverly bunch of coconuts" –softly rendered, so as not to bother Nicky and Max – never fails to make her smile. Soon, she will forget the dreams that made her cry out.

Less often, it's Daddy who gets her from her crib. He sings, too, but his voice comes from much further away. Her Daddy sings sad melodies, each change of pitch quavering as if he isn't sure where he wants the note to land. "*A la nana y a la buba,* s*e durma la criatura, se durma la criatura, el Dio grande que los guadre, a los niños de los males.*" She loves his songs, even if she doesn't understand, and they settle her as quickly as the bouncier melodies Mommy favors in the middle of the night. Years will pass before Kayla figures out that her father has sung to her a lullaby in Ladino, before she comprehends that the *Dio* of his song is God, the same God in whom her father no longer believes.

Even after Mommy or Daddy have returned to their room, sleep still evades Kayla. The dim light from the hallway lets her see just enough to scare herself again. She picks up her head and looks around, searching for the awful hurtful thing that's hiding in the shadows, looking at her, watching her, and waiting for its chance. Although she doesn't yet know about death, she fears death slinking through the closed window from the nearby sea, its salty smell ensnaring her even before its frigid hands close around her neck. She fears the ceiling of her small room caving in on her as she lies paralyzed, helpless to avoid the crush of falling plaster and wood. Most of all, she fears the monster in the living room creeping closer, its black and white ivory a field of mysterious power. Every night she knows it inches its way up the stairs, determined to rip her apart. She's the only one who can hear its footsteps and its threatening voice.

She doesn't yet have the words to explain how she's been selected.

CHAPTER 6

He does not remember how the affair began.

One minute, she wandered about his office, looking at its decorations, chatting. He'd gotten up from his chair. Was it he or Adrienne who locked his door? He couldn't recall. All he remembers is that he approached Adrienne from behind, putting his hands on her shoulders as if to give her a friendly squeeze, then somehow turned her and kissed her that first time. He hadn't anticipated her voracious response. He hadn't anticipated anything, but that's how it must have started. Her appetite overwhelmed him. That's how it certainly continues.

He violates the oaths of his marriage and his profession, yet cannot extricate himself from Adrienne's grasp. She is the spider into whose web he's fallen, against which he's powerless to escape no matter how hard he fights. The more he struggles, the more he feels ensnared. So he carries on with her over years, seeing her at a motel every month or two. She stops being his patient, stops seeing any psychiatrist, and never talks about depression or the lack of purpose in her life. Her husband leaves her for another woman soon after her affair with Nicky starts. Adrienne claims that her husband was ready to leave anyway and that their affair has nothing to do with the breakup of her marriage.

When he's home with Adel, he still feels great love for her, but now realizes that the love is mixed with pity and remorse, neither of which he feels for Adrienne. He pities Adel for her illness, a malady that can never be cured but, at most, can be ameliorated. He feels remorse for his lack of fidelity, for having led Adel into marriage and family, for having made a promise that he's betrayed. His sense of honor will not let him think of leaving Adel, and he could never leave his children. He must become two people, a loving husband and father at home, and whoever he has become when he's not home.

His two personas tear each other apart.

CHAPTER 7

Just two days earlier, the temperature in New York reached eighty-six and her neighbors were still wading in the Atlantic, but now a chill has settled over the area, a chill that reminds Adel that it's the World Series time of year. She knows that the World Series has started in Boston, but what happens to the Red Sox and Cardinals in the fall of '67 holds no interest. When the World Series doesn't involve the Dodgers – and now, without Sandy, they couldn't win the pennant – there's no team to root for, and when it doesn't involve the Yankees, there's no team to root against. This year, minus their ace, the Dodgers were crappy.

Baseball holds less interest for Adel as well since she had to give up the hope that Jackie, whispering just inside her left ear, would tell her by the fifth inning how each game would end. Jackie became insanely jealous, she recalls, when she'd fallen in love with Nicky. His messages of devotion to her and his tips had ended as suddenly as they began. As suddenly, perhaps, as Jackie's own career ended when he quit rather than play for the Giants. She thinks that she should have been betting on the games like crazy when she had the chance.

Just as well that she doesn't have to watch. It's good to keep the television off, turned on its rotating table so the screen faces the wall. Now, whoever's inside can't spy on her as she goes about her business. She spends every ounce of energy in running after the kids, and shopping, cooking, cleaning, washing the clothes, dusting the furniture, and paying the bills. Good thing that she spent years working at Norm's Diner. Almost everything she does now to take care of her family she learned at Norm's, under much more pressure. Norm taught her to cook and clean, to manage time, to assess needs, to shop wisely, and to keep the books. She'd learned an awful lot from him, the most important of all was that she could function in the outside world despite her bizarre thoughts. Without Norm's teaching, she would be at a loss now and unable to raise a family.

To be doing it all for Max, Kayla, and Nicky makes the strain of keeping herself together worthwhile. Nicky loves her in the way she wants to be loved, fully, with reverence, with passion, with enthusiasm. And the kids now are even more important to her than Nicky. What would she be, she wonders, if she'd never had them, if these two perfect, happy, wonderful, amazing creatures had never existed?

And thank God there are no more assholes to deal with like those who ate at the diner, the ones who treated her like shit when she served them. She's a married woman now with a family, a woman not to be treated like trash, not like just another fat girl to be made fun of. She recalls with great satisfaction how she punched out one of the worst customers at Norm's – fuckin' tried to kill him and almost lost her job because of it – and how the dickhead never came back. A brief smile flits across her face as she can still feel her fist smashing into the side of the moron's head and hear his gasp of shock. She can still feel the sharp pain in her knuckles and hand caused by the blow. It's a tiny little jump from that thought to wondering how it would have felt if the knife she'd held had cut into the bitch's heart.

Having dried and put away the lunch dishes, she comes into the living room to see Max once again climbing onto the bench of the Steinway. Kayla—her dark brown hair already shoulder length, tied up with a bright pink bow – sits on the floor on the other side of the room, looking first at *Goodnight, Moon!* and then glancing at her brother. Nicky had sworn that their future kids would take to the piano if it was there for them to see and touch and insisted on buying it when Max wasn't even three months old. How right he'd been! Since Max has been able to find his own way to the keyboard, he can't stay away, and Adel is pleased as well to see how her brother's efforts at the piano fascinate Kayla.

"Look, Mommy!" With the index finger of his right hand, Max plays "Mary Had a Little Lamb." Adel is impressed. The boy is not yet four and can already pick out a melody. She can hardly believe that her still chubby-cheeked son, not yet in kindergarten, plays the piano. If only her father could have been around to see this. Nate Miller had loved music too, mostly classical.

"Can I sing with you?" she asks.

Max grins, proud that Mommy wants to join him. He's learned that, when he controls the piano, he influences everything going on around him. So he plays the song again, louder, to make sure the piano dominates his mother's voice. Adel coaxes him to play it yet again, but she doesn't forget to turn to smile at Kayla, not wanting her to be left out. Kayla sees Adel's smile, pushes her book away, and crawls toward them.

"All right, now try with two hands." Max takes up the challenge. With the index finger of his left hand, he mimics what his right hand does, but an octave lower, hitting all the notes correctly. Then, without further urging, he plays the song again, but lets the fingers of his left hand hit different notes and listens to the emerging harmonies. Within minutes, he's making chords, and the harmonies blend well with the melody. After "Twinkle, Twinkle Little Star," Adel tells Kayla – who by now is on her lap, watching intently – that it's time for her nap. With sorrow, Adel explains to Max he must stop. Max protests, but when Adel reminds him that Kayla – his "lovey" – needs her rest, he goes in search of a book.

In just another week, the melodies and harmonies that Max coax out of the piano become more complex. They often push away the voices Adel still hears inside her head, frequently the voice of her mother telling her how bad she is. Max's music also pushes away the voices of others, the perennial chorus of strangers intent on making her hurt herself. The voices don't bother her as much as they used to, but sometimes echo endlessly from one end of her brain to the other. The voices make her stare into the distance and take her from the concrete world.

Early one December afternoon, Max again sits at the Steinway. Kayla kneels on the floor, close to him, playing with a doll. Adel watches, not wanting to interrupt. As Max plays, coaxing new melodies from the piano, Kayla looks up at him, listening intently, putting down her doll. A smile crosses her face, and now she picks up the doll and makes it climb the leg of the piano bench to sit next to Max. Max notices he has Kayla's rapt attention. He gets down from the bench and tries to kiss her on the top of her head, but she squirms away, grabs her doll, and toddles over to Adel for a hug. Adel must also hug the doll.

Today will be a special day for Max. Nicky's told Adel that it's time to take him to a real piano teacher. Yes, Max is only four, but Nicky has learned of a Sr. Cantelli who lives just blocks away and teaches children that young, if they seem mature enough. Adel has mentioned to Max the possibility of taking lessons, explaining to him carefully what that means, what piano practice will mean, and Max is excited. Nicky's got it arranged. Adel will walk the kids over this afternoon and see what Sr. Cantelli says.

After her hug, Kayla makes her way to the piano and reaches up to press the keys for herself. Adel thinks that it's cute how Kayla tries to act like her big brother.

CHAPTER 8

Before my sister became one of the world's most beloved prodigies, the piano was my instrument, not hers. It was as if I was necessary to pave the way for her to become the true star, that the plan all along was for her to ascend well beyond me, for me to fall back. And so I did. Whose plan? Damned if I know. Why should there be such a plan? I haven't the foggiest.

But I'm getting ahead of myself.

When I was four, just four I believe, my parents decided I'd be given piano lessons. My instructor's name was Mario Cantelli. Sr. Cantelli – I always called him "signor" – lived not far from us in Sea Gate. He was a tall, grizzled man with thinning white hair. He wore a coat and tie, even in his own house, and well-polished black shoes, and glasses tied to a lanyard around his neck. He must have made quite an impression upon me, because I can picture him now just like I saw him yesterday. I learned eventually that he'd left Italy years before the war. Dad liked Italians, maybe because of their common Mediterranean heritage, and they chatted in Italian on the occasional Sunday afternoons when Sr. Cantelli would invite his students and their parents to his house for informal recitals. Dad had learned Italian in the displaced persons camp after the war, nothing about which I knew then.

When I started lessons, Mom would push Kayla in her stroller as she walked me the five blocks to his house on Atlantic Avenue. Mom would sit in Sr. Cantelli's front room, from where she could watch the ocean laid out in front of her and hear, but not see, the lesson. She had books to keep Kayla occupied, and I don't recall Kayla ever making a fuss. What I remember is that occasionally, as I played for Sr. Cantelli, I could hear Mom singing softly, trying to mimic the music. It bothered the heck out of me, made it harder to concentrate, but Sr. Cantelli didn't seem to mind.

Now that I think about it, it could have been Kayla whom I heard.

I felt very important beginning lessons. I loved the piano and wanted to learn all there was to learn. I made progress immediately, impressing Sr. Cantelli and my parents. I was only six when I performed in my first recital at the Brighton Beach Jewish Center, a Chopin Waltz in E-Minor, which I'm sure you don't know from a hole-in-the-wall. But whatever. I never hear that piece now on the radio without flashing back to that Sunday afternoon and feeling nostalgia and pride. That recital was the peak of my career, but of course I couldn't have realized it. At six, I didn't even have the concept of a career; I knew only that more complicated pieces lay ahead and that I was eager for them.

By the time I was six, Kayla – not quite four – had begun studying with Sr. Cantelli too. And so, inevitably it now seems, it was Kayla who ended up at Bellington, who found herself admired by tens of thousands of fans. Everything that might have been mine if the genetic dice had rolled a different way was given to her. She had the unworldly talent, and I did not. As good as I was, Kayla was light-years better.

CHAPTER 9

It's much colder in Grenoble than Brooklyn, Adel thinks, as she tries to watch the Olympics. Then she turns off the television after a few minutes, uninterested and mildly sick. Following the skiers down the screen makes her dizzy, the dizziness brings on a headache, and the headache leads to nausea. She needs to get out of the house and enjoy her own sport.

Adel loves to watch the grackles, starlings, pigeons, gulls, doves, geese, ducks, and every other species of bird seen along the Atlantic shore, using the pair of Zhumell binoculars that Nicky gave her as a wedding present. Watching birds and cooking are her only hobbies, although cooking has become more of a chore. Watching birds is always a pleasure, though. She's been walking for exercise for years, and Dad taught her on their walks together to spy on the birds. She can get so close without them realizing she's there! Their first vacation – their only vacation because he died not long afterward – had been in the mountains of western North Carolina, just after she'd started on Thorazine. Every day they hiked and looked in the sky, looked in the trees, looked in the bushes to see what they could see. Every day, they ate peanut butter sandwiches and apples, then once more hiked and looked in the sky and the trees and the bushes. As she did then, she still records in her notebook everything she spots.

If Dad could only see her now, but he's buried in a casket in a cemetery and can't see anything. Poof! One minute Dad was there and said goodbye to her as she left for work, slamming their apartment door behind her, and the next hour Norm received a call telling him that Dad died in his law office, of all the miserable shitty places to die. She can't recall if she returned his goodbye that last day. She can't recall if she ever told him she loved him. It bothers her. If only she could bring Nate Miller back and tell him now. She'd be overjoyed if she could hear his voice again, just once, countering the thousand other voices that plague her. But all she can do is continue with the hobby he taught her and remember his love and care, the long evenings spent listening on the radio to the Dodgers games. With his help and the brain cleanser kicking in, she got a handle on her disease. He fed her the pills until she had the hang of it, so she constantly goes in search of birds and memories.

It doesn't matter to Adel what the weather is; if it's time to look at her birds, she's out of the house, dragging the kids. She walks briskly out to Lindy Park, takes in the view of the lower New York harbor and the Verrazano-Narrows Bridge, and makes the kids look too, although they rarely seem interested. More often, they want only to turn the center knob on the Zhumell, getting it out of focus. Then they'll go off to play with pretty stones they find on the ground. Kayla will occasionally put a particularly attractive stone into her mouth, but Max, ever vigilant, tells Adel at once so Adel can force Kayla to spit it out. On other days, Kayla might lie face down, pushing herself up into a cobra-like position. Max stands guard to make sure no one inadvertently steps on his sister.

On this particular afternoon Adel takes the kids straight to the playground, where they run around frenetically, playing a game that sounds to her like "catch the bad guys." She keeps half an eye on them while she scans the skies and beach for her birds.

Adel often has a running dialogue with herself, talking about ducks or sandpipers or any other birds that pop into her mind. Today, she breaks into rhyme. "Herons and egrets, birds of a feather, fuck together, fuck together," she sings, not caring whether her kids or anyone else's hear. "Birds evolved from dinosaurs, doo dah, doo dah, birds come from the dinosaurs, all the fucking day! All the fucking day! All the fucking day! Birds come from the dinosaurs, all the fucking day!" A few Sea Gate neighbors also walking in the cold, blustery February afternoon look at her askance, but most of them know she's harmless. No one much cares. If they're annoyed, they walk away.

Her kids now sit on a bench, Max with his arm around Kayla, trying to keep her warm. They're weary of chasing each other and tired of the see-saw and the slide and the monkey bars. They want to go home, and, shivering, they whine about their misery. Adel sees they've reached their limit. With the kids in tow, she starts back the half mile to their house on Lyme Avenue.

"The birds out here are beautiful because they're free," she says to them, apropos of nothing.

"What's free, Mom?" Max holds one of Kayla's hands and tries to pull her along, but she squirms out of his grasp and runs to Adel's other side.

"They can go wherever they want."

"Oh." Max thinks for a second, then adds, "But birds always do that, Mom."

"Not the poor birds in the zoo."

CHAPTER 10

She's now five, in kindergarten, but practices for an hour in the morning before school and in the afternoon for two hours as soon as she gets home. The piano stopped crawling toward her bedroom at night when she began her own lessons. Kayla has achieved in scarcely more than a year what has taken Max much longer to accomplish.

The piano is no longer a source of fear. Although still tiny next to its bulk, Kayla becomes the piano when she plays and the piano becomes her. The musical notes that she deciphers with ease, spread on the page before her, are messages sent to her from the heart of the piano. She understands only vaguely what a composer is, but she knows that the pieces written by Chopin differ in important ways from the messages called Bach, and both differ from the messages called Mozart. She loves them all. Whatever she learns, she loves. She feels the music has been written for her by the piano itself. Sr. Cantelli is the connector, the magician who finds the music that's rightfully hers and explains how it should be played. But Sr. Cantelli can't possibly know what she knows when she encounters the music; he can't possibly feel what she feels when she makes the music hers. He can listen to her, mark her progress, correct her mistakes, be amazed at the beauty Kayla elicits from the instrument, but that's all. Only she can know and feel as she does. Yet, he's absolutely critical for her development. The harder she works, the more beautiful music Sr. Cantelli will introduce her to.

Everyone fusses about her playing, as if she were doing something miraculous, and she wants to explain that what she does isn't difficult at all. What's difficult is when she can't get in her full practice because it's Max's turn. She tries to explain, but no one understands the ease with which she interprets the music, the facility with which her fingers strike or caress the right keys at amazing speed and accuracy.

Kayla has learned, not only to play well, but that she loves being the center of attention, that she deeply desires the power coursing through her when she plays, the power she holds over those who listen. The Steinway smiles at her, and it makes her smile too. When Kayla receives the accolades of her listeners, the piano's smile jumps to her face.

And she values Max's close attention and support. When he tries to make helpful suggestions about a difficult passage, she listens patiently and thanks him for his comments even when she senses he's wrong.

Although she'd very much like to practice on Saturday mornings, they are strictly for attending synagogue, not for practice. On every other day of the week, she's at the piano by six in the morning, but on Saturday mornings, her dad tells her she may not practice until the afternoon, when they get back. He reminds her that they are Jewish and that *Shabbat* is a day of rest, at least in the morning. She thinks, if *Shabbat* is a day of rest, then why not the afternoon, too, but is delighted to get back to practice when allowed, day of rest or not. It's hard to understand, but she complies. This is what her dad has declared, and her mom doesn't stand in the way. Kayla intuits that her dad is funny about religion.

They start out their walks to the synagogue as a group, but Kayla doesn't care to walk fast, and her dad becomes impatient. She knows her dad is losing it when she sees the veins pop out on his forehead. She loves to challenge him in that way and in many others, just to see him almost lose his temper.

Max tries to speed her up with orders such as "C'mon, Squirt!" but the more he urges her the slower she goes. She likes to get him riled up too. He never calls her "lovey" anymore. That stopped when she started lessons. Max's tone is often that of a put-upon older brother who must tolerate his younger sister's company.

Finally, her mom says "It's okay, Nicky, you and Max go on ahead, and we'll get there when we get there," and they continue separately to the Brighton Beach Jewish Center. Kayla loves these times when she holds her mom's hand and they walk as slowly as they want. They seldom talk, but Kayla is happy her mom is so close. Adel doesn't have her binoculars or notebook on these Saturday mornings, but still points out to Kayla the many birds she can identify.

When they arrive, the building seems gigantic to Kayla, its pink stone façade towering over her. Just to reach the three tall arched front doors requires a climb of twenty steps, an ordeal for her mom, who breathes heavily long before they reach the top. Once inside, Kayla hears the murmuring of prayers, but she and her mom must wearily mount another staircase to the balcony before they can sit. Men and boys down, women and girls up. From the balcony, she can see the men praying, using words that are meaningless to her, even when she hears them clearly. She can't see her dad and Max, because they sit in the very back. Her mom skims through a large-print Reader's Digest taken from her purse. Most of the other women, almost all wearing wigs, whisper to each other but not to her mom. No one follows the service. Kayla wonders why these women bother to attend.

And yet a strange calmness envelops Kayla as she sits next to her mom. While on the long walk she might become anxious about a nightmare or how the other kindergarten kids whisper about her, although she might worry that her dad and Max didn't really love her, such feelings disappear once she finds her seat and looks around. She admires the raised *bima* in the center of the floor below and the men standing around it, one of them chanting from the Torah. She studies the skylight and the diffused brightness it allows into the sanctuary, bathing everyone in a warm glow. She thinks about God, and what God might mean. God is something her mom has tried to explain to her, but only in a mocking way. Yet, God is the reason they all perform this *Shabbat* ritual. Kayla knows the prayers of the men below are their attempts to talk to God, but she easily sees her parents don't really care. If her dad cared, she wouldn't be allowed to practice on Saturday afternoons. Part of her understands that they bring her and Max to this synagogue on *Shabbat* because they think they have to.

Kayla's made up her mind that she must figure out God for herself. If God is connected with this synagogue, then God must have something to do with the feeling she has, once here, that everything is right in the world. She wants to be close to God. But how?

The chanting below is a simple melody that touches her and lays tracks in her mind. There's a logical order to it, she feels, phrases repeat in predictable ways, the melody suddenly takes flight around words that must be particularly important, and each sentence ends with the same resolving notes. The melody tells her that answers have already been found to questions she isn't yet able to ask. After the Torah is put away, the cantor's singing fills her soul with its beauty, and she can summon his vibrant tenor to mind at night as she settles down to sleep. When the men below rock forward and backward in their devotion, she wants to feel the same thing. She rocks until her seat squeaks and her mom looks up from the Reader's Digest and tells her to be still.

Kayla arrests her body's outer movement, but inside lets everything continue to sway. She wants to go to Hebrew school too, like Max, but girls aren't allowed. It's not fair. Max hates it, but she would love it. When she begs her parents, they laugh and point out that going to Hebrew school will reduce her practice time.

One day, she'll make the time and find someone to teach her what the words mean.

CHAPTER 11

He's told Adel that he'll have to work late, that the *Journal of Psychotherapy* has returned his most recent review article and demanded complicated revisions. That's true to an extent. He will in fact work an extra hour on the revisions after his last patient, but then he plans to meet Adrienne.

Nicky feels rotten about cheating, but he's helplessly drawn to his former patient. She's begun writing poetry again and often shows her poems to Nicky. He doesn't have a good feeling for poetry, his English still pragmatic despite twenty-five years in America, but he's eager to please, so offers his comments when asked. Adrienne chuckles at his struggling, puts the poems back into her purse, and undresses both of them quickly. They're not together for literary criticism. They make love with the lights on.

He's thought about seeking professional counseling himself. He knows he's not the first of his discipline to have an affair with a patient, but he feels that, if he does talk to another psychiatrist, word of his infidelity will spread. If he's so flagrantly violating the rules of his profession, anyone to whom he speaks can likewise break the rules.

As he leaves his office, his heart races. When he gets into his car, nausea overtakes him, a nausea so intense that he must try to vomit onto the parking garage floor. He only retches, bringing up nothing. His hands shake as they take the steering wheel, and he grips it that much harder to quell the tremors. Still queasy, he forces himself to drive to their rendezvous. At the motel, finally, his unease makes way for the rush of excitement and the anticipation of pleasure.

Sex with Adrienne is nothing like performing marital duties with Adel, which have become a chore. With Adrienne, he's in his late teens again, supercharged with hormones, and each time is new and brilliant, an explosion of nerves as if a nuclear bomb lights up his brain. He's addicted to this thrill. To give it up would be death, and he's not ready to die.

CHAPTER 12

Kayla sees her friend at the Jewish Center wearing a gold necklace with a six-pointed Star of David and asks her about it. The friend's name is Mary, and she's about a year older than Kayla. They often find each other in the back of the balcony on a Saturday morning when sitting becomes unbearable, and, if they keep their voices low, their mothers ignore them. Mary is everything Kayla thinks she herself is not. Taller, with curly blonde hair she constantly twirls around her fingers, Mary impresses Kayla as being a lot smarter and knowing the ways of the world. On this particular Saturday, Kayla must learn what hangs from Mary's necklace.

"It's the Jewish star. Are you stupid or something?" Mary holds it out so Kayla can get a better look. Kayla reaches out, but Mary pulls it back quickly, and Kayla's hand hangs in the air for a second.

"What's it for? What does it do?"

"Do? Nothing. It's for decoration. Don't you think mine is beautiful?" Mary holds it again toward Kayla.

This time, Kayla doesn't reach for it. She just leans forward a bit and considers her answer, not wanting to be thought stupid. "Yes, it's very beautiful. But why is it Jewish?"

"My Dad said it was the Shield of David. You know, Daveed Hamelkik. He was a king of the Jews."

"I didn't know we had a king."

"He died a long time ago. In Israel. Don't you know the story about how he killed the ugly giant?"

Kayla frowns, annoyed and embarrassed because Max must know this story, that it must have been taught in the Hebrew school she's not allowed to attend. "It doesn't look like a shield. It doesn't look like the ones I saw on *Dragnet*." She recalls a recent episode when two cops were talking about the badges pinned to their shirts.

"That's because it's magic. It protects you if you wear it. That's why I have mine on now, so the Evil Eye will stay away."

"The Evil Eye?"

"Don't look now, but the Evil Eye is everywhere, spying on us. Do you want to go downstairs and walk around the block with me? Our moms will be scared when they realize we're missing."

Precisely because she's been warned not to look, Kayla nervously surveys the balcony, expecting to see a large eye pop out of the heads of the chatting women. She sees nothing like that, only the women she knew were there, but the Evil Eye may just be hiding until the right time. "No. I'm going back to sit next to my mom. I'm going to ask her if I can have a Jewish star too, a Shield of David just like yours, only bigger."

"You can't, because your family's too poor."

"We're not poor."

"Well, mine already has all the magic."

With that, Kayla returns to the front of the balcony. Her mom is humming softly. Kayla takes her hand and squeezes it to say hello, then hangs on, just to be safe.

CHAPTER 13

She's been listening to her Zenith radio for two days and is afraid. The excited tones of the announcers on WOR are hard to distinguish from the chorus in her head, both telling her something bad is coming. Hurricane Agnes aims straight toward New York City, and nothing can stop her.

Nicky, who read the *Times* and studied the arrows decorating the maps of the country's East Coast, assures her the storm will swing out to sea long before it gets near them, but he's not a weatherman, and Adel knows otherwise. The birds have told her. They've vacated the skies around her house, and the surrounding waters of the bay are unusually quiet. So Adel knows, but she's learned not to argue with Nicky; she won't argue with him even when she's positive she's right. Nicky will say she's wrong and assume her illness is speaking, not the real, smart Adel, and she doesn't want to see that disgusted look cross his face, the look – partly of confusion, partly of exasperation – in which he asks himself why he married this nut case. She can't tolerate that look, it makes her ill, so she agrees with him.

Adel digs her fingernails into her arms before she realizes what she's doing and forces herself to stop. She reaches for her Marlboros continuously, lighting the next from the stub of the last. She swallows an extra Thorazine tablet just to make sure she's got enough on board, then wonders whether she should take yet another, but decides not. She's practical too, though, and checks to make sure the windows are all down and latched and that there's plenty of toilet paper and milk. Yes, the flashlights work and there are extra batteries. But what if the ocean comes into their house anyway, seeps in from under the doors? Where will they go? What if debris crashes through their roof and the wind picks them up out of their beds and tosses them into the water? She scours the basement for rope they can use to tie themselves to their beds, but finds none, discovering only a few electrical cords and decides they will do in a pinch. She brings canned food and a can opener and paper plates and four forks and paper towels up to the second floor too, stowing it all in the shelf of Kayla's closet on top of *Candy Land*. She should have bought a few gallons of water when she had the chance, but now it's too late. Fill the bathtub, she remembers hearing on the radio, and after a half-hour the two tubs hold as much as they can. Kayla is too busy practicing the piano to notice what Adel is doing, and Max is napping in his room. She wonders how her children can be so ignorant of the danger surrounding them. They have no appreciation about how harmful the world really is. You do whatever you can to avoid death, and yet it catches you when you least expect it. Her dad didn't expect to die so soon, so suddenly, leaving her without someone to watch over her. And now the hurricane is speeding right at her and her family, death's servant ready to wipe them out.

The wind picks up, as do the voices. "Eee-vil! Eee-vil!" they whisper, and she knows they're talking about her, she's done something wrong and must be punished, beaten so she'll never to do it again. She looks toward the grey waters turning black on the horizon, no longer still, and they're massing in anger, ready to punish her and her family. She fears for the lives of her children, who are innocent and good, who bring happiness and joy to her and Nicky and many others, and how can the voices want to harm them too? It's so unfair. She cries, despairing she was ever born to such misery.

An hour later Nicky's car pulls into the driveway, and he finds her sitting at the kitchen table with her head resting on her arms. He talks to her in a soothing voice, putting a kettle on for tea, and returns to stroke her hair and massage her scalp. She cannot find her voice yet, but his fingers feel so good, she almost purrs. Little by little, Adel comes around.

"The storm, Nicky."

"Yes, you were right. It is heading this way, but I think we'll still be fine. This house has stood up to many storms over the years, I imagine. It's sturdy, like the house I grew up in, also on the coast, also bearing its share of bad weather. In fact, I think this house is stronger."

The wind picks up over the evening until it's a roar, and rain cascades through the dark sky with a volume even greater than Adel imagined. The pounding of thousands of gallons of water on their roof reverberates through the house. Nicky and Adel put the kids to bed, tucking them in, assuring them everything will be fine, even as the house groans and creaks. Kayla cries, wanting her doll, which she can't find, but Adel spots Tina under Kayla's bed, reaches down to pick her up and hands her to Kayla. Kayla hugs Tina and lies down, squeezing her eyes shut. Then she opens her eyes and looks at Adel.

"Mommy, is the storm going to hurt us?"

Adel wants to tell Kayla that of course the storm will hurt them, because that's what Adel believes, but she knows she must not do anything to frighten her daughter worse than she's already frightened. So Adel lies.

"It will not hurt us." She wants to leave, but Kayla has more questions.

"But, Mommy, what if I need you and you're dead? Who will take care of me?" Adel returns to sit on Kayla's bed and engulfs her in a big hug before answering. "Kayla, I'll be here to take care of you, always." She means it, forgetting how death has marked her, ignoring that she's made a promise she can't keep. Adel's words comfort Kayla, who lies down again to settle herself for sleep.

Adel returns to the kitchen to listen to WOR with Nicky. The radio announcers warn Adel and Nicky at 10 p.m. that residents of shore areas in Brooklyn and Long Island should be prepared for power outages and listen for evacuation orders. Special mention is made of the danger of high tides along the shore at Coney Island. Junk flies against the house, pieces of wood or litter picked up by the hundred-mile-an-hour gusts. Agnes is worsening. We are close to the end, Adel thinks.

Nicky leans over and whispers to Adel, but she can't hear him through the din. Why bother to whisper, she wonders, when she wouldn't be able to hear him even if he screamed. He tenderly kisses her ear, but she still doesn't get it. When he touches her, however, she understands his meaning and is grateful as well as excited. She's never made love in the middle of a hurricane before. They hurry upstairs to their bedroom, and it's wonderful. Her fear subsides and now it's only Nicky she can think about and what he does to her. They fall asleep in each other's arms despite the noise and the danger. The voices go away while she sleeps, and for her the storm has disappeared.

It's about four in the morning when Adel's eyes snap open, fear gripping her again. Something's not right. The kids. She extricates herself from Nicky's embrace and sees he's still deep in slumber. She reaches for her blue robe and enters the hallway. Instinct takes her first to Kayla's room. She pushes open the door, and the dim light from the hallway falls upon Kayla's empty bed, no Kayla where she should be and no Tina either, and Adel knows the evil has gone straight for her daughter, and she is evil too and never should have let Nicky distract her with lovemaking. She almost calls out an alarm, but something stops her, a remnant of her brain staying rational, and she moves over to the door of Max's bedroom. There, in Max's bed, lie both of her children.

Kayla, in her red and blue Mickey Mouse pajamas, the ones with Mickey's arms spread wide in happiness, has crawled in with her brother, and they're both sound asleep. Max has his arm around Kayla. Mickey's joy leaps from Kayla's body into Adel's heart when she sees how her children have taken care of each other in the storm. Maybe Adel did something right after all, having these kids. She walks to Max's bed, reaches out, and gently shakes Kayla, telling her it's time for her to go back to her own bed. Kayla yawns, taking her thumb out of her mouth, and looks up at Adel, then over at Max, confused. Max, still half asleep, removes his arm from around his sister and turns over. Tina lies on the floor next to the bed, and Adel picks her up and hands her to Kayla for the second time that night.

After she puts Kayla back into her own bed, Adel descends to the kitchen and realizes the storm has receded. She starts the burner underneath the tea kettle and lights a Marlboro. The WOR announcers tell her what she already knows, that Hurricane Agnes has gone out to sea. Although the tide pushed in by the storm was high, it seems not to have caused a lot of damage.

CHAPTER 14

Max walks Kayla over to Sr. Cantelli's house for her lesson and, on this afternoon, at Sr. Cantelli's invitation, Adel comes as well. The maestro wants to talk to her. Kayla knows why and can barely contain her excitement. It's a secret between her and Sr. Cantelli – they've managed to keep Max in the dark – until her mom is told. After Kayla's lesson, they gather in the front room facing the ocean and deserted beach.

Sr. Cantelli explains to Adel that he feels he can no longer teach Kayla the way she deserves to be taught and thinks she should now be taught by one of the much more accomplished professors at Bellington. He wants to send her to the pianist and teacher Heinz Lindorf. Herr Lindorf has followed his exemplary performing career by making an even bigger name for himself by bringing gifted young students to a much higher level. Although Lindorf has never taken a student just seven years old, Kayla is so strong a pianist, so much a natural, so confident in her approach to music, that Herr Lindorf might just go along with the idea. Sr. Cantelli has been in touch with Herr Lindorf, who's agreed to audition Kayla if her parents will bring her in.

Kayla smiles broadly at Sr. Cantelli as he reveals his plan, then looks over toward her mom, whose face is turned away. Adel's staring out at the water. Kayla's not sure her mom has understood what Sr. Cantelli has said; sometimes you need to say things two or three times until she gets it. Her mom is humming something that sounds like "Hey Jude."

"Mom! Did you hear what Sr. Cantelli says?" Adel doesn't respond; she just looks out at the regular crash of waves on the beach and starts pulling the pudgy fingers of one hand with the pudgy fingers of the other. "Mom? Are you there?"

"Bellington. Hit-and-run. Tommy gun."

"Sra. Covo, it would be very good for Kayla." Sr. Cantelli, by now Kayla's close friend and the closest thing she has to a grandfather, frowns at Kayla as if to suggest that he cannot be held responsible if her mother inhabits another world.

"Bellington. Making fun. Hotdog bun." Adel's gaze lifts into the sky toward a flock of gulls.

"Mom! Listen to Sr. Cantelli! He's telling you something important!" Adel finally turns away from the window to look at them.

"It's like this, Sra. Covo. Herr Lindorf's spent much of his life teaching the most incredible young pianists, those with unlimited potential, and I haven't. I've never had a student like Kayla, and I've felt for quite a while she's beyond what I can teach and deserves better than me, deserves the best, now, as early in her life as possible. Herr Lindorf also has the energy of ten of me, and he also has connections to give Kayla a chance to compete and go as far as her gift takes her. Are you understanding?"

"Incredible?"

"Incredible. That's what I say."

"Where is it? Not anyway near Sea Gate, I'll bet."

"Bellington's in Manhattan, of course. On the West Side. Midtown."

"It would take a long time to get there by subway, yes? I don't drive."

"An hour?"

"Mom, come on! We can do it!" Kayla now fears her mom will say no and she'll lose the chance. She's assumed her mom would understand immediately about the importance of this invitation. How can she not understand?

"We'll let you know, Sr. Cantelli. It's something I need to talk about with Nicky. Her father. He's a shrink, you know." She nods as if she's explained the secret of the universe. With the promise to talk to Nicky, she leaves Sr. Cantelli's house and walks home with her children.

Kayla skips and bounces along the sidewalk, happy again, believing her dad will go along with the idea. She will try out for Bellington. Sr. Cantelli has been talking to her about it for months.

Max, ten years old, has remained steadfastly silent, having listened closely to all that Sr. Cantelli has said about Kayla.

CHAPTER 15

Nothing about his family escapes his eye, trained as it is to assess the quirks of behavior that suggest mental illness. He's known from the day he met her that Adel suffers from schizophrenia with auditory hallucinations, and he tries to make sure she stays on her medicine. He always watches for the possibility of serious side effects and weighs them against the benefits of medication. His former partner, Dr. Lack, writes most of the prescriptions for Thorazine but now sees Adel only once a year. No need to do it more often, given that Adel lives with Nicky.

Max strikes him as grounded and solid for a ten-year-old boy. He's intelligent, a prodigious reader, and a serious student, almost always getting A's. He religiously peruses the *Times* and wants to talk to Nicky about the Watergate scandal. But it's more than Max's interest in news and politics that makes Nicky feel close to Max. It's more than his intelligence and how well he speaks. It's also that Max is so helpful around the house, never having to be asked twice to lend a hand. He's turned out to be very useful in keeping an eye Adel.

If there's any difficulty, it's that Max seems jealous of Kayla's success, even though he professes great love for her and pride in her accomplishments. He'll occasionally take excessive time stopping his own piano practice when it's Kayla's turn, or he'll release the piano to her with a snide comment. Nicky and Adel have applauded Max's excellent grades and his awareness of what's going on in the world, but Nicky feels remorse that their praise for him pales in comparison to the accolades they heap on his sister.

Kayla worries Nicky the most, despite her dazzling talent. That she's brilliant, of course, cannot be denied. She displays an uncanny ability to hear music one time and then perform exactly what she's heard. And she is meticulous to a fault. She pays attention to every last detail of the music she's learning.

Nicky has often watched her practice on the weekends. In one session, Kayla is likely to repeat a short passage scores of times during a half-hour, doing nothing else, one hand at a time, not taking a break or even looking away from the piano. Each time she plays the passage, it sounds perfect to Nicky. When he asks her about the extent of repetition, she talks about things like holding her hand in precisely the same place to make it easier for her fingers, hitting the exact location on each key with the exact right amount of attack and pressure each time, listening to make sure she hears the subtlest differences in the passage on each run-through. She is attuned to the smallest variations in the curvature of her fingers, her posture, her breathing, and how each note makes her feel. Nicky knows that Kayla possesses the innate capacity to see things at a level of detail much beyond that of any normal human being and that this, more than anything else, explains what motivates and enables her to practice with such intensity.

But even as she shows a growing mastery over the piano, playing music he's been told should be impossibly hard for a seven-year-old, he feels uneasy when he watches her practice. A look comes over her face that reminds him of patients under hypnosis, so far away he fears she's not in the same world that he himself inhabits. Nicky thinks of it as a faint shadow; there's no true darkness, but a thin grainy film settling over her features, entirely invisible unless one were looking for it. It's not the look he's seen on other pianists he's watched on television. The others – he thinks of Andre Watts at Lincoln Center – may close their eyes, grimace with emotion, raise eyebrows, squint, stamp their feet, all depending upon what they're playing. Nicky doesn't know for sure whether these gestures are conscious on the part of the performers, but he suspects pianists like Watts know what they're doing and that there's a musical purpose behind it.

Kayla doesn't seem to be using her facial expressions to enhance the music. Her demeanor might best be described as contemplative. Whatever she's feeling is not apparent on her face until she's finished and her smile spreads from her face to the faces of everyone listening. When the music ends and Kayla rises to the applause, whether from the ladies at the Sisterhood of the Jewish Center or from a gathering of Sr. Cantelli's students, Kayla's smile is so intense, so beautiful, so mysterious that Nicky worries he's never seen her smile like that in any other situation. He gathers that performing is the only thing that brings Kayla joy and wishes she had more joy in her life than just the piano. He wishes Kayla was more well-rounded, like Max.

And then there are the other odd things about Kayla, weird things the family has come to accept without comment, weirdness such as her refusal to eat anything green – he's not aware of any trauma that might have induced prasinophobia – weirdness such as her recurrent nightmares of being chased and eaten by monsters. He worries these are not just mild quirks but indicators of greater significance. Of what, he's not sure.

When he hears about Sr. Cantelli's hopes for Kayla at Bellington, he's deeply concerned that the next level she strives for might be a stretch too far. She's obsessed with the piano, and Bellington will feed her obsession. The psychiatrist in him feels obsessions shouldn't be fed, notwithstanding a growing movement in his profession to use paradoxical techniques in treatment.

Kayla coerces him, however. She tells him squarely that if she doesn't get the chance to try out at Bellington, she'll stop playing the piano altogether. She's stubborn enough to do as she threatens. It bothers Nicky that he can be swayed by the belligerence of his seven-year-old daughter, but he knows she will give up what she loves if she cannot have it all her way.

He foresees that this won't be the last time she manipulates him in this way, but he cannot let her give up what she loves, so he agrees despite his fears. They'll go to Bellington and see what happens.

CHAPTER 16

Let me back up, kids, even though you know where I'm going and wishing I'd get to the point. I will, but in my own good time.

So I've mentioned Kayla's instructor at Bellington, Heinz Lindorf. As you might imagine, Kayla had to audition with Lindorf before he'd take her under his wing, so to speak. We all went into the city for the event. Lindorf, a German in his forties, had dark, unruly hair, a long nose, and hands twice the size of my own, hands as I learned later that spanned four keys beyond an octave. If anyone was genetically destined to be a great pianist, it was Lindorf; he had the hands to prove it. He explained in a thick accent before Kayla's audition that the slot for which she would compete was as a special student, something Bellington allowed on rare occasions at the specific request of one of its faculty, but the qualification made no difference to Kayla, nor to our parents. I wondered what he'd meant by "special" student, but I could see, if Lindorf accepted her, she'd be able to say that she studied piano at Bellington.

Mom, Dad, and I sat outside one of the practice halls after Lindorf led Kayla away. She looked excited, but not nervous. She even winked at me, and I could feel her confidence as if she'd whispered "I've got this" directly into my ear. In her mind, my seven-year-old sister felt she'd already nailed the audition.

The soundproofing of the practice rooms must have been extraordinary, because we could not hear her play. While we waited, dancers with harried looks emerged from a room across the hall, practiced a few ballet steps in front of us, and returned to the studio from which they'd emerged. From just those few seconds, I could tell Bellington was no joke, that it was as demanding a place in which to study as an artist could find. Lindorf and Kayla returned after a half hour. Lindorf extended his hand to Dad, who took it reluctantly. Lindorf didn't seem to notice Dad's hesitation.

"You have a most talented daughter, ja? She will work with me here once a week."

It was a statement, almost an order. Kayla jumped with delight and hugged Mom, and I just sat there wondering where Kayla's uncanny brilliance had come from, trying to figure out how Kayla could've gotten so far beyond my own level in such a short time. Lindorf and Dad went off for a few minutes to discuss financial arrangements.

I learned soon that Dad hated Lindorf because he was German. Dad made his feelings clear as soon as we were out of Lindorf's earshot. That Kayla's new teacher had left Germany as a child in the '30's and had no involvement with the Nazis – a point Mom offered in Lindorf's defense – mattered not a whit. Kayla of course was enthralled by Lindorf from the outset and cared nothing about his heritage.

I asked Kayla on the way back to Sea Gate what the audition had been like.

"Oh, Herr Lindorf showed me some pieces I hadn't seen before and asked me to play them. So I did. I wanted to study them a bit more before playing, you know, just read through them silently, but he said no, just play, so I played."

"What were they?"

"A few things by Brahms. Six pieces, and I picked three. The Sonata in F-sharp minor by Schumann. He said he likes the romantics."

"Were they hard?"

"I don't think so. He told me Schumann went crazy. Did you know that?"

"No."

I later figured out he'd given her extremely challenging music, pieces that I would have had difficulty playing after months of practice. Yet my sister couldn't even say whether they were hard. To her, it seemed like nothing about the piano was hard.

CHAPTER 17

Kayla's first formal lesson with Herr Lindorf is eye-opening. Before they begin, he has her drink a glass of cold water, lecturing her on the importance of drinking water if she wants to stay healthy and focused. Instantly, cold water becomes Kayla's favorite beverage. In his study sits his own Steinway, a grand, an instrument that produces a sound so much richer than that of the upright in her living room. Herr Lindorf takes the empty glass from her, has her sit on the piano bench, tells her to make herself comfortable, and asks her to warm up for a few minutes. She does so by playing the last piece she had learned under Sr. Cantelli's tutelage, a Scriabin prelude with a rapid three-against-two rhythm.

"Ja, not bad, but we need much work."

"Much work?"

When he tells her that her technique needs so much improvement he'll not let her play or practice *any* piece of music for three months, she doesn't object. Rather, she nods and asks him to explain precisely what he wants her to do. He lays it out, inscribing the plan in a notebook, detail by detail, making sure that she can decipher his handwriting. Scales, arpeggios, chord progressions, not just for warming up, but for the entire practice day. Every scale to be played perfectly five times in a row. Every scale to be played backward and forward, varying the tempo, varying the volume, varying the rhythm, over and over again, and, when she's run through the circle of fifths, she is to repeat everything in reverse order. When she's finished, she's to start again, always trying to bring new subtleties to the scales and arpeggios, experimenting with various combinations of speed, wrist movement, arm angle, hand posture, and finger pressure. He wants her to hear each separate note as music itself. She is to make the listener discover the music in each note. When her fingers, hands, wrists, and arms ache, she may rest for five minutes, not more. Then she must go back to her practice. The pain will get easier to deal with. Yes, she is already strong for her age and stature, he tells her, but not yet nearly strong enough.

Later, Kayla tries to explain to her parents and to Max what Herr Lindorf has demanded. She opens the notebook in which he's written the program she must follow and plays what she feels is a short example for her family, but they rapidly appear bored. She sees they don't understand, that they're disappointed she hasn't started on a new piece. Kayla herself, though, knows exactly why she must do as Herr Lindorf dictates. He has made her to see that she's only approaching the first step of what it means to be a great pianist. She has no urge to resist her new mentor, no desire to do anything else other than practice as he requires.

But Kayla's pain, as she devotes herself to this regimen, is intense. At night, when she's away from the piano, she holds onto Tina, crying, seeking solace. Tina cries with her. Then the pain slowly wears away, and in a few weeks Kayla has forgotten about it. At night, Kayla now regales Tina with her progress.

After the first couple of months, Kayla becomes ever more aware of the differences between Herr Lindorf and Sr. Cantelli, such that she finds it hard to imagine they could both be good teachers. Sr. Cantelli was always patient, but Herr Lindorf gets irritated, almost sarcastic, when she makes the smallest mistake. Yet, she worships Herr Lindorf, and it's not only because she finds his accent refreshingly different; she knows that he has her best interests at heart and is tough only because it will help her. She's devoted to gaining mastery and sees Herr Lindorf as the only way toward that goal.

CHAPTER 18

About a year later, Lindorf arranges for Kayla to compete in the twelve-and-under category of the Elmwood Conservatory Fifth Young Pianist International Competition, held at Carnegie Recital Hall. It will be her first serious competition.

The rules require her to select two contrasting pieces, one Romantic and one from a later period. Lindorf suggests Kayla might try a Chopin polonaise or ballade – she can choose whichever she feels most comfortable playing – and Gershwin's Three Preludes. She's never played the polonaises or the ballades, nor anything by Gershwin. None of that fazes Kayla, however. She'll have three months to master the pieces.

"Why did you pick that one?" Max questions her as she shows him the music and begs him to stop his own practice so she can have access to the piano. She holds up Chopin's Ballade in G Minor, Opus 23.

"I wanted something very different from the Gershwin." She hands him the preludes, which he flips open haphazardly to the second. "That's going to be showy and bright." Kayla continues. "I wanted a Chopin that was dark, but still beautiful." She pushes Max gently on the arm to signal he must now get up and make way for her more important practice. "C'mon Max! Time's up." She knows he's been purposely dawdling, but yet he lingers, still studying the prelude.

"Kayla, this piece is loaded with tenths. And look, at the end, that's an eleventh! Your hands aren't that big ... are they?"

"Sure they are." She leans over and, with her left hand, shows Max she can easily play eleven keys apart, the last chord of the second prelude. The flexibility in her digits is amazing; her hands can't be big enough to reach, yet they do. Max feels as if her fingers must have been stretched in the womb, that maybe there aren't real joints at all, just elastic.

"Now, move!" she orders, with only a half-smile. Max finally makes way for her, once again in awe of his little sister.

That Kayla will be judged makes everyone but her nervous. Kayla is confident, as confident as she was before her audition with Lindorf.

Her parents talk quietly about it, out of the kids' earshot, wondering if they've done the right thing allowing her into the competition. They were swayed by Lindorf's assurance that Kayla would benefit from the experience whether she wins or loses. They reason that, since almost everyone must lose, it will be a good idea for Kayla to learn how that feels now. But Lindorf has told them he doesn't think Kayla will lose. If she does, the loss will just make her work harder for the next competition. If she loses, she'll do more than survive; she'll thrive.

Max himself fears Kayla will come away from the competition disappointed, but keeps his opinions to himself. He too figures she'll learn soon enough that not everyone is a winner all the time.

The most difficult part of getting ready for the competition, as it turns out, is finding Kayla a suitable gown. Adel reveals herself to be clueless when, a few weeks before the event, Lindorf calls to ask her what Kayla is going to wear. After being made to understand what's required, Adel must then drag Kayla and Max around to a bunch of places in the city, looking for the right attire. Max thinks this shopping trip is a large pain and that he should have been left home alone, even if he's not quite twelve years old, to practice his own pieces. Had it been him, he feels, he would've picked the first thing that fit. He thinks Kayla, left to her own devices, would've done so as well.

But Adel is adamant. She requires Kayla to take one frilly thing after another into the dressing room, emerge with a smile, and wait for comments. Nothing seems right to Adel. When a saleslady finally asks Adel in exasperation what kind of gown she thinks would be appropriate, all Adel can say is "Dodger blue." Kayla and Max exchange glances and shrug, amused, while the saleslady runs off for a manager.

Kayla soon ends up with a blue gown.

CHAPTER 19

You don't know me well, sadly, and you don't realize how sentimental I can be about family matters. Someday, I hope, we'll be able to talk about these things calmly, as adults, but for now please just accept my word for it.

I still have a copy of a photograph Dad took of Kayla the evening before the competition, all dolled up for our own "dress rehearsal," her last practice before the event. I keep it in the center drawer of my desk at home. I did think of putting it in a frame and hanging it in my law office, but I have plenty of other great pictures of her there.

Your Aunt Kayla in this photograph is standing next to the Steinway with her usual bright smile, as if the piano had been invented just for her. Her dark brown hair falls to her shoulders. The blue gown has puffy short sleeves, and the high collar and sleeves are lined with a white lace. She wears white pumps. Nothing is gaudy or out-of-place. Kayla is just a beautiful little girl. You'll see it when you're here.

The next day would've been great but for one thing. Early morning, long before we were ready to leave the house, even before we'd had breakfast, the phone rang. Dad answered and, after a second, told us he had an emergency call from Bellevue Hospital about one of his patients, had to go, didn't know how long he'd be there, and would have to miss the competition. Before we could even grasp the idea that he was deserting us, he was out of the house.

Kayla was crestfallen, Mom stunned, and I ... well, I wondered. We all knew he'd been looking forward to the event, and I was shocked Dad would pull out, even for one of his damned patients. I knew back then about doctors being on call and such and some doctors having to fill in for other doctors. He couldn't have had someone else on call?

We didn't have time to argue with him. With Dad unable even to drive us into the city, we first found that we didn't have enough cash for cab fare and then struggled to get to Carnegie on time on the subway. It was a mile walk to the subway stop. We had to carry a large cardboard box with Kayla's gown.

But Dad's absence didn't affect Kayla's performance. When she played later that afternoon, I saw once again how thoroughly she loved what she was doing, how she lost herself in the music, how she transported herself into another world. Kayla's strength was amazing. How such a slight girl could make a piano roar! But she never overdid it; her strength and passion always made sense in the context of the entire piece. I remember well how the ballade struck a majestical and mystical mood from its opening octaves, how its volcanic energy seemed to break forth from the center of Carnegie Recital Hall itself, and how I hadn't wanted the music to end. And I remember thinking how I'd never heard anything as vibrant and buoyant as the Gershwin preludes. I can never forget Kayla's huge smile, both before and after she played, her graceful bows, and the audience's wild response, far beyond that given any other contestant. All of this no doubt led to the judges awarding her perfect scores. It was the first time in the history of the Elmwood Conservatory, we were told, that anyone had received such unanimous praise.

We sat next to each other on the subway back home. On the other side of Kayla, Mom sat, humming, pounding her hands on her thighs. Kayla herself was giddy about her wild success.

"Did you hear how they yelled, Max?"

"C'mon, Squirt. I was there. Yeah, they made a lot of noise."

"I could've done better."

"I didn't notice any clunkers."

"That's not what I meant, Max. It's never about just hitting the right notes."

That shut me up. I had no interest in arguing with her about what was important and what wasn't, so I buried my head in the book I'd brought and ignored her the rest of the way. We got back to Coney Island late in the afternoon and began the walk home. After a block, it happened that Dad was just returning from the hospital, or wherever else he'd been, saw us traipsing along Neptune Avenue, and pulled over to drive us the rest of the way.

Dad was excited to hear Kayla had won and expressed his sorrow again for missing the event. Mom, Kayla, and I were just very glad to get off of our feet. What a day.

CHAPTER 20

It's not long after the Elmwood Competition, when Max is just starting to absorb that Kayla is not only brilliant and amazing, but one in a billion, that he twice violates her privacy by snooping through her bedroom when she's away. He knows it's wrong, yet some internal drive – curiosity perhaps – overwhelms his reservations. He imagines that there, in her room alone, he will find clues to her genius.

He opens her dresser drawers, seeing nothing of interest besides nylon swimsuits and cotton underwear. He rummages through her closet, letting his hands run along the suede of her tan blazer, the wool of her pants, the rayon of her dresses, the cotton of her blouses – but these tactile efforts don't lead him to what he's looking for, what Kayla herself is made of and why she can so easily do what he cannot. Her clothes feel no different than his own.

He picks up Tina, her Tiny Tears doll, sits with her at Kayla's desk, barely resists the urge to change Tina's clothes, and after a minute or two of uncertainty puts her back where she'd been. He then lies on Kayla's bed, looking at the Beatles poster, closes his eyes, and tries to imagine being Kayla herself. What does she feel when she first picks up a piece of music? Can she not only hear the music in her head but also hear the multiple ways the piece might be interpreted? And how *does* her brain direct her fingers to find the right notes, always, with hardly a stumble even on first viewing? And what *does* make her smile so warmly when she performs, but never otherwise?

No answers come to Max's mind. He startles himself when he drifts off to sleep and has a momentary dream of falling into a black pit. Suddenly awake, his heart beating faster, he chest tightening, his mouth dry, he gets up and finds what Kayla calls her diary in the drawer of her desk. His hands shaking, he opens it carefully, but discovers only that she uses it to paste in animal pictures from magazines; other than captions – monkey, tiger – she's apparently never bothered to write anything.

Max opens her dresser drawers again, feeling certain he's missed something, but can't figure out what. He leaves her room, stealthily even though no one else is home, knowing his investigations were foolish and futile.

·　　·　　·　　·　　·

A week later, Max repeats the exercise, again hunting for everything and nothing, but this time the intrusion into Kayla's room is much shorter. Just entering her room causes Max much greater unease than the previous mission. Every item he touches fills him with anxiety and shame. He pulls his hand back after a split-second contact with her clothes, as if he'd touched a live electric wire. Just as he leaves her room, virtually repelled from her room, he hears Kayla and Adel returning from the Key Food supermarket, and he rushes downstairs to meet them in their living room. He wants to confess and beg Kayla's forgiveness, but can't bring himself to do so; he's not brave and he knows their relationship will be tarnished forever if he tells her what he's been doing.

Kayla stares at him for a few long seconds as if she senses his unease, as if a visible aura of guilt has settled over him. The moment passes. She smiles at Max and turns away, ready to help Adel stow the groceries.

Max wonders how Kayla could have known what he was doing in her room. Although it seems impossible, her look convinces him she knew, that among her other talents she has an ability to read minds and see directly into his, where everything must be clearly written. He remembers Adel telling them often about how she used to predict how Dodgers games would end, and he's always thought this was just another manifestation of her weirdness, but now he contemplates the possibility she actually hade that ability and passed her clairvoyance along to Kayla. He shudders at the ugly thought that his sister can read his mind.

In many ways, Kayla scares Max, even though he's older, stronger, and feels himself much smarter.

CHAPTER 21

There were so many odd things about Kayla we accepted, but that also worried us. She was an enigma. Yes, she was a star in the making, as shown by the Elmwood Competition. If only that were all she was. There were parts of her that didn't fit, or, perhaps more precisely, that we weren't comfortable with, that none of us understood, and that almost made her seem like she'd been born into the wrong family.

First, she had peculiar eating habits. Well, still has, as you'll see. From a very young age, before she could understand what it meant to be a vegetarian, she refused to eat meat, poultry, or fish. Eggs and dairy were okay. For a while, Mom would try to coax her into trying something she'd made – maybe chicken soup or chili or hamburgers – but Kayla would have none of it. Mom finally gave up. She prepared meat and fish dishes for the rest of us, but always made sure there were plenty of vegetables and fruits for Kayla. Kettles of tomato soup in cold weather, tomato soup with alphabet noodles, tomato soup with rice, and, if I never have tomato soup again, I won't miss it. But Kayla still prepares it, and I feel obliged to tell her how good it is.

But back to when we were kids. The meal plan was harder than it had to be, because green vegetables or fruits made her too nervous, so she wouldn't eat them, and then neither could we. So we ate red beans, garbanzos, corn, yams, potatoes, beets, turnips, or carrots. When Mom bought apples, they were Macintosh or Delicious. We didn't press for further explanations from Kayla. We adjusted. She was the star being born.

Second, Kayla had the habit of telling everyone her dreams. At first, these retellings were occasional; everyone does this from time to time. But her retellings increased, now that I think about it, as she began studying with Lindorf. Sometimes it seemed that Kayla had to tell us about her nightmares on a daily basis. I occasionally overheard her describing them to Tina, who would dutifully cry at Kayla's helplessness and the violence to which she was subjected. Kayla kidnapped, the kidnapper about to molest her. Kayla fed a poisoned candy bar. Kayla smashed to smithereens by a falling space ship.

And it was obvious Kayla heard things no one else could hear, reminding me of Mom. I remember once walking past Kayla's room and noticing her swaying like a palm tree in a tropical storm, her eyes closed. I stuck my head in and asked her what she thought she was doing, undoubtedly in the snotty voice only a big brother can muster. She opened her eyes – that tantalizing mixture of hazel and grey – and begged me to listen to the music, but I heard nothing.

CHAPTER 22

"God is a man who's a big Brooklyn Dodgers fan, but he hurts people for the fun of it."

It's one of her pet sayings no one understands. She connects god to the Brooklyn team that left town fifteen years earlier. It's not a god who's created the universe, looks after mankind, demands justice, or exudes love. It's not a god who makes rules; it's not a god to whom one offers prayers. Rather, it's a god who plots and schemes, a god who does nothing but make people miserable when he forces them into his idea of a character, and a god who's helpless to control the story he sets in motion. If this god could bring back the boys of summer and return everyone to the time of Jackie Robinson and Duke Snider, he'd have done so already. She doesn't know why god loves the Brooklyn Dodgers, but at least he has that one redeeming feature, the only trait they share. Adel knows god is a he. She's met him twice, but for the longest time now he's stayed away from her, and she wonders whether, quite possibly, his visits were only dreams. Well, if he ever existed, he's long since deserted her, and he can stay locked up in his office for all she cares. She's got better things to do than spend even a minute wondering about a god who so blatantly fucked her mind.

No one tries to talk Adel out of her beliefs in who or what god is or what he wants to accomplish or why, if he's god, he can't bring the Dodgers back to Brooklyn. When she starts in again about god, Nicky smiles and nods. Adel knows Nicky believes in no god at all, despite his religious upbringing. Adel doesn't blame him for abandoning all that, given what he's been through, and god never dragged *him* into an office crammed with books and pushed *him* down on a black leather sofa and started interrogating *him* under duress. Nicky would be singing a different tune now if all those things had happened to *him*, but, since they had not, then he's within his rights to insist there's no god at all. Nor does she mind that Max echoes Nicky's atheism and has never seen the point in the supernatural. Neither had Adel until she had her first personal encounter with god, and so it goes for many people, they have no belief at all until one day, when they least expect it, there *is* god, standing alongside them in the park or sitting next to them in the car or balancing on his head in front of them on the street or walking into their tent at a remote campsite. So Adel knows this happens, because one day god came slipping a note under the door of her apartment and, after she cautiously let him enter, sat with her on the sofa to chat. He wanted to talk to her about Nicky and listen to her dad's old radio. But she won't argue with Nicky and Max. They can believe what they want.

Kayla asks her about god from time to time. She refuses to accept Adel's explanations about the graying man with a mustache, the virtual stranger to whom she confessed her growing love for Nicky when a good girl would have kept her mouth shut. Kayla seems to think that god is some great force for good out in the far reaches of the universe, beyond the stars, buying into the traditional view packaged by the priests and the rabbis. Adel doesn't argue with her either, doesn't feel the need to prove to Kayla that she's wrong.

She, too, can believe what she wants.

CHAPTER 23

The telephone rings on a day when Kayla's at school, but Max happens to be home with the flu. It startles Adel. She has few friends, never connecting with the other women from the Jewish Center. But on the line is one of her closest friends in the world. It's been many years since they've spoken, but of course she recognizes his voice, more agitated than she's ever heard it.

"What is it, Norm? What's wrong?"

Norm is sobbing so hard she can barely make out his words. She waits, assuming that she'll understand soon enough. His crying doesn't seem at all strange. The more she listens, the more she thinks she's been expecting a call like this for years. As Norm calms down enough to a complete a thought or two, Adel finally comprehends. His long-lost daughter, Grace, has telephoned him from out of nowhere, and the call has upset him terribly, more than he can bear. Can he visit with Adel now? It's been so long, he knows, his fault entirely, but of all the people he's known through a long lifetime, Adel is the only one who will listen to him and not judge. In a minute, Adel calls the guard at the gate to announce a visitor.

Norm arrives much sooner than she expects, undoubtedly having phoned from nearby, probably on Neptune Avenue, where he must've pulled over only blocks away. He rolls up in an orange Plymouth Duster, a car that cost him a goodly share of his income from the diner when he bought it the year before Adel left his employ. Now it's little more than junk. Norm unfolds himself from behind the wheel, and from Adel's window he looks much shorter than he used to be. She sees the same bald, black head with a faint sheen of perspiration, but the posture is not erect. He sags and has difficulty with each step, as if he's forcing himself to wade through freshly poured cement. Adel runs from her house to embrace him. His once strong arms wrap themselves around her, but weakly. She wonders whether he can still hoist around the heavy kettles at the diner.

"Adel, you ... look great!" She hears the catch in his voice and knows he's lying but loves him for the lie.

"You look like shit, Norm. Well, fuck it all, come in, but try not to breathe too hard. Max's home with the flu. We got germs everywhere. It's a scare." She leads him inside and sets him down on the comfortable upholstered chair. Norm looks around at a house he's never visited. His face is still moist with tears.

"The piano?" he asks finally, as his glance settles on the instrument.

"Our Steinway. Both kids play. Every day." She's unaware that Max has gotten out of his bed and stands at the top of the stairs, listening, curious.

"Any good?"

"One piano sounds like the next to me." She starts to hum the main theme from *Jesus Christ Superstar* but Norm's next questions interrupts her.

"I meant the kids? Are they good at the piano?"

Adel thinks for a second before responding. "Max is very good, but Kayla's a fuckin' genius. You should hear her. She's super great and she's only eight."

Norm nods "You're so lucky to have your kids with you and they're doing well."

"So, Grace? She called?"

"How did she find me, I wonder?"

"Tell. Spell. Ring my bell."

"She asks, in this voice I don't recognize, she asks am I the Norm Williams who had a daughter named Grace. I should've hanged up, but I say yes it's me who's this who's this and then she started screaming like a banshee, swearing at me like she'd been saving it up her whole life."

"What's a banshee?"

"Wild animal, I guess."

"Was it her?"

"Must've been. Who else? Screaming I'm a drunk and how I'm a rat fuck for a father and how I beat her mother and how I'm a coward." He shudders, and tears roll down his cheeks again as he replays the episode in his mind. Adel hands him tissues.

"She's wrong, Norm. You're no drunk and you know it. And you ain't no coward. No coward's going to fight in both wars. No coward's going to do what you already done for your country and your friends."

It's as if Norm hasn't heard Adel. "I'm a coward, she says. All these years I've wanted to know what happened to her, how's she doing, maybe if she had children herself, and now to hear her, comin' at me entirely from out the blue, and she's just ripping me apart like I wasn't a human being. It's hard ..."

"Shush." Adel goes over to Norm and hugs him, not the happy hug of the hello, but a longer hug of consolation, a hug that tells him, no matter what, he has a friend who loves him and will do her best to make things easier for him. Adel doesn't understand for sure why Norm's wife ran away with their daughter years before, and maybe he did beat her, but he's not that way now and would never hurt a fly. She's never heard Norm to say a cross word to anyone. She knows his wife's leaving was one of the things that turned Norm away from booze and led him to religion. She knows as well that Norm – who in the kitchen rush occasionally called her Grace – saw in her something that reminded him of the daughter he lost. Norm had been like a father, most of all after her own dad died, and they needed each other's love.

For a long while, Norm cries and Adel lets him, holds him close and lets him empty his heart. She's unaware that Max has returned to his bed to fume about the injustice of it all, that Max is replaying in his head the conversation he's overheard, his mom explaining how he plays well but that Kayla's a fuckin' genius.

CHAPTER 24

So what I'm trying to lead up to is to explain how much, even though I loved Kayla, even though she loved me and treated me well, I hated her. Or at least a small part of me did. Well, hate is too strong a word. I'll think of a better word after I write down this little story.

What sticks in my mind even after all these years – could it really be 28 years? – was when Norm, Mom's former employer at a diner where she worked before she got married, showed up at our house. I eavesdropped from upstairs, and although I don't recall the exact conversation, I remember the gist.

Norm had gotten a call from his daughter. I don't remember her name, but he must've mentioned it. It had been decades since he'd lost track of her. What's stayed with me long, one of the reasons I remember at all, was Norm's crying. To listen well enough to hear him, I'd had to creep down a few stairs. He kept asking Mom why this had happened to him. All this made a big impression. I'd never given much thought to broken families until that afternoon.

But the point, the main reason I remember, is something Mom said. Norm asked about who played the piano, and Mom told him the piano was Kayla's and she was a star waiting to be discovered, she was brilliance personified, she was God's gift to music. Something like that, although she wouldn't have used such eloquent words. I use them now to underline that she told him Kayla was a genius and a prodigy, and how immensely proud she was of Kayla's accomplishments. Get it? Nothing about me! Not a word. No recognition I'd been the first at the piano, that I could play even before my first lesson. No recognition Kayla wouldn't have ever had a chance without my hard work ahead of her.

Now, rereading all this, I'm a bit ashamed because I want this letter to be mostly about Kayla's career, not about my feelings. And yet, I won't delete it. I'll let you try to feel, as I did, the embarrassment of being regarded so dismally by one's mother. The disappointment. And whether it was truly disappointment at what Mom said or disappointment that her assessment was accurate, I don't know.

So, as I say, hate is much too strong a word. If I was upset with anyone, it wasn't Kayla – who after all didn't ask to be born a prodigy – but with Mom. And, yet, how can you be upset for long with the woman who brought you into the world, who loves you, who took you to all your piano lessons, snow, rain, or shine, and who didn't always have all her marbles? You can't.

I think that was the afternoon when I finally faced the reality that I could never come close to achieving what Kayla had already achieved and that, at best, my role in the family would be one of fully supporting Kayla in her life's work.

If you understand this, then everything that came later between Kayla and me, and everything that exists now, can be seen in its proper light.

CHAPTER 25

After the Elmwood triumph, Kayla became an instant celebrity. A picture of her smiling, standing next to the piano used in the competition, appeared in the *New York Times*. Dad was the one who framed it, and it still hangs in my law office. It's one of my many photographs from Kayla's performing days that I can stare at when I'm thinking deep thoughts about pending business deals.

You'd think Kayla would've changed in some fundamental way when she had proof from neutral judges that she towered over the other extremely talented young pianists against whom she competed. You'd think she would've become haughty or self-absorbed or obnoxious. To her credit, Kayla remained modest, perhaps as modest in her behavior as she is today in her attire. The one thing different about Kayla, but only slightly, was the extent to which she bathed in the adulation of her audiences. That was everything to her, and, as her career progressed, the more she needed to have them jump to their feet and scream approval. She fed off this energy. It had to be one of the main reasons she worked so hard, as hard as the tyrant Lindorf demanded.

Right after the Elmwood, Lindorf insisted Kayla double her lesson time. Lindorf knew Kayla was exceptionally gifted, he told our family, but the competition had opened his eyes to even greater possibilities. He would see her twice a week, period. If there was choice involved, it was the choice of either complying or saying goodbye to Bellington. Lindorf assured Dad that Bellington wouldn't charge a dime more; special

Bellington scholarship money was available to see that Kayla continued with Lindorf for extra hours.

Kayla soaked up the praise, easily swayed by Lindorf's excitement. There was no question but that she would do as Lindorf instructed. And the family had to go along with the new arrangements.

The upshot? In a matter of months, we moved to Manhattan to avoid the hour-long subway ride. Lindorf found a sublet for us about a mile from Bellington; one of his colleagues had taken a two-year leave of absence.

Although Kayla was delighted to have twice the time with her mentor and a fraction of the commute, I was glum because I'd had to abandon the very patient Sr. Cantelli, with whom I'd grown quite close. I kept working with him right up until our move. I felt I was still making progress and could have made more if I'd stayed with Sr. Cantelli, but I didn't complain much. I hadn't wanted to interfere with Kayla's trajectory. I saw I wasn't the only one sacrificing something by relocating to the heart of the city. Mom would miss her bird watching along the shore, and Dad would have a longer commute to his office in downtown Brooklyn.

I continued to worry that Lindorf was being too tough on her. Every piece she played, no matter how good it sounded to me, was deemed deficient by Lindorf. The greater Lindorf's expectations, the greater a perfectionist Kayla became. Admittedly, Lindorf's demands and Kayla's inexhaustible energy and devotion paid off; her notoriety grew over the years. Kayla won most of the competitions she entered, including the Syracuse University International Chopin Competition at age ten, the Goucher College Young Pianist Competition at eleven, and the Musicfest French Composer Competition at twelve, when she performed the first movement of the Debussy Fantasie with the Orchestre Metropolitain. I recall there in Montréal how well her fingers swept over the keyboard, how flawlessly she executed the runs and brilliant trills, the excitement as the music rose to a crescendo, the shouts of "Magnifique!"

My role in Kayla's life changed after a few months of moving to Manhattan. We lived off West End Avenue on West 74th. (After two years, Dad bought an apartment in the building.) Mom was having trouble getting around, complaining about pain in her hips and swollen legs and ankles. The long walk to take Kayla back and forth to school, which Mom at first thought would be great for exercise, became problematic. Maybe it was Mom's way of protesting without saying so directly how much she missed the birds of Sea Gate.

In any event, at age ten, I started walking Kayla back and forth to Bellington; obviously, I'd been lectured by Mom and Dad to keep a close eye on her. Not only did Kayla have twice-a-week sessions with Lindorf, she insisted on going to Bellington every day to practice. That's when Dad took as out of the public school and arranged for tutors. We continued our education in the library and in vacant classrooms at Bellington, an institution only too happy to accommodate us on Kayla's behalf. I didn't mind being taken out of school, never having fit in. I was more or less a loner, finding it hard to make friends.

The changes in our lives could've been good for me. If I'd wanted, I had plenty of time to practice at Bellington. But, once I'd been forced to abandon Sr. Cantelli, I never found another teacher, and my own playing declined. I concluded – Mom and Dad never argued with me about the point – I was just a mediocre talent. I saw no further value in spending hours at the keyboard.

CHAPTER 26

She stares at the black and white ivory, aching to caress the keys, but holding back. She must first make sense of the flood of noises inside her brain.

There's a faint hiss, as if air is slowly let out of a balloon, and on top she hears a sound of women's voices. They chant in unison words she can't make out, reminding her of the chanting of the Torah she's heard in the synagogue, but these are definitely women's voices, not men's. Soon enough, the hissing and chorus fade and she hears quite clearly in their place her piano.

The Steinway produces a new melody. She holds her hands over its keys, her fingers poised, ready and eager to strike the notes that flood through her brain, but still she holds off, not wanting to interrupt the flow. She fears that, if she rushes, the magic will be lost. As she closes her eyes, immersed in the music springing to life within her, she sees the score materialize. She envisions everything as clearly as if the printed pages were in her hands: the musical notation, the melodies and harmonies, the arpeggios and scales, the clouds of sixteenth notes in the right hand now taken over by the left and now returning to the right, until the vision fades for an instant. The sounds trail away until there's complete quiet.

Kayla wonders if this is the work of God. She waits.

A full minute of nothingness passes while she breathes deeply, slowly exhaling on each breath so her heartbeat slows as well, until, by some strength of will within her, the music continues, the notations return in her mind's eye, even clearer now, brilliant, not only in black and white, but in bold hues of blue and green as well, demanding she touch the keys and set the strings vibrating. She lets her fingers fall onto the keyboard and plays what her heart has already heard and what her mind sees, music that, until a few minutes before, did not exist. Confidently, no longer afraid of losing the thread, she composes at the keyboard for twenty minutes. When she's done, the last pianissimo chord dissolving into the surrounding air, she rushes into her bedroom to put her hands on her blank music paper and a pencil. Back at the piano, she jots notes furiously with her right hand, continuing to play with her left hand and singing along although she's hardly conscious of her voice. The music takes shape on the paper until it fills many pages, all as envisioned.

An hour speeds by, but it seems like seconds only. She realizes after a few minutes of staring at the score that her mom will soon be home from the Fairway Market. Kayla doesn't want anyone to know yet what she's done. She doesn't understand it herself. She hurries back to her room and at her desk puts the finishing touches on her creation. Then she hides the music, which she thinks of it as a long prelude, in the bottom drawer of her desk.

CHAPTER 27

My fourteenth birthday was a day I'll never forget, for it was the day Kayla gave me as a present the music she'd composed just for me. It had been a secret; not even Mom or Dad knew she'd been working on something.

When she handed me the music, I must have looked stunned, because she said something like "Get a grip, Max. This is for you to enjoy."

I examined the score of a complicated piece in D Minor. Her penmanship had never been stellar, but I could see she'd tried with great effort to be neat. I didn't feel I had the sight-reading ability to play the piece credibly right there and then, so I asked her to play. She obliged with a smile. And this music, kids, was like nothing I'd heard before, although it did remind me of the Schubert quartet "Death and the Maiden" through its use of a five-note falling motif. But this was not written in the Romantic style. It was mysterious and haunting, its rhythm compelling it forward through exquisitely complicated runs in both hands, staying in D Minor only briefly, moving through a series of unexpected modulations, and ending in D Major.

When she finished, she turned toward me, waiting for my response. I rushed to hug her as Mom and Dad clapped. It was the best birthday present I'd ever received, and I keep it in a box in my closet. I still can't play it and gave up trying long ago. I think it hurt Kayla that I never worked harder to master it. But Kayla still plays it for me occasionally, usually to cheer me up when I'm depressed, and she doesn't need the music in front of her.

If you're wondering why I love Kayla as much as a brother can love a sister, this is surely part of the reason.

CHAPTER 28

Now that Kayla is a famous pianist, Adel is more enthusiastic than ever about classical music. She often thinks about how her father tuned their floor radio to the classical FM station when the Dodgers weren't playing, how he tried to teach her about the music, and how she'd then had only limited interest. She wishes she could tell Nate Miller how everything has changed. He would have been so proud of Kayla. He would have *kvelled*, something he'd never done for Adel herself.

She tries to keep up with what Kayla is playing. In a small, wire-bound notebook Adel keeps in her night table, not unlike the one in which she makes notes about birds, she writes the names of the pieces Kayla is learning, their composers, and the dates Kayla begins to study each. Kayla is a bird, that's the word, haven't you heard, Adel sings to herself. She also records when and where Kayla performs in her ever-increasing schedule of competitions and recitals. When Kayla practices at home, Adel listens closely, and when there's a pause, she'll ask Kayla what she's playing to make sure she can match the sounds with the pieces listed in her notebook. She's proud she can recall the name of the piece when she hears it months later, and she asks Kayla about the music to let her see she cares. Kayla is always gracious talking to Adel about the music, trying to explain what she feels her mother wants to know. The mother-daughter bond thrives upon the beauty Kayla creates.

Adel's noted many entries for Beethoven and Chopin, the composers that Herr Lindorf first wanted Kayla to concentrate on, but has now added Bach, Brahms, Bartok, Debussy, Poulenc, Prokofiev, Ravel, Schumann, and Scriabin. The last one Kayla has begun is Tchaikovsky, a piano sonata in C-sharp minor. While Kayla and Max are off at school, Adel sits at the

Steinway with her notebook and copies in the name of the new piece, very careful with the spelling. On the first page of the music, she sees that it is *allegro con fuoco* – allegro with fucking, must be, she thinks – and writes that as well. The music covers the pages, spilling into patterns across the staves, gibberish to Adel, but she stares at them anyway, captivated. The notes move around across the pages, like black ants actively working in their colony, pulsating and expanding into great big blobs of ink, disappearing, fighting with each other, fading into grey. Then the blackness turns without warning into a kaleidoscope of bright colors, iridescent reds and oranges, electric greens, and lightning yellows. She's hypnotized, enthralled.

Adel's never tried to play an instrument, so never learned to read music, and that's fine with her. She knows her eyes would never adjust, and the effort would be as futile as trying to read the newspaper. Before she became a nut case, she used to read a lot, but then printed matter became one of her many enemies. When the turmoil on the pages of Tchaikovsky finally scares her, she closes her eyes, takes a deep breath, and counts slowly to ten. She does what Nicky has told her to do.

Max, who'd come home for an afternoon nap, has been standing at the doorway observing Adel for minutes as she sits at the Steinway. She's so still Max can tell she's put herself into a trance.

"Mom? Are you all there?"

"What time is it?" She drops the music, reaches to pick it up from the floor, and the housedress she wears sags away from her bosom, revealing much more of her chest than Max cares to see. He turns away.

"Four-thirty, Mom. What are you doing at the piano? I was going to play."

"Just getting up now." She sticks the notebook in the front pocket of her dress. "I have to start supper. Your dad called to say he'd be late again. He's a hen; news at ten and then again."

"Figures. We don't see him very much these days."

She walks into the kitchen, then turns to stare at Max for a second. Max sits at the piano, intending to see if he can still play the Chopin E-minor Waltz by heart. Before he can begin to play, Adel says "Don't forget to pick up Kayla at 5:30."

"How could I forget?" he mutters, but Adel hasn't heard him.

CHAPTER 29

She decides to take off an hour to go to the park. It's late April, still cool, but the bright sunlight is too inviting for her to ignore. She needs to get away from the piano for a while.

She crosses into the park at W. 69th Street and walks down the shrub-lined path. Already there are yellow and blue flowers coming up all over, and she sadly realizes she doesn't know what they're called. A couple of teenage girls in jeans and t-shirts follow their dogs on leashes, and Kayla wonders why they're not in school. Then she remembers it's Saturday and, for normal kids, school is out. It is Saturday, *Shabbat*, and should be a day of rest, a day for just such walks.

As Kayla breathes in the fresh air and garden fragrances, she wishes she could take off an entire afternoon. She continues to follow the walkway, which curves to the left, then crosses West Drive and leads farther into the green expanse at the center of the city. In another few blocks, she comes upon a tulip garden in full bloom. In the years she's lived in Manhattan she's never been here – almost never walks in the park – and for a moment she's stunned by the buttery yellows, the dark purples, and the bright pinks forming a blanket over the ground. Kneeling at the edge of the garden, the cold damp of the ground seeping through her jeans, she peers at the flowers, focusing on a purple tulip whose petals have spread open wide. The insides of the petals at the bottom fade from purple into cobalt blue and surprisingly into a white circle around the center. Then she looks closer to examine what she assumes are the sex parts of the flower, the shaft of which is a pale yellow covered by a group of cream-colored protuberances. The names of these botanical parts escape her. She vows to ask her tutor to teach her botany.

The voices around her of children playing and the sounds of birds and traffic fade as the intensity of her focus increases. Consciousness of time ebbs away. After a while the colors change again. Every color – purple, blue, white, yellow, and cream – becomes suffused with a golden glow, as if the flower has its own sun bearing down on it or is lit by its own sun from within. The flower and she are connected, both part of a dream or a story, another dimension of reality far beyond what can be seen or touched, another expression of the Divine, at one with and the same as her music. There is no time. There is no forgetting or remembering. Kayla longs to merge into the Force who created them all, the flowers, the music, and herself.

CHAPTER 30

Kayla turns from a girl into a young woman in Max's eyes. One day, she's just his kid sister, a tyke, still just a wisp of a person. The next day, she attracts libidinous stares from the young men at Bellington. One day, her favorite way to relax before going to sleep is to cuddle with Tina. The next day, she's grown up and, although Tina still sits on Kayla's desk, the evening might bring a phone call from the young dancer at Bellington who's taken a liking to her.

Max now sees Kayla as a beautiful young teenager. He admires her long dark brown hair, which falls well below her shoulders; he marvels at her strength, the result of her enthusiastic embrace of the exercise regime Lindorf insists upon. Max even feels Kayla's smile has grown more mature, more compelling, more intriguing. There's still that innocence drawing people to her, strangers as well as fans, other musicians as well as her family, but there's also a hint of invitation. Max can't think of it in any other way. He senses in Kayla's smile the idea she might welcome someone to approach her in a not-so-brotherly way.

Max asks himself whether he's jealous that Kayla is attracting potential boyfriends and decides a brother can't be jealous like that. He knows she needs friends, even boyfriends at some distant point in her life. If he's irritated by Kayla's blossoming and the future romantic connections this foretells, it's because Max wants to protect her focus on the piano. It annoys him whenever he feels Kayla wants to do something other than practice, although she rarely wants to.

That dancer, Bryce, works out with them every morning. They've known him for a year before he starts paying close attention to Kayla, asking her about her music, about Lindorf, about her family, and Max notices that Bryce constantly has his eyes all over her. Kayla just eats it up, returning each conversational gambit, questioning Bryce about his dancing, then about his family and friends, and they often end up talking about the Mets or the Knicks. More than once, Max tells Kayla that they have to get moving, only to have her ignore his pleas.

Somewhere around then – Kayla is thirteen and well known in music circles now – Kayla grows tired of Max trying to get between her and potential boyfriends at Bellington. She broaches the issue as they walk up Broadway heading home. She carries a small leather satchel with the music she'd been working on, and Max carries the much heavier backpack full of their school books. A cold, early November wind blows dead leaves and other detritus around them as they walk.

"Max, you don't want me to get close to anyone my age, do you?"

"That's ridiculous. Where the hell did you get that idea, Squirt?" Max tries to sound indignant at her accusation, but fails miserably, knowing that he sounds more guilty than anything else. Of course, Kayla's right.

"It's not ridiculous at all. I can tell. What do you think's going to happen if I had a boyfriend?"

"Is there somebody?"

"No! How could there be? When would I have time to even consider such a thing?"

"I don't know."

"As much as I love what I do as a pianist, I also want to also have a life. Maybe have a boy love me some day. Don't you feel that way, too? I mean, about a girl? You're almost sixteen."

She hits Max in a sore spot, intentionally, because Max is shy with girls, has never been on a date, even though he's met plenty of girls his age at Bellington and there's a certain cute singer he's had his eye on. He blushes when Kayla asks him about wanting a girl to love him, but as they're walking fast and dodging cars on the cross streets, she doesn't notice.

"What I feel isn't the issue. You're too young to be thinking about boys, aren't you? You have a whole lifetime ahead of you. Isn't this the time of life when you want to keep working as hard as you can on your music?"

"It doesn't have to be one thing or the other."

"At this point, Kayla, it has to be one thing or the other. You're about to have your own Town Hall recital. Who knows what will happen next? There'll be more competitions! You have so much going on right now with the piano you need to keep your mind on. Don't you understand?"

Max, trying to sound like a smart, concerned older brother, comes across as arrogant and harsh. Kayla refuses to talk to him for the rest of the trip home.

CHAPTER 31

Now let's go back to the evening of Kayla's debut recital at Town Hall, February 18, 1980, the great triumph I described when I started writing this. Before we left Town Hall, Lindorf insisted on visiting us later at our apartment with two of his "friends." I could see Mom and Dad were drained by the drama of the day and didn't want company. But, as always, they deferred to Kayla, whose sense of her accomplishment gave her all that much more energy and who hated to disappoint her mentor. So it was planned.

Lindorf arrived with two people he introduced as members of a committee. The first was a small man named Robin Ziegler, dressed in a well-tailored dark grey suit and carrying a large shopping bag in one hand and a thin black leather briefcase in the other. The second was a tall, middle-aged lady, with short blond hair, introduced as Charlene Deerfield; she carried an elaborate fruit basket wrapped in red cellophane. The fruit basket was a gift for the entire family. From the shopping bag, Ziegler produced other gifts: two bottles of "fine Scotch" for Dad, a floral arrangement "straight from Ovando's" for Mom, and a Burberry leather wallet for me. I thanked them for the wallet, puzzled by why I should receive an extravagant present when it was Kayla who had performed. Oddly, there was no present specifically for Kayla.

"We wanted to share in celebration of Kayla's success, ja?" explained Lindorf.

Dad pulled in a few chairs from the kitchen so all could sit in our living room. "And what is it you'd like to talk to us about, Herr Lindorf?" It was

Dad's quiet, professional voice, a voice trained over many years to be matter of fact.

"Ah, see, I told you he was to the point," Lindorf said as he nodded to the others. "Herr Covo, this is about Kayla, of course, and what we do now."

"It's Dr. Covo, if you don't mind." The edge in Dad's voice was palpable, the professional voice he'd used just seconds earlier gone in an instant. He'd done all he could to put aside his hatred of Germans in dealing with Lindorf for Kayla's sake, but he could tolerate nothing smacking of disrespect.

"Quite right, Herr Dr. Covo."

"Why do we have to do anything now?" asked Mom. "Can't she just have one night's rest? You're a pest."

"Mom!" A look of horror crossed Kayla's face.

"Just a jest, no inquest." Mom just couldn't keep her mouth shut.

Lindorf ignored Mom's rudeness – he surely had long known by then that Mom was a bit "off" – and turned to my sister. I could tell he was pumped. "Kayla, do you wish to go on tour? As a professional? We can arrange, ja? Do you wish maybe also to record? We can arrange. You will have your picture on the album cover, of course."

"Hold on, hold on!" Dad rightly did not like Lindorf directing questions to Kayla when they should've been directed only to her parents. I could see the glow in Kayla's eyes turn to dismay. She was in thrall of whatever Lindorf wanted her to do, and the idea of a tour, the idea of recording, the idea of her photograph on an album cover, all tantalized her. Well, who wouldn't have been intrigued? "She's too young," Dad continued. She's still just a little girl. She's ..."

"Dad! Please. I'm almost fourteen. Mozart was touring when he was seven. I want to hear what Herr Lindorf is talking about."

A stronger father would've sent Kayla off to her room and told Lindorf and his stupid committee to go packing. Despite my pride at what Kayla later accomplished, I often wish Dad had done so. But he couldn't bring himself to stand in the way of anything Kayla wanted, especially when it was so obvious she was talented beyond measure, especially on the day of her greatest triumph. So Dad agreed to hear them out.

"I will let Herr Ziegler tell what is what," continued Lindorf.

Ziegler ostentatiously removed an envelope from his briefcase and unfolded about five sheets of paper, clearing his throat before beginning to speak. He had a high-pitched, affected voice, and I didn't like him from the start, wallet or no wallet. My immediate thought, later borne out to be on target, was "slime."

"These are agency papers for your daughter, Mr. and Mrs. Covo." I knew instantly he'd used "Mr." on purpose to rankle Dad.

"It's Dr. Covo, please."

"Yes, of course, *Dr.* Covo. Forgive me." I could have sworn he rolled his eyes as he spoke those words. "These are agency papers. They would be for one of you to sign, but of course both can sign."

"Agency?" I asked. I knew what agents were, but it hadn't occurred to me that official papers would be involved.

"Yes. So by these papers we are obliged to provide for the guidance of Kayla's career, to arrange for her performances, to engage her if possible in a recording contract, and to serve as her managers. We see to the publicity, we create her public image."

"Who is 'we,' Mr. Ziegler?" I had to ask, because Mom and Dad seemed at a loss for words, expressions of puzzlement on their faces.

"Well, as set forth here," he handed the papers over to Dad, "the entity is called Deerfield Entertainment III, Inc. It's a limited partnership under Chapter 5 of the New York Business Law, but you needn't concern yourself about our corporate form. Charlene here is creating the company just for the purpose of helping Kayla and putting out her own money to get it started. Aren't you, Charlene?"

"Yes, I am."

"And her companies I and II have also been created to help other young students at Bellington get their careers launched. Right, Charlene?"

"Yes. You know the Haitian violinist August Sorel? We represent him. He's studied at Bellington for years, our first project. And then there's Roberta DeLuca, the cellist, who's also studied at Bellington. She's with company II. So, Kayla, you'd be our first pianist. A great honor, I would add."

"You're all with Bellington, then?" Dad asked.

"Well, Dr. Covo, Herr Lindorf is with Bellington of course. I'm an attorney representing Ms. Deerfield and her companies, as well as a limited partner, and Herr Lindorf would be a limited partner as well. Ah, but we think of ourselves simply as the committee. Much less formal. We don't stand on ceremony."

Dad looked at the papers for a minute, frowning the whole time, then handed them to Mom. We waited while she read. She'd hold the papers close to her eyes for a second, then much further away, then close again, going through the same motions on every page. I could tell it was an effort for her.

"Fuck it all," she said after a while. "This says your company gets fifteen percent of bookings and fifteen percent for management plus fifty percent of any recording contract fees," Mom observed. "Isn't that too much?"

"First, that's net after our expenses, and it's standard in this business I can assure you," replied Ziegler. "There's a tremendous amount of work to be done, and we do it all, so Kayla can just concentrate on making beautiful music. We know the right people to introduce her to as well. Also, as her parents, you don't have to worry about things like booking her into hotels or transportation or arranging for the proper pianos to be delivered to the proper forums or any of the details of her career. You'll be putting Kayla's success in the hands of proven experts."

"May I see the papers, please?" I reached out to get them from Mom, but Ziegler grabbed them himself and glared at me while he put them back into his briefcase.

"That won't be necessary, Max. This is adult business. Mr. ... Dr. Covo, I'd like you and your wife to think about this offer very carefully. Opportunity knocks, you know? Kayla has a special gift from God, and it would be sacrilegious to deny her gift its full reign." My initial dislike for Ziegler grew immensely when he prevented me from looking at the papers, and with the invocation of God I truly hated him. I knew then, as certainly as I'm writing this today, that he was a phony and couldn't be trusted.

Dad glanced at Kayla. I could tell she intensely wanted to go along with the idea. She wanted travel and fame, true, but most of all she wanted to bring her music to as many people as possible. Music was the sole purpose of her life. Dad could see it in her face as well. "We will think about it," he said.

When they left, I told everyone in no uncertain terms what I thought about the committee. "They are going to run Kayla ragged and bleed her dry. Please, Kayla, tell Mom and Dad you don't want any part of this."

"But then Herr Lindorf will refuse me as his student!"

"You don't know for sure, Kayla. He may very well come back with a better offer." I had no idea how agency deals were supposed to work, but I felt the committee was trying to take advantage of my sister.

"Nicky, maybe we should ask Ben to look at the papers?" Mom had a good point. Ben was the lawyer who'd been the partner of my grandfather, Nate Miller. I didn't know him, but I'd heard Mom talk about him occasionally and assumed he'd assess the situation with common sense. Anything to delay this, I thought.

"I think Ben's a real estate lawyer, though, isn't he? Or wills and trusts? Is he the right kind of lawyer?"

"Any lawyer, Dad. Mom's right. Someone needs to look at that closely, someone with our interests at heart. There's something fishy."

"Fishy?" Dad had been an American for thirty years, but still got mixed up on slang.

"You know, fishy, not right, not kosher."

"Ah, fishy." It looked like Dad was about to say more, when Kayla spoke up.

"Can I say something?" We all turned to look at Kayla. If I remember correctly, she had changed into jeans and a Knicks t-shirt after the Town Hall debut. While we'd been talking about Ben and lawyers, she'd walked over to the piano, where for a second she caressed the dark wood like she was petting her child. "Herr Lindorf is a good man and means the best for me. He's brought me an awful long way from when I studied with Sr. Cantelli. Didn't you hear the audience today?"

"Yes, but ..."

"But nothing, Max. That's all that matters to me. Those audiences and giving them the music, letting them feel what I feel when I play. Nothing else would ever make me happy."

"You're so young to know what would make you happy." Dad's voice had turned professional again. It was a voice of reason, non-threatening, to be considered thoughtfully. "And there are parts of that ..."

"How do I make you understand? I'm your daughter, your sister, and you want to take this away from me?" She pounded on the upper end of the keyboard, and the discordant mélange of notes revealed the depth of her anger more stridently than her words.

"No one wants to take anything away from you," I replied, hoping Kayla would listen to me. I spent more time with her than Mom and Dad combined, and I knew what was best for her. I naively believed she'd agree with me.

"Forget this lawyer nonsense." Kayla's voice had as sharp and decisive a quality as I'd ever heard. "I'm going to tell Herr Lindorf tomorrow that one of you will sign. I will get the papers and bring them home and one of you will sign or ..."

"Or what?" I asked.

"I'll quit the piano."

"You'd never!"

"Try me."

And that was that. Mom and Dad didn't want to call Kayla's bluff, although I urged them to. I begged them to hold off signing. I argued as forcefully as I could, with as much skill as I could muster, that Kayla would never give up the piano because she *could* never give up the piano. I pleaded with them, I reminded them they were her parents and had a duty to tell her what to do, a duty to protect her from her own unwise desires. Mom and Dad heard me out, but to no avail. In their eyes, I was just a kid, and they probably sensed that part of me had been jealous of Kayla's success for a long time. But they offered me very personal and different reasons for their decision.

Mom recalled that her dad had supported her when she'd wanted to get a job. "Your Grandpa Nate didn't stand in my way," she said. "Parents have to support their kids. Plus, I had a bitch for a mother. I hated her enough to try to kill her, and don't want Kayla to hate me that way. So, let her fly. Let her try."

Dad's thinking was more complicated, to the extent I understood it. My folks had named Kayla for one of Dad's sisters mistakenly thought lost in the Holocaust; well, I've told you a bit about that story already, but at the time we're talking about here, February 1980, Dad's sister Kal was dead to him. I'm sure he felt Kayla was Kal's reincarnation. The highly educated man that he was, he never said as much, but I believe he saw Kayla as a vehicle to sanctify his sister's memory. To deny Kayla would have been to desecrate the ghosts of his murdered family.

It didn't make sense. I thought he could've put aside such an emotional reaction when the safety and well-being of his own daughter was at stake. But perhaps he intuited that Kayla's time in the limelight would be limited, and he didn't want to deprive her of her brief chance.

The next night, both he and Mom signed the papers.

CHAPTER 32

He should never have become a father. Although he loves Max and Kayla more than life itself, that's how he puts it in his own mind, he's lost when it comes to providing the strong guidance they need. He feels weak, powerless. He's allowed the outside world of contingency to push him and his family into waters for which he's unprepared. He's a capable swimmer in a still green bay, but a tide has swept him far from shore. He thrashes about, reaches for a hand or a rope, and the only thing he sees is Kayla's demonic hazel-grey eyes. No. Kayla's are the eyes of a genius that Nicky is unable to comprehend in the scientific, rational way in which he was trained. His psychiatric education did not prepare him to deal with prodigious children, least of all his own.

The rational part of Nicky knows instantly upon reviewing the contract that the deal is bad for Kayla. Every risk and doubt that Max urges upon him he already understands and fears. Yes, it would appear that the committee is a bunch of crooks. Yes, of course it would make sense to contact a lawyer, bargain, mount a defense, resist temptation. But he can't force himself to act upon what he knows. He fully believes Kayla's threat that she'll give up the piano forever if he doesn't go along with her demands. She's the most determined and stubborn person he's ever known, so obvious when she practices. These traits explain her uncanny ability at the piano and make it extremely unlikely she's bluffing.

Nicky cannot tolerate the idea that, by refusing to go along with the committee, he might push Kayla away from him forever. He cannot abide with the guilt he would feel if Kayla destroyed herself by turning her back on fate's gift to her.

He wonders what his own father would have done in a similar situation but then cannot imagine how such a situation might have arisen in his own family. What would Nicky himself have desired so strongly that he'd give up everything if he'd not gotten his way? His main desire, still not well formed at the age of fourteen, was to follow in his father's footsteps and become a doctor. His sisters, Ada and Kal? It pains him to think about how his family was murdered at Auschwitz. All they wanted was to live, not travel to the pinnacle of art.

Kal was the one with the artistic bent. What if Kal had demanded to be sent to a fine arts program at the Aristotle University, giving an ultimatum that she would otherwise give up drawing and painting forever. Dr. Max Covo would have found a loving way to steer Kal in what he considered the right direction and make it seem like Kal's decision. He would have taken her into his study and found an appropriate Talmudic passage to discuss. Perhaps it might be a passage about how a child must honor her father and mother and Kal would withdraw her ultimatum. But, just as likely, he might well have found a passage that convinced him to do as Kal wanted.

Nicky finds no guidance in the past, only the fantasy that Kal might well have grown famous as an artist, another Thalia. He forgets the last name of the famous Greek painter, but recalls that a framed reproduction of one her works hung in their house in Salonika. Kal could have been such an artist if she had lived.

He must do as Kayla demands. Her eyes pierce the raging waters to where he struggles. He reaches out, desperate to grab her hand lest he drown.

CHAPTER 33

Kayla has insisted her parents sign on the dotted line and she's excited about the prospect of going on tour, but she hides another feeling, from herself and from her family. It's easy to hide what she doesn't understand.

A small dot of fear lives on in her. It's not the adrenalin and quickened breath she's experienced before a performance. Those feelings tell her she's ready to bring the music from her heart into the world where others can love it too and love her as well. No. This pang of fear sits in the back of her throat, an ache that dries her mouth into a desert. It spreads from her throat into the back of her light hazel-grey eyes, pushing her to the brink of a headache. It creeps from behind her eyes to the skin of her scalp while she fights in nightmares against great dangers. When the ache has grown, it forces her awake, her eyes snapping open to the darkness of her room. She struggles to catch her breath, and her scalp feels as if thousands of ants milled about, digging holes into her skull.

She sits abruptly, pulling Tina next to her. Still in pajamas, she goes into the living room, puts Tina next to her on the piano bench, extends her hands over the keys, and practices in her imagination. It's dark, only the faintest glimmer of light filters into the room; it's hard to distinguish one key from the next with one's eyes. But Kayla can visualize everything she needs to see, can imagine herself attacking the grand opening chords of Tchaikovsky's G-Major Sonata, then deftly executing the complicated, ominous runs of the B-Minor second theme. Her body sways with the music she hears as clearly as if she were actually playing. As she practices, the gross tingling on her scalp subsides, her breath comes easier, and the fear retreats into the point in the back of her throat. Tina is content and doesn't cry.

In minutes Kayla can't think of anything she ought to be afraid of.

CHAPTER 34

Adel has signed the papers because Kayla wanted her to sign, and she had to sign to help her daughter; she didn't want Kayla to hate her like she hated her own mother, but she's pissed off and worried just the same. She's given up the reins on Kayla to a group of strangers. A loving mom should take better care of her little girl. Kayla needs her family to watch her back.

Herr Lindorf, she knows, has genuine concern for Kayla, but the other two are goons, two total fuck-offs, Max is so right about them. They're like many of the turds she used to serve at Norm's, the type who came in as if they owned the place, took one look at her, and judged she was a fat slob with no brains. She again recalls the asshole who out-and-out grabbed her tits, feeling he could be gross because he'd sized her up as below his station in life. What the fuck was he but some loser who swept the floor at a broken-down factory? She again recalls with pride how she'd punched him upside the head as hard as she could and damn near lost her job because of it, but he hadn't been the only one who'd looked down on her. She'd heard the whisperers calling her names and telling her how bad she was. If those voices had come with bodies, they would've looked exactly like the rest of this fucking committee.

With Kayla's first tour in the planning stages, Adel asks herself why she was so wimpy as to cave in to the demands of a not quite fourteen-year-old. She could see the agency papers gave the committee too much money and all the power, but she couldn't bring herself to say no. If she'd had the courage to say no and argued with Nicky then maybe he wouldn't have signed either and things for the Covo family would be the way they had always been.

It's not just her loss of control that bothers Adel. It's also that she knows Kayla will become a victim like Adel herself at the same age. She remembers too well the intense sexual need that flooded through her. Kayla, once freed from the nest, will put out for every guy who comes her way. Maybe it's happened already, although it's hard to see how Kayla can had time to fuck boys given her demanding schedule. But going on the road will be different. A new room every night in a different town, a mess of taxi drivers, busboys, waiters, stage managers, an army of pricks who'd like nothing more than to ravish her innocent daughter. In a distant corner of her mind, Adel dimly recalls her own violation by someone she thought she loved. Kayla, as beautiful as she is, as much as she looks on the outside like a woman, is still a child. She still loves her doll! Yet, the hormones, the spidery chemicals her body manufactures. She'll give in to their unrelenting demands.

Charlene – that dyke! – has explained to her over and over how Adel can go with them on the road to keep an eye on Kayla, expenses paid by the committee, but Adel doesn't want to tour herself. Despite her interest in Kayla's music, Adel's place must be in the home, cooking, cleaning, paying bills, and seeing to Nicky's needs.

It can't work.

CHAPTER 35

Despite my misgivings, things did not start out badly.

Our routine hardly changed. We continued to walk back and forth to Bellington, and Kayla practiced like one obsessed, both at school and at home. So engrossed was Kayla in her music that she often got up in the middle of the night to sit in front of the Steinway, pretending to play but not making a sound. I watched her once for a full ten minutes when she didn't know I was awake. She had Tina sitting next to her as if the doll could listen and judge.

I prepared for my high school equivalency tests and worked on college applications. I gave no thought to applying to colleges outside of the city, feeling instead I needed to be around home. So I examined the brochures of Columbia, NYU, CCNY, and Fordham, among others. I was most interested in Fordham, because it had a campus at Lincoln Center, spitting distance from Bellington. If I could attend college there, I could stay as close as possible to Kayla. And I'd thought about a career in law even back then. In part, I put my mind toward law because of that pathetic Ziegler. I wanted to understand what could empower someone to bring contract papers into a stranger's house and act so scurrilously. I wanted to be able to fight people like Ziegler. In my fantasizing about the future, I could better protect Kayla and other innocent people if I too were a lawyer.

The first tour arranged by Charlene was modest enough. Kayla would play a solo recital at the Columbus, Ohio, Jewish Community Center on a Sunday evening, continue with a matinee recital at the First Presbyterian Church in Indianapolis the following Wednesday, and give recitals Friday and Saturday evenings at the University of Chicago School of Music. Lindorf recommended a program only slightly less demanding than the one she'd performed at Town Hall, and Kayla agreed.

Both Mom – whose arm we had to twist – and I would accompany Kayla. Completing the entourage were Charlene herself – to get things in order, she said – and a young woman named Renee Gottschalk, described by Charlene as someone being groomed to be Kayla's road manager. We were given to understand that Renee, a former student of Lindorf, had been on many tours, could arrange things for Kayla, and act as the obligatory chaperone. Charlene's exact words were, "Renee will always be able to keep her out of trouble."

I didn't think much of Renee. She was tall, like Charlene, and also had short blond hair. She could've been attractive if she'd tried, but dressed indifferently and her most distinguishing feature was her empty facial expression, as if she were not quite conscious or as if whatever difficulties she'd face in life had drained her of emotion. I don't think I ever saw her smile. Automaton is the word that came to mind. She'd answer questions with the fewest words possible, not wanting to talk unless forced to do so. A great traveling companion, I told myself, about the equivalent of sitting next to a department store mannequin.

Given that I didn't like Charlene or Renee and that Mom wasn't the easiest person to talk to, Kayla was the only one with whom I could converse during the tour. And we did talk quite a lot. On the surface, Kayla seemed her usual happy self, especially when she played. But something had changed in her, a change so slight it was hard to perceive.

The first problem had nothing to do with a change in Kayla, however, but with the way Charlene treated her. In Columbus, the five of us had gathered for dinner at the Blackwell Inn on the night before the concert. We sat around a table overlooking a small garden, Mom tapping her finger against the window and humming to herself, Renee peering into the napkin on her lap, Charlene consulting notes she removed from her bag, and Kayla perusing the menu. When our waiter arrived, and it was Kayla's turn to order, she told him she didn't want anything on the menu, but asked if the cook could manage a vegetable plate including a baked potato, stewed tomatoes, mashed sweet potatoes, and applesauce. Charlene jumped all over her.

"What? That's not a proper dinner! There's no protein. Order the salmon." The waiter looked back and forth between Kayla and Charlene, confused.

"No, Charlene. I'm a vegetarian."

"She won't gobble green, either." Mom added. "Reminds her of puke, I think."

"That's unacceptable," Charlene bristled.

"Don't eggs have protein?" I asked, trying to sound innocent. "She eats those in the morning."

"Chill, Max. If I don't get what I want, I won't eat."

"Green is gross. The grocer's green is grossest. The grocer's grossest is *charoses.*" Mom understood that Kayla was being challenged and, in her unique way, was trying to defend Kayla.

Happily, the waiter saved the day. "Well, Miss, I'll have the chef prepare a dish exactly as you request. We're pleased to oblige." He took the rest of the orders and left.

"Kayla, no wonder you're so skinny," Charlene huffed. "I had no idea about your strange eating habits. I think you'd better reconsider."

I couldn't stand Charlene – or anyone – criticizing Kayla. "Excuse me, but don't you think that's Kayla's business, what she eats and doesn't eat?"

Kayla looked at me, telling me by her glance that she could handle things herself, but said nothing.

"Well, Max, *you* are not managing Kayla's career, are you? We've invested quite a bit of money in Kayla's future. Don't you think her health, her well-being, her appearance are matters for us to think about?"

"What she eats is her business. Period." I wanted to tell her as well that her conduct was outrageous, but I'd said enough. Charlene ignored me for the rest of the evening.

The second problem did involve a change in Kayla, though, and emerged the following afternoon, at the concert venue. We'd been listening as Kayla practiced on the Steinway set up for her when, five minutes into her practice, she stopped in mid-phrase, unhappy.

"This G is definitely out of tune." She played a G high on the register. "It's flat about an eighth of a step."

The manager was upset. "We've just had the technician here this morning to make sure everything was good."

"Bring him back, immediately. This must be fixed or I can't play." The manager ran off, presumably to the telephone in his office.

Now, a couple of things struck me as odd. Kayla had never complained before about a concert piano's tuning. It was possible the technician had made a slight mistake on that G, and Kayla's super-sensitive sense of pitch detected it, but the Steinway technicians were highly trained; I felt an error was unlikely. More significant, however, was the tone of Kayla's voice. Other than members of her family, she rarely ordered people around. When she wanted something, from Lindorf, from Opal the photographer, from her tutors, she usually added "please" and a smile. Here, there was neither a "please" nor a smile. My impression was that Kayla was nervous as she began her first professional tour and that she was trying to quell her jitters by asserting authority over others. I liked the idea of Kayla taking charge, but I worried about whether she was dealing with much more than the usual stress.

The technician returned in an hour and worked on the tuning again, with Kayla close by his side. He didn't detect any error as far as I could see, but made fine adjustments anyway until Kayla was satisfied. When he left, Kayla finished her practice, and we returned to the Blackwell.

At Kayla's room, I asked whether we could chat, and she invited me in.

"What was that all about today with the tuning?"

"You didn't hear the G was a bit flat? Like about five cents' worth?"

"No, nor did anyone else. And you know, he was using the Sanderson tuner, these guys know what they're doing, so I don't see how it could've been wrong."

"It was the weirdest thing. It sounded wrong, it *was* wrong, even when he showed me that the Sanderson was telling him it was right. But then, finally, it sounded okay. I'm sorry I made everyone go through the trouble of bringing him back, but I couldn't have played otherwise."

"Are you nervous, Kayla?"

"No more than usual. No more than before the Town Hall recital."

"You'll talk to me if you need to?"

"Of course."

I went to hug her goodnight, but she pushed me away. "Good night, Max," she said.

Because I wasn't ready for her push, which was probably harder than she'd intended, she almost knocked me off balance. I smiled wanly and left.

CHAPTER 36

The recitals on this first tour are magnificent in Kayla's view. Her entrance onto the stage to the enthusiastic applause is not so much a walk as a bouncing of energy and excitement. She's as full of anticipation as a bride eagerly opening her arms to her new husband.

Kayla scans the audience for the most interesting and most deserving faces, even as she smiles broadly to all. Love radiates from every end of the hall, adding to her supreme confidence. She will return that love twenty times over by reaching into the soul of the music, in the place music meets God. She will bare the music's beauty to the audience, because they've come to her expecting no less, and they will worship with her at the shrine of her art. As she sits at the piano, she falls into a trance, losing consciousness as a separate being. She is so relaxed and yet focused that the audience disappears, and the music takes over. She lives only because the music wills her to live.

When she concludes, the ovation brings her back into the concrete world. She loves her audience as she unleashes her jubilant smile, as if she were smiling to her lover's returning from a long absence. She basks in the returned affection. The audience wants to love her, but she wants even more to love the audience, and she does, every last person there fulfilling her desire to the point of blinding exhilaration, like the discharge of lightning during a summer storm. The world explodes for her in the seconds after she concludes a piece, when she's flooded by the roar of adulation. The world explodes for her, as she thinks about it later, very much like the orgasms she's recently started giving herself.

Kayla laps up the attention from the press and saves the reviews, all generous and outstanding, even though she feels they lack full understanding of what she does. The *Chicago Tribune* writes as follows:

"Fourteen-year-old pianist Kayla Covo, on her first professional tour, performed works of Beethoven, Chopin, and Ravel with exceptional grace and power at the University of Chicago School of Music Concert Hall last evening. This young lady, who hails from New York, was impressive in her mastery of the program, displaying a musicality suggestive of a much older performer. She is a special student of Heinz Lindorf at the Bellington School of Music.

Covo's first selection, Beethoven's Pathetique Sonata, was played with a great range of color and authenticity, making this overplayed piece into something new and immensely enjoyable. That set up an amazing performance of the Appassionata Sonata, where the great sound Covo elicited from the Steinway and her virtuoso rendition of the electric third movement stood in stark contrast to her rather slim frame and, dare we say, her little-girl smile. The second half included three Chopin etudes and Ravel's *Jeux d'eau,* all of which were met with the knowledgeable audience's enthusiastic approval. We hope Miss Covo continues in the path toward pianistic perfection she's already on and will return soon to the Chicago area for more performances of the same caliber."

She appears on a Sunday morning local television show after her last recital, a show in which the word prodigy is bandied about and in which she performs a Chopin etude on a piano whose tuning is less than perfect.

"So, Kayla, when did you start playing the piano?" Every interview begins the same way, but she responds as if it's the first time she's heard the question.

"Well, I don't remember, exactly. I think I was two and started to play when my brother Max began his lessons. He's very good too, you know."

"Incredible. Two years old! A real prodigy for you! How long do you practice every day?" That's another question she must field every time she's interviewed, and she's delighted to give the same answer every time.

"Oh, as long as I can. Maybe ten hours?"

"What are your plans, now?"

"Keep getting better."

"Will you stay on tour?"

"If Herr Lindorf, my professor at Bellington, wants me to. He's looking after my career right now."

"What do you think of Chicago?"

"It's amazing! I'm so happy to be here." She flashes her million-dollar smile directly into the camera, and thousands of viewers feel that the smile is meant just for them alone.

For a while, Kayla has forgotten that ache in the back of her throat.

CHAPTER 37

It barely occurs to Adel that Charlene is cold and bossy and that Renee is unresponsive. At best, they're like pieces of furniture, familiar and useful, but not people she'd ever consider friends. At worst, they're agents of the devil, the people who are taking Kayla away from her and placing Kayla in danger.

Adel doesn't perceive that her own actions have taken a sharp turn toward the bizarre, that the stridency of her humming has increased, that she often engages in conversations – some muted, some not – with persons unseen, that she more frequently swears at no one in particular. She doesn't pick up on Kayla's worried looks. She ignores Max's concerned questioning about whether she's stayed on her medicine. The truth is that she doesn't know. Medicine is just another dirty word, shorthand for how people are always plotting against her, wanting to capture her, tie her down, and put her into a state mental hospital.

All but Kayla have conspired. Kayla, her brilliant and beautiful daughter, what Adel wishes she herself might have been, is still on her side. What pleases Adel most about this trip is how happy Kayla is and how the audiences adore her. Adel loves the music Kayla brings out of the piano, and her familiarity with it comforts her and makes her feel more at home, where she'd rather be. She still wonders why she let herself be coaxed into going on the tour, but Charlene insisted Kayla would benefit and that Adel would relax once she saw Kayla in good hands.

Ah, the music. Adel has to fight hard not to sing along with the lilting melody of the slow movement of the Pathetique. And she sweats profusely with nervous energy during Kayla's performances, almost as if it were she, Adel, on stage, continually judged.

At the tour's conclusion, Nicky meets them at La Guardia, and Adel feels as if she's been away for years. But is he looking at her now with longing or disgust? He speaks to her, but she can barely comprehend what he's saying. Something about the damn brain cleansers. She understands he's reprimanding her about how she needs to get back on the meds and how, once she does, she'll be okay. But she's okay now, already, isn't she? She's angered that they figured out somehow she'd not been taking the brain cleansers. Max must have snitched. Of course she had to stop, because she'd been taken off Thorazine and placed on Haldol and got the shakes so bad it was hard to hold a cup of tea without spilling. She's been much better without the meds, but then she's confused about which meds exactly. Her family's conversation buzzes around her, whispers tap at her ears, and nothing makes sense.

"I'm upset none of us made sure she had her Thorazine, too, in case she couldn't deal with the Haldol." Is Nicky speaking? His voice sounds more than anything else like an angry beehive.

"At home she was pretty good about staying with the program," Kayla says. "Now I see what happens when Mom stops. It's ugly."

"Right. Psychosis. Hallucinations. Loss of affect."

"Meaning?"

"No emotions. Like a zombie."

Although they whisper, she can make out some of the words. Adel knows they're talking about her, she's the only mom in the car, that much she's sure of, and the word zombie makes her bridle. She wants to say she hasn't clawed her way out of a grave, but the thought vanishes before she can speak, and she no longer remembers what they were talking about. She hums the melody of that Beethoven song she loves. She doesn't notice how Kayla glances at her, then looks to Max with a pained expression.

"Would she become violent, Dad? Before she could be locked away?" asks Kayla.

"Most patients with schizophrenia don't become violent, but some do. If she feels especially threatened by something – rightly or wrongly – it's not impossible."

Violent! Adel understands violence. Someone is going to hurt her. Her bitch mother's going to come back into her life with that whipping belt, with its hard metal buckle, about to put the pillow over her mouth and nose and press hard, cutting off her breath. There's Louise, right now, climbing in through the back window. Adel panics; she tries to unlock the door of the moving car and throw herself onto the pavement, to safety.

Nicky pulls over and grabs Adel's wrist. "*Cara mia*," he murmurs to her as she screams and fights to pull away. As he holds Adel down, Nicky reaches into the glove box, removes a pack of cigarettes and a lighter, flips them to Max, and tells him to light one. In seconds, Nicky places the lit cigarette into Adel's mouth and she inhales. The smoke calms her in a few seconds. Between drags, she hums Beethoven.

"Kayla. Max. Listen. If you're afraid, and I'm not around, if you think your life or anyone's life is in danger, call 9-1-1."

CHAPTER 38

Following the success of her first tour, Kayla foresees a career in which she'll have the chance to bring her music to people all over the world, and she intensifies her practice, working at the piano up to twelve hours every day. She meets with Herr Lindorf three times a week at a minimum, but stops by to see him more often when she needs advice on a particular issue. She builds up her repertoire, adding Rachmaninov and Khachaturian and Joplin. As she explains to Max, she wants to be able to reach people who might not like one kind of music but could respond to another.

"But Joplin? Is that really classical music?"

"What difference does it make? It gets people moving, doesn't it? I'm adding *The Entertainer* and others to my list of encores. You'll see what a commotion that makes when the audiences recognize *The Entertainer.* They'll go crazy."

"And the press? The critics? Do you think they'll still take you seriously if you suddenly start into ragtime?"

"They loved *The Sting* when it came out, didn't they?"

"I'm not sure we're talking about the same critics."

"It doesn't matter. I'm learning to play them all. This week it's *Maple Leaf Rag.* Besides, they're great warm-ups. And the critics? Well, just wait. You'll see. It'll get me even more notice."

"And how does Herr Lindorf feel about this Joplin business?"

"Ha. I haven't told him, but he'll love it too when he reads the reviews."

Kayla loves the notice she receives in the press. When she's alone with Max, as they continue their tradition of walking together to Bellington even though Kayla is old enough to walk by herself, she not infrequently raises the topic.

"Max, don't you think I did a good job in the Channel 9 interview with Michele Marsh?"

"Sure." He's not much for talking when he's intent on watching the traffic as they cross the numbered streets.

"It's exciting to be on TV!"

"I wouldn't know."

"Oh, you do know. There must be thousands of people watching me, and some will come to one of my concerts someday. It's ..."

"Don't get a big head about it, Kayla."

"Max, I'm not ..."

"I mean, sure, it's great you're on TV and all, great that you can spout off the names of these news anchors, and we're proud of you, but that's not really the point of your music, is it? To be on TV?"

"No, it's not the point. I just thought it was neat, that's all."

Kayla can't help but be annoyed with Max's attitude; she feels he should give her one hundred percent support. Without saying more, she speeds up to create a space between them. He lets her get ahead, even though it wouldn't be difficult to catch up.

CHAPTER 39

After her first tour, I deeply regretted my loss of influence over Kayla. The days when I could make a pianistic suggestion to Kayla without getting a disgusted, patronizing look had long since passed.

She had others now to look after her career and direct her – others whom I distrusted – and she could get from them whatever support she wanted. They may not have been the most pleasant people in the world, they may have been crooks, but they at least seemed to know about setting up tours, arranging for TV and radio interviews, and getting their star performer to the right spot at the right time. It boiled down to Kayla just not needing me. As more people came to know her name, I'd be known, if anything, as her older brother. This is how it must have felt for Nannerl Mozart, an accomplished musician in her own right, when the world's attention focused on her brother Wolfgang. I read somewhere that the two grew far apart later in life. I dreaded that happening to Kayla and me.

One great annoyance was how her managers played up Kayla's maturation into a young woman. They believed she couldn't be promoted any longer as a child prodigy but would win more hearts and sell more tickets as a very attractive teenage girl performing in alluring attire. In short, they tried to make your Aunt Kayla into a sex symbol.

I remember well the session in Opal's studio for a new set of publicity photos. It was shortly after Kayla's first tour, and she didn't mind my tagging along. Charlene was there, in charge, and she'd brought with her a variety of dresses, wanting to see how Kayla looked in them. They were form-fitting, some had low necklines, the longer skirts had slits up the side where Kayla's legs might show as she reached for the pedals and the shorter dresses and skirts were, well, just short. Kayla loved trying everything on and wanted the committee to buy them all. The colors were as flashy as the styles: bright warm oranges, hot pinks, deep naughty reds, cool metallic blues. Kayla was ecstatic. As I watched, Opal and Charlene posed her provocatively. In one pose, Kayla wore a silver gown with a low bodice, and they pulled one sleeve a bit off of Kayla's shoulder.

"Try to look dreamy," Opal instructed. "Pretend you're on your way to bed and just starting to undress."

"Opal!" interrupted Charlene, nodding my way as if I was there to ensure decorum. Then she directed an order to Kayla. "Just try to imagine you're playing something slow and heart-rending."

Kayla was not cut out to be a model, too fidgety by a long shot. But she never complained. From what I could see, she tried hard to give them what they asked for. In the off-shoulder shot, Kayla's expression is somewhere between beguiled and bemused. In another sequence, they posed Kayla leaning back against an upholstered chair, wearing a floral-patterned gown with a V-neck. Charlene told Kayla to have a very slight smile and to imagine she was seeing a friend enter the room. It took long minutes for Kayla to tone down her smile, but she managed. That became one of the best shots the committee used in the coming publicity.

What truly rankled me was the absence of photographs with a piano. The previous sets all had pianos; Kayla might sit at one, stand next to another, or there were pianos in the background. At this session, I saw nothing to suggest Kayla was a musician. I mustered the nerve to ask about it.

"Well, Max, the committee now feels that people know Kayla's a pianist. It's been all over the news. It would be superfluous. You know what that means, don't you?"

I don't suppose I could have hated Charlene any more than I already did, but her condescending tone always made me want to tear out her throat and feed it to pigs. "The only reason we're all here is because Kayla is a pianist, so why no pianos in the pictures?"

"Too much detail," said Opal. "We want now to just focus on Kayla as a person."

"It's all right, Max. I'm good with this. Relax." Kayla decisively ended the discussion, so I sat again, muttering, swearing in my mind.

The spread of proofs that came back from that session was amazing. I've kept quite a few in my scrapbook. Of course, I'll show you when you're here. I'm not sure Kayla even knows I have this particular scrapbook, as I never take it out when she's around. So, Joseph and Rosina, let's be clear about one thing. You're not to mention it.

My favorite photo now – my favorites change from time to time – is the one in which she's wearing a blood-red long, sleeveless gown, standing against a grey background. The shot is taken from behind, and Kayla turns back toward the camera over her right shoulder. She looks like she's about to walk out of the frame and is inviting someone to follow her.

CHAPTER 40

It's confusing and exciting. Adel examines the spread of photographs Charlene has brought to the apartment and feels gratified that Charlene asks for her opinion, as well as Kayla's. Kayla's a beautiful young woman, and, poring over the proofs, Adel marvels such beauty could descend from such a dumpy looking mother. She wants Charlene to use all the photographs in the next round of publicity, but Charlene laughs and says they need to select just a few. So Adel thumbs through and divides the proofs into piles for yes, maybe, and not sure, ending up with more than half in the yes pile, a quarter each in maybe and not sure. How can she decide when they're all so good?

"What do you think?" she asks her daughter.

"I like this one," Kayla says, pointing to the photograph of herself wearing a long blue gown, a warm smile on her face.

As they debate the merits of various poses and outfits, Adel hears the voice of her mother whispering in the back of her head, reminding her that she's a slut. For a minute, she thinks Louise is actually in the room and turns her head abruptly to see if she can catch a glance of the ghost, but nothing's there. Kayla and Charlene pretend not to notice.

"You're a slut, Adel. You're a slut, Adel." The whispering grows louder. First there's one Louise whispering, then two, then ten, then a large group of Louises in unison, repeating the accusation. It's the same chorus Adel has heard thousands of times.

Adel shakes her head to rid it of the voices, but shaking only makes the voices more threatening. She pushes her chair back from the table, runs to her bedroom, and slams the door. Kayla and Charlene look at each other and shrug sadly, then move photos from pile to pile. As they do so, they hear muffled cries from Adel's room. Kayla knows her mom is screaming into her pillow.

CHAPTER 41

And so, kids, I began college and became absorbed in my studies, taking as much writing, political science, and history as I could cram into my schedule. I figured that's what pre-law students needed. Just as Kayla wanted to excel as a pianist, I wanted to be the smartest one in my class at Fordham, get into the best law school, have the most exciting legal job, and become a judge down the road. I took eighteen credits at a time. Dad had breezed through college in a few years and I vowed to myself I would do the same. Eighteen credits a semester were nothing, I decided, and looked for ways to take even more. As hard as Kayla worked at the piano, I would work harder as a college student.

To be honest, I also developed an attitude of know-it-all with Dad. Now, you might think that this is a diversion from my story about Kayla, but it ties in later. You'll see.

Maybe I'd always been a know-it-all like that, a natural-born American as opposed to an immigrant. I remember vividly lecturing Dad about the presidential election in 1980. He was a Democrat, had been so since he'd achieved citizenship, and supported Carter's re-election. Just to antagonize him, I found reasons to support Reagan, and we'd debate until Dad just gave up. I couldn't be content to let him win any argument, especially involving politics. Looking back, it seems clear that my disdain for the way Dad thought had much to do with Kayla. I knew he'd dropped the ball by letting her get mixed up with Charlene's committee. I had to prove to him that I was smarter.

It was around then that Dad asked me to help him at his office. He needed someone to go through his charts and redact names and other personal information so the charts could be used in a study. He'd pay me three dollars an hour, he said, if I spent every Saturday with him in the office until the work was done.

I tried to get out of it, not wanting the bother and not needing the money because I had a fat allowance anyway. But he almost begged, so much so that I succumbed, dubious and annoyed, but feeling I had to oblige him.

As it turned out, the exercise, which spread over four weekends, taught me a lot about his practice and necessarily about him, too. Of course, I read everything as I looked for names to black out. His patients were wealthy businessmen, their wives, their disturbed children, but every so often I found the records of a charity case, as Dad called them, someone who would receive his care for free. Rich or poor, many of his patients seemed the victims of trauma: Holocaust survivors, women who'd been raped, children who'd been molested by their parents, older relatives, teachers, priests, and rabbis. I read about uncontrollable lashing out and about marital infidelity and depression. I read the copious notes Dad put into his charts about the medications he chose for each patient, the discussions he'd have with them concerning benefits and risks, and the adjustments he inevitably made.

In short, I realized Dad cared deeply for his patients' welfare, as if each patient had been part of his extended family. I saw clearly that Dad internalized his patients' problems. When they suffered, he suffered with them.

Perhaps he cared for them even better than he cared for Mom, Kayla, and me.

CHAPTER 42

The tiny dot has gradually grown into a lump of bitter, foul-smelling coal at the back of Kayla's throat. A few months after the conclusion of the first tour, just as she's resumed the comforting rhythm of walking to school in the morning, exercising, practicing, and walking home, the committee is determined to push her onto the road again. They want her to start on a major tour the next spring. She wants to tell them that she needs more time at home, time to relax and be a kid for just a little while longer, but she doesn't know how to say this without sounding ungrateful. She's aware only that her parents signed the agency papers, making Charlene her manager, and that she's obligated herself to do as they ask.

Kayla knows that she forced her parents into it signing. She could have said no, but she insisted. Now, everyone's trusted her, everyone's counting on her. Yet, at her next session with Lindorf, she tries to raise her concerns. She's just about to leave his studio when she turns to him, swinging her ponytail around, and points to the Chopin B-flat Minor Sonata she's begun to work on.

"Herr Lindorf, don't you think it will be quite some time before I'm ready to perform this on tour? With everything else I'm trying to learn? Perhaps next spring is too soon?" She wants her words to be interpreted as a plea that her mentor will put a stop altogether to the plans for the second tour, but he doesn't pick up on her meaning.

"Ah, you're making fast progress, ja? You learn all this quickly and many more. And you have much time to prepare. But wait to you get to the last movement. How do you say? *Gespenstich* ... ghostly, yes."

"I've looked at it already. Yes, ghostly, but ..."

"So I know you will make that ghost appear in the concert hall. It's the return of the corpse from the funeral march, ja?"

She knows what she can do. Learning the piece is easily within her grasp. She's already figured out how to evoke – at the highest levels – the stirring climax of the first movement, the pathos of the walk to the graveyard, the beleaguered spirit from beyond. She has no concerns about failing. It's not that at all. The audiences will love her as much as they loved her before. With that lump of coal feeling, though, she's just not ready to commit to another long trip.

"But maybe I'd play this sonata even better, much better, if I had, perhaps, a year between tours? Couldn't I perform in a few local competitions for a while? Spend more time in the recording studio?" Her voice has faded almost to nothingness, so afraid is she of letting Herr Lindorf down. But there, she's said it. After one tour, she's grown weary of traveling and needs a long rest. It's so obvious what she needs, isn't it? What more could she add? How can he not see?

"Ja, time off from touring is good. But it won't improve your playing. And too much time off is bad." He hands her a plastic bottle of water on her way out of his office. "Here. Drink up on the way home. So, we talk about schedules again next session, ja?"

She nods, not so much because she's agreeing to raise the issue again, but because she sees her instincts are on target. The committee won't understand. She vows to give up the idea of dodging the next tour and to be a more faithful servant. She'll pull Tina into bed with her at night and Tina will help her cry when she feels like crying.

She's taken two steps into the hallway when she turns again because Herr Lindorf has one more thing to say. "Now, please to remember, at the beginning of the Chopin, *agitato, doppio agitato!* Da-dit dit-dit-DAH. Da-dit dit-dit-DAH. It must be as if your heart is bursting with fear. *Verstehst du?*"

"*Ich verstehe.* See you Tuesday, Herr Lindorf, *und viel danke.*"

"*Bitte.*"

CHAPTER 43

So Charlene started planning your Aunt Kayla's next tour not very long after we returned from the first. Kayla showed me a list of venues and events. This time she'd be away for two full months. She'd even make an appearance with the Los Angeles Philharmonic near the end of the tour, playing an as yet undetermined concerto. Lindorf wanted her to get ready both the Grieg and the Schumann. The cities also included Houston, San Antonio, Phoenix, San Diego, San Francisco, and Vancouver. To accomplish all the preparation, to learn all the new pieces she'd be expected to play, would take many months of work. She'd have to work harder than ever, but Kayla seemed to luxuriate in hard work. Yet, I worried.

"Don't you think this is a bit much? It looks exhausting." I didn't see how any human being, even my prodigy sister, could handle the flood of new music, the pressure to excel, and the grind of travel. I knew from even the short tour we'd shared that travel could take a lot out of one, and I had seen the effect of the pressure on Kayla.

"Charlene and Herr Lindorf don't seem concerned. Well, yes, it's ambitious, but if I'm going to get my name known around the music world, this is the best way, don't you think?" The words spoke of confidence, but Kayla's tone suggested reservation. I thought she was trying to convince herself of the wisdom of the proposed trip. I didn't want her to go if she wasn't fully committed.

"I don't think Mom or I will be able to go with you. That's an awfully long time away from your family."

"I wasn't counting on either of you coming. I know you've got college and Mom ... well, she's better off staying here. God, we don't want a repeat of the problems we had with her. But I'll have Renee all the way on this trip and Charlene for part of the time." She failed in her attempted smile, undoubtedly trying to imagine months with the robotic Renee and the overbearing, insensitive Charlene.

"I don't think Renee's much protection for you."

Then her demeanor turned on a dime, as they say. Kayla looked startled, then angry. Her attitude of resignation to a difficult trip disappeared. "Why do I need protection? Do you think someone's going to attack me?" On top of the anger, perhaps I should've caught a hint of concern in her voice.

"No, of course not. Just speaking generally." We let the matter drop.

In fact, though, the idea of her being attacked was exactly what I feared soon afterward. Kayla's new set of photos ostentatiously marketed her as a sex-symbol. I couldn't say that outright, though. Instead, when we next spoke about the planned tour, I again tried to point out the difficulties. I told Kayla I thought Renee seemed pretty inexperienced for all the touring she'd supposedly done before she'd quit. And then I added that Renee struck me as totally weird, like she lived in a different world and couldn't be trusted.

"Do you really want to spend months with her as your main companion?"

"Well, she's quiet, true, but she knows her way around airports and hotels and venues. C'mon Max, what's really bothering you? I thought you'd be excited for me. Aren't you?"

"It's a great opportunity, yes, but it'll be grueling and a long time for you to be gone. And, well, I just hope you're not being taken advantage of. It's not only Renee I'm concerned about, but the whole committee, the whole arrangement."

She shook her head in obvious dismay. "You're not my father, Max!"

"I'm not trying to be your father. I'm trying ..."

"You never liked Herr Lindorf, and you hate Charlene and Robin."

"I don't hate them," I lied.

She continued as if she hadn't heard me. "You worked hard to convince Mom and Dad not to let me sign with them, but thank God they didn't listen, and now, since you lost that battle, you're fighting to override my managers. You want to sabotage me into becoming a second-class pianist."

"That's ridiculous."

Kayla surprised me by crying. I moved to where she sat on her bed and tried to put my arms around her, but she pushed me away, just like she'd pushed me away in her hotel room during her first tour.

"Stop with the hugs! Hands off! What I need is your support. I'm going to do the tour, you know. I want to feel that you're there with me in spirit, needing me to succeed in a big way. Can't you give me that?" She reached for tissues.

"Okay. You have my unreserved blessing, for whatever that's worth." I didn't know what else to say and got up to go to my own room. I thought our conversation was over, but she spoke again, in a much softer, almost pleading timbre.

"Max. Please don't go yet."

I turned to face her again. "Well?"

"Don't go away angry at me."

"All right. I'm not angry. It's your career, and I'm only your brother who loves you and worries about you."

"And I love that you care about me so." She dried her tears and smiled at me, that beautiful Kayla smile that always wrapped me around her little finger.

I sighed, knowing I could no more dissuade her from going on the tour than I could've performed on the tour myself. "Tell me. What will you play? Has it been decided?"

"Let's talk about it. I'd like to hear your suggestions."

CHAPTER 44

He lies next to Adel, who's gently snoring, but Nicky feels too keyed up to sleep. He's not sure what's bothering him the most: his continued guilt for the affair with Adrienne, his concerns about Kayla going off on another tour, his fears Adel will stop taking her meds – all of these, from one second to the next, grab his attention in a never-ending cycle and prevent him from drifting off. He takes a few deep breaths to help himself relax and then, in the darkness, allows himself to imagine he hears singing, chromatic, accompanied by a single acoustic guitar picking a slow counterpoint.

"*Nani, nani, nani kere el ijo de la Madre. De chico se aga grande. Ay el durmite el alma que tu padre viene.*" Go to sleep, the voice urges him, as it sways and lifts, "because your father is coming." It's his mother's voice he hears, come from nowhere, retrieved from the memory neurons in his brain that settled into a quiescence fifty years earlier, a voice of comfort, a voice filled with a promise he can close his eyes and be safe. Then he remembers the rest. "*Avrir no vos avro, no veníx cansado, sino que veníx de onde nuevo amor.*" "I will not open my door to your father," he can hear her sing, "because he comes not from work but from a new lover." Nicky can't remember the last time he thought of this lullaby, but now the darkness is rich in memories and he's helpless to fight them off.

The line from *Hamlet* comes to him. "To die, to sleep, to sleep, perchance to dream." How does the rest go? He cannot recall, but remembers Hamlet contemplating suicide to escape the burdens of his existence. It takes nothing to "shuffle off this mortal coil" – ah, yes, that was one of the key lines – if one acts resolutely.

He's not ready to die, but the thought of bringing on his own death strikes him as plausible, more plausible than ever. He feels dead already. There's just the question of putting on the finishing touches.

Nicky gets up quietly, whispering to the still-sleeping Adel that he's going to take a long walk, puts on his pants and jacket and a pair of sturdy boots, and leaves the apartment, intent on hiking into the park. He knows it's not safe at night; the park harbors gangs of marauding teenagers who kill just for fun and scores of addicts who'd knock him into the next world for his inexpensive watch. He walks on, not caring about the danger, almost wanting someone to challenge him with a knife so he can feel himself alive again.

The failed effort to sleep has left him depleted and unsure of anything. He needs time to think. This is the only way for him, away from the office, away from the apartment, away from the stress of Kayla's career, away from the craziness of the woman he married and still almost loves. He just wants time to think. The brisk walk in the cool air makes him feel more like himself, and he decides he's not ready to die. There's too much to do first.

Then another memory, something he hadn't thought about in thirty-plus years. His Uncle Avram – his mother's brother-in-law—hanged himself just as the Nazis entered Salonika, leaving three children and a widow and no note. Nicky recalls how his father solemnly broke the news to him and his sisters, even as his mother rushed across town to comfort his aunt. Nicky's father had been a straightforward man; was gentle and caring, loathe to speak ill of anyone, but not a person who would sugarcoat such a nasty story. He didn't try to explain why Uncle Avram ended his life, didn't try to connect it to the war, to the fear of the Germans, or to anything else other than that he'd decided it was his time. No one would ever know why. Nicky recalls his disbelief that such a thing could happen, that a parent would abandon his children that way.

As he walks, another memory: he thinks of the evening, a year later, when he nearly ended his own life by hanging himself with the leather straps of his *t'fillin*. They were designed to make a tight knot, and it would have held. A young girl had barged into his room at the rectory where he was hiding at exactly the right time – or maybe the wrong time – and he'd had to put away his suicide plan. Apparently, he needed first to fall in love with Dora and then fight and kill with the *andartes* and then watch Dora die from typhus. Some great plan of the cosmos had required their deaths be so ordered. In the inevitable calculation of misery to which his life was subject, he'd added Dora's death to those of his own family in the gas chambers and to those of the people he himself had killed with his Mauser.

Then the part of Nicky wanting to heal others took root, and he made it to America, learned English, got his education, became a psychiatrist. The good part of Nicky fell in love with Adel and fathered two remarkable children. If there was a purpose to his having been spared from death, it had to be Max and Kayla. Now, as he walks through the darkness, he sees that the good part of him has diminished. He'd promised to be true to Adel for the rest of his life, but he's been too weak to fight off his desire for Adrienne. He's given in shamelessly to the myth of sexual conquest, yearning to prove to himself ... what? He isn't sure.

He grows cold as the wind picks up. Getting his bearings, he heads back home. He's sorry no one has accosted him with a knife or even panhandled. It's going to be another ordinary day. He'll have to leave for the office soon, with a full schedule of patients lined up.

He cannot keep seeing Adrienne, as much as he loves her. He needs to say goodbye to her forever to give the good part of himself a chance to recover. He must eliminate everything from his life that is not pure. He will call her today.

CHAPTER 45

It wasn't until the middle of June 1981 that Charlene – smoking and looking annoyed while she waited for Kayla to say goodbye to each of us – stood next to a Lincoln Town Car parked in front of our building. I was having an incredibly dull summer because of the baseball strike.

"She's here, Kayla," said Mom, looking down from our window. Kayla had been rushing around, trying to find a few more things she needed to bring with her. The last item she stuck into her large handbag was Tina. Tina hadn't been along on the first tour, but Kayla probably figured that two months without her would be too long. "Make sure you call us when you get to Houston."

"Yes, Mom."

"And call us every other night the whole time you're away, like you said you would. If you could, you should, be good. Don't be crude. Don't be lewd."

"Yes, Mom. No, Mom."

"Come here for a hug goodbye." Kayla obliged, but once in Mom's grasp Kayla struggled to escape. Mom clung fast, and it took a few seconds before Kayla pushed free. Then it was Dad's turn.

"Kayla, we're all very proud of you. You'll make sure to have someone clip the reviews for us and send us copies of the programs?"

"Of course, Dad. You know I will. That's one thing Renee gets paid for."

"Then be well. Bring me my chariot of fire."

"Bring you your what?"

"Never mind." He hugged her, and she turned her toward me.

"Max ...I'll miss you."

"Same here."

"Thanks for everything. Thanks for suggesting the Schubert Impromptu. Thanks for, well, just being there."

"Call me if you need anything." I had no idea what I might be able to provide that Kayla would need. This time, she let me hug her and kiss her on the forehead. I tugged on her ponytail and grabbed one of her suitcases.

When the family had loaded her into the Lincoln and said our polite goodbyes to Charlene, Kayla was driven off, and we wouldn't see her for two long months. We looked at each other, crestfallen, missing her even before her car was out of sight.

"Well, she flies away. Chirp, chirp. Fuck a duck."

"She'll be OK, Adel. Renee will make sure."

"Where is Renee anyway?" I'd thought her chaperone would be in the car when Kayla was picked up.

"I guess they're to meet her at Kennedy."

"There are flocks of seagulls and egrets at the airport, you know. Rocks and flocks and docks. I hope Kayla looks for them."

"I'm sure she will. What do you all say to going out for brunch? I'm hungry."

So Kayla was gone not even two minutes, and Dad was planning to take us to a restaurant. I guess this was Dad's way of softening the blow, reminding us we couldn't stop living our lives just because Kayla was a star, well launched on her way to greatness. We crossed Broadway and headed uptown a few blocks to Sarabeth's.

There, in a brightly lit room, the highly polished floor shining up at us with its pattern of dark brown circles, I sat across from my parents. We looked at each other, we looked at the pedestrians passing on Amsterdam Avenue, we looked at our menus, and again at each other. I don't know why they were so quiet, but I was thinking hard, trying to find the courage to raise the topic I'd been worrying about. Then Dad reached out his hand and turned Mom's chin toward him, and she blushed, smiled, and looked down. His gesture and her reaction disrupted my chain of thought; I was confused, if not mortified. What kinds of parents do this sort of thing in front of their seventeen-year-old son? Yet, as I thought about it, I realized

Dad had been paying more attention toward Mom in that way. I wondered whether I could make him pay attention to me.

We ordered, and, as the waiter left, I ventured into the subject most on my mind.

"Dad, what kind of arrangements were made to handle Kayla's money?"

"What do you mean, handle?"

"Account for. Invest. Manage. You know, handle."

"I think they set up a bank account for her."

"You think?"

"That was my impression."

Mom played with her spoon, tapping it against the side her water glass, and appeared to ignore our conversation.

"Dad, don't you think we need to know exactly what they've done? We really need to check the numbers and make sure she's not being cheated. Do we even know if she made anything from that first tour? And from her recordings?"

"I ... I don't know."

I put my glass back on the table with enough force to slosh out a few drops of water. "We need to find out, for Kayla's sake. When we get home, if you don't mind, I'm going to draft a letter for you to send to Herr Lindorf, demanding the information, and the bank account number, if there is an account, and there better well be, and authorization to look at the account."

"Kayla hasn't told us to do any of those things," Mom interjected. So, she hadn't been ignoring us after all. "It could be like green food for her. She hates peas. Fuck peas, if you please."

"You don't understand, Mom. Kayla's only fifteen, and if you and Dad won't look after her interests, who else will?"

"Well, don't get unpleasant, Max."

"Dad, I'm not ..."

The waiter arrived, bearing our orders of shrimp and chorizo quesadillas and crab cakes. As he placed the dishes and refilled our water glasses, we suspended our conversation. Then he walked away.

"We'll write the letter, as you suggest," Dad continued, calmly, "but it must be polite, and we will do so only after we talk to Kayla and get her consent. She has to agree. When it comes down to it, it's her life we're talking about. Food's here. Let's eat."

"It's a treat," finished Mom.

CHAPTER 46

She knows something's wrong. It's a feeling unlike anything she experienced when Nicky drifted away. When his lovemaking had become less frequent, she took this as a sign they were just getting older. Nor had she worried when she perceived Nicky paid her fewer compliments or his kisses became less ardent. Nor had she worried when she realized Nicky was holding her less often at night. She'd heard enough on her favorite shows to understand that romance in marriage often fades over the years.

It's the opposite now that worries her.

Nicky doesn't seem himself when, on a Tuesday night, he interrupts her listening to the CBS Radio Mystery Theater to encourage her into their bedroom. It's so out of character for him. She asks over breakfast the next morning whether anything's wrong. He looks uneasy, but protests that all's fine and wants to know why she might think otherwise.

She lets the matter drop.

CHAPTER 47

Kayla did as she'd promised, at least at the beginning. She called when she arrived at her hotel in Houston, then every other night for about a week. I was spending all of my time in school, in classes or at the library, so I didn't talk to her myself. But Mom and Dad assured me she sounded fine.

Then Kayla wasn't calling as often as she promised. Once she forgot it was the night to call, once she had to leave early for a performance. When no one heard from Kayla for four days and I could feel the tension mount in our apartment, I picked up the phone myself, gave the operator the number of the hotel (in Phoenix, I think), and within a minute had Kayla on the line.

"Max!" Her voice sounded genuinely happy, but weak and groggy. I'd woken her from a nap.

"We haven't heard from you, Kayla, and the folks are climbing the walls." I pulled the phone into my room and closed the door. "What's going on?"

"Nothing. Just dozing off."

"How's everything? We haven't seen any reviews or programs."

Her voice picked up a bit more energy in her effort to assure me that things were fine. "The concerts have been wonderful, and I'll talk to Renee about sending the stuff she's supposed to send. Great reviews."

"Go on."

"And the audiences are so excited and happy, makes me happy. I played at least two encores at every event. Last night, three. I worked in *The*

Entertainer and they loved it, like I knew they would. Almost added *Maple Leaf Rag*, but I was bushed."

"I can imagine. But what about all the rest of it? Renee?"

"Renee seems hardly there, you know? Well, I guess you do know. I meet her in the morning after I've already practiced for three hours. She hands me airplane tickets and tells me where to be at a certain time. Oh, but there's one strange thing."

"What's that?"

"She doesn't listen to any of the concerts. She's at the venue, but stays in the dressing room."

"I told you there's something off about her. I've been telling you since we met her. She acts like she's had a lobotomy."

"Could be, yeah. But she's getting me around okay."

"You don't have anyone to talk to."

"Well, there's Tina, of course, but real people, no. It doesn't matter, because I practice most of the time or I'm performing. When I'm not practicing or performing, I'm reading, eating, or sleeping." There was a slight pause. "I did see a movie by myself one evening, though."

"That can't be very safe."

"The theater was right next to the hotel, and I was back in bed by nine."

"What did you see?"

"*Chariots of Fire*. I'd been thinking about it since Dad mentioned something about it, right before I left. Cool music."

"What's it about?"

"Olympic runners and their belief in God."

"Any good?"

"Fair. This main character – I forget his name –says he believes God made him for a purpose, to run. I've thought about that myself and feel God made me for a purpose, too. My music."

"I see."

"But, to be honest, I fell asleep near the end."

"You do sound tired. I should let you get back to your nap."

"No more nap, but I need to get back to practice."

"OK, Kayla, take care. You know best. Love you."

But she'd hung up. I can still see myself that evening in my bedroom, holding onto the phone, looking at it longingly, as if I wished Kayla would climb out of it and be back home with us.

Of course, I shared with our folks most of what Kayla told me. They were satisfied that she sounded well, even if tired. When I mentioned that Kayla went to the movies by herself, though, Mom was upset.

"She's going to get into trouble! There has to be some boy involved."

"No, I don't think so," I responded, but she'd placed a seed of doubt into my mind. Or maybe the seed had always been there.

"She's fifteen, boys are a normal thing to be interested in," mused Dad.

"She's attracted boys down at Bellington, you know," I chimed in, unable to help myself.

"See, Nicky? Maybe we should call Renee or Charlene and complain."

"But Adel, we don't want to get Kayla into trouble or annoy the people who work for her. Let's not worry about this one incident. Seems totally harmless."

"Maybe the next movie will be different! Maybe she'll just slip away from Renee and hit the bars. Someone would buy her a drink and then ..."

"Relax. Let's see what happens. We can try to call her more often if she doesn't call us. Max, thanks for taking charge here and putting a call through."

I didn't tell them about Kayla's comments about Renee, because I wasn't sure whether Renee was good or bad for Kayla, as strangely as Renee behaved. Nor did I tell them about Kayla feeling that God made her for a purpose. Kayla had said similar things before I hadn't paid attention to. When she said it this time, though, it struck a chord. Kayla saw herself as a missionary, like the runner in *Chariots of Fire*, Eric Liddell. I'd seen the movie and knew what Kayla was talking about. I'd pretended not to, because I'd wanted to hear her talk about it.

CHAPTER 48

She knows she hasn't been calling as often as she promised. She doesn't want her parents and her brother to hear the fear in her voice. They've sacrificed too much to listen to her doubts, and they wouldn't understand anyway. The sense of dread that she feels more often now is not about a lack of confidence in her ability to play. The music still comes from her as easily as ever. The hours of practicing fly by. When she's lost in practice, she's lost to the outside world, but very much in her own. She's a Navy Seal on a secret mission, trained to fight and win. If she's hiding, it's from the bad feeling in the back of throat. The bad feeling returns only when she stops practicing.

She doesn't want anyone to know she's afraid of her own doom. Something awful is about to happen to her just because of who she is. She doesn't fear a falling asteroid wiping out her city or any other massive calamity such as earthquake, fire, flood, or virus. It's more the recognition she's become a public figure, that the sexy posters are spread over every city in which she's going to appear, and that tens of thousands of people can look at the picture and imagine doing dreadful things to her. If she could stop all the publicity, the photo shoots, the TV appearances, she would.

Max and her parents don't need to worry about her wandering around. Other than *Chariots of Fire*, she's stayed a virtual prisoner in her suite when she's not practicing or performing, not even venturing to the hotel restaurants as long as the room service people can get her vegetarian food in the appropriate colors.

CHAPTER 49

Around this time, Norm became a big concern for Mom. Mom received a call from Tricia, the black woman who'd been Mom's co-worker at the diner, and learned that Norm was in poor health. He was about eighty-two, if I recall. Tricia told Mom that Norm wanted to see her, but a sick man in his eighties couldn't just jump onto the subway. Norm lived in Harlem. Would Mom care to visit? Tricia, who'd been taking care of Norm, put Mom on with him for a few seconds; all I could hear was Mom repeating his name.

When Mom told us she was going to Harlem to see Norm, Dad tried to nix the idea. "It's not safe for you up there."

"I'll be all right. I know where he lives. Remember? I spent a few nights there myself after Dad died."

"Yes. And I brought you there and brought you back. It's not a place where a woman should travel alone. The place is crawling with drug gangs and there are robberies on every corner, even in daylight."

"Nicky, don't lock me in a cage!" Mom was getting quite upset, and I felt I should intervene.

"I can go with her," I said. "We'll keep our cab waiting while we visit. We'll keep a careful lookout, promise," I argued. "OK, Dad?"

"Fine," he grumbled. "But be careful."

We arranged to go the next day, and Tricia would meet us there.

Why do you need all this detail? You kids are probably wondering if I've gone off my rocker. You're probably wondering how I can recreate conversations that happened so long ago. Well, they are recreations, of course. They're the best I can do, so stay with me. To understand what happened to Kayla, you need to also understand what happened around her in the family, and a big piece of that is what happened to Mom, and for that ... well, just read.

CHAPTER 50

Norm's voice over the telephone doesn't sound right. It's like his voice box is filled with fluid and his lungs can barely gather enough air for words. Adel hasn't talked to him in a long time, but now regrets their separation. She could've talked to him about Nicky. He would've understood her concerns. She could've asked his advice about Kayla and explained Max's worries that Kayla was being taken advantage of. She could've confessed her own fears of Kayla starting in with sex. She could've trusted in him not to laugh at whatever she had to say, crazy as she was, because he'd known her forever and had seen her through the rough times. He would've accepted with love whatever she said. His main response would've been "Praise be to Jesus." He would have let her talk it out.

And now it's too late. The time to talk to him alone, to share her gravest doubts, has passed. She can visit him now only with Tricia and Max there too, and, even if they weren't present, she doesn't think the very sick Norm would be able to talk to her like the father she needed.

She looks for something to take to Norm, for remembrance's sake. Then she spots the baseball Jackie Robinson signed for her at Norm's Diner, at a meeting Norm set up just to please her. It's the thing she loves most in the world. She'll give her Jackie Robinson baseball to Norm. It will lend him strength to face the end.

CHAPTER 51

Norm was far from the robust man that Mom always talked about. Death's approach does that to a person, I guess. It eats them up, diminishes them to mere skeletons of what they'd been, long before the inevitable. Norm was unable to sit up. His apartment looked neat and clean, which had to be due to his friend Tricia's care.

"Norm! You look like shit," Mom announced, as direct as ever.

"Sure good to see you too, Adel. You look as slim as ever."

"Slim enough to fill the double Xs. What the fuck are you doing, crapping out on me like this?"

"Doing what God says we must all do some day. Won't be much longer that I'm for this world. Soon I'll meet my Lord Jesus in Heaven. I see you brought your boy with you. Matt?" He looked over at me and lifted a hand in a weak salute. His face was haggard, his voice dry and remote, his eyes cloudy.

"Max, not Matt." She nodded in my direction, then turned back to Norm. "Why didn't you call me when you got this sick? I could've come and made you some dinner, you know. Chili. Chicken soup. The things you taught me to cook. I love to cook. By the book. Hook or crook."

"Didn't want to be worryin' you, the truth. You got your own family. 'Sides, Tricia here been lookin' after me, ain't you, Trish?"

"You don't need much looking after, Norm." She reached over and plumped up the pillows Norm had been lying on, giving him a better vantage of his visitors. Tricia looked over at Mom and shook her head, mouthing "not long."

"So how's that darlin' daughter of yours? Kate?"

"Kayla. She's famous, Norm. She's on tour playing the piano like she was Van Cliburn. And she's had her picture in the papers and been on television, too." She pulled a newspaper clipping from purse and handed it to Norm. He tried to read it, but couldn't seem to focus. He handed it back in a few seconds.

"Lord of mine! She's somethin' special then. You should be proud." A coughing fit overtook him, and we waited nervously until it passed; when it ended, he spit into a used handkerchief produced from under his pillow. "And what about you, Max? Still playing the piano? You was pretty good too, I recall."

"I started college already, Mr. Williams. I don't have much time for piano these days."

"College! Well, that's somethin' I never done. Most schoolin' I had was Navy teachin' me to peel potatoes, which I already knew how to do. You're smart. You'll be good at college, I bet, if you work hard. You gonna be in business some day?"

"Lawyer, I'm pretty sure. I'll be the guy putting the bad dudes in jail."

"Dudes, huh? We need more lawyers to keep 'em out, I think. Don't be one of those damn white persecutors trying to put all black men in the clink." Having delivered his solemn advice, he turned to Mom. "I'm glad y'all come up to visit with me. Adel, I been wanting to tell you somethin' for a while, now's as good a time as any, I guess." He paused for a few seconds while he closed his eyes, whether because he was in pain or thinking how to say what he wanted to say I couldn't tell. Finally, he opened his eyes. "You been like a daughter to me, Adel."

"Norm, you *were* my father after Dad bought the farm."

"If I called you Grace once by mistake, I done it twenty times. When she got took away, I didn't know how I'm gonna survive, but Jesus finally come into my life, and I made a new life for myself, and then finally one day you and your dad walked into my diner. Never forget it, long as I live, which ain't gonna be too much longer." He chuckled at his own joke.

"I remember that night. Cold as hell froze over. Fuckin' froze my ass off just walking the two blocks from our apartment."

"I woulda never hired you if you hadn't been a big Jackie fan and knew all his stats."

"Used to hear Jackie talk to me all the time. In my head."

"In your head, shit. You was talkin' back to him out loud half the time."

"Well, being a nut case and all, what you expect? But now, it's all ended, too many pills, the brain cleansers, pills and thrills and spills. Good God."

"Nut case nothing. I always told you not to call yourself a nut case. You're as smart as a whip and you done good at the diner. I'd have liked you keep it goin' but then you got your own life and Nicky come along. You been happy?"

She ignored the question and reached into her bag again. This time, she pulled out the baseball she treasured more than her wedding ring, more than the china set Dad's old friend Elie had given Mom and Dad as a wedding present.

"Here, Norm. The ball Jackie signed for me. Will you keep it for me? Hang onto it?"

"You're sweet to think of that, but it's yours and you gotta keep it. I'll always know it has a good home. Here, let's hold it together for second." He reached out his hand, Mom sat on the edge of his bed finally, and together they held the ball for a while without talking. Then Norm coughed again, and Mom returned the ball to her bag. I could see Mom's tears on her face, and she wiped them away with her sleeve.

When Norm could speak again, he repeated the question that Mom hadn't answered. "Are you happy, Adel?"

Tricia had gone into Norm's kitchen by then, and when the conversation had gotten personal, I should've excused myself too, but I couldn't.

"What's happy, Norm? You got your Lord, and I got my family. I miss the birds at Sea Gate. It's not the same in the city, never will be. I'm closed in all the time, trapped." Mom glanced at me, then back at Norm, as if she wanted to say more.

He coughed again, so violently this time that I was scared he'd die in front us. But he pulled through it; when he was done, he wiped off his mouth and continued. "When I'm gone, I got some money put away for you. You're in my will, 'long with my church, of course."

"Oh, Norm, I couldn't take money. We don't need that."

"Nonsense. If you can't use it, then you give it to a good cause. The Audubon Society. Whatever. Ain't much. Few hundred is all, but I always wanted to do more for you."

"Thank you." She cried again.

"You're a good person, Adel. No. More than good. Special. C'mere and gimme a hug, will you? And then get the hell outta here." He seemed to pull every ounce of strength he had into a smile.

She obliged him. It wasn't one of those perfunctory hugs where people just go through the motions. She half lay on his bed, covering him with her immense body, so much so I feared she might press the few remaining breaths out of him. This hug was for keeps. After an eternity, Mom got up, sobbing openly, and Norm waved a feeble goodbye. I took her hand and led her out of Norm's apartment.

She said nothing the whole way home.

CHAPTER 52

She has two more concerts in Vancouver and then she can make the long flight home. It's been, as Max said it would, a grueling two months. As soon as she catches her breath, it seems as if she's running uphill again, with no horizon in sight and multiple obstacles in her path, but city by city she continues to thrill everyone who comes to hear her play. City by city she reaps great reviews. Her concerts sell out weeks before she appears. The audiences come to expect at least one Scott Joplin rag as an encore. *Maple Leaf Rag* is her favorite. So exhilarating to play when she's already bursting with happiness at how she's performed. She encourages the audiences to clap along.

Early in the morning of the next to last concert, Kayla hears a knock on her door and through the peephole sees Charlene standing next to a tall, very dark black man sporting a goatee and wearing a diamond stud in his left ear. She lets them in.

"Sorry to bother you, Kayla, but here's someone you need to meet. This is August Sorel." The man smiles and takes her hand before Kayla even realizes she's extended it. His hand is cool and confident, smooth and strong. He wears casual tan pants, and a royal blue polo shirt reveals a muscular physique. She almost forgets to let go of his hand and immediately thinks he's cute.

"Ms. Covo, the pleasure is all mine. I heard you play last night and you were magnificent. Loved that rag in particular. I've got to look into playing Joplin tunes myself."

"Thank you, Mr. Sorel. I've heard a lot about you but never have had a chance to hear you play. I hope I will, very soon."

"August, please."

"Then call me Kayla."

"Kayla it shall be. I'm fortunate to be here in Vancouver when your schedule brought you to town too. When I found out you were here, I begged Charlene to take me to meet you. As you can see, she's cooperated."

They sit in Kayla's suite for a few minutes chatting. He throws out the idea that perhaps they play violin and piano sonatas together someday, just for fun. Nothing serious, he assures her. Charlene smiles throughout but keeps silent. Kayla assures August it would be her honor to accompany him. She discovers he lives in Manhattan, too. Small world, she thinks.

CHAPTER 53

Nicky wonders whether he should have let Adel go to Harlem, even with Max as a bodyguard, and then wonders whether he should have taken off from work to go himself, with both Adel and Max. Norm had been an important part of Adel's life and, through Adel, had become a friend of his too. The times he'd meet Adel at the diner, waiting for her to clean up, eating a hamburger Norm would shove in front of him while he waited, seemed too many to count. Norm would never take a penny, but it wasn't Norm's generosity that impressed Nicky as much as his patience. Nicky had never encountered a person as calm and understanding with someone suffering from schizophrenia as Norm was with Adel. True, Adel's symptoms retreated when she kept up with her Thorazine, but even then there were myriad problems Norm overlooked.

It was easy for Nicky to understand what had made Norm the man he became. Norm never made a secret of his devotion to Jesus and how Jesus helped him turn his life around. Norm admitted – "before Jesus come into my life" – he'd been a drunk for a long time and that booze had been his escape as he tried to forget his own traumas. He turned to alcohol, he told Nicky, to dull the pain of the loss of his two close friends within seconds of each other during the First World War, to bury the humiliation he suffered from the bigotry of the white soldiers and, later, from the abandonment by his wife and daughter. Only his strong faith could have enabled Norm to step away from his addiction. Unlike some of Nicky's patients who'd kicked addictions but, in the process, become judgmental about the weaknesses of others, Norm developed great empathy. He was perhaps one of just a handful of people who could accept a schizophrenic employee in a job requiring substantial contact with customers. If anyone could rightly have been called as a saint, Norm was that person.

Nicky recalls how Adel had lost it at the news of her father's sudden death. The violent potential that infected Adel, an abused child, had burst out raging when Norm had had to tell her of Nate Miller's fatal heart attack, and suddenly it didn't matter that Adel was on Thorazine. Probably no drug would have stopped her from trying to kill Norm then, when Adel needed to strike out at the world that so badly treated her. Norm was the only person within Adel's reach; also within her reach were a phalanx of sharp kitchen knives. Luckily, Norm was strong enough to disarm Adel. The episode only made Norm love her all the more.

As Nicky himself fell under Adel's spell, he was impressed by the effect Norm had on Adel's self-image. He could see that Norm's patience and love for Adel enabled her to achieve more than Nicky thought possible. If this then sixty-year-old man from an entirely different culture could turn Adel into a productive employee, teach her to cook, and entrust much of his business operations to her, then Adel could also be a good wife and raise the family Nicky urgently wanted.

Although he regrets he didn't go with Adel and Max to Harlem, he realizes he's needed more in his own office, taking care of his own patients.

CHAPTER 54

It's the last performance of the tour. From all accounts – the adulation she receives at the end of a performance, the reviews, the laudatory comments of Herr Lindorf based on a recording – the music has gone spectacularly well. She's gone far beyond delighting her fans. She's sent them home raving with superlatives.

But the last piece of her concert at Chan Center is the Chopin B-Flat Minor Sonata, with its ghostly final movement. The music takes her own breath away, as if she's run a marathon with a world on her back, collapsing at the end. The audience rises to a thunderous ovation, stunned with the beauty of the sonata, hoping to hear more. But Kayla cuts short her bows, her smile less glowing. She walks off the stage quickly and into her dressing room, telling the manager she won't perform encores this evening, not even *Maple Leave Rag*. For long minutes, she hears the clapping and shouting until, finally, the disappointed audience realizes she will not appear again.

It's the first concert in which she hasn't returned to treat her fans to an additional morsel of delectable music and of herself.

CHAPTER 55

It wasn't long after our visit to Norm's apartment that I found myself waiting anxiously on the evening of Kayla's expected return, looking repeatedly for the Town Car to turn up our street. After many impatient peeks, I decided Kayla would arrive sooner if I occupied myself doing something other than waiting.

I sat at the Steinway and improvised minor-key melodies. I hadn't felt like playing anything particular in the classical repertoire, knowing Kayla might walk in and hear me playing something in a way much inferior to how she herself would play it. Improvisation was different; whatever I played would be correct. Soon I relaxed and lost myself in my own music, forgetting time. Mom wandered in to listen, pleased to hear me playing. It had been a good long while. Then the door banged open, and there was Kayla.

"Hi, everybody!" she yelled. "I'm home!" We rushed to her. I beat Mom and gave Kayla her first hug in two months. She felt great, alive and warm in my arms. Mom's turn was next, and Kayla was all over her with kisses.

"Kayla, you lost weight!"

"Not much, Mom, maybe a bit. But you'll feed me and fill me up again!"

Kayla wasn't alone. Renee stood quietly at the open door, along with four large suitcases.

"C'mon in, Renee. Let me help you with those." I reached for two of the suitcases in her hands. Renee walked into our apartment, leaving the other two behind, and Kayla grabbed them herself.

"Mom, you remember Renee? Can she stay for dinner? We sent the car away."

"Well, sure. You're welcome to stay, Renee. We can all play today." Kayla knew Mom would do as she asked.

Dad got home shortly afterward, as delighted as the rest of us to have Kayla back. Two months had been awfully long and, despite the occasional phone calls, we'd been kept in the dark about the tour. We'd never received copies of the reviews, despite Kayla's promises. So, at dinner, Kayla showed them to us, and we pressed her to talk about what the two months had been like. She happily gave us tidbits of the cities she'd seen and people she'd met. The traveling and performing had tired her, she admitted sheepishly. She wanted a little rest, away from the piano entirely, but for a few days only.

The fatigue had been worth it, she claimed. She described in detail each venue's idiosyncrasies. She critiqued her own performances, mentioning a mistake she'd made in San Diego on one of Scriabin's preludes. The critics overlooked her tiny misstep, she recounted with a smile, and the television interviewers laughed away her admission that she could've done a better job. The high point of the tour had been performing the Grieg concerto with the Los Angeles Philharmonic, a true honor to share the stage with such illustrious musicians.

And then came the dropping of the other shoe, the significance of which I realized only much later:

"And also, well, guess who I finally met? In Vancouver? August Sorel. Charlene told him to be at my concert, and then the next morning Charlene brought him up to my room to talk to me!"

"I'm sorry, Kayla, remind me who he is again?" I knew I'd heard the name, but couldn't place it.

"The violinist! He's only twenty, but he's already so famous!"

"Ah, the Haitian. Right. Charlene mentioned him the night they came here to sign you. Deerfield I if I recall."

"Yes, and he happened to be in Vancouver at the same time as me. Imagine! It's a beautiful city, mountains all around. Guess what? He'd like us to play together. Just think, I might be able to make music with August Sorel."

"Great news, Kayla. Don't you think so, Adel?" But Mom was busy dishing out more food and said nothing in response to Dad's question. Turning to Kayla, he asked "Hadn't you met him before at Bellington?"

"It's amazing, but no. I think he's on tour almost constantly."

I recalled then a picture of the black violinist performing a jazz medley at a Bellington recital. Hadn't Kayla been there with me? I couldn't remember. But, in that memory click, I could see him. Tall, dark, goatee, long black fingers caressing the strings. I'd been impressed with his virtuosity but hadn't been a big fan of jazz so had never searched out more of his music and knew nothing about his classical repertoire. I couldn't see Kayla turning to jazz, despite her current infatuation with Joplin, nor could I see her accompanying Sorel in a classical repertoire, but I didn't say anything for fear of dampening Kayla's enthusiasm. I'm sure it was a great honor for a famous violinist to express an interest in an up and coming fifteen-year-old pianist, if it was only music on his mind. But why shouldn't it be? There might be many talented violinists who'd love to have Kayla play with them. But Kayla was a soloist in my mind, and I couldn't fathom anything else for her career.

As I mused, Dad tried to draw Renee into a conversation.

"What was it like traveling with Kayla?" he asked.

"All right." Renee sounded if she was unaware she *had* been traveling with Kayla. I wondered why Kayla had wanted Renee to have dinner with us.

"Was Kayla a good girl?"

"Mom! Don't ask questions like that!" Kayla almost choked on the piece of baked potato she'd just put into her mouth. But, in the end, the embarrassing question didn't matter, because Renee's responses were entirely favorable, if predictable. Kayla was easy to watch over, very dedicated to music, not interested in anything else. Kayla had always been where she was supposed to be, when she was supposed to be there. Kayla was a pleasure to work with. Kayla had tremendous talent. Renee said all the right things. Perhaps that's why Kayla had wanted Renee with us that evening. In those two minutes, Renee pronounced more complete sentences than I'd ever heard her put together before. Still, she had the demeanor of a dumb machine.

I didn't ask her why she never watched the concerts herself.

CHAPTER 56

It's only the day after Kayla's return, and Adel feels the world spinning around her when she tries to see what will happen next. The spinning dizzies her. When she moves around the apartment, she bumps into furniture she sees but can't avoid. As if the answers are just outside her building, she's repeatedly drawn to the living room window and must hold the sills to steady herself. When she opens her eyes, she stares for long minutes across the street, trying to discern the future.

She's learned to trust her intuitions in whatever form they come. In the days before she started on meds, she could often foresee how the Dodgers games would end, almost as if she'd lived through them before. It wasn't only baseball, though. She felt she could sense when any momentous world events would occur. She recalls with sorrow how she saw, going into labor with Max, that the day would bring tragedy. Like most clairvoyants, she completely forgets the times when her intuitions were wrong.

Exactly what's happening now she can't say, but events are coming together in a way that don't occur just by coincidence. She suspects god is at it again, creating complications just for the sake of his own amusement. That's the only sensible explanation. She counts Kayla going on tour for months as one such complication, Norm's illness as another, and Nicky's strange behavior the third. She sees that Kayla meeting August is one of the twists in the fabric; the world starting to spin around her is yet another twist.

She wants to be ready for the terrible things that are surely going to happen, the cataclysms that will change her life forever. Now she knows she must prepare herself, not only for Norm's death, because anyone can see that coming, you don't need to be clairvoyant, but for the other bad things just hiding around the corner, the things she can't quite see clearly yet. She recalls from her sophomore English class the line from *Hamlet*: The readiness is all. It's a line that Nicky mentions to her occasionally to prove that he's well read.

Across the street, the building seems oddly aglow, taking on a salmon pink-orange wavering light. It can't be sunrise or sunset, because she's staring at it in the dark of night. The building does more than glow, however; she can feel heat pouring from it. The building burns, and its conflagration penetrates her window, scorches her skin, and quickly reduces her intestines to crumbling bits of charcoal. She scratches her arms to make sure she's not dreaming; when her arms bleed, she knows she's awake. What the fuck? Fuck a duck.

Then she realizes the building is sending her a message.

CHAPTER 57

She doesn't scream at being mistreated, not even when the sharp, cold metal pierces her body. But, for the first time, for the last time, she cries real human tears.

CHAPTER 58

Kayla writhes in her bed, fighting the sheets and blanket. In her dream, she finds herself beset by a mob of angry girls, and they push her, scratch at her face, grab yank out great chunks of her hair, every yank causing intense pain. The girls are younger than she, perhaps nine or ten, and they are wasting away, nearly skeletons, so Kayla feels she should be able to escape, but she cannot. She tries to fight them off, but her arms feel like lead. Her attackers gouge out an eye, laughing at her helplessness until Kayla forces herself to wake up.

It's getting light, her room is quiet, and she hears her father making breakfast. She has to pee. She swings her legs out of bed and notices her door is a few inches ajar.

Looking down, she sees it and screams.

Kayla's scream pierces through the apartment with more decibels than anyone would imagine her slender body could produce. She screams with all the horror commensurate with stumbling over a dead body. In fact, a dead body lies before her.

In the small space between the door and the jamb, Tina lies smashed beyond recognition, her once smooth puffy cheeks crumpled and pierced, her hair pulled out and piled next to her head, one foot twisted nearly off and hanging by a thread, her dress cut into strips, and a kitchen knife plunged into her belly.

The screams bring the family to her door in seconds, Adel in pajamas, Max in shorts, and Nicky dressed for work. They stare at Tina, at Kayla, now sobbing uncontrollably, and at each other. Adel gasps and runs back to her room, slamming the door. Nicky forces Kayla to sit on her bed and puts his arms around her until her sobs subside into shallow, ragged breaths. He doesn't try to make her talk. He rubs her back, encouraging her to breathe deeply. He rocks her. He hums the melody of a Sephardic lullaby.

Slowly, ever so slowly, Kayla calms down. After a long while, she reaches over to her night table, picks up her Star of David necklace, and puts it on. She buries her face into Nicky's shoulder and cries again.

Meanwhile, Max has gingerly picked up Tina and removed it from Kayla's line of sight. He stands at the door of Kayla's room, watching his father and sister, saying nothing.

CHAPTER 59

Nicky always worries about the safety of his family, but his concerns have centered about random encounters on city streets, not things that might happen just among the four of them in the confines of their home. As he holds his daughter, whose body heaves with sobbing, as he offers his handkerchief, he has never been so scared. Someone has ravaged the doll who gave Kayla so much comfort.

After Kayla has put on her Star of David necklace – an item Nicky has forgotten about – he questions her gently. "Do you know what happened?" He cannot bring himself to say the doll's name.

"No. I just ... when I got ..." She cries again.

"You heard nothing unusual?"

"I had a nightmare just before I woke up, Daddy. A crowd of young girls. They were killing me." If she were his patient, he'd pursue the dream angle, asking her to associate freely. But just now he can't put himself into professional mode with his daughter. Instead, he seeks to comfort and counsel her solely as a loving father.

"I don't think you should go down to Bellington today, Kayla. Take one day off. Only one. You need to rest."

"I need to practice."

He doesn't argue, tells her to get dressed in that case, and leaves, closing her door. Outside her room, he picks up Tina from the table in the hallway. Wondering what to do next, he carries Tina into the kitchen; strands of her hair flutter to the floor as he walks. He removes the knife from her belly and places it into the sink to be washed and restored to its drawer. Tina must be discarded, he realizes, but it would be unfeeling to drop her into the trash. He should have asked Kayla what she wanted done with Tina's remnants.

Nicky uses a grocery bag as a makeshift casket. Then he carries the bag into his own bedroom, where Adel lies on the unmade bed, humming, oblivious to his entrance. He places the bag on the top shelf of his closet, a temporary morgue.

CHAPTER 60

I should've asked her why she didn't want to watch Kayla's concerts. Maybe, if I'd asked her, Renee could've told me something about how frightening it can be to walk out on that stage and be the sole object of attention of hundreds of strangers. Maybe if we'd had such a conversation, I would've seen much earlier what was about to happen to Kayla. I should've done many things when there was still time.

When you kids think about how you might someday desperately need each other, please keep all this in mind. Don't be afraid to ask the right questions and listen carefully to the answers.

On Kayla's third tour things took a decided turn for the worse. The second tour had been such a critical and popular success that the committee decided the next extravaganza should be in Europe. Both Charlene and Renee would accompany Kayla, who'd perform in London, Edinburgh, Frankfurt, Warsaw, and Rome. When the tour began, no one in our family expected Kayla to call regularly. Instead, we tried to reach her at her hotels when we thought she might be available. On almost all our attempts, phones rang in empty rooms. Charlene called occasionally to assure us everything was all right, but she never had Kayla with her. Mom and Dad were understandably frantic with worry.

I finally reached Kayla late one Sunday evening in Warsaw. The connection was poor; I could barely recognize her voice, which was more remote than the five thousand miles between us could explain.

"Are you all right, Kayla? You sound weird."

"I'm worried about someone listening in."

"What? Someone's in your room?"

"No, but what if someone's listening in on the call? As in wiretapping?" The comment made me shudder.

"Very unlikely."

"Max, Poland is communist."

"Of course, but still. Why would anyone want to listen to the conversation of a classical pianist performing with the Warsaw Philharmonic?" There was only static over the line for a few seconds, and I feared we lost the connection. Then I heard Kayla's whisper slightly above the background noise.

"Someone's been following me."

"Someone's been following you? You're kidding, right?"

"No, Max. I saw ... this man, in the audience in London, then ... Scotland, and again in Frankfurt. Now in Warsaw."

"Obviously he's a big fan," I suggested, with little hope she'd agree. I was starting to fear she wasn't joking. Mystified, I grabbed a pencil and took notes.

"He didn't look like a fan. I know what fans look like. This one, he just stared at me. Never clapped once. Not once, in the five or six concerts I saw him."

"Holy shit."

"Gives me the creeps."

"Did you tell Charlene or Renee?"

"Yeah, but they don't believe me. They said they didn't see anyone who fit my description." There was a long sigh, followed by long seconds of quiet. "They said how it must be my imagination."

"I believe you. What does this man look like?"

"Very, very tall. Probably six-six or more, but hard to say exactly from the stage. He stands out, though. Very white skin. Almost albino. Angry eyes."

"You could see his eyes?"

"He always sits up front. Second or third row. I could see enough to tell he was dangerous. Very dark eyes, almost black."

"Have you tried to point him out to Charlene or Renee from backstage?"

"Yes, in Frankfurt. They looked and still said they didn't see him. Then I looked, but the crowd was leaving, it was all confused, and I couldn't see him anymore. They just don't believe me."

"Bizarre. Utterly fucking bizarre. Do you want to come home? If you do, just say the word. Tell Charlene you're tired or sick. You can cancel. Tell them..."

"No. I have three more concerts, one here and two in Rome. I want to finish."

"*Can* you finish? Isn't this affecting your playing?"

"I don't think so. I can still focus on the music as I play, although as soon as I stop I'm totally aware of him."

"I want you to come home, Kayla."

"You always want me home, but I'm going to stick it out."

We tried to find inconsequential stuff to talk about for a minute, but couldn't, so we hung up. I'd called from the private phone Mom and Dad had installed in my bedroom, so they weren't aware I'd reached Kayla, and I elected not to tell them.

I was scared for Kayla. Now, reading through the notes I'd taken as I write to you, I can see that I wanted to believe her, to know she wasn't hallucinating. I knew there were plenty of times when sociopaths stalked famous artists. Just blocks from where I lived, less than a year earlier, John Lennon had been shot dead by Mark David Chapman, a fan for whom he signed an autograph. I remembered Kayla, who loved the Beatles, had been traumatized by Lennon's murder, could barely speak for days. But Lennon surely hadn't been the only famous person to be murdered or attacked because of his celebrity. In the back of my mind, I thought the actor Sal Mineo had been stabbed by a fan hiding near his house.

So, what Kayla said was possible, but I ended up feeling she wasn't being followed. That Charlene and Renee couldn't see this guy and that Kayla had supposedly lost him in a crowd, despite his height, cut against the reality of what she was seeing. As my rational side dismissed her story of a real music stalker, my fear grew for Kayla's sanity. I knew schizophrenia was largely genetic and typically presents during teenage years, when Mom said her own illness began. If Kayla was becoming ill, then what should be done? You'll think I should have confided in Dad, and you'll be right, but I hesitated. I didn't want Kayla to feel that I'd betrayed her. I wanted to wait until she came home, when we could talk face to face.

It's peculiar, but even as I worried about Kayla's sanity, I never worried about inheriting schizophrenia myself. I was built more in Dad's mold, strongly rational. Sexist that I was, I thought daughters were more likely than sons to get the mental illness genes from their mothers. (Sorry, Rosina.) Now I wonder about the signs in myself I might've overlooked. I'm sure your mother has a long list.

CHAPTER 61

Something new has bothered her ever since the horrible thing that befell Tina. She's tried to talk to Nicky about it, but she can tell by the look on his face that whatever she says is not making sense. That's how he is with his patients, she figures. He'll listen, he'll say the right words, but inside his fuckin' gigantic brain he's above it all.

As she lies down for her afternoon nap, she recalls their last conversation about Tina.

"Nicky, what happened to Kayla's doll after … you know?"

"I put her in a paper bag, and she's in the top of our closet."

"Oh no! We have to get rid of her! I can't sleep in the same room as a dead doll."

"We'll dispose of her properly, it's just …" He paused to gather his thoughts. "You know how important she's been to Kayla, so I think we need to let Kayla decide. I didn't want to ask her about it when she was so upset."

Adel feels that she herself should get out of bed, grab the carcass, and drop it down the garbage chute. She should watch it disappear like a turd down the toilet, but she's afraid to touch the bag. She lies there, feeling Tina's obliterated eyes on her. She can hear Tina's scratchy voice, which sets her nerves jangling. The lifeless doll is not lifeless at all but angry, and now Tina's shrieking pounds in Adel's ears. It's her mother telling her how bad she is, a mother so ashamed to have brought Adel into the world she must remind Adel constantly that she's a worthless cunt.

"What were you doing in the park, bitch?"

"Nothing. Just went for a walk with a friend. Daniel, from my class."

"You're hooking, aren't you? You're trying to sell your disgusting body, aren't you?"

"Of course not. What a terrible thing to say!"

"No one will ever want to touch you, pig, let alone pay you for it. You disgust me."

"I'm going to my room to study."

"And you can stay there all night. Forget supper. I'm not feeding a hooker. The angel told me not to give you anything to eat, so there."

It's been years since Adel chased her mother away with a knife, but that hasn't stopped the nasty, crazy voice from piling on the insults and reminding her she's worthless. Now the hideous verbal assault comes from the dead doll. There's no way to silence it.

She forces herself to get up, grabs a jacket, and leaves the apartment.

CHAPTER 62

Before Kayla could get home from Europe, I resolved to get to the bottom of the agency contract. Kayla had reluctantly approved the letter I'd drafted for Dad to send the committee. I'd drafted it ultra-politely, a simple inquiry about accounts and revenues and such, but we received no response. As far as we knew, no account had been opened in Kayla's name, and she'd never received a dime from her hard work. Two weeks after mailing the letter, I again broached the topic to Dad. He listened to me and asked what I thought should be done. How was it possible, I wondered, that he'd have no clue about what to do for his daughter? Had his parents been so inept in dealing with his needs?

"Like I said at the beginning, Dad. We need to consult an attorney, and the longer we wait the worse everything will be. We should've done this long ago."

"But how?" I'm sure I must've sighed in frustration. "You pick up the phone. You make an appointment. I don't know. I've never called a lawyer, but it can't be rocket science."

"My insurance company has lawyers to defend doctors against malpractice claims, but I've been lucky. I've never met any of them."

"What about Grandpa Nate's old partner? Mom mentioned him when they marched in here with those damned papers." I'd known before I started the conversation that I'd head in this direction.

"Ben Brody. I haven't spoken to him in years, and I doubt he's still practicing. He was old even before Mom and I married."

"Do you have a better idea?" I couldn't understand why Dad was making this so hard.

"No."

We agreed to call Ben. Then it turned out Dad didn't want to call himself, but wanted me to call. I think Dad was embarrassed that he'd allowed Kayla to get into this mess – I was sure it was a mess – and wanted me to be the one to talk to Ben, because I'd argued against the contract in the first place. I was glad Dad wanted me to take the lead role, because I desperately wanted to prove myself right. I wanted to be the fixer or at least the one who finds the right champion to fight. If I was headed for a legal career, this was the best way to start.

I found a number in an old Brooklyn Yellow Pages for Brody & Miller, but it was out of service. Then I started working my way through the Ben and B Brody's in the Brooklyn White Pages and, on the fifth call, got lucky.

"So this is Max Covo, Mr. Brody. C ...o...v...o. Dr. Nick Covo's and Adel Miller's son. You remember them, I hope."

"Nick and Adel's son! My word! I haven't seen them since a short time after their wedding, when they moved down to Sea Gate. How are they? I hope you're not calling to ..."

"They're fine, Mr. Brody ..."

"Please call me Ben."

"Thanks, Ben. They're fine, but we do have a problem needing a lawyer, and we thought you'd be a good person to talk to."

"I'm happy to chat with you, but I haven't practiced law for ten years. I'm eighty-four."

I thought for a second before answering. "Ben, you know our family, and Dad says we can trust you. Mom wanted you from the first."

"Quite a young lady, your mother. God, did she love the Dodgers. I never really thought she'd have a family, but I'm glad she did. So, Max, how can I help you?"

"You've heard of my sister, Kayla Covo, the pianist?"

"Kayla Covo! I've heard the name but never put that together with Nicky. She's his daughter? She's Adel's daughter? My word! Nate would be so happy to know."

"Yes, we're that Covo family. The legal issues are about Kayla. Look, I'd rather talk in person if you don't mind. May I visit you at your home? Tomorrow? Or whenever's convenient?"

He gave me the address. Two subways and a walk. Not a problem. Then I remembered that lawyers need evidence. I pulled together for my visit with Ben the news clippings and reviews we'd collected. And some photographs.

CHAPTER 63

Kayla is pulled in opposite directions.

Her love for her music grows daily, and she pours herself into her practices and performances as if her life depended upon them. The piano is her refuge and protector. As long as she is there, bringing to the world the genius of Beethoven or Bach, she doesn't see herself as a victim.

But the other insidious pull grows daily. The awful feeling in the back of her throat, the hard lump cutting off her breath, the intractable dryness in her mouth – all are linked to her nightmares and her fear when, having finished her performances, she sees staring at her the tall, angry man with black eyes, the man who wishes her death. Before he kills her, he will rape her, and death will be welcome then.

Paradoxically, her fears blend into her burgeoning sexual desire. Kayla lies in bed, night after night, obsessing about her stalker, unable to get to sleep. As she does so, what starts as a tingle throughout her body mounts slowly but surely until she must satisfy herself, images of the stalker dominant, but images of other men take his place occasionally as she desperately finds release. Afterward, her sleep is rough, unrestful. When she must drag herself out of bed in the morning, the expression coming to her mind is that she's been through a grinder.

There's no one to talk to about her libido, which scares her almost as much as the music stalker. She finds it hard to imagine her mom really knows what sex is about, even though she's had two children. All her mom would do is tell her to stay away from boys. Nor can she talk to Charlene or Renee. They're concerned solely with making sure Kayla holds up her end of the bargain, her bargain with the devil. They refuse to admit they too have seen the angry, threatening man. Rather than admit the truth, they would rather have Kayla think she's crazy. Well, she's not crazy.

Now the devil is coming to take her away.

Kayla still grieves over Tina, even though she knows Tina wasn't a real person. But Tina possessed the power of a real person, the power to listen to her fears and longings. Tina's tears were real. On the previous tour, Tina helped her get past the dark moments, the nights when Kayla fell into bed exhausted, wanting never to get up. In the mornings, Tina would be there to cheer her on and prompt her into her routine.

Longing for Tina makes Kayla so sad. No angry, staring man followed her when Tina was nearby.

CHAPTER 64

Ben's home was a townhouse in Borough Park. His nearly bald head showed more brown liver spots than wisps of white hair. Although he appeared frail, I could see he paid attention to keeping everything neat and orderly. I learned he was a widower for years and that a son, who lived out on Long Island, looked in on him. He sat me down in his living room and offered me a cup of tea, which I accepted.

"So, what can I do for Kayla? I'm curious why you'd want to call consult with someone long into retirement, albeit an old friend of the family."

"Kayla's being taken advantage of by the people who are supposed to be guiding her career, and I'm very worried about it. And, who better than a family friend to look into it?"

"You'd better explain." I felt relieved that I seemed to have piqued his interest.

"My folks signed off on an agency contract for Kayla. We don't even have a copy. It's all been very mysterious. Kayla's earning a lot of money for them – at least that's what I think, given how many concerts she does, she's doing right now in Europe – but she hasn't seen a cent. They must be ripping her off."

"My word! Extraordinary! How is it you don't even have a copy of the contract? That's mighty careless, if you don't mind my saying."

He was damned right about our family's carelessness. I was bitter about my own role in letting it happen. I explained about the night Lindorf and the others arrived with the proposal, how they tore the papers from Mom's hands before I could look at then, how I pleaded with our parents not to sign, Kayla's ultimatum, and all that had transpired since. Ben listened, then excused himself, retrieved a pen and a yellow legal pad from a drawer, and had me repeat the story while he took notes. I wanted to tell him also of Kayla's strange call and my fear she was developing paranoid delusions, but couldn't bring myself to do so. I felt it wouldn't do to complicate things.

"Well, what do you think?"

"I don't know, but you do have cause to be worried. Bellington, you say? I can't imagine a school as famous as Bellington getting involved in shenanigans like this."

"Lindorf is on their faculty, but this committee seems to be outside Bellington, even though Kayla still practices there most of the time. She needs to be close to Lindorf." I took a sip of the cold tea. "Can you do anything to help us?"

"I was thinking, before you arrived, that I'd have to refer you to other attorneys. But I'm intrigued, so much so I'm delighted to be involved."

"What do you charge?"

"For Adel's and Nick's kids? *Bupkis. Nada.* Zilch. But, you know, you get what you pay for." He laughed, and I relaxed for the first time during the visit. "How old is Kayla now?"

"Only fifteen. She won't turn sixteen until next May."

"She knows you're talking to a lawyer?"

"No."

"I couldn't ethically claim to represent her without her consent. Do you think you can get her to agree?"

"I ... I don't know. Isn't there some way you can just represent me? As her interested brother?"

"I don't think that would work. If there's a scam, which sounds likely from what you tell me, we may have to litigate, and I'd have to bring in another lawyer. I want everything to be as clean as a whistle. Hmm. I could represent your folks, if they consent. They signed the contract. Surely they consent, right?"

"Dad probably. Who knows with Mom? She's not all there, as you know. But I think if she was having a good day she'd approve too."

"Well, let's call Dr. Nick first. That seems most logical. There's the phone. Get him on and I'll talk to him."

Dad was likely seeing patients then, but I dialed his number anyway and left a message asking him to call Ben as soon as possible. In twenty minutes, Dad called back, and I listened to Ben explain how he could represent Dad, in Kayla's interest, because she was still a minor, and then heard Ben mumble a few times before he hung up.

"What did he say?"

"Your father is afraid, because word of any legal inquiry will get back to Kayla."

"Well, yes, I suppose that's obvious. So?"

For a few seconds, it looked like Ben was at a loss for words, biting his lower lip as he thought. "He's afraid Kayla will get angry if we go behind her back. All she agreed to, he argues, is that a letter be sent to this committee. If you don't mind my saying so, it's almost like she's the parent and your dad is the worried teenager. He's insisted we not do anything, unless and until Kayla agrees. He also said that you need to be the one to talk to Kayla about this. Until that happens, my hands are tied from approaching the committee in any way."

"Just like Dad."

"How soon can you talk to her?"

"She's in Warsaw, going to Rome soon. She'll be home in about two weeks. I don't think I can do this on the phone, not the way she sounded when I spoke to her recently. She's worn out, and she has to focus on the music. I'll have to wait until the tour's over and she's here."

"Well, so be it. I'm sorry this is difficult, Max, but if we're going to do anything, we have to do it strictly kosher."

"Of course."

I started to see the drawbacks of my intended career. Ethical rules tied your hands. Things had to be done by the book.

• • • • •

Now, please remember that this is all happening long before email. I did try to reach Kayla a few times by phone, to no avail. I think I intended, not to talk about lawyering at all, but just to see how she was. I'm not sure what would've happened if I'd spoken to Kayla. The hotel switchboards would connect me to rooms where Kayla's phone rang until I gave up. I supposed that Kayla could've been sleeping through the noise, but the constantly frustrated efforts to contact her magnified my worries. In short, I was scared shitless, half-fearing that Kayla had done herself in. I also tried to reach Charlene and Renee, with equally little success.

Although I didn't want to talk to him, I could think of no other way to get news about Kayla's European tour than by approaching Lindorf himself. He was difficult to reach as well. The Bellington operator always claimed he was busy with students, and he didn't return my messages. When I had enough, I marched down – all right, I half ran – to Bellington and planted myself outside his office for an hour until he showed up. I tried to keep my voice level as he approached.

"Herr Lindorf." He looked up, a cloud of concern passing over his face as he recognized me.

"Max! Is something wrong? You look like you have seen a ghost."

"Something wrong?! I haven't been able to reach Kayla, I can't find any news about her tour, and I need to know, my family needs to know, what's going on?"

"Nothing is going on. *Gornicht.* I have spoken to Charlene just last night, ja? Kayla is doing fine. Why are you so worried?"

"I just ... just wanted to hear from my sister, my parents want to talk to her, and she doesn't call home. Why can't she keep in touch? Why can't Charlene or Renee make her call? Why can't even Charlene or Renee call us or answer their phones or return my messages?"

"Ah ... come into my office. We talk a bit, ja?"

I sat in his dusty and cluttered office, where framed photographs of many of his students lined the walls. There was one of Kayla beaming, standing next to Lindorf, taken right after her Town Hall debut. There was even a photograph of Renee holding a bouquet on some stage, but not smiling. I caught sight also of a framed headline from 1956, a review of a concert Lindorf himself had given.

"So ... you are not liking Kayla being on tour in Europe?"

"That's not right, Herr Lindorf. I want her to be a success. My family wants nothing more than for her to be a success. But Charlene and Renee should make sure she calls home. She's still only fifteen."

"Ah, fifteen, a beautiful age. When my daughter was fifteen ..."

"Excuse me, Herr Lindorf. We have to focus on Kayla." Looking back, I'm sure that he thought me rude. "How *is* Kayla doing on this tour? Really?"

He was clearly peeved that I'd interrupted him. He gestured with his hands as if I was the orchestra and he the disgusted conductor; he was calling a halt to a bad bit of music. "Max, as I am trying to tell you, my Katerina at that age had none of that, how do you say, *Selbstbewusstein.* That confidence from within, which Kayla does have. Kayla, she is fifteen, but is mature like an adult. And Charlene is saying she ... Kayla ... excelling every performance. Quite remarkable, she is saying, ja? Energy going through the roof, she is saying. Reviews are excellent, she is telling me almost *jeder Tag.* You think I am not checking up on my best student, on the most incredible talent I've ever taught?" He rummaged on his desk, found a large envelope, pulled out a raft of clippings, and handed over a few. "So. *Da. Da. Da.* Read for yourself."

Why Charlene sent them only to Lindorf and not to our family annoyed the shit out of me. I glanced at the clippings from London and Edinburgh and confirmed they were excellent, with phrases – yes, I still have them – such as "demonstrating a musical awareness far beyond her years," "eliciting new insights into Chopin despite the fact his works have been played for more than a century by the world's best pianists," and – the one that got to me – "reminiscent of and in many ways better than Rubinstein." Better than Artur Rubinstein? A thrill of pride engorged me. How could it not?

"OK, these are fine. Better than fine, truly amazing, but what about Frankfurt and Warsaw? What about Rome?"

"Well, just as good." He pulled out more from the envelope. "Here are all. I read the Frankfurt, Charlene knows the Russian and Italian. Here's from Roma." My high school level Spanish did not allow me to translate for myself, but I could make out *bellisima* and *bravura* and *virtuosima* in the Italian.

"I'm still worried. Kayla should call us regularly."

"I will mention to Charlene, ja? But they will soon be home. Two more nights. You will see soon for yourself."

That was all I could get out of Lindorf. I felt better having read the English-language reviews, but they'd been written before I'd spoken to

Kayla and heard how paranoid she sounded. And, yes, the Italian review was good, too, but I didn't trust Lindorf to tell me the truth about the others.

"All right. I'm sorry to have disturbed you, Herr Lindorf. But I do have one other question."

"Ja?"

"Renee. I see her picture there." I pointed, as if Lindorf had forgotten where Renee's picture hung. "Why did she stop performing?"

A cloud of anger passed over Lindorf's face, but he recovered quickly. "A very good student. Promising. But nothing like Kayla. Renee never had enough, how do you say, *Begeisterung*. The zeal, you know. The passion? That's what Kayla has that marks her above everyone else. *Begeisterung*. That every ounce of her life is committed."

With that, I left and headed back uptown. I thought Lindorf and the others who were supposedly nurturing her career had either overestimated her zeal or misunderstood it. Behind Kayla's passion was something else, something ominous, something other-worldly.

•   •   •   •   •

I resolved to go to the airport to meet Kayla on her return. I didn't want her under the influence of Charlene and Renee – who lacked the slightest compassion for my sister – more than a second longer than necessary. Kayla's flight was expected at Kennedy at around six the next night. At dinner, I brought Mom and Dad up to date on everything I'd learned, Lindorf's assurances, the *bellisima* and *bravura*, everything but my concerns about Kayla's mental status.

"I miss Kayla. How can she follow the Knicks when she's in Europe? Does she even know they beat the Pistons in overtime last night?"

"Probably not, Mom, but ..."

"Seems like Kayla's flown the coop for a year. Oh, dear! What a bear!" She drummed her fingers on the table, causing the plates to rattle, as if she herself was pounding out the last notes of the *Appassionata*.

"Right, Mom, it does seem like a very long time. It's not a year, but it could just as well be if Kayla's changed a lot." I was trying to warn them, I guess, to expect that the returning Kayla might not be the same Kayla they'd known.

"She doesn't call us. It's like we're not even family." Mom took the serving spoon and started to dish me a second helping of chili, but I grabbed her hand gently and pushed it away.

"No more, Mom, although it's delicious." I'd not been eating well, nervousness wreaking havoc with my appetite. "So, here's my plan. I'm going to out to Kennedy and meet her as soon as she comes through Customs. I'm going to stuff her and her suitcases into a cab and talk to her on the way back here. I'm going to tell her we never received a response to our letter to the committee and about my conversation with Ben."

"Won't she be tired, though?" asked Dad. "Maybe that won't be the best time for her to consider what's in her best interest. Maybe you should let her get acclimated to being back at home for a few days before talking to her about your concerns, or maybe ..."

"Our concerns, Dad."

"Okay. Our concerns. What I mean is, if you want her to be receptive, she has to be in the right frame of mind."

"I'm not sure she'll ever be in the right frame of mind or even what that means. Look, Dad, no offense, but you put this all on me. I had to be the one to talk to Ben. You said so, right? So now I'm going to do what I feel I have to do. I'm going to talk to her as soon as I can."

"Well, here's money for cab fare." Dad withdrew a handful of twenties from his wallet. I took it without comment.

"Max, shouldn't you bring Kayla some kind of present, you know, to give her when she gets off the plane?"

"Great idea, Mom. What did you have in mind?"

The question stumped her. She sat thinking, then lit a cigarette. "Maybe she'd like a new Mets sweatshirt? Her old one is getting ratty. You could probably get one at the airport while you're waiting." She took a deep drag, then blew smoke through her nostrils, closing her eyes. "She'd be a women's medium now. Our little girl's growing up."

Kayla had been a medium for about two years, she filled a medium nicely, but I didn't have the heart to correct Mom. "Sure, fine. One new women's medium Mets sweatshirt coming up." Dad reached into his wallet again, but I assured him I had enough money. It was settled.

CHAPTER 65

Charlene and Renee insist on delaying their return from Rome for one day to sightsee, and Kayla reluctantly agrees. They walk through the Forum, gawk at the Coliseum, listen to their guide droning on about how many Christians were killed there, how many lions were brought there to kill the Christians, and how big the crowds were. All Kayla can do is pray she can get out of the sun, which is making her dizzy, get back to her hotel room for one more night, and then get on the airplane to ferry her across the Atlantic.

She refuses to dine with Charlene and Renee at Ditirambo, much to their annoyance. Kayla knows where to meet them in the morning and goes up to her room to draw a bath. While immersed in the hot water seasoned with Aveeno salts, Kayla closes her eyes, trying to relax, but she sees still the face of the angry albino man who wants to hurt her, and the tingling sensation, now expected, returns, and she touches herself again, then stops, afraid she hears noises. As she towels herself dry, she tries to process everything happening to her. He can't be a figment of her imagination. She knows he's real, because, if he weren't, she wouldn't be able to conjure up his appearance so readily, to see him so distinctly, as if she'd been staring at a photograph of him for her entire life. Charlene and Renee, who think she's crazy, are just wrong.

What has she done that could make someone hate her so much? She's been invariably polite every time she's been interviewed, she's patiently signed autographs for people who wait for her when her concerts end, and she's complied with everything Charlene and Renee have demanded. She's given every ounce of energy to her practice and performances and knows she's innocent of any misconduct. Her biggest crime is not a crime at all, just something that she won't talk about to anyone, how she satisfies herself, in the last few nights with the pressure of a pillow between her legs.

All Kayla wants to do is forget for a while that she's become a world-famous concert pianist, but the next morning Charlene contrives to prevent her from forgetting. Charlene talks to a flight attendant about Kayla as they board the 747 at Da Vinci Airport. How can Charlene not understand how tired she is? Kayla settles into the first-class seat, fastens her seatbelt, and tries to hide behind a magazine. Then she changes her mind about the magazine and decides to feign sleep. She closes her eyes and puts her head on a pillow jammed up against the window. She's so exhausted following a restless night she's actually about to doze off when she hears her name mentioned over the speaker system amidst a bunch of Italian. The English translation is all too clear; they are "privileged" to have with them Kayla Covo, who has just performed to such good reviews in Rome. The last thing Kayla wants is to be a celebrity on this flight. She just needs to sleep and let everything seep away – the excitement, the fear, the doubts – so maybe she can regain her balance before she gets home, and yet her needs are ignored. The plane lumbers down the runway and finally separates from the ground. As soon as the seatbelt sign is off, the aisle fills with people wanting to say hello to Kayla and get an autograph. Charlene, in the next seat, is beaming, reminding her to be pleasant and sign.

Kayla hides her anger. Charlene's her boss, and Kayla isn't ready to disobey, no matter how tired. The rush of fans and the curious subsides after a half hour, and Kayla is finally allowed quiet, but now it's useless. She's too riled up to sleep.

In the concert hall, she loves her fans. But, on this morning, when she wants only to be home, to be back with her family, to be out of the limelight, the fans are cancer cells, growing uncontrollably, multiplying voraciously, eating her from the inside out.

CHAPTER 66

I took the E train to the Jamaica station and transferred there for the short run down to JFK instead of wasting money on a taxi. I'd formed the idea that, despite the cash Dad seemed to have in substantial supply, his practice was precarious, perhaps because he focused too much on writing papers and charity cases and not enough on paying patients. With my certainty that Kayla was being cheated and our family would need to bring in a lawyer other than Ben – a lawyer paid by the hour – I wanted to be cautious with the dollar. But I also wanted more time to think about what I might say. I worried anything I did say would upset her, that a suggestion she slow down would be interpreted as another example of my jealousy.

I left our apartment early enough to make it to Kennedy with more than an hour to spare, bought the Mets sweatshirt plus a large bouquet, not thinking about how we'd manage to carry the gifts as well as the suitcases. Only after I planted myself in the line of people waiting for arriving passengers did I realize I'd have to confront Charlene and Renee as I met Kayla. A minute later I noticed Ziegler also waiting, just a few people down the line. Damn if he wasn't the last person in the world I wanted to run into. Ziegler hadn't seen me, but there was no way Kayla could get to me without first being accosted by him. I hated the idea of physical confrontation, but I couldn't let him derail my mission. So I approached him, getting his attention by punching him in the arm, undoubtedly a bit harder than politeness called for.

"Mr. Ziegler. What a pleasant surprise. What are you doing here?" A stupid question, I know, but I had nothing better.

"Yes? Do I know you?" He looked annoyed, rather than angry.

"Max Covo. Kayla's sister. That's why you're here, isn't it?"

"Max ... Oh, yes. So, you came to say hello to her? Well, we have the Town Car waiting outside, and we're all going to meet Heinz and have a quiet dinner together, so ..."

"No, you're not, Mr. Ziegler. Sir. I came to get Kayla myself and take her straight home. So go have your dinner without her."

"Oh, no, Max, that won't do at all, and who are you by the way, you snot-nosed high school kid, to tell me what to do?" I'd managed to get him angry, which improved my mood. Happily, I realized I could get into this guy's head. What an asshole. His self-importance couldn't comprehend that a teenager might tell him what to do.

"Well, we'll see. We'll let Kayla decide when ..." And at that moment I saw Kayla pushing a luggage cart through the swinging doors, into the waiting crowd.

"Kayla!" I yelled, jumping, waving the flowers. Ziegler actually tried to pull down my arm, and I yanked it away. "What the fuck? That's my sister, shithead!" Ziegler's face flushed a dark red, and he tried to get closer to Kayla while avoiding me. I followed on his heels, grabbed at the back of his shirt, and pulled him around, all the while yelling Kayla's name. She caught sight of me and smiled. Ziegler stared at me with disgust, then turned again toward Kayla.

She looked a total mess, dark circles under her eyes, her hair uncombed and pasted to her head in sweat, her shirt half-pulled out of her jeans, her body slumped, leaning on the luggage cart for support. It didn't take a nuclear engineer to figure it had been an unpleasant flight back from Rome.

"Max! You came to meet me!" When she smiled at me, it's no exaggeration to say my heart fluttered. I'd been without that smile for so long, and it reminded me about everything I loved in Kayla and why I was so concerned; it was the smile I'd have given my life to preserve. Then Ziegler pushed between us.

"Kayla, hello. Welcome back. I'm taking you to dinner with ..."

"No, Kayla, I'm taking you home."

I shouldered Ziegler out of the way and smothered Kayla in a hug, which she returned without much strength. She smelled of light perfume, perspiration, and bad breath, and I held her closely as long as I could. When she finally pushed herself away, I noticed Charlene and Renee had wheeled up their luggage carts behind her. While hundreds of happy but tired passengers and their welcoming parties swarmed around, the five of us stood, looking at each other, assessing the situation. I was pretty sure I could take out Ziegler in a fight, but I didn't want a fight. As much as I wanted to smash his smart-ass face, these were the people whom Kayla's career depended upon, and I knew it would be a mistake to burn bridges. I realized too, if we were headed to litigation, it wouldn't help our cause if I became violent.

"Max, hello. So nice of you to come to meet Kayla." Charlene tried to be the voice of reason. "But we already made reservations for dinner at Oceana. You're … you're welcome to join us, if you want."

"Ms. Deerfield, that's very generous of you, but our folks are anxious to see Kayla, and I can see Kayla needs rest. It was surely a grueling trip. We'll take a cab back to our apartment. Won't we Kayla?"

Kayla was torn. She wanted to please me, she was exhausted, she probably wanted nothing more than to take a hot bath and sleep; yet, she wanted to please her handlers. The image came to my mind of a lion trainer wielding a long whip inside a circus tent, the lion forced to jump onto a stand by the threat of the whip cracking alongside its head.

"Well … I …"

"Here, these are for you." I gave Kayla her flowers and the sweatshirt. "They're from all of us. Mom and Dad want to see you, *right now.*" I grabbed the handle of her luggage cart and started pushing it to the door marked "Taxis." Ziegler got in the way, and I bumped his knee hard, forcing him out of the way. "Oh, sorry, Mr. Ziegler. Sir. I didn't see you move there." I tried to adjust the direction of the cart, and he moved again to block its way. I hit him again with the cart, as hard as I could dare. "Get out of our way. Sir. Kayla, tell him you're going home with me."

Kayla decided the right way. "It's OK, Robin. We'll do dinner another time. Please give Herr Lindorf my regrets and tell him I'll be by to see him in a couple of days. I do need to rest." She attempted a brief smile, then grabbed my arm, squeezing gently. "Let's go, Max."

A deflated Ziegler stepped aside. I wanted to kill him. No, not quite exactly. I wanted to rip his ears off first and stuff them down his lawyer throat and then kill him.

We all managed to say polite goodbyes, and Kayla gave Charlene and Renee perfunctory hugs before we headed out. The three of them stood speechless as we left. We got into the long taxi line, and Kayla squeezed my arm again, then closed her eyes and leaned her head against me as if I were a pillow. No, more like I was a crutch, the only thing preventing her from collapsing. It made me feel good, to be honest. It excited me that I could still be a comfort to her.

We said nothing as we stood in the cold, dreary December afternoon. After we made it to the front of the line, I helped the driver load her heavy suitcases into the trunk, then took two smaller bags and the gifts into the back seat. Kayla sat there, head back, eyes closed.

CHAPTER 67

"Why did you do that, Max?" She sounded more tired than perturbed, her voice as scratchy and depleted as an overused vinyl record. Her hand was like a block of ice, as if her blood had gone into hiding. Her hand needed warming, and I was relieved she didn't pull it away. I studied her hand in the dim light of the cab, wondering once again how that hand managed to do what it did.

"I've worried about you, Kayla, since when we last spoke."

"What last time?"

"You haven't called us."

"I'm sorry. It's just ... it's so insanely busy. But what did you mean last time we spoke?"

"The man who'd been following you?"

"What man?" She sounded genuinely confused, and for an instant I wondered whether I'd imagined that telephone conversation.

"You don't remember telling me about this guy who showed up at all your concerts, very white skinned, very tall, angry, always stared at you, never clapped?"

"God. Did I really tell you that?"

"You know you did, Kayla. Don't pretend."

"I don't ... maybe it was just a bad dream. I had horrible dreams. No one wanted to listen to them. I was in a pool of water, and there were sharks, and ..."

"Kayla, stop it." Her evasions made me worry all the more. "There's something else I wanted to talk to you about, and it couldn't be in front of the others."

"Go on."

"You've never seen a cent of the money you're earning, right?"

"They give me cash, when I ask for it, if I see something I need or want."

I sighed in frustration. "Not what I mean at all. Where's all the money going from your concerts? We wrote to Deerfield for an accounting and they never responded. You approved the letter."

"Well, probably because ... I don't know. They tell me it's going into a bank account under my name."

"Did you ever see a statement?"

"No, but I trust them. Why would they lie?"

Was she that innocent? She was fifteen, she'd had some of the best tutors you could find in Manhattan, and, with all her traveling, she must've known something about how the world works. I stifled my sarcastic impulse. Kayla's fragile mental state – for now I was convinced something was wrong in her mind – would not take well to anything other than sweetness, concern, and reason.

"Look. If there was an account under your name, Mom and Dad should've been told about and be in control of it. Right?"

"I guess." She sounded utterly disinterested, but I had to press on.

"Of course. If there was an account, the committee would've responded to our letter and shown us how you were doing, right?"

"I don't know."

"They blew us off, Kayla." I paused in the hope that simple sentence would penetrate. "They blew us off, and the only logical conclusion is there's no account in your name or they're cheating you in some other way."

"Oh, well, maybe the letter just got lost, the mail these ..."

"Kayla, listen. I know you love Lindorf. He's taught you well, he's set you on an amazing career. He's a great teacher. But, when you work for someone like you're working for this committee, they need to treat you fairly. We don't want you to be taken advantage of, even if they're helping you."

"Helping me? They're doing everything for me! Do you think I'd be touring Europe and playing with the Warsaw Philharmonic without them?"

"But you're doing all the work! You're the one practicing ten hours a day. You're the one performing. You have the talent, they don't."

"Well, Herr Lindorf..."

"He's not out there doing these concerts either. And, as you know, his former students have not all made it to great careers, Renee being a case in point. Can't you see what he did to her?"

"Ridiculous. He didn't do anything to her. She quit of her own will."

"After he pushed her too hard, I'll bet. What I'm trying to say is that you need to think more about your own interests, not everyone else's."

"Is that so?" Her voice had grown even more tired by this time. She rested her head back again, closing her eyes. I leaned over and kissed her on the side of her head through her wool cap, and she smiled. Then I put my arms around her lightly and kissed her head again. I struggled to find the right words.

"Now listen, please. Say it's all right for Dad to hire a lawyer to look into what's happened so far. We don't even have a copy of your contract."

"They'll hate me if you do this, Max. Everything I've tried to do will come crashing down." She opened her eyes and looked at me, the smile gone. Somehow, the long trip back to the West Side had passed by way too quickly. We were already on the FDR Drive and would be home in minutes. I needed to get this resolved.

"They won't hate you. If they ask, just tell them the truth, that your parents signed the contract, you're a minor, and you have to do what they say."

"This is this all because you're jealous, isn't it?"

There it was. I knew she'd think there were ulterior motives in whatever advice I tried to give her.

"No, of course not."

"Then?"

"We love you. Just accept that."

She fell silent, head back, eyes closed again. I assumed she was still thinking rather than trying to doze. We turned the corner onto our street as she looked up and spoke.

"You're dying to be Perry Mason. Okay, then. 1 accept. Go do your lawyer thing."

"Thank God."

"You don't believe in God."

"Just an expression. But thank you, then."

"Max ... there's one more thing."

"Yes?"

"There's something you need to know." The taxi had stopped, 1 paid the fare, and the driver went to the trunk to start with the luggage. We remained briefly inside.

"What's that?"

She hesitated. "There really was a man staring at me. I'm sorry 1 just lied to you. There really is someone following me, Max, and it's awful. I'm so scared."

Tears spilled from her eyes as we got out.

CHAPTER 68

Kayla went up to our floor while I struggled with the suitcases. By the time I got everything into our apartment, Kayla had composed herself and was sitting in the living room, sipping a cup of tea and chatting with Mom and Dad. She'd managed in a few minutes to comb her hair, change her clothes, and take on an entirely different demeanor from the girl I'd just held in the taxi. Being home again had poured new life into her, perhaps, or she was working hard to create that impression.

"So, in Rome, do you realize we had only a couple of hours to rehearse the Mozart concerto? And the Maestro, Andrea Papi, wanted to do it differently from the way I wanted to play it. Well, what a battle! But I convinced him, and ..."

"Him? You said her name was Andrea, I thought."

"Oh, Mom, that's a male name in Italian. Anyway, the orchestra was amazing, they were so receptive, and Maestro Papi hugged me, he was so happy it worked out, and the audience was super, too, you know, they're very warm, the Italians." After a few seconds, with a mischievous smile, she added, "Great lovers, too, I hear."

"Kayla!" Dad pretended that he was shocked at her comment, but I felt he was faking mortification for Mom's sake. "Let's not talk about lovers, great or small. You're still a child!"

"She's old enough to be thinking about it, think and do, sticky glue, aren't you?" asked Mom. Kayla continued to smile, but said nothing.

The subject made me ill; I wanted to turn to a safer topic. "I hope you rest up for a few weeks, Kayla. It must be overwhelming, not only with the constant practice but all the travel and the different languages every time you stop."

"Oh, it's not bad. They interview me in English. Then they run subtitles in the local language when they play the interviews on TV."

"There's lots of birds in Rome, right?" asked Mom. "I hear there's bird shit all over, from the starlings. On those plazas? And millions of doves and crows and gulls. I wonder if I can see them in Rome some day."

"I didn't pay attention to the birds, Mom. I'm sorry."

In a few minutes, Kayla had drained her tea and begged to go off for her bath and a good night's sleep. When she left the living room, I filled in Mom and Dad about her agreeing to let Ben intervene on her behalf with the committee. Again, I hid Kayla's fear that she was being stalked by a strange, dangerous man.

"How did she seem when you brought up the subject?" asked Dad.

"Worried. She's afraid that bringing in a lawyer will ruin everything. As expected." I lowered my voice. "It's very good I met her at the airport. That piece of shit lawyer Ziegler was there to take her and the others to dinner, and Ziegler wanted to start a fight when I objected. I had to bat him out of the way, had to bump him twice with Kayla's luggage cart. Not hard enough to hurt him, I don't think. Regrettably." I hoped I might have another chance.

"Then you'll work with Ben?" Dad asked.

I nodded.

"I heard last week on WQXR that gulls have been attacking doves in Rome. Did you know?" It wasn't clear whether Mom was asking me or Dad, but neither of us answered.

I promised to call Ben the next day.

CHAPTER 69

She cringes when Kayla talks about Italians being good lovers. Fifteen is nitroglycerine in a martini shaker. Although Adel's own desire has been tamped down over the years, she recalls well what her body did to her at Kayla's age. Took her into a boy's apartment when his parents weren't home, knowing full well what was going to happen, wanting it to happen even as she didn't want it to happen.

She has to protect Kayla from life's dangers, but most of all from the danger of sex. Kayla isn't emotionally ready, just like Adel wasn't ready at fifteen. Yet Adel had been helpless and Kayla will be helpless too. Kayla's still just a little girl who must travel all over creation without her mother there to keep a proper eye on her. Adel can see Kayla parading before hordes of men reaching for her, pretending to love her, but getting ready to mutilate and maim. It's a shame, they'll kill the dame.

Max can be violent, too, like his father. Why would he have destroyed the doll if not to send a warning to his sister?

CHAPTER 70

I was about to call Ben the next morning when our phone rang. It was Tricia calling to tell Mom of Norm's death.

I found Mom in the kitchen, staggering to a chair, the phone dangling from its cord. A small voice squeaked out of the receiver. When I found out what had happened, I assured Tricia that Mom would be okay, promised we'd attend the funeral, got the details, and thanked her for calling. Then I turned toward Mom, who was banging her head on the table, crying. Kayla came out of her room, I filled her in, and she helped me stop Mom from hurting herself further.

"Sit up, Mom. We're sorry about Norm."

"Fuck. He never found Grace again, so I had to be Grace for a long time. Fuck."

"Yes, Mom."

"The only boss I ever had. Taught me a lot. So much I forgot. A good man with a pecan."

Where the hell was Dad, I wondered, on a Saturday morning? Then I remembered he'd gone to his office to catch up on paperwork. I thought we should let him know about Norm. He'd want to return. I let his office phone ring about ten times before hanging up.

"Here, Mom." Kayla found Mom's Marlboros and lit one for her. As always, Mom calmed down with the infusion of nicotine.

"Did you know about his Grace?"

"You mentioned her," I said uncertainly.

"Lost, forever. And his buddies killed in No Man's Land, and his wife disappeared, and it turned him into a drunk. He was a mess, a state of undress, in jail hundreds of times, stuck with the slimes, but then he found Jesus. Norm never believed me that god was just a middle-aged man with too much imagination, stuck in a messy, crowded office."

"Norm's faith in Jesus helped him a lot, though, didn't it?" Kayla observed soothingly. The night's sleep had done her wonders, her voice had lost the scratchiness from the night before, and her presence helped Mom immensely. Mom seemed to be slowly getting under control, as Kayla rubbed her back and gently massaged her shoulders.

"It was like he could talk to Jesus, but of course he couldn't because Jesus is someone else's story."

"Still, if Norm believed," said Kayla, "then it made sense for him and helped him. It wasn't fiction for him. But I didn't even know he was sick, Mom. I'm so sorry."

Of course, Kayla couldn't have known Norm was dying, as she'd been on tour when we'd heard how badly he was doing. If Kayla had been calling home as she was supposed to, she would've known what was going on with her family, but she was caught up in her own drama. Whoever had written her story had made sure she was away and out of touch.

"Came back from war very bitter. A black man. My Dad called him a Negro, told me it was bad to call him a black man, but I did anyway."

"We know."

"What's going to happen to me now?"

"Well, nothing. We'll go to the funeral and pay our respects."

"Why do my friends always die?"

I had no idea what Mom was talking about. Norm had been the only friend who'd died, not that she had many friends. I made everyone chamomile tea, and we fell quiet, sipping. Chamomile was supposed to have a calming effect, but I felt anything but calm. Indeed, a wave of nausea passed through me. If I felt so poorly, and Norm hadn't even been my friend, I could imagine how Mom felt. He was her friend, her second father, and with his death – I can see much more clearly now – the skimpy fabric of her world was being ripped, never to be repaired.

In a couple of minutes, Mom stood abruptly, looking around as if coming into her kitchen for the first time. "Where's your dad?"

"His office, I think." I called again, let it ring a long time. When he picked up, he sounded out of breath. He promised to be home as soon as he could, but a patient he needed to see on the weekend was almost as this doorstep, too late to cancel.

We got Mom into the living room, onto the sofa, and then Kayla caught my glance and nodded toward the Steinway, suggesting I play for Mom. In a way, that was odd. Kayla was the pianist, and I was a hacker by comparison. But I trusted Kayla's judgment. She needed to hold Mom, whom she sat next to. I thought for a minute, wondering what wouldn't sound trivial to Kayla and yet would have a shot of cheering Mom. I settled on show music, knowing Mom loved *West Side Story.* At least, with those tunes, I wouldn't be competing with Kayla. I'd just started "Tonight" when Mom excused herself to lie down.

After Mom closed the door to her room, I couldn't help but make note of the obvious. "She's taking it hard, isn't she?"

"She lost a close friend, a father figure, so sure she's taking it hard."

I walked into the kitchen with Kayla to wash the tea cups. "We saw him recently. Mom and I. At his apartment in Harlem. I didn't think he'd last the day. Mom made a special point to tell him how proud she was of you, of what you've accomplished." I tried to keep the jealousy out of my voice.

"That was sweet of the two of you."

"Kayla, is she supposed to say the Jewish prayer for somebody who dies?" The word – which of course I knew – wouldn't come to me. "Like, because he was a father figure."

"*Kaddish.* You're an airhead, Max, because Mom doesn't believe in God anyway. You can't pray to nothing."

CHAPTER 71

We attended Norm's funeral at the Abyssinian Baptist Church a week later. The place was crowded with mourners, and we were the only white faces. This was the first time I attended a church service, and I felt remarkably ill at ease. Or perhaps not so remarkable.

It wasn't just that I was bothered at the incessant invocations of Jesus, the Savior and Creator, the frequent assurances Jesus was coming soon to save our world, or the scores of times they repeated that God is Love; it wasn't even the three people who approached me on my way to and from the men's room to ask whether I'd found Jesus. I could tolerate all that for an hour of a Saturday afternoon, particularly to support Mom. What drove me nuts was looking at the faces of the worshipers as they transported themselves into otherworldly bliss, eyes closed, sighing or shouting "Amen" with every breath. I wasn't sure where these worshipers thought they were, but it wasn't in the real world. Meanwhile, Dad looked down at his feet, and Mom hummed to herself, not seeming to hear anything going on around her. Only Kayla, in a too-short black dress, looked interested and respectful.

Through the eulogies I learned Norm Williams was revered for having given so much of his money to the church's upkeep, meanwhile keeping himself in near poverty after he'd closed his diner. Many of his friends came forward to speak about how Norm, "a reformed alcoholic," had helped them attain sobriety themselves, how he'd answer the telephone at any hour and talk them through a bad time. One spoke about how Norm lived for many years with a mother of a friend killed near him on the battlefield and how he took care of her in her dotage. Only when people mentioned the diner in Brooklyn did Mom perk up, nodding.

Following the service, a hearse drove the casket over to a cemetery on 153rd Street. I hadn't realized there *were* cemeteries in Manhattan. We walked over with most of the others, heard a few more speeches, saw Norm's casket lowered, observed as friends threw bouquets into the grave, and then ran into Tricia, who wanted to thank us for having come to the funeral. It wasn't until Mom saw Tricia that she cried.

"He was a good man, Trish. Made a hell of a beef stew. And much more he could do."

"Amen to that, Adel."

"I'm gonna miss him. You know, he found Jackie Robinson for me. And Jackie brought Rachel along too, to meet me."

"I was there, hiding in the kitchen, but peeking through the door. Saw the whole thing. Never forget it."

Just then, Kayla, who'd been standing next to me, looked toward the cemetery entrance, gasped, and bolted in the opposite direction, taking off like a sprinter. With speed like that, she could've qualified for the 1980 U.S. Olympic team. In Kayla's panic to get away from whatever she'd seen, she stumbled about ten steps into her run and smacked down on her knees. But before I could react, she was up again, running as if her life depended upon it.

CHAPTER 72

Nicky listens to the preacher, remembering other religious leaders to whom he'd given ear. He feels he's lived a very long life to have heard the voices of so many. A rabbi in the Great Synagogue of Salonika, an imposing man, dark and bearded, and absolutely sure of himself as he sermonized in Ladino. An Orthodox priest in Athens who tried to tell him his life depended upon turning his faith toward Christ the Savior, a priest who demanded he accept the sacrament in return for being hidden from the Nazis, but who ultimately relented, allowing Nicky to refuse conversion and still be hidden, allowing Nicky even to fall in love with his daughter. A rabbi in a small town in New Jersey who for a while rekindled his interest in studying Talmud, knowing Nicky had lost his faith during the war.

They were all good men, much worthier of salvation than Nicky, yet one had been gassed at Auschwitz; the next, bereaved of wife and daughter, had succumbed to typhus in war-ravaged Athens, to be buried in a shallow grave on the side of the Acropolis; and the last had drifted into senility.

None of this makes sense to him. Nicky cannot reconcile these and other gruesome events of his life – particularly those innocents who died at his hand during the war – with the concept of a good and all-powerful deity. He listens once more to a man of faith, the preacher assuring his flock that Norm now sits at the feet of Jesus for eternity, but Nicky knows better. No one comes back to life, the end is bitter. As *Koheleth* teaches, all is futile and wearisome. The missing can never again be counted.

CHAPTER 73

Dad and I both ran after Kayla. She ignored our calls to stop.

She headed for the exit at the opposite side of the cemetery, but we caught up with her before she could make it. I grabbed her arm, which she yanked free. She blabbered about someone slicing off her fingers and held her hands under her armpits. Then I got her in a bear hug, tightened my grip as she struggled, and forced her over to a bench. She struggled like a woman possessed, which I guess she was. Dad grabbed her from the other side, and we held on. My lungs were heaving with the exertion. Mom and Tricia hustled over as fast as they could, their mouths also gulping at the air.

"Kayla, what's wrong?" I managed to ask.

"I *saw* him again. That man!" She jumped up, but Dad and I forced her back down. "He's *here*. Oh, let me go! I need to get away!"

"What man? What are you talking about? Again?" Dad glanced around, as did I, and I saw nothing abnormal. No exceedingly tall, very white man. No angry person glaring with terribly dark eyes, nothing that should've scared her.

She looked at me in desperation, as if I needed to explain to Dad, not her. Her fear turned her beautiful face into an ugly mask, her features taking on an unhealthy purple tint, as if she'd been battered.

"Tell Dad now, Kayla," I said. "He needs to hear it from you."

"Tell me *now*? Something you know about, Max? What the fuck's going on."

It took a minute for Kayla to calm herself enough to talk. While we waited, I noticed we were near a tombstone that looked as if it had fallen from the moon, its face covered with blotches of red, black, and green moss. If the dead person's name had once been carved into its face, the letters had been obliterated by the elements. I doubted those charged with the upkeep of the cemetery had a clue who was buried there, nor was there a sign anyone had cared for the grave in ages. Burying the dead was a barbaric practice, I mused, a waste of precious space. As my thoughts turned to how I'd insist on cremation, Kayla finally revealed her secret. I felt great relief that I no longer had to hide what she'd told me.

"Dad ... Mom ... I was followed all through Europe."

"Followed?"

"A horrible man coming to my concerts. In the audience. He stares, just stares at me. Wants to hurt me. And now I just saw him over *there*!" Kayla broke down again.

"Max?" Dad looked at me with as much confusion as annoyance.

"She mentioned it to me near the end of her tour. I was going to tell you, honest, but I wanted to talk to her first and ... we've had limited time, you know, so ..." I didn't know what else to say. I felt I'd betrayed both Dad and Kayla by not telling him sooner.

Dad ran his hand through Kayla's hair and massaged the back of her neck. "Listen to me. I don't see anyone here staring at you. The only people I've seen in the cemetery are the people who came over from the church."

"I *saw* him! I swear, it was him and ... I heard him. I heard him growl that he'd kill me. I heard him. And I *saw* him!"

Mom and Tricia had been standing close by, listening. Mom said, "I think maybe I've seen him, too. Yes, I believe I have." Her voice was firm.

"Adel, maybe ..."

"What did he look like?" she asked Kayla.

"Very tall, very white skin, black eyes."

"Yes, exactly. I did see him too. So let's go home, sweetie," she said, kissing Kayla on the nose. "I'll make you a cup of hot tea and we can talk about it there, okay?"

Of course. Mom wouldn't fight with Kayla about what Kayla thought she saw. I shouldn't have been surprised. Mom just walked right into Kayla's hallucination – if that's what it was – as if it had been her own. Her genuine acceptance of Kayla's fear enabled us to walk out of the cemetery together and find a taxi. I sat in the front and the three of them crammed into the back, Kayla between our parents.

They each locked their doors.

CHAPTER 74

The drive back to their building takes forever. She sits with her eyes closed, aware no one is talking. She keeps trying to pull the hem of her dress down over her knees with no success. Although she knows she's in the cab with her family, she feels utterly alone. It's as if the others are trying not to breathe for fear of disturbing her. She's embarrassed both herself and her family. She can still see the outraged stares of people in the cemetery, mourners offended by her outburst, an outrageous affront to the dignity of Norm's funeral.

Kayla presses her fingers over her eyes until stars dance behind her eyelids. After a minute, she's no longer sure she saw the tall man. The rational part of her brain kicks in for an instant, and she realizes that the man – because there was a man in Europe, of that she's sure – couldn't know she'd be in a particular cemetery on a particular Saturday afternoon. Even if he'd known she lived in Manhattan, he couldn't have followed her, couldn't have known where her apartment was. But then – the opposing thought creeps back – how could she have been so sure just minutes ago it was him? She hadn't been thinking about him at all, but about Norm and how God had turned his life around. She'd been wondering about God's presence in everyone's life right before she saw her stalker.

She reaches toward the top of her blouse and feels under it the shape of her Magen David, then puts her hands back to her side. No one in the cab notices her gesture.

God is a He, a Father who created her and gave her the gift of her music. She's believed this as long as she can recall. She's grateful for this gift, as well as for the strength to believe in God, but wonders why God also created the man who's following her.

CHAPTER 75

When we got home, Mom made tea as promised. We sat around the kitchen table, sipping, our ritual bridge to a semblance of normalcy. It took a while before Dad again asked Kayla about what had frightened her.

"Do you want to tell us one more time what you saw?"

"I ... I must've been mistaken. I'm sorry." Kayla sounded so fragile and vulnerable that I felt like crying.

"You ran off like you'd seen a ghost," Dad continued.

"Yeah, didn't I, though? I must've been upset because of the funeral."

"We were all upset, but you were the only one who, well, bolted away," I pointed out. As distraught at Kayla was, I didn't want her to escape scrutiny with a lie. I wanted Mom and Dad to see how troubled she was, that she'd been tormented repeatedly by this imaginary evil man. "You were the only one who saw anything." I ignored that fact that Mom had pretended to see the man too, and Mom, in her motherly wisdom, said nothing to contradict me.

"Nerves, I guess. I'm tired from the tour." Kayla didn't quite sound as if she believed what she was saying.

"Kayla," I responded gently, "you told me about the stalker while you were in Europe."

"My imagination got carried away with itself. In Europe and here. That's possible, isn't it, Dad?"

He looked at her for a long moment, then reached to take her hand, removing it carefully from her teacup. "I'd like you to see someone professionally, Kayla. Just talk to someone in my specialty, totally private, I promise."

"No."

"You need help. Maybe some medication, may ..."

"I said no!"

"But ..."

"Just 'cause you're a shrink, Dad, you won't make me a patient. I know what shrinks do. I'm not going to load myself up with medicine that will make me foggy. I'll never be able to play again if that happens."

"You know, brain cleanser has helped me a lot, Kayla."

"But, Mom, you're cr ... you're not ..."

"Sure, you can say I'm crazy. You know I'm a certified nut case, but it can happen to anyone. It's not a crime, rain or shine. Brain rot happens in children of nut cases, everyone knows. So why don't you ..."

Kayla pushed her chair back with enough force to tip it over. She grabbed her teacup off the table, smashed it into the sink, then ran into her room, slamming the door.

"Well, fuck a duck."

"Adel, take it easy. The question is what do we do now?" Dad picked up the fallen chair and returned it to its proper spot. Mom and I watched as Dad methodically picked the broken teacup pieces out of the sink and disposed of them. I realized Dad had very few answers when it came to my beautiful, talented, sweet, and deeply disturbed sister.

CHAPTER 76

A few days after Norm's funeral, Kayla heads to Bellington to practice, but before she actually gets to school, she'll make a short detour. If Herr Lindorf looks for her and doesn't see her practicing, he'll assume she's working at home for a change.

She's been thinking about this for quite some time, but hesitated. Each time she gets up enough nerve to walk down W. 67th Street from Broadway, she keeps going past the door that she intended to open, not even looking at it, hurrying her pace in the hope that no one inside might see and recognize her. After the episode in the cemetery, however, something has changed. She knows she's being followed, but her family thinks she's insane, and thus no one wants to protect her from this stalker. All her dad offers is consultation with a shrink and the promise of deadly medication, a prospect she cannot contemplate. This is the morning she walks down W. 67th Street and opens the door.

Inside, she easily finds the person with whom she needs to talk to. He introduces himself as Rabbi Berenbaum and invites her to sit with him in his office. He pours her a cup of strong French roast from a coffee maker on his shelf, offers her milk or cream, which she declines, and they sip for a minute until she finds the nerve to speak.

"This is hard for me, Rabbi."

He nods slightly, assuring her that he knows whatever she wants to talk about must be hard. He's there to try to answer her questions, he promises. He smiles to encourage her.

"I'm Jewish, but I'm really not."

"Please tell me in more detail what you mean." His voice is warm and accepting; she feels its embrace, its capacity to hold her steady, even as she sags.

"By blood, I'm Jewish. Both parents."

"Then you're Jewish. Even if only your mother is Jewish, so are you."

"But they never really taught me Judaism or let me experience it fully. My family isn't observant," she continues with a bit more confidence, starting to get used to this young rabbi with whom she's making her first contact. "My parents, my brother, none of them believe in God. I'm not sure if they believe in anything, to tell the truth."

"And that bothers you."

He does not question her but announces what to him is obvious, and it sounds like he's confirmed her right to be bothered by her family's lack of faith. "They're so different from me, I wonder how we're all part of the same family."

"It's not unusual, unfortunately, for only one member of a Jewish family to embrace the presence of *Hashem* and for the others to doubt."

"It's more than doubt, Rabbi. My father, a Holocaust survivor, willfully decided to deny God. I can't blame him, really, given he lost his entire family. His parents. His two younger sisters. Countless cousins, aunts, and uncles."

"Yes, I know survivors like your father. They might believe in *Hashem* if they could see only good in the world, but of course there's isn't only good in the world, and they focus on the bad. That's what trauma often does. It takes away the power to see the good."

"And, my mom's mentally ill and thinks that she talked to God in his office, her version of God being a man with a mustache and a lot of baseball pictures on the wall. The Brooklyn Dodgers, specifically." She can't help but laugh as she explains Adel's theories about who God is and what he does to amuse himself. "I don't know if you're a baseball fan."

"No, not really, but I've heard of the Dodgers."

"Yeah. My mom's obsessed with them."

"You know, mental illness reveals a part of *Hashem*'s reality. In our community, we see every aspect of reality as a manifestation of *Hashem*'s goodness."

"How can a person's illness show that God is good?"

He ponders for a moment before answering. "There's no easy answer, Kayla. When our movement was founded, the so-called rational Jews in Europe called us mentally ill. Why?"

"Why?"

"Because we danced and sang in a way that disturbed others who weren't used to our ways. We learned at a very early stage of our development that attaching the label of mental illness to a person was, let's say, a lazy way of dealing with *Hashem's* creation of the world in his own image."

"But you didn't answer my question."

"I was getting there. What I mean is that you need to start with first principles. The person in front of you who's crazy by your definition – and definitions change – that person, your mother, for example, stands before you only because *Hashem* created *Ha O'lam*, this universe, from nothing. And you stand there, looking at your mother – laughing at her perhaps – only because *Hashem* created you from nothing. Those are first principles, Kayla."

"First principles. In the beginning, God created heaven and earth."

"Quite so. *B'Reishit Bara Elohim et Ha-Shamayim v-et Ha-Aretz.* Those words were given to us by *Hashem. Netzach Yisrael Lo Yishaker.* The God of Israel does not lie. If you start with those principles, take them into your heart, then you'll see the good in any situation. Does any of this make sense?" He deliberately closes a large volume in front of him. Kayla assumes he's been studying the Talmud.

"I hear you. I don't fully understand." She pauses for a second, then takes a deep breath and lets the words spill out, the main reason she's sought counsel this morning. "Rabbi, I have to tell you something else."

"Go ahead."

"Can you promise not to say anything to anyone?"

"You know that a rabbi keeps confidential anything he hears unless a life is at stake."

"All right, then. I fear I have a mental illness, too. I see what my mom's become and I'm afraid I'll end up as ... as hopeless as she is. I hide it from everyone as best I can, but now other people are seeing it in me and it can't be hidden."

"Tell me, please."

"I see someone who's going to kill me, a scary person who follows me everywhere I go, and I know he's going to kill me after he tortures me, and most of the time I feel he's real, he *is* real, I know I've seen him stalking me, but part of me knows he's not real. I see him as clearly as you see the Talmud in front of you, and yet, he has to be a hallucination, right? No one else sees him. My mom pretended to see him, too, but she was lying." She tears up, but it's not from sorrow as much as it is from relief. This rabbi is the first person to whom she's confessed this deep an understanding of her mental status.

"You should talk to your family about this, Kayla."

"I do talk to them. They want to help me. But my dad wants me to see a psychiatrist and start on medication. I can't."

"Why can't you?"

"They've given me so much, Rabbi. They've sacrificed so I could play the piano. I know it's not my fault, they'd be so disappointed if I had to give up my career."

"I'm sorry, Kayla. You're a pianist?"

"I told you I was Kayla Covo."

The rabbi shakes his head. Until this instant, it appears to Kayla, he hasn't understood to whom he was talking. "Forgive me. Kayla Covo. Yes, come to think of it, I have seen your name and probably your picture somewhere, but I've never given it much thought. What you'd call classical music isn't my interest, sorry to say."

"Well, my point still is I can't admit to my folks I might be ill. I can't let them medicate me, because that would end my performing life. And the ability to perform is everything to me."

"You mentioned a brother. Do you want to tell me about him?"

"Max is very much like my father in many ways, a pure atheist. He tries to look after me as you'd expect a big brother to, but can be overbearing. I often feel oppressed when he's around, like he needs me to give him something I can't. Like he needs me to accept something from him I couldn't possibly accept. What I'm trying to say is that he's much too close and so I do talk to him, but ...." Her voice trails off, her conscious mind uncertain about what really needs to be said about her relationship with Max.

"Maybe he's the one who needs a psychiatrist? People are so complicated."

"I guess. It has very much to do with the piano, I think, because he studied it first and, well, I shot past him almost as soon as I began."

"I see. Jealousy rears its ugly head. So, tell me how you think I can help you, Kayla. I don't think you're here just to chat with me one time. There's more."

"I want to be closer to Judaism. I know there are people who ..."

The rabbi waits a few seconds to see if she's going to continue, but, again, she's at a loss for words, not sure what she knows. "Closer to Judaism is exactly why we're here, Kayla. To help people like you. To help any and all Jews draw closer to the practice of true Judaism, to the proper worship and celebration of *Hashem*. Closer to Judaism so that they may live the fullest possible lives according to the will of *Hashem*. Closer to Judaism is what we're doing right now, with this conversation. You're welcome here always."

"I will come back."

He hands her a small printed pamphlet with a list of service times and other activities of the West Side *Chabad*. "And any time you want to talk more about your situation, we'll sit down and study together. We'll see what insight and comfort the sources might offer."

She stands, ready to be shown out. She needs to get to school and start her practice. She plans to think about everything he's told her, starting with first principles. She thinks about the beginning and what there might have been before the beginning.

CHAPTER 77

I'm pretty sure it was the week after the funeral. Kayla was gone early, her bed made. She'd mentioned that she was going to get up very early to practice at Bellington. At about nine, I walked down to the Fordham library to study. When the librarian paged me at three in the afternoon, I knew something was wrong. He led me to a cubicle and put through the call from Dad.

Kayla had "gone missing." Lindorf had called, wanting to talk to Kayla and wondering if she was home. Of course, we'd thought she was at Bellington. Lindorf had explained to Dad that he'd scouted around Bellington, all her favorite practice rooms, all the other practice rooms, and no Kayla. He'd not found anyone who'd seen her, either. Did I know where Kayla had gone? Did I know anyone else we could call? I had no idea on either score.

As if Kayla being AWOL wasn't enough, Dad told me about the other "weird thing." He didn't know where Mom was either. She'd left home at about ten, saying she was running down to the grocery, and hadn't come back. He'd checked in vain at the grocery and with our neighbors. He wondered if Kayla and Mom might've gone off together, but we couldn't imagine where. Then I flashed on that scene from the cemetery a week before, when Mom had told Kayla she, too, had seen the stalker. I wondered whether they might have gone back there.

"Why would they do that?" Dad asked. "Kayla was scared out of her mind there."

"That's why she might've gone back," I offered. "She might've thought she could face down whatever she thinks she saw there, prove to herself she's actually fine, prove to us she doesn't need to see a shrink. I don't know, but I don't have any other ideas. I bet they're both there, wandering around, convincing themselves it was just a case of jittery nerves." Even as I spoke, I knew none of this made sense. Mom had been gone for, what, five hours already? Kayla all day? I kept thinking about all the studying I had to do, how far behind I was in my courses, and now this interruption. "Let me hop in a cab and check it out. I'll call you from the cemetery, one way or another. Maybe by then you'll have heard from one of them."

"Okay."

In the cab up Broadway I wondered what the hell Dad had been doing all day in the apartment by himself, with Mom not back from the grocery. Probably immersed in the *Times* crossword puzzle, as usual, or reading one of his psychiatric journals from the pile on his night table. Either way, oblivious when it came to his family. But it was so creepy that both Mom and Kayla should've gone missing within hours of each other. The ridiculous thought crossed my mind – a B movie script at best – that Dad had done away with the both of them. I had to laugh at myself; Kayla's paranoia was catching.

At least half of my hunch had been right. Call it brotherly intuition.

After I'd gone only a few steps into the cemetery, a few funerals taking place on this Saturday afternoon, I saw Kayla. She sat on the same bench we'd all sat on the week before. Nor was she alone, but her companion wasn't Mom. Kayla sat close to a tall, slender, very black guy with a goatee. She was talking to him, a broad smile on her face. Now I felt like a fool, chasing after my sister, finding her, and getting ready to interfere with her …her what? Date? She picked up a black guy in the few hours she was away from home and was already on a date? In a cemetery? (And please. Don't rail at me for calling him a black guy. It's descriptive only.)

I glanced at the ancient tombstone on which I'd focused while holding Kayla down the prior Saturday and wondered how many similar trysts had played out before it over the centuries. As Kayla saw me, she said something to her companion, and her smile changed to a look of confusion.

"Kayla, where the hell have you been?"

"Where the hell have I been? What are *you* doing here, Max?"

"Looking for you, obviously. You've gone missing in action."

"Missing? But that's absurd. I mean, I went to school this morning, like always."

"No one's seen you there today."

"That's because I ran into August, and we went to practice together, and then we left to have lunch, and then we decided—well, I asked him—to come here. It's not far from where he lives. This is August Sorel, Max. August, my crazy meddling fool of a brother, Max."

Despite her insult, I extended my hand toward Sorel out of habit and politeness, but was not pleased. "Yes, I've heard Kayla talk about you. You practiced with Kayla? Practicing what, if I may ask?"

He ignored my question. "She's an amazing accompanist." Kayla beamed as if President Reagan had invited her into the Oval Office and presented her with the Medal of Freedom.

"No. I didn't know she ever accompanied anyone. Have you, Kayla?"

"Well, not until today. But we had a good session! A great session! We worked on an easy Beethoven sonata, you know the one in G? Da-da-da-da-da-da-da-da-da-da-da-da-da-dah-dah. Dee-dee!" She sang the first two bars, and I knew the one she meant. I couldn't help but be pleased for her delight in the music, and her smile comforted me, but I found nothing positive about the new ... relationship? ... connection with Sorel. I had no idea what I was looking at, what it meant, how it might tie into everything else.

"That's great, Kayla. Listen, let me call Dad and tell him where you are. Will you be coming home soon?"

She looked quizzically at Sorel, who shrugged his shoulders. "I guess."

"Okay then, I'll be right back."

I found a pay phone in about half a minute. I left a message on our answering machine and returned.

"So ... August ... you're not thinking of turning Kayla into an accompanist, are you?" I tried to keep my voice light, smiled as if the whole thing were a big joke. "I mean, are you?"

"Actually, I *have* been looking for someone new for the last six months. I think she'd be great, if she wanted to do it. She's so talented. She'd bring my music to such a higher level, I'm confident to say."

"Oh, August, do you think so? Max, August's an incredible violinist, and we had such fun playing together!" Kayla looked up at me with the little-girl smile that could have melted all the ice in Antarctica, waiting for my blessing, but I stood dumbfounded.

Finally, August broke the silence. "Well, it's getting late. I think I'd better get back to Bellington and a lot more practice before the day ends. Share a cab? Drop you guys off on the way?"

We walked back to the street, hailed a cab, and the ride down Broadway to our apartment was quiet. I'd decided not to say anything about Mom's disappearance until I was alone with Kayla. When the cab stopped, August leaned over and kissed Kayla lightly on the forehead. She squeezed his arm. Every muscle in my body tightened.

"See you tomorrow," they said to each other, in perfect unison.

CHAPTER 78

Birds fly near Adel's head, too near, so close that she smells them, a nauseating essence of rotting fruit. She hears their breathing, a chorus of hissing as they snap at her. She waves her hands to ward them off, but they return. The hissing evolves into whispering, a message she's heard many times. She's a whore, she'll never come to any good, she'll never make her mother happy. She's stupid, she's fat, she's ugly, she's disgusting. Even as she tries to bat them away, she takes inventory: house sparrow, house finch, eagle, common grackle, red-winged blackbird, northern cardinal, common yellowthroat, each bringing its own message of hate. They were her friends and now they're trying to hurt her.

For a few seconds, the onslaught slows, and she feels the need to record their appearance. Where's her notebook? How can she bird watch without it? Where are her binoculars? She spins, once, twice, checking to see if she's dropped them behind her, but they're gone. Without her props, Adel is lost, and she sits down on the curb in front of Weber's Real Kosher Meat to cry. Passersby on 12th Avenue avert their eyes.

Then she picks up her head in time to see a very rare Connecticut warbler swing through the air over the parking lot across the street, turning to get a bead on her. It swoops down to pluck out her eyes, but at the last second veers away, and she's left grasping at empty air. She puts her face down on the street next to the curb and licks at the dirt.

CHAPTER 79

As soon as the taxi drove off with Sorel and she no longer had to keep up pretenses, she substituted her smile with the look of anger.

"What's eating you?" I asked.

"Nothing, Max ... except that my big brother had to track me down and bring me home, like a baby, when I was having a pleasant afternoon with a friend." Her voice, laden with sarcasm, started to break. She stormed past the doorman and jabbed at the elevator button. I barely got there in time to get in with her before the door closed.

"Look, I'm sorry if I interrupted something, but we were worried. Dad had to call me at the library. You snuck out this ..."

"I didn't sneak out! Shit! Who the fuck do you think are you, anyway? My bodyguard?"

"I didn't ..."

"I'm free to come and go, dammit! I went where I always go! You don't own me. I'm not your fuckin' *girl*!" I was shocked at her vulgarity, so unlike her.

"We're your family," I said, trying to keep my voice low and even. I thought about the pile of books I left at the library and about my upcoming exams. I wondered – not for the first time – why I couldn't have been born into a normal family, where I could just pursue my own interests, spend time as I needed to and not have to worry about a crazy mother, a prodigy sister going crazy herself – rude and ungrateful on top of everything else – and a father too preoccupied to do the hard job of being a good husband and parent.

The elevator door opened at our floor, and there was Dad, waiting, wanting to talk. I half expected Kayla to wall herself away in her room, but she surprised me by sitting at the piano, still bristling.

"Kayla, why did you just take off without telling anyone where you were going?"

She ignored Dad and began the Chopin B-Minor scherzo with an overabundance of brutal energy. The *sforzandos* were needlessly strong, rattling the dishes in the china cabinet. We listened, letting her work out her emotions. In the lyrical middle section, she exaggerated the change in tempo, slowing to a snail's pace, pregnant with danger. When the piece returned to the initial theme, Kayla attacked it with even greater frenzy, at a speed that left me breathless. No concert pianist would dare play it that fast, but she struck every note brilliantly, as if she'd been practicing nothing else for her entire life. She pushed the piece almost to the end, but in the middle of the final chromatic scale – I'll never forget the eerie feeling of discombobulation – she stopped cold and whirled around, glaring.

"Where's Mom?" With her anger directed at me, I'd not had a chance to explain.

"Mom is ... We don't know. She left this morning and hasn't come back yet. I looked around the neighborhood, the doorman hasn't seen her, the people in the grocery haven't seen her, no one's seen her since she walked down the street. We thought she might have been with you."

"Holy shit!"

"Right," Dad continued. "The two of you missing in one day. Hard to believe. What motivated you to go back to the cemetery? If you'll pardon me, isn't that kind of ..."

"Gross?" I volunteered, unable to restrain myself.

"If I wanted to go back to convince myself I'd not really seen anything last week, would that make sense?"

"Maybe. It made enough sense for Max to think to look for you there."

"And if I asked August to come with me because I didn't want to go alone, would that make sense too?"

"Yes."

"Well, then you've heard the truth. Max scared the shit out of me when I saw him walking up. I didn't know for a second whether I was imagining him or what."

"Why August? Why not go back there with me or Max?"

"Come on, Dad, I was at school. I'm a pianist, remember? He's a violinist. I told you about how we met in Vancouver, right? Well, now we're playing together. At least we were earlier today. Whether he'll want to make music with me anymore, after the heroic rescue by Max, I don't know."

"There's a lot going on in your life now, isn't there?"

"Put that aside. I can't believe we're talking about me, when Mom's missing and she's certified crazy. Don't we need to call the police and have them look for her? Shouldn't we tell them there's a nut loose on the street?"

"I wish you wouldn't call her a nut," Dad said.

When the phone rang, the three of us jumped for it, but Dad got there first. He listened for a second, then said, "All right. We'll be over within the hour."

"Mom?"

"Brooklyn Police. Saves us a call, a bunch of calls. They picked her up in Borough Park a little while ago. Literally picked her up out of the street. She was near where she used to live, near what used to be Norm's Diner. We have to go to Brooklyn to get her. You guys coming?" Well, of course we were.

On the way, I asked Dad if Mom had been keeping on her meds. He didn't know, and his ignorance made me want to lash out. How could he not know? He was a psychiatrist and her husband, so if he didn't know, who *would* know?

Dad drove like a maniac, if you'll forgive the trite expression, and I tried to brace myself against what I was sure would be a horrific accident. But we got across the Brooklyn Bridge without killing ourselves and in another ten minutes drove up to a three-story brick building displaying an NYPD logo and a sign telling us we'd arrived at Precinct 23. The desk sergeant, a black woman, had a weary look on her face. When we explained who we were, the look changed to a frown.

"You're her family? Why'd you let her out? She's committable, you know. Come this way."

As we walked into the innards of the station, the sergeant described how they'd found Mom, lying against the curb near the corner of 52nd Street and 12th Ave, talking to herself. She'd swung at the officers who tried to get her into the patrol car, but they handcuffed her and, by the time they reached the station, she'd calmed down and they'd taken off the handcuffs. They found our number in the small phone book in Mom's purse, but Mom had asked them to call a friend named "Trish" and they'd found her number too. Trish had arrived at the station a half-hour before we did.

Mom sat on a chair in the corner of a small conference room, staring at the floor, muttering. Tricia sat and watched her from a few feet away.

"Well, at last," sighed Tricia. "Excuse me while I find the Ladies."

"Mom, it's me, Kayla." Mom looked up, smiled for an instant, then grimaced.

"Do you know where you are, Adel?"

Mom reached into her pocket for her Marlboros, which had been crushed. From the pack she extricated a bent cigarette, broke off the end, and looked for matches. Dad kept some on hand for just such situations. Mom dragged smoke deep into her lungs, trembling, but said nothing. She looked around at us as if trying to make sure we were her friends.

"I'm going to call Dr. Lack," Dad said. "Max and Kayla, wait here."

Where else were we going? I couldn't take all this drama, suddenly dizzy and fighting nausea. I pulled a chair from the table and fell into it. I put my head on the table, afraid I might vomit. Then I heard Kayla singing softly. I looked up, and she was holding Mom's free hand, kneeling on the floor in front of her. She sang a song from *Cats*, which had just opened. Dad and Mom had seen and loved it.

"Memories, all alone in the moonlight, I can smile at the old days, I was beautiful then, I remember the time I knew what happiness was, let the memories live again."

I couldn't understand how Kayla had learned the song and couldn't remember when I'd heard her sing as sweetly. More miraculously, Mom began singing too, coming out of her trance. They sang together, Kayla harmonizing or at least trying to against Mom's uncertain melody. So engrossed was I in their singing that I began to feel better myself.

"If you touch me, you'll understand what happiness is, look, a new day has begun."

When they finished, Kayla hugged Mom, and both were crying. Dad cleared his throat from the doorway, and I looked around to see him and

Tricia watching. But Kayla and Mom didn't notice. They whispered to each other. When Kayla stood, still holding Mom's hand, she took away her cigarette and stubbed it out in an ash tray.

Kayla looked at us and spoke in a low, matter-of-fact voice. "I think she's okay for now."

"Adel, do you know where you are?" Dad asked again. He pulled a chair and sat in front of Mom. Mom rubbed her eyes, as if she was waking up, perhaps from a bad dream. She seemed to ignore Dad and looked directly at Kayla, who was standing next to him.

"The cops picked me up. We're in Brooklyn, right?"

"Right, Mom," Kayla answered. "Why did you come to Brooklyn? Do you remember?"

"Sure. I wanted to see Norm's Diner. He died."

"He died, yes, I'm sorry. We went to his funeral. So, you came to Brooklyn to look at the diner. Did you find it?"

"Not really."

"What happened then, Adel?" Dad continued.

"I walked around. It was the old neighborhood, Nicky. When we first dated, you came to the house and picked me up. Do you remember?"

"Of course. Did you go back there?"

"I walked up and down the block seventeen times. I counted."

"Seventeen, very good. And then what?"

"Seventeen is four squared, you know, plus one. I was the one."

"All right. Then what, if you don't mind telling us?"

"Then thousands of birds came at me. It was ... they wanted to hurt me, but I shooed them away. I tried to hurt them. I tried to bite off their heads. I threw lightning bolts at them, but nothing worked. They kept coming."

"Birds. And lightning. And then what?"

"I don't remember. Just the cops. And the handcuffs, and the patrol car. And so here I am."

"You haven't been taking your meds, have you?" Mom didn't respond, but we all knew the answer anyway. The question was so obvious that Dad didn't need to ask it.

"What's going to happen now, Nicky? Do I have to go to jail?"

"No. We want to take you home with us."

"Where's Trish?"

"I'm here, Adel. What can I do for you?"

"Take me with you? Please? I don't want to go back ... to go back to ..." Mom was becoming agitated again. She pulled her hand away from Dad's.

"Adel, you'd be best ..."

"Dad, wait ..." Kayla put her hand on his shoulder. "If Trish has room, I can go with Mom, for just one night?"

Trish looked uncertain but acquiesced in Kayla's suggestion. "Your mom can sleep on the sofa, and you'll need to sleep on the floor next to her. If that's okay and if you promise to take her home tomorrow morning, then sure."

"Dad?"

"Adel, if Kayla goes with you to Trish's house tonight, will you come back with her first thing tomorrow? You have to get back on your Thorazine."

"Turn your face to the moonlight." Mom choked back tears as she tried to sing; her voice was croaky at best.

"Is that yes? You'll do whatever Kayla and Trish want you to do? You'll stay with Kayla and Trish? You won't run away?"

"Will you sing for me, Kayla?"

"Sure, Mom, whenever you want. Any show tune. We can do *Fiddler* or *Man of La Mancha* or anything else you. Will you behave?"

"Do they have to put the handcuffs back on?"

"No handcuffs, Mom."

"Well, let's go."

So Trish left with Mom and Kayla in tow, and Dad and I headed back toward his car.

•   •   •   •   •

We were just about to get in, when an older, short man with red hair, wearing a cheap and tattered business suit, rushed out of the station and called to us.

"Dr. Covo! Wait!" He drew up, short of breath. "I'm Detective Harrington. You were here to see Adel Miller?"

"My wife, detective. Mrs. Adel Covo."

"Yes, of course. You and I met before, a long time ago, at her father's funeral."

"Ah, yes. Harrington. You arrested her once, didn't you?"

"Sure. When she smacked that asshole at the diner who grabbed her ... when she smacked the asshole. Charges dropped, of course. I was surprised to see her here again. She'd moved away ages ago. Neighborhood changed a lot since then, too. I was wondering if there was anything I could do. I see she's not well."

"Thanks so much for asking. Norm Williams just passed away. They were close, and it's gotten to her."

"Norm! Oh, wow, that's too bad. He was some guy. Closed up years ago, and, although the place was a dive, it had a certain charm. I loved his chili. Nothing like it anymore around here. Norm gone, huh? A shame."

"Adel's taking it hard."

"I understand. Norm kept an eye on her, 'specially after her dad died."

"He did. Gave her away at our wedding, too. So, I appreciate your offer, but I don't think there's much you can do, Detective. Unless you see her wandering around again." Dad reached into his wallet and took out a business card. "If you do, please call me."

"He might have to call you at home, Dad." I offered. He seemed to have forgotten I was with him.

"Oh. My son, Max. Yes, let me give you our home number." He found his pen and jotted the number on the back of the card.

"Was that lovely girl your daughter?"

"Yes. Kayla Covo. You've maybe heard of her? A classical pianist?"

"I'm not a classical music guy, other than the 1812 Overture with the cannons. I'm more into country, Kenny Rogers and stuff." Dad had no clue about country music. "But, it's great to see you and Adel had kids, and nice ones, too." He looked at me, smiling. I guess he was nearing retirement. I couldn't see him chasing crooks or drawing his gun. He was simply the nice neighborhood cop everyone wished for, the precinct's Mr. Rogers. "She's a handful sometimes?"

"Kayla?"

"Your wife, I meant."

"Sometimes. Well, we've got to go, Detective Harrington."

"Good to see you again, Dr. Covo. And nice meeting you, Mark."

"Max."

CHAPTER 80

Adel sings again with Kayla on the drive to Trish's house, both of them in the back seat, but it doesn't take long before Trish joins in from the front. Trish doesn't have a great voice, but then neither does Adel tonight, so it's all right. Kayla's beautiful soprano keeps them close enough to the right key.

Adel recalls how Trish came into the station and tried to hug her and she pushed Trish away, fearing Trish was another bird come to torment her. Now Trish is taking her home, if only for one night. Adel remembers when Trish, so long ago, had been there for her when her dad died. She hasn't thought about this for years, but it seems like only yesterday Trish came to their apartment that first night, when Adel was in shock, trying to hurt herself. Trish slept with her, holding her until dawn, her body warm and sweet smelling. Trish held her tight, murmuring softly from the Bible, until Adel fell asleep. What was it now? Ah, yes. "Let not your heart be troubled." Adel can almost hear it again, and, in a flood of long-delayed gratitude, she cries once more. Why had she never thanked Trish properly?

She will sleep with Trish this night only and then Kayla will take her home. She's promised.

CHAPTER 81

We headed back to Manhattan, my mind reeling. I didn't know what question to ask first. The lights of the Brooklyn Bridge sped by as I tried to organize things in my mind.

"What's going on with her, Dad? It's more than just the medicine thing, isn't it?"

"It's never just the medicine."

"So what is it?"

"It's Norm, like I said to the cop, as well as not taking her meds. And all the stuff with Kayla. Life's catching up with Mom. That's probably why she complains occasionally of pains in her chest, in her arms, in her back."

"Life catching up? They cause physical symptoms?"

"I've seen this kind of thing since I first dealt with schizophrenic patients."

"Explain."

He thought for a while before responding. "Patients with schizophrenia will have their somatic complaints and odd behaviors, but they can function reasonably well for a long time if they stay on their meds, have support from family and friends, and they're ... oh, maybe a bit sheltered. But you can't shelter someone forever from life's problems. And then ..." Whatever he was thinking got him off track. I grew impatient.

"And then what, Dad? Sheltering from life's problems. You said it was impossible to do that forever."

"Ah. Well, there's something else about Mom we never told you kids. Always thought you were too young. You must never mention it to her, what I'm going to tell you."

"I won't say a word, but what the hell are we talking about, anyway?"

"Mom was raped as a teenager."

"Raped?" I couldn't have been more surprised if he'd said Mom had grown up on Mars. I'd read rape wasn't a sexual crime so much as a crime of violence, but I still felt – undoubtedly misogynistic – that only attractive women were raped.

"On a date. For whatever reason, I think memories of her rape have surfaced. The rape pushed her over the edge of overt mental illness. Or maybe it's other abuse Mom endured as a child that's resurfacing now. Or a mixture."

"Raped. I can't believe it, and yet, I have to. How old was she?"

"About Kayla's age, I think. It was a boy she cared for, but, as it so often turns out, he wanted only one thing."

"Shit, Dad. That's horrible." I was seeing Mom in a new light. More than just odd, she was a victim. Someone she trusted had taken advantage, probably because she *was* a mental case. And she had to deal with the consequences ever since. Part of me admired how she overcame as much as she did, to live as close to a normal life as she could, schizophrenia and all. But my selfish part was disappointed in her for letting herself get into that situation.

"So, when I say life catches up, I mean the bad things that happened decades earlier keep happening, and no one can fight them off forever, least of all the people with mental illness. Things that all human beings have to deal with, like the death of friends, like the illnesses of children, take on a whole new dimension of difficulty."

"I think I understand, but tell me why now? Why, suddenly, is this long-ago rape affecting her so much, and why didn't she want to come back with us tonight? She should want to be back with her family, in her own home, in her own bed, where she's safe. I mean, Trish is virtually a stranger compared to us."

"I don't know why exactly now as opposed to any other time. Kayla going wild at the cemetery? That by itself is traumatic. I wish I could tell you."

"Mom seemed so afraid at the police station."

"Yes, and what happened today is obviously also tied in with Norm. The diner's where Norm adopted her as his pet project, where she began to see she could live and function in the world, and it's where she and Trish became friends. She went to Brooklyn to find her way back to the diner and maybe thought she'd find Norm there too. As for coming home tonight, maybe she just wanted to prolong the mourning period by staying with Trish, who was also close to Norm."

I couldn't put my finger on it, but I felt Dad didn't believe his own explanations. He could see, as I could, that Mom had been afraid to come home.

"And what about Kayla? What's going on with her seeing people who aren't there, with her deciding to be an accompanist instead of a soloist? What's going on with her and August? Doesn't that concern you?"

"What is it, Max? What are you more concerned about? Kayla's paranoia? The course of her career? That she might have a boyfriend?"

"He's a *man*, Dad, and ... well, I have nothing against blacks, but, you know ... it's not very common at ..."

"So the main thing you're worried about is his dark skin?"

"You're distorting what I said."

"I wonder." We sat in silence for a minute.

"Look, Dad, I'm not a racist." It seemed the most logical defense, but to my own ears I sounded weak.

"I'll take you at your word. Not a racist. Fine. So, yes, I am obviously worried about paranoia. You heard me tell her she needed to see a psychiatrist. Yes, I'd be concerned about her adjusting her career plans on the spur of the moment, but we don't have enough evidence yet to say that's what's happened. And, yes, I'm concerned about her taking up with *any* boy or man, but I think we'd be hopping the gun ..."

"Jumping the gun."

"Right. Jumping the gun. We'd be too hasty in interpreting this as a big problem."

"You're telling me, once again, that you won't worry about Kayla at all until she's in really big trouble, isn't that what you're saying?"

I was miffed and let my voice grow large. No one else but me ever looked out for Kayla and, although I was her brother and wanted to help her, I needed to have a life of my own.

I know I was very rude to Dad that evening, on that ride back home from Brooklyn. Replaying that conversation, I can see I was trying to hide my embarrassment at having expressed racist thoughts. You've got to understand, kids. I was an arrogant, heavily-opinionated teenager, and I was thrashing around, far out of my element, overcome by emotions I didn't understand.

My snide comment clearly hurt Dad. His hands tightened around the steering wheel, as if trying to choke the life out of it.

CHAPTER 82

Oddly, when Nicky gets into his room and lies on his bed, he seldom thinks about Adel or Kayla or Max for more than an instant. If he mulls over the events that plague his family, he knows he'll never fall asleep. He'd learned to sleep even during grave danger while fighting with the partisans in Greece. He'd learned to sleep holding a rifle, in forests crawling with enemy soldiers. The problems his family now faces will still be there in the morning.

He doesn't blame Max for being rude. Nicky has learned after decades of practicing psychiatry that teenagers excel at rudeness and love to show off their skills, their verbal jabs and hooks. If anything bothers him, it's that Max's comments hit the target. He'll do something about Adel tomorrow when she gets home with Kayla. He'll talk to Ben himself about what must be done to protect Kayla's interests. He'll push harder to get Kayla into treatment. Maybe his former partner will give them a family rate. He'll take Max to a Knicks game.

Then his thoughts turn to Adrienne, and he realizes once again how much he misses her, even though it's been years since he ended the affair. It's good that he put her out of his life. He couldn't deal with the complexities of another relationship on top of everything else. He's heard she's married, with two children. Good for her. He's heard she still publishes poetry. Good for her. Still, he wishes he could recapture the way she made him feel.

Then his thoughts drift to Laura, whom he's not seen in the twelve years since her father managed to hang himself. That suicide surprised him. He hadn't thought Lyle had the energy to end his life. It bothered him deeply but he'd received a thank-you note from Laura for the effort he'd put into trying to help. There were other patients who'd also taken the easy way out. It was something psychiatrists most feared, a hazard of the profession.

Then his thoughts briefly turn to Ezra, who'd left his care, gotten involved with narcotics pushers, and ended up in the Attica Correctional Facility.

The idea crosses his mind that he should have gone into internal medicine, when at least most of the patients who wanted to kill themselves took their time doing so with alcohol, cigarettes, and painkillers. Just as he recalls the last study he'd read in the New England Journal, about smoking and health, he drifts off to sleep.

CHAPTER 83

The next morning, Dad asked me if I'd like for him to make breakfast. He offered to fix cream cheese omelets, his way of saying that his anger at me of the evening before had passed, and I was happy for a truce, so I readily accepted. I didn't deserve his forgiveness, of course. It was I who should've begged him to forgive me.

I put on a new pot of coffee and flipped through the *Times* to pass the time until we ate. The world didn't seem a very safe place. Countries were testing nuclear weapons. The Italian Red Brigades had kidnapped a U.S. Army general. Israel had annexed the Golan Heights. I opened the sports section, only to see the Mets had traded away one of their best hitters and looked as anemic on paper as any Mets team I could recall.

Before the first omelet could be prepared, the door opened and Kayla and Mom came striding through, smiles on their faces. They looked as if they'd just returned from a shopping spree. They also looked like they slept in their clothes, which they had, but otherwise nothing was amiss.

"Good morning!" Dad cracked a few more eggs, and I set out additional dishes. "Hungry, Kayla?"

"You bet, Dad!"

"So, Adel, how's Trish?"

"Her place is small, Nicky. She has three cats, did you know? And a fish tank."

"No, I didn't know. Does she have any family living with her?"

"Her husband died. She has two sons in the army. Norm was in the army too. He told me. His friends died. Blood and guts. It was nuts. And then he was in the navy at Pearl Harbor. More friends died."

"Right, I think I heard about that. He was a lucky guy to have been off the *Arizona* when the Japs attacked. Adel, will you take your pill now, please?" He reached for the small bottle of Thorazine on the counter and shook one out for her. Mom glanced at it, then at Dad, then back at the pill.

"I'm going back on?" She looked doubtful.

"If you don't mind. You never should have stopped, Adel."

He put the pill in her hand, then poured a glass of orange juice and handed it to her. She swallowed it with a small sip. "There, how's that?"

"Good, Adel. Now, remember, one before bed, and one at breakfast, every day. You promise, right?" She ignored the question.

"Say, Mom, did you know the Mets traded away Lee Mazzilli?" I asked.

"No kidding! Who'd they get?"

"Some minor league pitcher named Ron Darling. From the Rangers. Big shot guy who went to Yale, supposedly. Who cares? I don't even know if Yale has a baseball team. He's not going to replace Mazzilli."

"One bad year because the guy's injured and they dump him!"

"Yeah. Doesn't make sense. Buying a pig in a poke."

I immediately regretted my metaphor, because Mom went "oink oink" and laughed bizarrely, a hysterical "Eeee!" like the scream of a trapped animal. I feared she'd wake our neighbors, but she stopped after a few seconds.

"A pig in a poke is a prick on a bloke." Mom laughed crazily again, Kayla stifled her own laughter, and I couldn't help myself, but guffawed. Mom was too much. The three of us were falling apart, it seemed, but Dad's face showed concern.

"Adel, kids, maybe ..."

"Well, it's always what did you do for me yesterday," Mom continued, determined to keep the conversation on baseball. "You know what happened to Jackie after the '56 season, don't you?"

"Sure. The Dodgers traded him to the Giants." Everyone in our family knew, because Mom brought it up constantly, more than two decades after the fact. It still rankled her, always would.

"*Tried* to trade him. He quit, rather than play for the Giants. Made my stomach turn, burn, and churn. So his numbers were off a bit. Big fucking deal."

"That's life, Adel," said Dad. "Baseball's a tough game, and it's sad, but that's how people are. Speaking of yesterday, did you know Kayla went missing?"

"Dad! It's not true!" Kayla pretended to be upset. "I was practicing at Bellington with August, the violinist, you know, I've mentioned him, and we ... well, I left with him to go back to the cemetery. But, you see, Dad and Max didn't know where I was, so Max came hunting for me, figured it out, he's pretty smart, of course."

"Then you had to come looking for me."

"Isn't that funny, these two guys," Kayla waved her hands at Dad and me, "having the two of us missing on the same day!"

"C'mon, let's eat our omelets before they get cold."

"Cold is old, so let's be bold. You're right, Nicky. Let's eat."

Everyone tried hard to create a sense of normality, but we all knew our world was abnormal and our lightheartedness only an act. Baseball remained the main topic. Once again, we talked about how Jackie had had a pretty good year in 1956 and should never have been treated so shabbily, and Mom presented us again with all his statistics. By unstated agreement, we swept under the rug the scary events of the preceding week.

Thinking back about that morning, I imagine Dad worrying about Kayla, Mom, and his patients; Kayla afraid for her life, trying to find an escape from her torment, and beginning to dream about when she'd see August again, contemplating how she might make the transition from soloist to accompanist; Mom thinking about how Norm might have prepared *his* cream cheese omelets. And, me, I don't have to imagine what I was thinking about. I still worried about the books I left at the library the day before and my exams.

As we washed up, the phone rang. Dad and I glanced at each other, anticipating that no good could come of a call at ten on a Sunday morning. I answered. It was Ben.

After a few pleasantries, during which I said nothing of the horrors our family had just suffered, he got to the point. "So, listen. I've made contact with Charlene, told her I'm representing the family, and explained to her, as nice as I could, our concerns."

"And?"

"She wants to have a meeting. The four of you, and me, and the entire group of them, her so-called committee. Can you all get over to Bellington this afternoon? It has to be at Bellington, she says. I wasn't going to argue the point, although doing it there doesn't make me happy. I'd rather have picked a neutral place."

"Hang on."

I told Dad, who agreed and went off to talk to Mom. Then I found Kayla sitting at the piano, staring at music. Scriabin preludes, I noticed. For her, pretty simple stuff, but I wondered the particular prelude she was looking at was the one on which she'd made an error in San Diego. It seemed like years ago that she'd been on that tour. I was relieved she wasn't looking at a violin sonata, but then realized we probably didn't have any around.

"Kayla, Ben's telling us Charlene's group wants to meet with us this afternoon, at school. Can we do it, please? It won't be bad, I promise. Ben's very diplomatic."

"Shhh. I'm thinking. Whatever, yes, just let me concentrate."

I returned to the telephone. "Can we say three? I've got work of my own to do first."

"Three will be fine."

"What's our plan?"

"Charlene said she'd bring a copy of the contract, apologized, thought we had one, she said. Ha-ha, what a liar. Of course, I don't believe her. She's going to show us bank accounts, and so on. She pretended to be surprised we hadn't contacted them earlier if we were concerned. Said it wasn't necessary for you guys to hire a lawyer. Said it was a waste of your money.

Said everyone there was a bit dismayed at the lack of trust, but we'd clear it all up at a meeting."

"And you think...?"

"I don't think much of anything, although I'm finding their shenanigans more interesting than I imagined. Who would've thought I'd get involved in a legal case again and one concerning Adel's family? We'll hear them out, perhaps ask a few questions, thank them for their time, and then we meet separately to decide what to do."

"What do I do at this meeting?"

"Take careful notes. Got it?"

"Got it."

"And watch them closely."

CHAPTER 84

I walked Kayla down to school, like the old days, then went over a few blocks to the Fordham library and found my carol. My notebooks were still there, the books had been rearranged, but otherwise were okay, and I worked until about two-thirty. Then I stuffed everything into my backpack, returned to Bellington, found the room Charlene had specified, and entered to see Ben, Kayla, and our folks. The Bellington people hadn't arrived. Kayla looked unhealthily pale, as if she were on death row, about to be executed for high crimes against society. Mom wore her usual jeans and sweatshirt, but Dad had put on a suit and tie. Ben finished explaining, again, how he expected the meeting to play out.

By five after three, no one from the committee had appeared. I started to complain, but Ben shut me up, explaining this was a common ploy, we shouldn't fall for it by getting bent out of shape, and it meant nothing except rudeness. Kayla bristled, but said nothing.

At a quarter past, our three adversaries – that's how I thought of them – entered. Charlene and Ziegler looked mildly annoyed, and Lindorf appeared confused. After they introduced themselves to Ben, Ziegler cleared his throat and reached into his briefcase for a bunch of papers. As directed, I took notes.

"Let's get down to business and stop this waste of time. You're concerned about our arrangement with Kayla, I understand. Kayla, you're happy with the performances we arranged, the tours, how we take care of you?"

Before she could answer, Ben interrupted, his voice authoritative. "Cut the crap, Mr. Ziegler. We're here because you never provided to Kayla or her family a copy of the agency agreement, which we demand to see right now, and because as far as we can tell Kayla hasn't received a penny of the revenues for all her hard work and celebrity."

"Well, Mr. Brody, if you want to act like that, fine. Here's a copy of the agreement for you." Ziegler tossed the papers across the table, and they fell in front of Ben. Rather than pick them up, Ben just stared at Ziegler. Ziegler tried to match the stare, but after a few seconds gave up, and began rummaging again through his briefcase. Score one for the good guys, I thought. Ben finally picked up the agreement and read through it slowly, making his own notes. No one said anything. Charlene drummed her fingers audibly on the table, the disgust on her face probably unfeigned.

"All right. I'll reserve comment about the utter lack of fairness of this for later. Meanwhile ..."

"Fairness! What do you mean, Herr Brody?" asked Lindorf. "You are saying this is not fair?" I glanced at Kayla, who looked down at her shoes, the paleness of her face suddenly supplanted by a red tint.

"I'm not saying anything, Herr Lindorf. We're here to get information. Ms. Deerfield mentioned there were bank accounts. We need to get our copies of the bank statements, now."

Ziegler took more papers out of his briefcase. This time, instead of throwing them across the table, he got up and handed them to Ben. "Thank you." Ben spent long minutes examining them, making more notes.

"I have questions."

"Go ahead," said Charlene, the distinctly sour look still on her face. "This is my company, so I'll speak for everyone."

"The account is in the name of 'Deerfield Entertainment III.' It's not in Kayla's name at all. How is this Kayla's money if it's not in her name?"

"Charlene, let me ..."

"No, Robin, I'll answer, and keep your mouth shut unless I ask you to say something." She turned toward Ben. "Mr. Brody, it's understood by all of us that this is Kayla's account."

"Understood? Ha-ha. Good one. That has absolutely no legal meaning. This is a scam if I ever saw one, but let's pretend what you just said makes sense. Next issue: I see substantial withdrawals. I haven't added them up, but they look like you're withdrawing most of the deposits, and what's left in the account as of the end of March is not quite $7,500. You're saying that's all Kayla has earned after three tours?"

"We have expenses. Travel. Hotel. Marketing."

"Where are the documents showing these expenses? The checks? The payees? Where are the documents showing your company taking its cut?"

"We didn't bring those. That's not ..."

"I was very explicit. I told you I wanted every scrap of paper relating to this business arrangement."

"Well, you didn't ..."

At this point, Lindorf interrupted. "Wait. What you are now saying? They are telling me all the time Kayla is making good money, great money, they are saying this, ja? But you are saying no?" Lindorf's German accent thickened as he got excited.

"Herr Lindorf, have you seen these bank records?"

"No, I am not seeing bank records. I am worrying about music, *nicht wahr*? Let me to see, please." Ben handed the bank account across to Lindorf.

"Look at the number I circled, last page."

"Seven thousands, four hundreds." He looked at Charlene. "This is what you are saying she's earning *this whole time*?"

"Heinz, it's not what it looks like, it's ..."

Ben cut her off, disappointing me because I wanted to hear how she was going to explain herself. "I'm afraid it is what it looks like, Herr Lindorf. Your colleagues here – and you, by association, if you're part of this business – have been cheating Kayla, it does so very much appear."

I would have let her go on. I vowed to myself then that, if I ever had a similar situation in my future life as a lawyer, I'd keep my mouth shut. Give the crooks enough rope to hang themselves was the motto already cementing itself in my mind.

"That's nonsense," blurted Ziegler.

Charlene said "Shut up, Robin!"

Lindorf pounded his hands on the table, pushed back his chair, and rose. "Kayla, please to come with me to my office? I want to talk."

Kayla looked from Lindorf to Ben and then to me. At least she still wanted my advice on something, I thought. Lindorf wanted privacy only because he had something to say that he didn't want Ziegler and Charlene to hear. Kayla had to hear it, though. I nodded my head slightly, and Ben confirmed that Kayla should honor Lindorf's request. "It's okay, Kayla," he said. "Go ahead. We'll come for you before we go home."

Lindorf extended his hand to Kayla, who clasped it, then turned a murderous glare at Charlene. They walked out together without further comment. As soon as the door closed, Charlene took up the argument.

"I don't know who you think you are, Mr. Brody, but you've slandered my company. It's outrageous for you to sit there, not knowing a thing about how we operate, and tell my client we're cheating her. We can have you disbarred for that, you know."

"Charlene, maybe ..."

"I told you to shut up, Robin. You and your fucking legal advice." She turned again to Ben. "You're wrong, Mr. Brody, and if you keep going down this road, we'll be able to sue you for ...for ..."

"Interference with business relationships," volunteered Ziegler in his high-pitched voice.

"Hold it! Hold it right there!" This was the first time Dad spoke, and I was not only rooting for him, but wanted him to pound Ziegler into the floor. I wanted him to choke the life out of that little shit. Dad was the kind of guy who, if provoked, would turn violent. There'd be no better time than right now, I thought. "Lindorf just looked at the bank statement, and you could see he was shocked. Ben's right to believe you *have* been cheating Kayla."

"I don't think you can complain, Mr. Covo. You signed the agency agreement. You ought to know exactly what we're required to do and what we're not." Charlene's ace in the hole, apparently, was the fine print in the agreement. I cursed myself for the hundredth time for not being able to convince Mom and Dad to consult with Ben before going along with the damned thing.

Ben jumped to Dad's defense. "Well, let's see. Ms. Deerfield, it's black letter law that fraud voids a contract." Ah. It was so good to have a lawyer like Ben there. I immediately put black letter law into my arsenal for the future, right next to giving crooks enough rope to hang. "I see fraud here. It's a contract of adhesion. That makes it voidable. I see embezzlement. That's criminal. Any judge or jury in New York would award punitive damages against you, personally, as the manager of this company. You've surely enriched yourself unfairly on Kayla's sweat and blood. That's just my initial assessment. In a few days, we'll be ready to file an action."

"Bullshit, Mr. Brody, and you know it."

"You want to fight us in court, Ziegler? My word! Think about the publicity this'll generate about how Bellington is stealing from its students with the aid of its lawyer. God, it will be fun to make you look like the fool you are, in front of a jury. And lawyers can go to jail, too. And, Ms. Deerfield, the *Times* would be fascinated by hearing what Bellington is doing under your direction. The *Post*, the *News*, the *New Yorker* and ..."

"This has nothing to do with Bellington."

"Oh no? Where are we sitting right now, at your demand? Bellington's making this room available for you to conduct your business is, isn't it? Hmm, Bellington could be named as a defendant, just on that basis. A co-conspirator. That's Chapter 24 ..."

"Robin, let's get out of here. I've heard enough."

Deerfield and the punk lawyer stormed out, made a big show of trying to slam the door as they left, but they couldn't do that right, either. It popped open. As soon as they were gone, both Mom and Dad laughed, obviously enjoying the spectacle, and I had to chuckle as well.

"You were magnificent, Ben! Why the hell didn't we bring you in at the beginning?"

"Never mind past mistakes, Dr. Nick. What's done is done, but we have to decide what's next."

"Is the contract as bad for us as Deerfield says?"

"It's not good, if you want the truth. But, like I said, we have strong leverage on Deerfield. And the fact Lindorf was surprised – shocked, I'd say

– is great for us and bad for Deerfield. She and Ziegler kept him in the dark too."

"I just hope this doesn't spoil things for Kayla." For once, Mom wasn't trying to rhyme.

"Adel, I think this will be great for Kayla."

"We need to talk about it, Ben." Dad stood and helped Mom out of her chair.

"Right. So, let's see if Kayla's done with Lindorf and go back to your apartment."

"Sounds like a plan," I said, standing as well, stuffing the legal pad into my backpack. I'd filled three pages with notes.

I knew there was a reason I've saved these notes all these many years.

CHAPTER 85

We waited outside Lindorf's office in the noisy hallway, plenty of Bellington students milling around even on a weekend afternoon. At last the door opened to show Kayla saying goodbye and hugging her mentor. As she turned from Lindorf, she wiped away tears. She looked surprised to see us.

"Dad. Ben. The meeting's over already?" Lindorf followed Kayla into the hallway, curious as well.

"They cut it short, Kayla," replied Ben. "Walked out in a huff. I kind of enjoyed it. Brought back memories of many negotiations in my legal beagle days. Kind of made me feel young again."

"Oh, no. They walked out?"

"Kayla, don't worry. Herr Lindorf, can you tell her she has nothing to worry about?"

"Correct, Herr Brody. Kayla, you will always be my student, if you want. Nothing will take that away, ja? We will work out this thing with Charlotte or tell her to go flight a kite."

For the first time that afternoon, Kayla smiled. "Yes, exactly. Herr Lindorf, I'll be here tomorrow morning to start working again and maybe we can discuss some new ideas I have."

"Very good." He walked down the hallway and disappeared around a corner.

In minutes, we caught cabs and headed uptown. I shared one with Kayla and asked her what Lindorf had said in their meeting.

"He was very sorry. Had no idea what was going on."

"Do you believe him?"

"I do. He's devoted to his music, to teaching, and to me. I think he just trusts everyone else to handle the business side fairly. He never even asked me about money before because he assumed things were going fine."

"Did you tell him that you'd hooked up with August?"

"Not yet. I'm not sure what I would say about that. What do you think?"

But the taxi pulled to a stop in front of our building; we had to pay and get out.

•   •   •   •   •

We gathered in our dining room, where Ben began the post mortem, pulling out the contract. "Deerfield shall be paid thirty percent of all bookings, minus expenses, as a management fee."

"I remember," said Mom. "We all read it the night of the Town Hall recital."

Gesturing with the papers, Ben continued. "Well, then it goes on to explain how much Deerfield is allowed to take out for expenses. It's very broad and detailed." He read for a bit before continuing. "The way they've drafted this, anything that might arguably accrue to Kayla's benefit, regardless of how speculative, is an expense they can deduct from her earnings before taking the management fee. My word! That's way too generous for them."

"So, what does it all mean?" asked Dad.

"Well, it means …" I think that Ben caught himself before coming right out and saying how stupid Mom and Dad had been to sign. "Interesting … wait a second." Ben looked at the last two pages of the document. "Well, this says right out how either party may terminate the contract with a month's notice, undoubtedly drafted that way so they could protect themselves if Kayla wasn't drawing large enough audiences. Dr. Nick, you and Adel are still the parties, so all you need do is send written notice to Deerfield that the contract has ended, and it ends."

"Wait a minute," I said. "It can't be that simple. Can it?"

"Ending the contract? Yes. Getting back what Kayla deserves, not so clear. In fact, it's downright problematic."

"There must be some provision for checking the numbers, though, isn't there?" I'd heard Dad talk enough about his work with accountants over his years in practice to know at least that much.

"Yes, Max, but … it's cumbersome. It's written to give Deerfield almost unbridled discretion, as I said, and by the time an actual accounting might be finished, years would pass. Part of the reason this contract is so …" He hesitated again, trying to be diplomatic. "Well, it's offensive to me."

"But there has to be something good, too. Doesn't there?" Kayla voiced the question that all of us were thinking.

"The good thing is that Deerfield doesn't want this to blow up in her face. It would be embarrassing. I think she'll want to settle."

"How much … how much do you think they owe me?"

"I'll have to study these bank statements a bit more, but they took into this account …let's see … more than three hundred thousand dollars. My word! Seems you've been quite busy, young lady. Let's say the legitimate costs incurred were twenty percent. I'm just guessing."

"Leaving at least two-hundred forty," I volunteered.

"Quite correct."

"Thirty percent of that is seventy-two thousand, leaving one hundred and sixty-eight thousand."

"Again, quite correct. You've got a good head for figures, Max."

Presented with my calculations, Kayla finally began to see what had happened. "And they said I had seven thousand? Not one hundred and sixty-eight?"

"Yes, Kayla, I'm sorry to say that's what's left in this account."

"Shit on a stick." No one was surprised at Kayla's swearing.

"And there's always the possibility they didn't run all the revenues through this account. The way Deerfield operates, I'd say that was likely. I'd guess that they put money through this account only for the sake of appearances. We can find out for sure through discovery, but I don't think we'll need to go that far."

"What do we need to do?"

"Well, Dr. Nick, I propose to write a letter to them today, laying out the facts and demanding a settlement of two hundred thousand dollars, payable at once, and terminating the contract. Of course, as long as everyone is willing and I can get your signatures, Nicky and Adel."

"Kayla?" asked Dad.

We waited while Kayla thought. She took the contract from Ben and read parts of it he indicated. Then she studied the bank statement for a minute. It seemed like we waited forever, but finally she assented to Ben's proposal.

"Yes. Let's do it. I feel terrible about this for Herr Lindorf, though. He's going to be in trouble, I bet. They're going to cheat him like they cheated me. But Herr Lindorf assured me he wanted us to do what we thought best. You heard him swear he'd never give up on me as a student, and he told me in his office he'd do anything he could do to make this up to me. He was mortified."

"All right. By tomorrow morning, my letter will be delivered."

"Ben, what do we owe you?" Dad asked.

"Ha-ha! Nothing, of course. I'm doing it for Adel, and for the old times with Nate, who was a great partner and friend, and for you, Dr. Nick, and for all of you." As this last bit came out, he was looking straight at me.

"We need to do something for you. You've been too kind to take this on, seeing as we ought to have called you before we put our names on the damned thing." Ridiculously, Dad had reached for his wallet.

"Well, put that away, Dr. Nick. My word! The thought I'd take money. But I have an idea. Kayla, would you play something for me right now? Something you love? My own private concert will be more than sufficient payment."

"Of course. Great idea." She moved to the Steinway, waiting for inspiration. Then, she knew. "Got it. This is short, and I've often played it as an encore."

She treated us to a smooth and emotional rendition of Schubert's Impromptu in E-Flat Major. Kayla's fingers flew over the piano, and the melodies sang out, along with thousands of other notes making up the background. Her smile grew as she whirled her way through the piece. It was over in minutes, but we would've listened for hours. When she stopped, Ben stood and clapped. The rest of us did likewise.

If you think Kayla, fifteen years old, might not have wanted her family to applaud her in her own home, that she was well beyond needing such affection, you don't understand her yet. Kayla loved to be loved. Her smile lit up the room.

CHAPTER 86

She's a soldier, fighting whom or for what unknown. She's in danger as bullets whiz by, and she knows a mortar is about to slice her to bits. She holds a gun but can't get it loaded or maybe it's loaded but she can't fire it or maybe it's not even a gun. Then she sees a soldier rushing toward her. For a second, she fears he's the enemy, but before he reaches her she realizes that he's one of her own. She's about to warn him to get down when he plows into her hard, knocking her flat.

She turns to see Nicky still deep in sleep, gets out of their bed, and dons her bathrobe. Disturbed by her dream, she wants to fathom its meaning. She steps into their living room and stands by the window, looking across the street.

Free association is what the shrinks call it. The first thing coming to her when she thinks about the fighting in her dream is that she's in high school, struggling with a teacher or a friend, she can't be sure. She pounds her head on a table in the school library, bright sunshine hurts her eyes, her entire body convulses in pain. The pain springs from the center of her body, and she feels the blood trickling down her legs from where she's wounded. But then she's no longer in the library, she's getting on a bus, then walking through a large ominous park at night, and people follow her, whispering nasty things. She feels enormous hunger, a craving for nourishment that's denied her. She sees herself grabbing a large knife from the drawer in the kitchen and turning around to face ... what?

The train of thought stops as bright red lights flash before her eyes. She blinks, looking out the window to see if police cars are speeding by, but the street is empty of traffic, nothing unusual.

Dr. Lack told her once to just let go, to not fear what she might coax from the back of her mind, that she can know the bad thing was in her past, she can put it aside and, by doing so, live her life without being controlled by it. She should take deep breaths, he says, letting her breath out slowly. She should gently rub her arms, her thighs, massage her head with her fingertips. She should run her fingertips back and forth lightly over her closed eyelids.

Go on and embrace the memory, she tells herself, and remember what stood there in front of you, as you held that blade, perfectly shaped and honed to slice through flesh. Let the association have its sway. Don't censor anything, she can hear Dr. Lack's guiding, gentle voice. But as she stands at the window, facing across the street, she sees nothing. Her hand is empty.

Her thoughts turn back to the dream. When a friend attacks her, that can only mean that he wants sex. So the dream is about a friend who wants sex so much that he will blast her to bits if he doesn't get it. The soldier doesn't remind her of Daniel, her rapist. Does he remind her of Norm? Of Nicky? Of Max? Little by little, the dream fades.

In a minute, Adel cannot recall why she's standing in her dark living room staring at the building across the quiet street. She yawns. There are still a few hours of sleep ahead.

CHAPTER 87

She returns to the *Chabad* outpost, feeling vaguely that she needs to talk something out with Rabbi Berenbaum. She recalls, when she last spoke to him, she'd mentioned Max, that he was overbearing and oppressive. She hadn't thought about Max that way until she heard the comment spring from her lips. It still bothers her. She wants to explore the meaning of this feeling. Is it true? Is Max actually overbearing and oppressive? And, if it's true, is this contributing to her stress?

Kayla is pleased the rabbi seems happy to see her again. She sits in his office in the chair where she'd sat before, and she takes the cup of strong coffee he offers her. Finally, she explains why she's there, but slowly, with substantial embarrassment. She doesn't precisely desire a Jewish interpretation of her concerns, but she anticipates this very thoughtful, caring rabbi will find one.

"You're in close contact with him every day?" Rabbi Berenbaum asks.

"Well, yes."

"I can imagine how upsetting it must be if you feel he doesn't have your best interests at heart. That he's trying to manipulate you for some purpose not serving what you really need. But why? I can counsel you better if I understand more. Why would he be like that?"

Reluctantly, she must say what she feels, if she's ever to get it off of her chest. "He's jealous of me, Rabbi. Jealous of what I've achieved. Jealous of my fame, jealous of the attention I get. Jealous of my talent and ability to work intensely hard. I can't think of any other reason."

The rabbi's warm eyes seem to twinkle as he responds. "Our tradition speaks to those emotions directly. We can learn a lot about sibling rivalry from the Torah."

"We can?"

"Esav and Yaakov, of course."

"Who are they?"

"Did you never learn the stories of *B'Reishit?* Perhaps you were taught the names Jacob and Esau?"

She grimaces, completely at sea and embarrassed at the same time. "I was taught nothing."

"More's the pity. So I'll explain simply. They were the sons of Yitzchak, whom you might know as Isaac. So Esav is the older, Yaakov the younger. Esav felt Yaakov stole what was rightfully his, the special blessing from Yitzchak for a firstborn son. In a way, that's what happened. Yaakov pretended he was Esav and got away with it because Yitzchak was blind. The deception, the loss of this blessing, caused immeasurable pain for Esav."

She thinks for a second. The firstborn loses out to the second born, and it causes him pain. This must be what the rabbi is driving at, that she's caused Max horrible suffering by being herself, as good as she can be. "That's terrible for Esav. I see ..."

"Please wait. You might not yet see where I'm going with this. Esav's calamity, his pain, his loss were all intended by *Hashem.* Yaakov, despite his own faults, which were considerable, had to accept what *Hashem* decreed, that he was to greatly surpass his older brother. Yaakov had to accept *Hashem*'s purpose arranging things so. Now, it would seem that *Hashem* has willed that *you* have the talent, the drive, the opportunity to achieve what Max cannot. Following me?"

"Maybe. But must I accept Max's jealousy? His trying to control me? I feel at times Max wants to be me. Or become so close to me I can no longer say I'm my own person."

"If you believe in *Hashem,* then you have to see Max, with all his problems, as *Hashem*'s creation too. And, must you accept? You will decide. But let me go on with the story. You must hear the whole thing."

"All right."

"So Yaakov, the younger one, the gifted one, *Hashem*'s choice, what does he do in regard to his older brother, whom he has cheated, who is very angry with him?"

"Hide?"

"Very good. Yaakov indeed hides, for twenty long years, but circumstances drive the siblings together again. He must meet the blood relative he's supplanted and, as it happens, must meet Esav on Esav's own land. Yaakov cannot really know what Esav is thinking, but prepares an enormously generous gift for his brother. They find a way to co-exist. They kiss."

"Must I therefore make such a gift to Max? Is that what you're telling me? To make up for what I stole ... even inadvertently?"

"Ah, no, not precisely. But there's still more to the story."

"I'm sorry."

"In the process of preparing his gift for Esav, in the midst of great risk to himself, Yaakov wrestles with an angel of *Hashem* and becomes severely injured. This wrestling – why Yaakov is renamed Israel, he who wrestles with *Hashem* – this wrestling brings about a major shift in Yaakov's life. He loses a part of himself in this struggle with *Hashem*'s emissary. He must limp for the rest of his days. But the outcome, with respect to Esav, is that the brothers find a way to reconcile. Quite an unusual family. On what could be the field of battle and death, Esav and Yaakov kiss. Together, years later, they bury their father."

Rabbi Berenbaum stops, and Kayla knows the story has finally come to an end. It's time for her consider its meaning carefully, to see how she might apply this story to her life.

Part of the message – one that will grow inside her over the years – is that she must prepare some type of gift for Max. She has no idea what that gift could be. Whether she can ever find the right gift, she won't know for a long time. But, at this meeting in the *Chabad*, she begins to understand better Max's sense of having been cheated, the sense that he is owed. It makes no difference, really, whether she intended to cheat him or take his birthright.

Part of the message is that her own struggles are like Yaakov's struggles with the angel. The wrestling match is an excellent metaphor for the way she must fight the stalker and the ever-present fear he engenders.

But the last part of the message is one she cannot consciously accept as she sits there. The full meaning of Rabbi Berenbaum's teaching won't become accessible to Kayla until many months pass.

If Yaakov had to limp for the rest of his days, what does that mean for her career?

CHAPTER 88

Kayla and I began walking together to school again. She bubbled with new excitement, telling me how she had decided to accompany August professionally and about the repertoire he wanted them to work on. Lindorf was pleased with the arrangement and committed himself to helping Kayla become the best accompanist she could, as long as she vowed to continue performing solo as well.

I tried to talk Kayla out of giving up a career as a soloist, because that's what I saw happening, but she insisted she wasn't giving up anything, she was only "expanding her horizons." Whether those were Lindorf's words to her or vice versa, or whether perhaps they had come from August himself, I never learned. I was just sure my years of sacrifice for Kayla were being wasted.

Ten days or so after the meeting with Charlene's committee, Ben called in triumph to announce that they had agreed to his demands. The agency contract had been terminated; there would be no official accounting, but $200,000 would be paid to Kayla within a week. Kayla had to promise to maintain absolute confidentiality. Ben set up a bank account in Kayla's name, with Dad having power of attorney until Kayla turned eighteen, and within a day the money landed in the account as promised. The speed with which Ben resolved the matter should've pleased me, but I was, inevitably, annoyed. Unable to accept that what I'd started had met with rapid success, I thought Ben's demand had been way too low and that we could've gotten more for Kayla if we'd only been tougher.

Nonetheless, Kayla was pleased to have things resolved. She urged Dad and Mom to invite Ben for *Shabbat* dinner – an event we seldom celebrated ourselves – and they agreed. Dad presided, saying the blessings in Hebrew and teaching us a *Shabbat* melody without words that he remembered from his childhood. He called it a *niggun*, one he had learned and sung often as a child. Kayla was the first to pick it up, then Mom, then Ben, and I had no choice but to join. Of course, everyone praised Ben to the heavens for his assistance with the Deerfield group, and he modestly accepted our thanks. Before he left, Kayla played for him again, this time a few Joplin tunes. Ben was almost bouncing as I escorted him to Broadway, making sure he could catch a cab without being molested.

Mom seemed to be continuing to take her meds after her embarrassing episode in Brooklyn, but once in a while would stop what she was doing and stare at nothing, muttering. Dad talked to me one evening about maybe starting Mom on a second or third round of anti-psychotic drugs just hitting the market. It wasn't the kind of thing fathers and sons usually talk about, how to quell the craziness of wife and mother.

What still bothered me greatly was Kayla's fear of someone following her. She'd refused to talk to a psychiatrist and refused even to mention her fears to Lindorf. I had good reason to continue to worry. I could see on our walks that she might turn suddenly to check behind us, how she'd duck into a doorway, ostensibly to tie her shoe, but actually to hide. I told no one about these troubling behaviors. As long as Kayla wasn't doing anything *really* crazy, as long as she wasn't hurting herself, then some eccentricities could be tolerated. Or so I thought. There were no more explosions like Kayla's freak-out in the cemetery.

Within a short time of the settlement between Kayla and Deerfield, a plan was set in motion for Kayla and August to tour together. The first tour of this new violin and piano duo would begin in the late summer of '82. Kayla had a new agent, an entertainment lawyer named Phaedra Freeman recommended by Ben, and Freeman arranged for a new chaperone, a paralegal in her office named Annie McGrath. But Freeman had to negotiate with Deerfield, who still represented August. Freeman, from what I could tell, was a no-nonsense lawyer. She settled with Deerfield on a new contract for the tour, one with every protection for Kayla that was absent from the monstrosity Dad and Mom originally agreed to.

Kayla worked very hard on her new repertoire. She and August would perform six sonatas and vary the program for each performance. Kayla showed me the music one evening, which included Beethoven's Kreutzer sonata, the Franck sonata, and sonatas by Haydn, Mozart, Grieg, and Bartok. Either the Beethoven or the Franck would bring each program to its conclusion. I looked closely enough at the scores to see the piano parts of both the Beethoven and the Franck were extremely difficult. By then, I have to confess, almost everything looked difficult to me. My pianistic skills had slid from meager to negligible.

"Have you learned these all already?"

"Well, you mean, just to play through with August? Sure. Not a problem. But ..."

"But?"

"There's so much more to just playing them through and staying together, you know? We have to get in sync with our interpretations."

"I assume he's played these before and has his own well-settled views."

She shook her head. "It's not like that. You see, he has to listen to what I say."

"Do as you say?"

"No. Listen. We have to communicate." I must have looked puzzled still, because she pulled me over to the Steinway and handed me the music she'd been studying. It was the second movement of the Beethoven sonata, a theme and variations. "I say to August like here, measure 19, we need to add a bit of *rubato*, so he asks why, and I explain it will nicely set off the following phrases, making them sound like variations on the variations. So he says, well, let's try it and see how it sounds, and we play it that way. Or try to. We have to get our *rubatos* in sync. Well, maybe he says, mmm, no, doesn't sound right, so we work it around for a while. When we both feel it's right, we play it again the same way about ten times. Until it's second nature for us, like we could do it in our sleep. Or, if we never feel it's quite right, we put that idea on the shelf and move on to another idea. You see?"

"Sort of."

"The main thing making this so fascinating for me is the communication. It's similar to learning to play with an orchestra, but the soloist has to take more direction from the conductor. After all, the conductor's got scores of musicians. Much harder to manage them, harder to change them around. With the violin sonata, with August and me as a pair, we're equals and we can adjust much more to each other's good ideas. Now do you see?"

"Yeah, I guess. But, Kayla, we've talked about this before, and I still don't understand why you want to give up soloing. You say you're not giving it up, but here you are, spending months getting ready and then a two-month tour, so aren't you giving up almost an entire year to do this little experiment?"

She sighed, telling me without words that I knew so little about music I'd always be a difficult student in her eyes. "No. I'm not giving up anything. This is broadening my ability to make music. August's teaching me in a way Herr Lindorf can't, because August's getting on the stage with me. His success directly depends on me, and vice versa. I have to work more closely with him than I've had to work with anyone else. That's *why* Herr Lindorf thinks it's a fine idea. Herr Lindorf is helping me with all the new pieces, most recently on this." She handed me the Franck, opened to the second movement, where I saw copious marginal notes I didn't understand. "You see? I take the problems I first discuss with August to Herr Lindorf for further thought. And everything I learn in these sessions I can use throughout my career as a soloist."

And then she hit me with her heart-melting smile, and I couldn't help be caught up in her excitement, despite my doubts. "I see you're committed to doing this and, well, I'm looking forward to hearing the two of you perform together. On stage. At your venues. Wherever you go."

"Really?! You're going to come listen to us on the tour?"

"I was thinking about it. I haven't heard you on tour for a long time, but I'd love to be there when the new, improved Kayla does her thing."

She came over to hug me. "You're so sweet. As soon as the schedule's set, we'll decide what we're performing at each venue and then you can pick whichever ones you want to go to. It will be super to know you're in the audience."

CHAPTER 89

I was surprised when Dad asked me around that time to accompany him on one of his Sunday walks in the park. Usually, he'd bolt out of the apartment early in the morning, walking by himself. He might be away for hours and, upon return, say he'd gotten wrapped up in thoughts about various patients and forgotten the time. On this Sunday, however, Dad wanted to talk to me. So we hustled out. When we hit the street, I realized I'd almost have to run to keep up with him. His strides were long and fast, as if he were hurrying to catch the last train out of Paris before the Germans arrived.

Casablanca? Never mind. I'll explain when you're here.

So back to the park.

"What the heck did you want to talk about?" I was already breathing hard, trying to keep up with him, and we hadn't gone even a hundred yards.

"Kayla, of course."

"I should've guessed."

"What's going on with her?"

"With this guy she thinks is following her? With August?"

"It's all wrapped up together, isn't it? You want a pretzel?" He paid a vendor for two. Now holding our snacks, we resumed our walk, but at a slower, much more reasonable pace. "I've heard of fans, weirdos as you might put it, stalking celebrities. It's not impossible. Maybe what she thinks is happening *is* really happening."

"Look, Dad. I should tell you. She's been acting afraid on our walks to school, too, like she still sees someone or feels someone's presence. She'll hide in a doorway. She'll run into a building we're passing."

"*Was* anyone following her? Or acting suspicious?"

"It's New York! Hundreds of people roam the streets, and lots of them look like they could've just escaped from a zoo. So, no, I haven't noticed anything standing out."

"Which brings us to August. Don't you think it's more than a strange coincidence that Kayla's making such a major shift in her career around the same time she's seeing a stalker?"

"Is there a connection? I don't know. I've talked with her quite a bit about what it means to her to be an accompanist. She's got reasonable explanations. She tells me it's like music as a conversation instead of music as a soliloquy. Stuff like that."

"I regret not having much musical knowledge."

"Well, you know a lot more Shakespeare than I do. Anyway, I think Kayla would say she's learning more about music when she performs with August. It's not only the performance but the getting ready to perform, analyzing the music. And there's no question August is a major talent and much better known than Kayla. If you take Kayla at her word, she's expanding her musical knowledge and fan base at the same time. Makes sense, right?"

"Okay."

"This could easily be happening even if Kayla wasn't in fear for her life."

"Perhaps. So, music as conversation, you say? Not only does it make sense, as you explain it, but sounds like a good thing. But that still doesn't explain why this is happening now instead of two years from now, say."

"Well, let's not ignore the more obvious explanation."

"Which is?"

"She's attracted to August. She's a girl, he's a guy. He might be a hunk in her eyes. That diamond stud in his ear. Who knows? But I have a strong feeling it's that chemistry thing. Hormones and all."

"This is a delicate question to ask a brother, but I have to ask. Do you think he'll take advantage of her? She's not even sixteen."

"I don't know. It bothers me August is part of the Deerfield operation. He's mixed up with thieves."

"If they're thieves, he could be a victim himself."

"Doesn't strike me as the victim type. I've lots of concerns about him, but who knows if that's only because I'm a big brother. You're right. You probably shouldn't have asked me."

Of course it bothered me to think about Kayla with August. It bothered me ever since I saw him kiss the side of her head in the taxi.

Dad led me over to an empty bench and we sat.

"Here's what I think," he said finally, after painstakingly finishing his pretzel in small bites, savoring every morsel. "She's afraid to go on the stage herself."

"Because ..."

"Because she's paranoid. The love affair she's always had with her audiences has been derailed by fear or evolved into fear. She wants him up there with her because, subconsciously, she feels he'll protect her. She needs to put her trust into someone who's going to be right next to her every minute she's performing."

"An interesting theory."

"Which you say with a hint of disbelief. But, still, I have an idea."

"Go ahead."

"You told her you'd try to attend some of her concerts. I think we should be there, at least one of us, for all of them. We can take turns. I'd have to cancel some patients, you might miss a class or two, but we ought to see how this plays out in person. Be there for her if she needs help. Keep an eye on August. What do you think?"

I considered for a minute. "To be honest, if one of us has to be at all her concerts, I'm thinking it might screw me up at school." I laughed bitterly, remembering I was a week late in turning in an essay on police use of force. "I'm always behind, rushing to finish a paper, cramming for a test I should've been studying for weeks earlier."

"You've got to learn better time management if you're going to take eighteen credits again, Max, but we'll work it out to minimize the disruption. Or you take only fifteen credits next fall. Are you up for it?"

"Whatever you think best. She'll be delighted one of us will always be there. It might help her relax and put this stalker idea out of her mind. But ..."

"But what?"

"What if she objects to your being there? She might feel it's so out of character for you, Dad. She might feel you're there only because you believe she's ill."

"I don't think she'll object. But, if she does, it's a free country. Anyone can buy a ticket."

"That's what scares her the most," I said.

CHAPTER 90

Something bothers Nicky intensely, gnawing at him since it happened. The ravaged doll triggers traumatic memories of the war in Greece: visions of a dying girl in a yellow smock, riddled with the bullets he's just fired from his Mauser semi-automatic, are never far from his consciousness. He'd break down if he tried to talk with anyone now about what happened to Tina. He would lose it, go on a rampage, be overtaken by an urge to strike out he wouldn't be able to control.

Yet, he never stops pondering who destroyed Kayla's beloved doll and why.

Nicky knows he's not personally responsible. But that leaves only three others who might have done it. Each possibility profoundly troubles him.

Adel? He should've been aware if Adel had gotten out of bed that night to sneak into Kayla's room, so he deems her unlikely as the culprit. Not impossible, though. The attack eerily echoes Adel's assault on her mother as a teenager.

Max? Nicky considers him a better possibility, Max, who might have allowed deep resentment toward Kayla get the better of him. Nicky's seen excessively jealous patients do the strangest things. Max has always had a small chip on his shoulder due to Kayla overtaking him so rapidly at the piano. On the surface, Max protects his sister, but Nicky feels Max does so to hide his deeper negative feelings, and he greatly overdoes the protective older brother bit. Plus, he's always keeping his eye on her, literally as well as figuratively. Nicky has noticed Max stealing inappropriate looks, not doing it so blatantly or so often that others would have to notice, but Nicky sees all. His powers of observation, honed through years of practice, don't miss a thing.

Nicky can't say anything to Max about these observations, of course. To call it to Max's attention would be to acknowledge yet more family pathology. But it's possible whatever had been building up in Max – sexual tension, jealousy, his lack of close friends – erupted one night in murderous rage. Tina – a surrogate for Kayla – was the only available target to take the brunt of his anger. It wouldn't be the first time in psychiatric history that someone harboring repressed anger destroyed a doll.

Kayla? He has to admit the possibility that Kayla herself destroyed her doll, the Kayla slipping into schizophrenia. A compelling voice could've commanded her. Yet, her main psychotic symptoms – an imaginary stalker – are visual, not aural. More importantly, he believes the truth in Kayla's blood-curdling screams. They rattled him to the bone. The utter shock and disbelief of her screams couldn't have been faked, so if Kayla was the culprit then she acted entirely at a subconscious level.

He's feared getting to the bottom of the mystery for too long. Maybe when it happened he should've commanded a family meeting, thrashed everything around until someone admitted guilt, and dealt with the consequences. Now, all he can do is ponder.

CHAPTER 91

As Dad had correctly assumed, Kayla was happy that one of us would attend most of her recitals. She didn't see it as a threat. Instead, she half-chastised him, saying "you've come to very few of my concerts over the years."

"Have I?"

"Like you don't know? But there's plenty of time to make it up to me. I hope you'll be pleased."

"I'm sure I will. Now, where and when are you performing?"

She ducked into her room for a second and emerged with a leather folder, from which she pulled a few pieces of paper.

"Boston, New Haven, Baltimore, Atlanta, Miami, Birmingham, Memphis, Cincinnati, Buffalo, whew, and then ... the last performances are here in New York, at Avery Fisher Hall."

I jotted notes as fast as Kayla could speak. "Ten cities!" I couldn't help but exclaim. "In how many weeks?"

"Five. Do you think five weeks is too long? Many artists go on the road for much longer."

"You came back from the last tour very tired."

"I know, Max."

Dad took the papers from Kayla with a smile and turned to me. "Well, let's divide up the list, Max. We can do ten cities and however many concerts that means."

Dad and I worked through it with Kayla's advice as to what she and August would be playing at which concert. That was more for my benefit than Dad's, because I knew most of the music. We had months to work out a sensible schedule. As it turned out, I decided to attend primarily the weekend performances, not wanting to miss classes, and Dad agreed to attend most of the weekday performances. It was the first time, I thought, Dad actually sacrificed some of his practice on Kayla's behalf. With our decisions recorded, Kayla promised to have Annie reserve the necessary tickets as the tour grew closer.

CHAPTER 92

As the months in preparation passed, it became obvious Kayla and August were more than partners in music. They began dating, and neither of them tried to hide that they were greatly attracted to each other. Kayla turned sixteen, still too young to drink in New York, but they attended plays and operas together. August had plenty of money and, dressed to the nines, would pick Kayla up for an evening out on town. He was making a big effort to impress Mom and Dad. Kayla herself became more of a beautiful woman with each passing day. She had stopped exercising for a while, but now started again. Her skin had a healthy glow, her dark hair warm and luminous, her skin glowing as well, her smile overpowering. I'm sure August saw the same things. He was enraptured.

At Kayla's suggestion, we invited him for dinner one evening. Dad used the opportunity to get August to talk about himself and his own family.

"I was born in Port-au-Prince, but our family moved here when I was only two. So I know only a smidgen of French from my folks talking around the house, but otherwise I'm more American than anything else." He didn't see offended by Dad's questions.

Dad considered this for a second before responding. "I came here at a much later age, seventeen, and it took a while to get the hang of English. You're lucky you didn't have that problem."

"True."

"What do your parents do, if I may ask?"

"My father's an engineer with IBM. Travels a lot. My mother stays home taking care of my two younger sisters."

"And you live with them?"

"Of course. We live in Hudson Heights. West 190th."

"Way up there."

"A very pleasant neighborhood."

"I was the older brother of two younger sisters, once. They didn't make it through the war, though."

"I'm so sorry, Mr. Covo."

"Dr. Covo, if you don't mind, August."

"Of course. I'm sorry. Dr. Covo."

And thus it went for the evening. Dad did a good job getting August to talk, about his violin, his particular interests in music, his siblings, anything and everything. Fortunately, Mom didn't act out that night, and I contributed what I hoped was a polite remark every once in a while. Kayla beamed the whole time. God, was she pretty, eyes only for August. Nothing he could say would strike her wrong that evening. I felt strange, however, knowing I'd never had a girl come to our home for dinner. I ran through my mind the short list of girls I knew from Fordham whom I might date, if only I had time and inclination and wasn't so nervous about girls. Which among them, I wondered, might be invited to meet our folks? I thought I'd never invite any.

"How are your preparations for the tour?" Mom fussed about getting dessert served, while Kayla and I sat listening.

"Dr. Covo, your daughter's exceptional. She'll be the best accompanist I've ever had in my short career."

"Oh, August!"

"Don't be modest, Kayla." He turned back to Dad. "When we play together, it's like every day we're playing something new, that there's a spirit and meaning in the music I hadn't discovered before, and she helps me see it. It's an incredibly rewarding experience."

That's when Mom entered the conversation, placing the dessert dishes in front of us. "Do you sing?"

"Do I sing?" August smiled broadly; he knew about Mom. "Yes, Mrs. Covo, sometimes I do sing, but not in front of people if I can help it. It's more like for the shower."

"What's your favorite song?" she continued. "I like the Broadway shows, you know? *Cats. The Fantasticks!*"

"I'm a big Leonard Bernstein fan, so I'll have to say *West Side Story*."

"One of my favorites too, August." She pronounced his name like the eighth month, with the accent on the first syllable, but he didn't seem to care.

"I like the reprise of "Tonight" the best, when the gangs join in. It's in the style of a canon."

"A cannon? The only loud boom I remember is at the end, when Chico kills Tony." Her comment stopped us in our tracks for a few seconds. Fortunately, Mom didn't notice. She was listening to "Tonight" in her head. Then someone changed the topic.

After a while, we cleared dishes from the table, and Kayla and August talked about how they were heading to a friend's apartment for a small party. Kayla went off to fix her makeup, Dad stepped into the kitchen to help Mom with cleanup, and for the first time August and I were alone.

"Look, August, I want to ask you ..."

"You want me to be good to Kayla. I know. You're a big brother." He said this, not in a condescending way, but was relaxed, almost conspiratorial.

"Well ..."

"You don't have anything to worry about. I wouldn't do anything to hurt her. She's a precious flower."

"A precious ..."

I'd begun to ask him what he meant, but stopped when Dad came back in looking for more things to clear from the table.

CHAPTER 93

In mid-September, I chose to attend the first recital, in Boston, a city I'd never visited. Rather than fly, I took an early train, arriving at North Station at about ten in the morning, having a whole day ahead of me to take in the sights. I walked the Freedom Trail for hours, not really seeing very much, because my mind was elsewhere, then took the subway to Cambridge and milled about Harvard Square, wondering what the big fuss was about. I was sure the Fordham education I was getting was every bit as good as what Harvard students got. It was at Harvard Square I first saw the posters advertising Kayla and August's recital. I saw one pasted on the front wall of the Out of Town newsstand, and then I saw them all over the place.

The Deerfield people were still doing the publicity, which made sense given August was their client. As a result, they still emphasized Kayla's sexuality. She wore a black dress revealing substantial cleavage and her Star of David necklace. They'd managed to capture a dreamy look on her face as sat at the keyboard, her right hand on the keys, but her face toward August holding his violin, his left hand on her shoulder. The image screamed that August owned Kayla. The poster's header announced "A Collaboration of Giants!" and, in smaller type, "World-famous violinist August Sorel and beautiful accompanist Kayla Covo perform works by Mozart, Grieg, and Franck," then giving dates of three performances at the Berklee Center. The poster drove me nuts. August "world famous" and Kayla "beautiful"? She was, of course, but that wasn't the point. My anger at the Deerfield people kicked in again, modified only slightly because I knew Kayla would at least be paid.

I got to Berklee with an hour to spare. I wanted to see if any of the other concert-goes matched Kayla's description of a very tall, albino man with very dark eyes. I didn't expect to see any such person and wasn't surprised when no one remotely fit the description. I just wanted to be able to tell Kayla that I looked, if she asked. Then I thought to strike up conversations with other young men milling about, without letting them know my connection to the performers. I wanted to find out if they were there because they were physically attracted to Kayla. But my plan was ill-conceived from the outset, because all the men were with women. I couldn't spot one single man, young or old. Well, I wondered, who but me goes to a concert by himself?

When they first stepped onto the stage, I saw with relief that Kayla wasn't wearing the black dress with the scooped out front she'd worn for the publicity shot. She'd donned a much more conservative sleeveless, golden, floor-length gown, with a modest slit up the side. She'd need the freedom of that slit to work the pedals. Perhaps the gown was a bit tight in front.

August and Kayla were starting these Boston programs with Mozart's E-Minor violin sonata, well known to lovers of classical music as a composition he'd written in Paris around the time of his mother's death. The program notes explained that the E-Minor was the only one of his many violin sonatas written in a minor key, suggesting that grief underlay the music. As I listened to the first movement, I couldn't have disagreed more. Kayla and August, playing crisply, precisely, yet sweetly, allowed tons of happiness to seep through. They brought to mind Mozart's playful ingenuity more than his loss. I felt the first movement as a great tribute to the life of Mozart's mother. The second movement, with its beautiful but pathetic melody starting in the piano, took us closer to Mozart's sadness over his mother's grave, yet, with Kayla playing, the music conveyed a sense of hope.

What struck me from this first piece I'd ever heard Kayla and August perform together was how well they knew each other and responded to each other's emotions. It didn't sound at all like the tentative steps of a new duo. They played with supreme confidence. From one glance at Kayla's face, I could tell she loved doing this as much she loved solo performing. Perhaps even more. At the end, the audience rose for a standing ovation. That kind of response to the first piece of a concert was unheard of. Where could the audience go from here?

Kayla got up to stand next to August for their bows. Her face glowed as she looked at August, and for a second I feared she'd forget the audience, but she then turned to her admirers. Kayla and August had to bow multiple times before walking off stage to regroup. The audience didn't want to sit.

When Kayla and August returned to the stage a minute later, they performed the Grieg G-Minor sonata. This was primarily a showpiece for August, but the piano part was much more complicated than in the Mozart. Again, by bringing out the sonata's lyricism and mystery, they showed they were completely in touch with each other musically and fully comfortable in the Romantic mode. As I listened, entranced, I loved my sister more than I ever had before and felt I would've died for her. I stayed with her through every note, almost as if I was inside her, feeling the music with her, almost as if I was playing it myself, stroke for stroke. When the impetuous third movement ended, the audience once more rose in unison, yells of "Bravo" and "Brava" filling the hall. Kayla smiled as if the audience was her secret lover. I couldn't detect a hint of fear. Maybe this would all work out, I told myself, wanting and needing to believe.

At intermission, I stood near others in the lobby, trying to eavesdrop, eager to hear comments about the performance. I could catch only fragments, given the noise and my desire not to be obvious. "Beautiful!" was one word I heard a number of times, which reminded me of the posters, but they might well have been talking about the music, not Kayla. I also caught "Black and white," "Haiti," "extraordinary," "where did we hear her name?" and "doesn't sound Jewish," among other things. I remembered to look for very tall, angry men with very dark eyes, finding none.

Following intermission, they played the Franck, a violin sonata I made it my business to listen to a number of times that spring as I studied for my exams, sitting in a room in the Fordham music library with earphones clamped around my head. Kayla and August hit it out of the park. I'd been listening to Kayla play for my whole life, and yet once again I stood in awe of her ability to make the hardest passages flow effortlessly from her fingers and bring the emotion directly to the listener without drawing attention to her virtuosity. Following the last movement's final exhilarating coda in A Major, the audience went wild. I'm running out of superlatives here, and I confess to contributing my part to the craziness. I could no more have stayed seated than held my ground in the middle of a tornado. Inevitably, Kayla and August played an encore, choosing a rondo from another Mozart sonata, bringing the recital around full circle. The music must've been marked *presto*, but Kayla and August played it at an even faster rate, not missing a note. I can't recall which sonata this came from, though it might've been in C Major.

Afterward, I went backstage and turned a corner toward their dressing rooms, happening upon them kissing, locked in an embrace. They pulled back as soon as they sensed my presence. Before I could say anything, Annie appeared, and Annie and I kept saying inane things like "incredible" and "amazing," repeating ourselves ad nauseum.

"Enough!" August said finally. "Thanks to your sister here I never played the violin so well!"

Kayla smiled like she believed it, but wanted to compliment her partner. "You were outstanding, August." They kissed again, briefly. Then she turned to Annie and me. "He's the reason the audience came, right? Everyone wants to hear August Sorel."

"Nonsense," I said. "They've known about you since you were a child, Kayla, and this was your first time in Boston. That audience was here for you as much as for him, and you didn't disappoint them, for sure."

Everyone was tired, and we decided to get back to our hotel and catch up on rest. There were two more concerts to go in Boston, and then they'd get on the road again, and I'd take the train back to New York. I felt sure Kayla hadn't thought about anyone following her. She carried herself with ease whenever August was near. After all my doubts, it dawned on me that this was the right solution to Kayla's problems.

CHAPTER 94

The radio's been talking about the Battle of the Bulge, but she's not exactly sure if it's good or bad. The announcers don't seem to know either, from one minute to the next. Because there's a war on, her dad's not home, working late again at the Navy Yard. She wishes he were there, because she can talk to him. He brings a bit of peace to their home. She knows the war is a bad thing and a lot of people have been killed, which makes her sad, but at least her dad, even though he wears a uniform, doesn't have to go away to fight. He can be a lawyer not far from home, and she can see him every night, unless he works late, and on most weekends. She's much luckier than her friends in the second grade whose dads are fighting with real guns and bullets. One of her friends sadly tells her that she lost her dad and cries. It takes Adel a while to understand that lost and died mean the same thing.

On this night, Adel is blue. Her dad told her "blue" means "sad" and she doesn't quite get that yet, because her Dodgers wear blue and they make her happy. But her dad would say that tonight she's blue. The witch has sent her to bed again without dinner. She can't remember what she did to get herself slapped so hard on the face and starved, but it must've been evil. She feels shame and knows she's worthless. She feels guilty for making her mother have to hit her. Her mother is the one who takes care of her, so it's very bad to hate her so. But she does hate her mother.

She knows about evil because her dad took her to see *The Wizard of Oz*, and she was so gleeful near the end when Dorothy melted the wicked witch. She didn't feel sorry at all. She wants to throw a bucket of water on her mother, but knows what she saw in the movie was only pretend, knows that throwing water on her mother would bring on the most severe punishments – certainly the belt, its metal buckle gouging skin out of her bare bottom – and again no food. When she's all grown up, a big girl, she's going to eat everything in the house and then eat everything in the city and then eat everything in America, and it will make her feel so good.

Her dad's given her a beautiful doll for her birthday. She names her doll Myrtle. Myrtle has curly, light red hair. She wears a light grey frock with a white ribbon tied in a bow around her neck, and white socks and little white booties. She loves Myrtle and pulls her into bed, under the covers, where she can whisper to her and no one can hear.

She tells Myrtle she's going to kill her mother, even though she's supposed to love her. When she kills her mother, it won't be with a bucket of water.

CHAPTER 95

When I got home late Sunday night, Mom and Dad were waiting, wanting to hear from me what I thought. I shared with them my relief that things had gone well and took from my pocket the Boston Globe review of the first recital. It's here in my scrapbook, so I'll quote it in full.

•   •   •   •   •

Boston, September 18, 1982. By Anne Guilford. Boston concertgoers were treated last night to an uncanny display of symbiosis between two very young, but mature, performers at the Berklee Performance Center. The Haitian-born violinist, August Sorel, has teamed up with teenage piano sensation Kayla Covo, both based in New York, at the beginning of an American tour, and the results in the estimation of this reviewer were outstanding. They've chosen an ambitious group of violin sonatas to perform in Boston, including Mozart's E Minor, the Grieg G Minor, and the Franck. Sorel and Covo seem to have been made to enhance each other's performances, working together as if they were one mind and body, playing with focus and high energy, eliciting both the pathos and joy inherent in each of these pieces. They are confident in handling the most difficult nuances of these well-known compositions. The audience responded with great enthusiasm to the artists' flair, consistently rising to its feet to express its profound appreciation. We hope Sorel and Covo return often to Boston if they can continue this kind of bravura collaboration.

"What does all that mean, Max?" I'd lost Mom, who never read newspapers, let alone music reviews.

"This reviewer loved it."

"What's bravura?"

"Just means great performance. This is very, very complimentary. Hard to imagine better."

"Ah, so I thought. You read it so nicely, too."

"Any sign of fear?" Dad asked me.

"No, I didn't see any."

"Do you think she's over her hallucinations? Have they passed for good?"

"Hard to say, Dad. She seems comfortable with August there. I think that's a big difference."

"All right. I'll see for myself this week. Where am I going again?"

"New Haven."

"Right. I can take the train, too."

"Can I go with you, Nicky?" asked Mom.

"I don't see why not, Adel."

"I haven't seen her play in a long time."

"Then let's do it. One condition, however. You have to swear not to hum during the concert."

"Okay, Nicky. No humming. I swear on the lives of the ducks in The Lake."

CHAPTER 96

She's euphoric, the only word in her vocabulary to come close to the exhilaration of three outstanding performances. She's felt the giddiness of the audience's love and admiration before, but now, with August, the sensation has intensified. He's done so much for her playing and been so complimentary, as if he'd been waiting for her his whole life to make him a more complete musician.

When he knocks on her hotel room door, she's waiting for him. He said he might stop by to chat. Her heart pounds as she opens the door, afraid of what will happen and determined to let it. He steps inside and, without fanfare, without so much as a word, he pulls her close to him and kisses her deeply. It begins. It's exactly what she expected and wanted.

A new world opens to her, one she only imagined before, one she was afraid to enter, but one into which she now vaults with her whole being.

CHAPTER 97

Mom and Dad had been required to stay overnight in New Haven, as the concert ended too late for them to catch a train. They got home the next morning, but I'd already left for Fordham, so didn't see them. By the time I got home that evening, Mom was already in the hospital. Dad told me what happened.

"She was okay at the beginning of the concert. Really. She paid attention at first, but then her mind was off somewhere else. I got her Diet Coke at the intermission, but she didn't touch it, and she zoned out during the second half."

"Asleep?"

"That might have been better. No. Staring off into space as if she wasn't aware she was in a full auditorium. She kept her promise not to hum, but she tapped her shoes on the floor to the point where people turned and glared. I whispered for her to stop, but she didn't get it. So, during the Beethoven, I got her up and we walked out. I'm sure the people around us were overjoyed to have us gone."

"Then what?"

"Well, we waited outside the doors to the hall so I could listen. When they were done, I took Mom around back to see Kayla, but Mom was decompensating fast. I had sedatives at the hotel, so I told Kayla I had to get her back to our room. In the morning, I got her to the station with difficulty, and there she started acting out, worst I've ever seen her. Swearing, calling strangers names, carrying on loudly about Reagan being a piss pot. Have to agree with her there. Anyway, I gave her another sedative, my last. She quieted down, but when we get back here she started up again. She was banging her head against the front window to the point I thought it would break. I gave her a cigarette, but it didn't help."

"Crap. Then what?"

"I called Dr. Lack. I mean, what else could I do? He told me to get her down to Bellevue, where he checked her in for a three-day involuntary stay. He's there now, checking up on her."

"Crap again. How many times can I say crap?"

"I know."

"How was Kayla? I mean, could you tell anything from you saw and heard?"

"She was very much as you described. I don't know those pieces, didn't care for the Bartok, just pounding and frenzy if you ask me, but my musical opinion doesn't count. The first piece, Haydn, was more my style, and then, well, it was too difficult to follow the music and watch Mom at the same time. But Kayla looked fine, and the audience loved everything."

"Mom's skipping her meds again, obviously."

"I confess I haven't been keeping track as I should. I'll to talk to Lack about maybe changing them. Maybe something else will be less disagreeable than Thorazine. Maybe get her into a trial of a new antipsychotic. I've said that before, though, haven't I? But maybe this is the time."

"What do you want me to do?"

"You might call Kayla, wherever she is. Fill her in and tell her not to worry. Tell her Mom's under good care. That's about all you can do. You're seeing their concert this weekend in Baltimore, right?"

"That's the plan."

"Okay, then I'm heading to the hospital."

CHAPTER 98

He ponders what he has to do to get his life back in order. There's too much going on for him to grab hold of. Kayla's paranoia and Adel's worsening leave him drained even before he gets out of bed in the morning. By the time he walks into his office, he's sweating, from anxiety, concern for his family, and frustration at his ineptitude. He can do nothing to avert the coming crises, whatever they might be.

He frequently cancels his afternoon patients because he lacks the stamina to pay attention and respond appropriately. He transfers patients to his former partner and puts others on hold. His income drops. For the first time in his career, despite all the drugs he's had at his disposal, he begins to self-medicate.

So far, the anti-depressants don't help.

CHAPTER 99

The events of the next month and a half now are a blur in my memory. Mom was released from Bellevue but still struggled, posing a major distraction for everyone. Dad took more time off from his practice to be with Mom at home. He arranged with Tricia to care for Mom, too, paying her handsomely; Tricia moved in with us, occupying Kayla's room while she was away. I was torn, wanting to study, behind on getting papers to my professors, but needing to follow Kayla around the country.

Living with Mom became a nightmare. She'd grab a shoe and start pounding it on the walls of our apartment, or she'd take all the silverware and hide it in her underwear drawer, or she'd sit for hours talking to a window. At times she thought she was in school and kept mentioning Daniel, the boy whom Dad told me had raped her. Dr. Lack, who'd taken care of her for twenty-five years, did try a few new anti-psychotic drugs, settling on perphenazine, which had to be injected. For all I could tell, it just made Mom more jittery and confused.

Kayla knew what was going on with Mom, but couldn't do anything to help and had to focus on her music. I can't imagine how she could concentrate, knowing that Mom was in such a declining state. Yet, things were going well on her tour. Audiences flipped out, reviews glowed, and, when I heard Kayla and August play, I couldn't criticize as much as a note, nor notice any progression of Kayla's paranoia. I stopped scanning the audiences for the tall angry man.

Two things did change, though, as the tour went on, and they might well have been related. Kayla's outfits became more daring, more revealing, and her relationship with August deepened. I was sure they were intimate. Maybe it was the way they looked at each other. I confronted Annie at one point on the subject, but she assured me I must be mistaken, that she was keeping careful watch over Kayla, and that Kayla was not misbehaving. Annie couldn't be so sure, I thought. It's impossible for one person to watch another for twenty-four hours a day. Annie would need to sleep. She couldn't know everything. But I held my peace. I didn't say anything to Kayla, either, giving no hint of my misgivings.

I felt a sense of loss in recognizing Kayla was old enough for sex. I'd held onto the illusion too long of Kayla always being under my immediate protection, and it was inevitable that, when the illusion faded, I felt more than a twinge of disappointment. To be honest, I felt jilted. I didn't dislike August, and if she wanted to give herself to him at the tender age of sixteen, I couldn't prevent it. I knew at some point he'd move on past Kayla in his musical career. I could see he'd reach the point where he no longer needed her. I knew she'd be devastated, but things were going to play out as they would. I could just watch and wait.

It seemed forever, but the tour began to draw to a close. Dad made it to Buffalo for the last performance featuring the Franck, and then we waited in New York for the final weekend of recitals, with the Beethoven Kreutzer Sonata as the finale. Posters of Kayla, with the low-cut black dress, could be seen all over Manhattan. "Exquisite Duo Returns to New York!" shouted large print.

Deerfield insisted that both August and Kayla stay at the Waldorf when they got back to the city until their last concert had concluded. We thought this odd, but Kayla assured us, based on what August told her, that such was occasionally the practice in the elite music community. Deerfield didn't want their being home to change anything about the successful routine that August and Kayla had developed on the road. They would pretend they were still traveling.

We considered whether it was safe to bring Mom to one of the performances, then decided against it. The last thing we wanted was a scene. She seemed to be acting out less on the perphenazine, the drug finally taking effect, but she couldn't sit for more than a minute before needing to get up again. Tricia, ever the good friend, would watch over Mom while Dad and I attended the concerts. We'd get everything straightened out once Kayla was back at home. Or, at least, that's what we thought.

CHAPTER 100

He's so beautiful when he's naked and when he's inside her. She smiles in the darkness of her hotel room when she realizes the longing she's felt for years is being miraculously fulfilled. She responds to his touch as if she were his violin; the fingers that cause such a pleasant vibrato make her skin sing with joy. The metaphor – even though she imagines it trite – amuses her because she knows it's so true.

Is he likewise her Steinway? Even as unpracticed as she is, she knows that she's more than succeeded in raising from him the flood of emotions comparable to what she can extract from the piano. God created in August a Chopin scherzo, a Beethoven sonata, a Scriabin prelude, a Bach invention, all rolled into one amazing and loving person. Under the sheets, her fingers manipulate an imaginary piano, running through the opening measures of the Franck second movement at breakneck speed.

When she's warmed up her fingers, she reaches for him.

CHAPTER 101

We never made it to the last planned performance. The Friday night concert went very well, and Kayla seemed exuberant when we talked to her by phone Saturday afternoon. When we saw her briefly backstage before the Saturday night concert, she was excited, yet composed. And then ... well, there's no way to capture it in a word.

Kayla and August were at their best in bringing home the Kreutzer. By now, I'd heard them play it so many times I could anticipate every nuance. If anything, August's sound was fuller and more vibrant than usual and Kayla's virtuosity beyond belief. At its conclusion, they bowed to a roaring audience leaping to its feet at the final chord.

And then I saw Kayla's trademark smile change in an instant to a grotesque grimace of fear. She screamed. It took the audience a second to realize what was happening. August turned toward her, one hand still clutching his violin, and Dad and I ran toward the stage as if we'd been expecting this all along. Kayla ran off stage, still screaming. Someone yelled for the police, someone for a doctor, someone fainted, and I thought I heard a woman's voice somewhere from above us calling "Nicky." August followed Kayla offstage, calling her name. Dad and I were slowed by the audience, which had filled the aisles, many running for the exits as if Kayla had shouted "fire." The public announce system clicked on, urging the audience not to run but to walk to the nearest exits. If anything, the announcement induced more fear. When Dad and I at last got backstage, perhaps three long minutes after Kayla's scream, our confusion only grew.

August was with Charlene, who was talking to the police on the phone, but Kayla was not to be seen.

"What happened?" I shouted, grabbing Charlene by the arm.

"I don't know. She stormed out before we could stop her."

"You let her go?" I couldn't believe their stupidity and spinelessness. "Which way?" Charlene pointed with the phone toward an exit, and Dad and I both ran for it, hoping we'd find Kayla right outside.

We were shocked by our sudden entry into the cold fall night, but we were even more shocked that we didn't see Kayla where we'd hoped. People milled around the plaza as if nothing had happened. We questioned bunches of people who must've thought we were crazy, but no one admitted to having seen Kayla. True, this was New York, where strange behavior is so common no one ever notices. But not to have seen a screaming young woman in a concert gown?

I sent Dad east, I went west, running up one block and down the other, calling her name, drawing bemused looks from passersby. No sign of Kayla.

I finally gave up and went back to Lincoln Center; Dad arrived a few minutes later, alone. He'd learned a woman running on Broadway had disturbed a driver's attention and there'd been a rear-end collision, but the onlookers couldn't give a coherent account of whether Kayla had been the distraction. We checked at the Waldorf, where she hadn't been seen. We called home and talked to Tricia, who'd not heard from Kayla either. We ran down to Bellington, talked to the night guard, who'd not seen her. He let us inside, though, and escorted us down the hall to knock on the door of Lindorf's empty office.

Nothing.

Checked her usual practice rooms.

Nothing.

Checked the room where she and August often practiced together.

Nothing.

CHAPTER 102

Adel will not remember the dream but will wake with the knowledge that she's been tormented by an overpowering and malicious force. As she sleeps, she pulls at her hair one minute, then digs her fingernails into her arms the next.

In the morning, she'll be bathed in sweat as if compelled to run miles under a broiling sun. She'll recall only the pieces of Myrtle left behind after her mother had smashed the doll with a hammer, the feeling of gut-wrenching disbelief that she's been victimized yet again, helpless to fight and helpless to escape. She's only eight years old. Where could she possibly go?

In the morning, she'll feel that the punishment is the exactly what she deserves, that her pain is her inevitable birthright.

CHAPTER 103

Dad called home again to find that Kayla had still not shown up and to caution Tricia against saying anything to Mom. We'd tell Mom ourselves in the morning if Kayla hadn't materialized.

At the police station, we filled out paperwork. Finding recent photographs of Kayla wasn't hard; they were posted all over town, and soon every patrol car in Manhattan had been informed and was looking for her. We denied knowing about anyone having threatened Kayla and said nothing about Kayla's imaginary angry man with dark eyes. We told the police that Kayla had been known to be jittery and nervous lately, a white lie.

When we'd done all we could at the police station, they encouraged us to go home and keep our phone lines open. But when we got back to the apartment, Tricia had already disconnected the phone. Word had leaked out about Kayla, and the phone hadn't stopped ringing. Although Mom was still sleeping, Tricia was afraid the incessant calls would wake her. Dad hooked up the phone again, set its ringer on the lowest setting, called the police to find out what he should do, and learned that an officer would come by shortly to field calls all night, if need be.

Kayla might call, in distress, needing help. Or a kidnapper might call demanding ransom. The police still thought someone – a deranged fan, perhaps – might have abducted her from outside Avery Fisher Hall, a crime of opportunity.

Neither Dad nor I could sleep. He came into my bedroom and sat on my bed as I sat at my desk. I couldn't remember the last time Dad had been in my room. We kept hearing the phone ring and the officer answer, talking in a low voice for a second or two before hanging up. Reporters and quacks, the officer told us in the morning.

Dad and I had to talk, if only to confirm to each other that we'd actually seen what we thought we'd seen.

"Something in that audience triggered her." Dad's comment was painfully obvious, but I didn't have the heart to point that out.

"She couldn't have screamed louder if she'd seen a dead child rise from the grave or ..."

"Must you?"

"Sorry. But you have to agree no one's *ever* heard Kayla scream like that. Much worse than in the cemetery. And then she ran ..."

"Like her life depended on it."

"Exactly."

"But where?"

"Back to the cemetery?"

"I don't think she'd run there at night."

"We checked with August's folks?"

"They were the first ones August called. And he called them repeatedly. If she'd shown up there, we'd know by now."

"Do you think she's ... would she try to hurt herself, Dad?"

"I hope not. She's been so happy on this tour."

"Would she have gone to Brooklyn? Maybe back to the police station where we picked up Mom? Maybe ... maybe trying to find her way to Ben's house?"

"She's never been there."

"But she could've gotten his address from the phone book?"

"All right. It's two in the morning, but let me call him." Of course, Dad woke Ben up, but Ben had already been told by Annie what was going on, and no, he hadn't seen or heard from Kayla. He offered to do whatever we needed him to do, but of course there was nothing.

Thus it went through the night. An idea, a recognition of how ridiculous the idea was, but a call just in case, getting us nowhere. At six, we woke Mom, who looked horrible, but we brought her into the kitchen, made her sit, and told her Kayla was missing. We didn't talk about the screaming or the look on Kayla's face, just that Kayla had left the recital hall abruptly, letting no one know where she was going, and no one had heard from her since. Mom remained quiet for a while, and, when she spoke, she made no sense.

"Do you see the fire?"

"No, Adel. What are you talking about?"

Despite myself, I glanced in the direction Mom had looked, at our front window. Nothing going on, a regular Sunday morning.

"It's burning red hot. It's sending signals. Can't you feel them? Can't you see the fire? I even smell the ashes." She wiped sweat from her brow.

"Tricia, maybe you can help me get Adel back to bed."

"Sure, Dr. Covo."

Together they maneuvered Mom back to the bedroom. I thought for sure she'd be returned to Bellevue before long.

Dad emerged a minute later. "Well, nothing more we can do here. Let's get back to the police station, in case they hear anything there. Maybe we can help search." The officer who'd spent the night would stay at our apartment to keep answering our phone and noted that a relief officer would be by shortly. In thirty minutes, Dad and I were back at a conference room at the station, finding out that New York's finest had no clues. Yes, she may have run across Broadway through heavy traffic, and yes that probably caused the accident, but from there she left no trace. They were doing a building-by-building search. They were checking with the cab companies to see if a fare matching her description had been picked up near Broadway at about that time. All we could do was wait.

So that's what we did. We sat and waited for about ten minutes, until Dad and I looked at each other and said what we'd both been thinking for a while: "August." Neither of us had said more than a word to him the night before, but if either of us was going to do anything useful, talking to August in depth was obvious. Sure, the police had questioned him, twice, once right after Kayla's disappearance and once that morning. He'd not seen anything unusual in the audience and had no explanation for why Kayla might have bolted. No, he'd given the police no suggestions as to where she might've gone. The police had done what they felt needed to be done to rule out August as a participant in Kayla's disappearance, but Dad and I felt we might be able to get more out of him.

A short time later, after a call to August's parents to find he'd gone to Bellington, we barged into his practice room. He didn't look pleased with our intrusion.

"C'mon, August," Dad said. "Let's go where we can talk more comfortably."

He took us to a quiet alcove, and we sat on facing benches. "So, Dr. Covo, Max, I've told the police everything I know, which isn't much. Can you tell me what's going on?"

I filled him in. "The hospitals have been notified, her picture's in every squad car on the street and in the hands of every cop on the beat."

"What do you want me to do? Join the search? If I thought that'd help, I'd be out there right now."

"Had she been acting strangely?"

"The police asked me, Dr. Covo. And the answer's still the same. No." It could've been my imagination, but I thought August averted his eyes when he answered.

"Did you have any concerns yourself about her mental stability? You knew what happened in the cemetery that day."

"No, I swear I didn't have real concerns. I thought she'd mostly gotten over that thing about the angry fan. The stalker. How could we've performed as well as we did during the tour if she was ... you know ... bothered?"

"I don't know, but sometimes patients ... people ... can carry on much of their normal life, even when they're sliding downhill." Dad's tone was professional. He knew an accusatory approach would cause August to shut up. "You say you didn't have real concerns. Had she talked at all about her fears?"

"Of course. There were times she did, right from the day when Max found us in the cemetery. But she assured me she felt better and guessed it was only her imagination. She swore she wasn't seeing him again. Wasn't even thinking about him, unless I brought it up. I had no reason to doubt her. Didn't you hear her *play*?"

"She's a genius at the piano, that's a given." I tried to keep my tone friendly, following Dad's lead. We had to play August was well as he played the violin.

"Max, I'm not sure what a musical genius is, but Kayla feels the music like no one else I've ever played with. It's like I was the only one who could speak a language and then, from nowhere, a wonderful person appears at my side with whom I can speak the same language. It's a miracle."

"I don't believe in miracles," Dad said firmly, then continued in a more subdued voice. "You've spent tons of time with her over the last half year."

"Of course, Dr. Covo."

"When you weren't talking about music, what were you talking about?"

"It was almost always music. When it wasn't music, it was ... let's see ... what she thought of different cities she's visited, how she feels she was cheated by Charlene, how ..."

"You don't think she was cheated, I gather?"

"I don't know, Max. I listened to her tell her story, I've heard Charlene tell a different story, and I've decided to be agnostic. I really didn't want to talk to Kayla about it, because it was a distraction."

"Was?" I pounced on August's use of the past tense.

"Is. Was. Will still be."

"What else?" Dad continued, struggling to maintain control.

"Shit. How can I remember six months of conversations now?"

"Try. Humor me, August. We're talking about my daughter's life at stake."

"Okay, let's see." August frowned and thought for a few moments. "We talked about the weather, the programs we'd play, the acoustics in the various venues, and well ..."

"What?"

He breathed deeply before continuing, steeling himself. "We did talk occasionally about her family, her mom, you, Max."

"What about us?"

"Oh, God." I noticed August had begun moving the fingers of his left hand as if they were on the violin. I wondered if he actually heard his violin then, even as he spoke to us. "What you were like to live with, how you supported her music, how maybe ... well, Mrs. Covo wasn't always there all the time mentally, you know ..."

"We know."

"How ... let's see ... where she used to live in Coney Island."

"Not quite Coney Island, but close enough."

"We talked about her outfits, I know."

"What about?"

Here, he smiled briefly and stopped his fingering long enough to crack his knuckles. "What I liked her to wear. Whether I thought her outfits were too ... not conservative enough?"

"Too sexy, you mean?"

"Well, yes." He fingered his imaginary violin again, at a higher speed. Very distracting. His digital manipulations called to mind the last movement of the Mendelssohn concerto; now I was sure he could hear whatever he was fingering.

"And what did you think?" I had to know.

"Kayla's beautiful. Anything she wore would've been fine. Did I think some of her clothes were sexy? Well, sure. Didn't you, Max? But that's not why people loved her ... love her. It's because of her music."

"What else?"

"Should she wear jewelry? Should she wear that star necklace? You know the six-pointed star. She called it her ... *Mogen daveed?*"

"Right. A Jewish star. Literally it means Shield of David."

"I liked it. Wear it if it makes you feel better, I said."

"What else? Think!"

"We talked about Haiti and how I feel I have nothing in common, really, with Haitians, other than skin color. We talked about food, how she was a vegetarian who couldn't eat anything green. But since I ate with her all the time, I knew all that. She tried to explain her dislike of that color but couldn't."

I was impatient to move the conversation along. "You must've talked about her dreams, because she always talks about them." A glance from Dad told me I'd done the right thing, that this was the questioning that needed to happen. His message: I should continue.

"Now you mention it, Max, she did talk about dreams. Often, there were monsters chasing her..." He acted as if a light bulb had lit up his brain. "Oh, I see, monsters and all. Never thought about it before in relation to the other stuff."

"You didn't connect her dreams with her fear of someone following her?"

"With all respect, Dr. Covo, I'm not the psychiatrist. No. I didn't make that link. She never acted too concerned about her dreams. Let me see. One day, she dreamt she was Miriam, the prophetess, being chased by Egyptians, about to be pushed into the sea. Very Old Testament. Another time, she dreamt she was Joan of Arc, ready for battle, knowing she'd die. Very New Testament. I mean, people have all kinds of dreams, they remember some, they forget most, and then they live their regular lives and the dreams fade away. That's how Kayla struck me. She talked about them and moved on."

"Did she ever talk about other famous people?" I asked. "Like … presidents or queens or rock stars? The Beatles? How they dealt with over-exuberant fans? John Lennon?"

"I don't recall anything of that kind. But, look, Max. I'm happy to answer your questions, but I don't see their point."

"The things she said might give us a clue about where she's gone, don't you think?"

"But if someone's kidnapped her, then what she talked about is irrelevant." August pulled a used handkerchief from a pocket and wiped his hands with it. I couldn't tell whether they were really sweaty. I saw no film of perspiration on the rest of his body. If he was nervous, it was only his hands that gave it away.

"No reason to think she's kidnapped," I said. "We haven't had any ransom calls. She ran, she wasn't grabbed."

"But after, if she was abducted …"

"I don't …"

"You can't …"

"For *any* reason …"

"Do you feel she's been abducted? Is that what you're trying to tell us? And you're just going on with your practicing?" I finally allowed indignation, something close to hatred, into my demeanor.

"I don't know. I'm practicing because it helps me to keep my mind off of Kayla for a while. I couldn't stand to lose her."

"You couldn't stand …?"

"Dr. Covo, I love Kayla. Haven't you realized that?"

CHAPTER 104

"I don't believe him," Dad said as soon as we'd gotten away.

"I'm with you. He knows more than he's telling us. If he loves Kayla, he has a damned peculiar way of showing it."

Despite my earlier feeling August was the answer to Kayla's problems, that he would settle her down, that his continued presence would nurse her back to sanity, by now it was obvious I'd been naively wrong. His confession of love was a ruse. If he really loved her, he would've run out of Avery Fisher Hall without a moment's hesitation and caught up with her before she vanished. His so-called love meant only that he lusted. He was just a man entranced by being close to a sexy, beautiful girl for months, working with her every day. Right now, she was great for his career and great company, too great, but at bottom August was only for himself. Guys like him are narcissists; they get bored and move on.

"And, he knows something important he's not telling us. He knows a lot he's not telling us." Dad and I agreed on that score.

"We'll find out," I assured us both.

"You know, it was all I could do to stop myself from choking the life out of him when he talked about loving Kayla."

"Me, too, Dad."

"If Kayla wasn't in danger, I would have."

Then I had an idea, ill-formed and ill-conceived though it might have been. "Tell me. What would you think if I tried to follow August? Maybe he knows where Kayla is, which could explain why he doesn't seem terribly worried. If he knows, he might lead us to her, right?"

"That's using your brain."

CHAPTER 105

A knock on the classroom door, and it slowly opens. Cringing from behind a chair she's pulled into the corner of the room, her moaning having subsided for the moment, Kayla looks out at the woman who enters. She's young, maybe late twenties, but it's hard to tell. She's dressed in a long flowing skirt and a long-sleeved white shirt, wearing what must be a wig of dark brown hair. She's pregnant and she's carrying a small duffel. There's a look of concern on her face.

"May I please come in?" Kayla makes no response. "You're Kayla, right?"

"Please close the door behind you."

The woman obliges and backs up to the door so as not to seem a threat. "I've brought you clothes. These are mine, but you're welcome to them. They don't fit me anymore." From her bag she takes a pair of grey woolen slacks, a pale green shirt, a white blouse with long sleeves, a dark green sweater, plain white underwear, white socks, and worn-out tennis shoes. "I think these will work for you." She begins to walk toward Kayla, holding out the clothes as a peace offering.

"Is there anyone else with you, hiding outside the door, I mean?"

"No, of course not. It's just me. I'm Sarah, by the way."

"I know who you are, Sarah. I've seen you before. You're the rabbi's wife."

"The *rebbetzin*, yes. Please come out from the corner, Kayla. Please get off the floor. It can't be very comfortable. There's no need to hide."

Slowly Kayla emerges, naked. The scraps of what she wore have been stuffed into a waste basket. Sarah hands her the replacement clothes and turns her face away while Kayla dresses. When Kayla is dressed, she says "Thank you," and Sarah turns back to face her.

"Can we talk?"

Kayla nods and they sit on two folding chairs pulled back from a table.

"Do you want to tell me what happened? You don't have to. But perhaps if we know what happened to you, we can help you."

"I need a place to hide."

"*Arei miklat t'hiyena lachem.*"

"What?"

"It is written in the *Chumash*, in *B'midbar*, the fourth book – called Numbers in English – that *Hashem* commanded the Israelites to create cities of refuge." Sarah pauses contemplatively for a moment. "You're welcome to stay here as long as you need to."

"I am?"

"Of course."

Sarah's soft, caring words are feathers of light caressing Kayla, who's overcome with emotion, tears of gratitude spilling down her cheeks. She had hoped with so much longing they'd take and keep her. She had prayed as hard as she could. With the tears, she feels a strange calmness, a lifting of a tremendous burden, the weight of which she couldn't measure until it was gone. She rushes to Sarah, who returns her long embrace.

CHAPTER 106

I had no clue how to follow someone, particularly someone who knew me and who, if he was trying to hide anything, might well be watching out for me. I could spy on him from a block away as he left Bellington, maybe use Mom's binoculars, but he'd get lost in a crowd, and the binoculars would attract unwanted attention. I decided to station myself near the front entrance of the school and wait. If he appeared, I would try to stay close to him, hoping he wouldn't notice. To my surprise, the strategy worked.

When he left late in the afternoon, he seemed lost in thought, paying no attention to anything around him. He walked up Broadway a few blocks, then crossed at West 69th and entered the Christ and Saint Stephens Episcopal Church. I waited a few seconds, then followed him inside. A concert of liturgical music was about to begin. I paid a five-dollar entrance fee and found a seat in the last row. I could make out August sitting close to the front. It dawned on me that I was unlikely to find Kayla in this church, and I was annoyed at myself for having thought I could become a hero by playing the detective.

I assumed Kayla was hiding and didn't want to be found. Unless we found her, though, we couldn't help her, couldn't get her the psychiatric medicines and counseling she needed. I was about to get up, approach August, apologize, confess my stupid plan, but decided to wait. Maybe Kayla was, after all, hiding in the church and would approach August. Maybe, they'd go off together into one of the side chapels. I could confront them there. As my eyes adjusted to the dimmed lighting, I scrutinized every row looking for Kayla, in disguise perhaps. But I saw nothing, no one who looked like Kayla. No one approached August. Organ music by Bach filled the room, and later a choir sang hymns with a piano accompaniment. The pianist wasn't Kayla, but a man in his sixties.

Despite myself, I listened more thoughtfully to a hymn, glancing again at the program pushed into my hand when I entered. "Dear refuge to my weary soul," went the first sentence. I'd never heard it. Some concertgoers sang along in soft voices, and I felt a twinge of regret that, although many could find solace in God, I could not. If I'd ever needed something divine to comfort me, some essence to which to pray, that late afternoon was the time, but belief in the supernatural was beyond my capacity. I ruminated on the theme of belief and disbelief as the concert washed past me until I nearly forgot why I'd come.

When the concert ended, I rushed toward where I'd seen August. For a second, I couldn't spot him. Then I did see him, turning from a clump of people with whom he'd been talking. He appeared greatly surprised to see me approach. I got within two foot of him before I stopped my charge.

"Max, what the heck ..."

"August, we need to talk again."

"I already told you ..."

"Let's get over to the side, where it's quieter." I motioned him over to a dark chapel.

"How did you know I was here?"

"I followed you."

"You followed me? Why didn't you just come back in and interrupt my practice again?" August was steamed, and I didn't blame him.

"I thought you might lead me to Kayla."

"You thought ... I said I didn't know where she is." He started to walk away, but I grabbed his arm and got myself in front of him.

"Wait. It was stupid of me. I'm sorry. But I think there's more about Kayla's disappearance you're not telling us."

"And what would that be?"

"You have an idea where she's hiding." The expression on his face – like the proverbial kid caught with his hand in the cookie jar – told me I had guessed right.

"If I did, why wouldn't I tell you?"

"Because Kayla doesn't want to be found by us." I had to keep guessing, had to press in any way I could. I pretended to know what I didn't know. Incredibly, my ploy worked. We sat on a pew along the wall of the chapel. The crowd from the concert had thinned. He grabbed a hymnal lying on the pew near him and thumbed through it until he found what he'd been looking for. I waited until he read the hymn, not caring what it was, wanting only for him to tell me what he could about Kayla. When he replaced the book, he turned to me.

"You don't like me, Max. Why don't you admit it?"

"Nonsense. Why ..."

"I can see the way you look at me, because I'm black, you don't think I'm good enough for Kayla. She can see it in your eyes as well."

"That's ..."

"Nor do you like that she's stopped soloing. That's also very obvious, and she's told me you've tried to talk her out of accompanying me."

"She can do whatever she wants with her career. I'm just worried about her, we all are, and if you know where she is, tell us. Or if you think you know, tell us. Whether I like you or don't like you is irrelevant. We're her family, we love her, and we need to be there for her. She's sick, and we need to make sure she's taken care of." I could sense August was weighing the pros and cons of telling me more. Well, if I had to beg him, then I would. "Please, August. Please, help us. Do I need to get down on my knees?"

"No," he said, apparently startled by my offer. My willingness to prostrate myself did seem to have the desired effect. He took a deep breath. "I will tell you more, then. Kayla's a very troubled girl, much more severely disturbed than even you realize. I have no idea how she pulls it together for performances. When we're alone together, she's almost a different person than the one who performs so well on stage."

"How so?"

"Hearing things."

"Like?"

"A choir singing, for example. Someone talking to her from another room."

"And you've never said anything to us about this?"

He shook his head, but I couldn't tell whether it was with remorse or defiance. "Maybe that's the selfishness in me. When she plays, all those things disappear. As long as she keeps playing, it's only her music she hears, the music from her heart. And I wanted that. Still want it. Badly. To be able to play with her, in that world we create together. You're not a musician, so you wouldn't understand."

I wanted to smash his head on the floor. Who the hell was he to tell me I wasn't a musician? Who the hell led Kayla to the piano in the first place? Who made it so interesting for Kayla that she made it her life? Who helped her with the fingering on the Chopin B-Minor scherzo when she only seven, when she still might seek my help? Didn't he know our history? But it wasn't time to pick fights.

"What do you know that would help us find her, August?"

"I don't know. But one of the imaginary people she hears is a man she called the *rebbe*. That's the same as rabbi, right?"

I knew the term referred to the leader of a Hasidic cult, but not much more. I told August as much. "Did she say anything else? Like, is this a real *rebbe* she believes she's talking to? Or a fictional *rebbe*? I mean, did she talk back to him?"

"Once or twice."

"What did she say?"

"Forgive me, *rebbe*."

"Forgive me, *rebbe*, and you said nothing?"

"I felt I should let her say whatever she had to say, to whomever she thought she was speaking. No one else could hear her but me."

"Forgive me, but you're an asshole. Incredible. Was that all?"

"No." He looked down, closed his eyes.

"Then?"

"She said once, 'There was so much blood, *rebbe*. I ...'"

"Go on."

"'I washed my face in his blood. Forgive me, *rebbe*.' That scared the shit out of me, I'll be honest with you. I grabbed her, and she looked like she'd been in another world and was only then recognizing I'd been in the same room. But she came out of her trance like a light switch had been flicked off, and said, as if nothing had happened, 'Let's go through the third movement of the Franck again, August.' It's the *Fantasia*, you know, Max."

"I know." The blithering idiot was trying to teach me stuff I knew. "Get on with it. What happened next?"

"I told her it was a great idea and let's try playing it a bit more slowly and more mysteriously than usual." In seconds we were practicing as normal."

"How long ago?"

"A month."

"During the tour?"

"Of course. What does it mean, Max? Do you know this *rebbe*?"

"I never heard her use the term. I never heard her talk about washing her face in someone's blood. Jesus f ... What I mean is, how could you hear that and then just let her turn the conversation back to music? Are you fucking crazy yourself? Are you the dimmest fucking wit in the world?"

"I didn't know what else to do. I thought once we got back on track, maybe this would go away. For a while, it worked."

Yeah, I thought bitterly, it worked fine. Thank you, August.

"What do we do now?" he asked.

CHAPTER 107

Nicky sits at his kitchen table with Adel, barely aware she's talking to him. She's been complaining about something, but, although he understands her words and can see she's upset, he has nothing with which to comfort her. Tapped out. That's it. A perfect expression to describe how he feels, empty of energy, emotion, solace, self.

He recalls what the young teenage Nicky would have prayed. "*Ezrat avotenu*," he would've beseeched, seeking help from the God of his ancestors. But that God vanished for him in an instant, even as his family vanished into the Nazi death machine. Folded up in the trunk of a car in Athens, he decided that prayer was no longer an option. He decided that he alone, Nicky Covo, not a supreme being, would take charge of his life. And that decision had worked for so long, but the inner resources upon which he relied were now rapidly leaking away.

Adel has said something again, but her words still don't register. He tells her to go back to bed. He doesn't watch her as she shuffles out of the kitchen.

CHAPTER 108

The room in which Kayla has been hiding fills with a score of women, most of them strangers to her. These kind women in long black or grey skirts form a circle, arms around each other's shoulders. Sarah leads them, and they dance and sing with unfeigned happiness. Kayla sits outside this circle, on a chair against the wall, in semi-darkness, staring at her lap. She half expects some further degradation to fall upon her, but she listens and finally lifts her head to watch. These women are there for her as a human being, as a Jew, and want to help her. They don't care a whit that she's a famous pianist. It's a relief. Their communal support, their shared chaotic joy, push the evil far from Kayla. She's safe, safer than she's felt in years. She's lifted up by the sweet music, by their purpose to help her heal; she's a vapor, a ray of light, a breath, a word, a thought in God's book.

The singing reminds her of the Sephardic *niggun* her father had taught her family, but the spirit here is a million times larger than any she ever felt around her family table. She can't stop crying in gratitude for the love she feels and the growing knowledge that she must make a major change in the direction of her life. These women will protect her with their love and their *Chabad* rules and faith. They will hold her up.

They invite her to come inside her circle. With some trepidation, she approaches. One of the women leaves her spot in the circle, hugs Kayla briefly, then positions her in the center. They continue with their dance and song, but now crowd ever closer until she's swamped in a massive hug. She feels at home. This is home. This is where she was meant to be. She reaches for each of these women in turn, hugging and kissing as many as she can.

She would like to thank them, but she's without words. Yet she senses that words aren't necessary when the meaning is clear.

CHAPTER 109

I rushed home to talk things over with Dad, hoping he'd understand what Kayla had meant. I told him the whole story, how I waited for August, how I followed him into the church, how I listened to the concert, and what August told me. At the end, when I relayed Kayla's hallucinatory conversation, Dad turned white.

"What is it?"

"It's just ... never mind. But, tell me again about that hymn."

"Nothing, just a hymn."

"Dear refuge to my soul, you said?"

"Dear refuge to my weary soul, but I don't see ..."

"Hold it!" Dad jumped out of his chair and ran into the kitchen for the telephone directory. I followed, thinking he too had lost his mind and that I was the only sane person left in the Covo family. He flipped through a few pages, started pushing his finger down a column, and barked out, "Got it! Write this down: 37 West 65th. C'mon!"

He didn't wait for the elevator, but ran down the four flights of stairs, so I had no chance to ask him what the hell was going on. Once on the street, he ran toward Broadway. I'd never seen him run so fast and had trouble keeping up. Dad grabbed a cab on Broadway, narrowly managing to avoid getting crushed by a speeding car, then yelled at me to hurry. Finally, we were in the cab together, I'd caught my breath, and I asked him if he'd gone completely mad.

"I think I know where Kayla might've gone. There's a *Chabad* not far from Lincoln Center. It's possible she's hiding there."

"A *Chabad?* You mean ..."

"The *rebbe* thing."

"Well, yes, but ..."

"And the hymn. Refuge for the weary soul, right?"

"But that's just a coincidence."

"Fine, a coincidence. If Kayla's seeking refuge, and she knows about this *Chabad* house, maybe she headed there."

The lights cooperated, and we neared our destination in two minutes. "We could've called. You had the number in front of you."

"How do I know they'd tell me the truth on the phone?"

"Wouldn't the police have already talked to them? They scoured the area."

"The Nazis couldn't find me for months, hiding in plain sight in a church."

The cab swung up to the *Chabad,* a narrow seven-story building tucked into the middle of the block, next to a Chinese café on one side and a small apartment building on the other. Dad marched up to the door and walked inside as if he owned the place, and I followed. A young bearded man – maybe early thirties – wearing a long black coat, a white shirt, and black hat sat reading at a front desk. He was clean-shaven but had those long side fringes of hair.

"Yes, *shalom.* Welcome to *Chabad* in the Sixties. It's too late for our *mincha* unfortunately but you're welcome to stay for *maariv,* which starts in about a half hour."

"Thank you, but we're not here for prayer today. I'm Dr. Nicky Covo, and this is my son, Max. We're here to ask if you might know where our daughter Kayla is."

The man looked at us closely, then looked at the front door, then back at us.

"I'm Rabbi Berenbaum. Sol Berenbaum."

"You're the *rebbe?*" I asked.

"Heavens, no! But I'm the spiritual leader of this outpost. I hate to do this, but may I see some identification?"

Dad handed over his driver's license. Berenbaum looked at it briefly and returned it.

"So she *is* here!"

"Come to my office. We'll talk there."

He locked the front door, then led us down a hallway. The walls were decorated with kids' drawings. They looked like Biblical scenes in bright colors. I could identify what I thought was Noah's ark, and there were renditions of Hanukkah candles burning and dreidels spinning. Well, why not? Hanukkah had just started, unobserved as always in our family. Whatever else these decorations meant, I understood there were plenty of kids involved in this religious group, kids being force-fed beliefs of magical powers in charge of the world.

Rabbi Berenbaum's office was surprisingly neat. It surprised me because I naturally assumed that irrational people – the Hassidim particularly – couldn't be expected to be orderly. Everything about this place surprised me. A rabbi who looks like he just got out of rabbinical school. A place where Jewish children gathered and made art together. When we seated ourselves, Berenbaum told us what we hoped we'd hear.

"We know where Kayla is."

"Which is?"

"She's living here. Hiding would be the more appropriate way to say it."

"Can we see her?"

"I don't think she wants to see you right now, I'm sorry to say."

"Why not?"

"She's very ill, Dr. Covo, at least in my judgment. Now, I'm not a doctor, and I understand you're a psychiatrist ..."

"You've learned about me?"

"Kayla's told us a lot about your family over the past two days."

"We're here to take her home. We're here to get her the care she needs."

"I'm sure your intentions are the best."

"So you have to let her go."

"Let her go?" He laughed, entirely inappropriate given the circumstances. "We're not keeping her prisoner. She came here of her own free will, and she hasn't wanted to leave. I've talked to her about it. I've urged her to call you, to let you know she's all right, but she refuses."

"Refuses! You could have called us yourself."

"But then I'd be violating a confidence. She trusts us here."

"She's been here before?"

"A few times over the past year."

"We'd never heard her talk about this place."

"All the same. She stopped by on occasion in mid-day. She came once or twice to part of a *Shabbat* service. Once, she came to talk to me and explained who she was. I don't listen to classical music, I don't go to concerts, so I didn't know her from a hole in the wall. But she's Jewish, so that didn't matter at all. She showed me one of the fliers from a concert, and I could see she was who she claimed to be. And once, later, she came and we discussed the story of *Toldot* in *B'reishit.* You know the story of Yaakov and Esav."

Dad ignored the clear attempt at diversion from the purpose of our visit. "Why did she come here in the first place? Certainly not to study Torah?"

"Why does anyone come?" He paused for a second or two, readying himself to give the spiel I'm sure he'd given hundreds of times. "Jews come all the time, looking for answers, looking for community. They're looking for a glimpse of the Eternal's light. They're looking for meaning in their lives, looking for that which they've not found elsewhere. Some are troubled, deeply troubled, like Kayla, some merely curious, exploring all kinds of spiritual possibilities. I take it from Kayla that you, your family, aren't religious?"

"True, Rabbi Berenbaum."

"A shame."

"I survived the Holocaust." For Dad, that explanation of how he'd lost his faith was all he needed to say.

"Yes, I know." Rabbi Berenbaum paused, then turned to me. "And you, Max, you're very much like your father, aren't you? Jewish, but not a believer in *Hashem?*"

"My beliefs, sir, have nothing to do with why we're here. All respect. Can we talk to Kayla, please? If we could talk to her, perhaps she'd come home with us."

"I'm worried about the stress such a meeting might have."

"Rabbi, forgive me for asking, but are you a father?"

"Oh, yes, Dr. Covo. I already have two, with another on the way."

"As a father, can you appreciate how I feel now, when my own child, my own flesh and blood, the best part of my life, is afraid to see or even talk to me?"

"Of course, I understand. It's most disturbing. No father should have to live through that."

"Then can please you help us?"

"All right." He sighed. He probably thought that he'd never get rid of us unless he at least told Kayla we were here. "She stays in a room upstairs. Let me see what she wants to do."

"Thank you."

We waited for a long time, quietly. I wanted the next sound I heard to be Kayla's voice. I wanted that so badly that, for a few minutes, I prayed. To whom or to what I prayed, I don't recall. To fate, I guess. What I recall is that my entire being ached for Kayla's welfare and for her returning to our family, and I felt I had to reach for some power outside myself.

Then, finally, she was there.

"Dad! Max!" Kayla half ran, half stumbled, into the office. She was crying and looked horrible, gaunt, as if she hadn't slept in days. She wore borrowed clothes, a long greenish skirt, a white blouse buttoned all the way up, tennis shoes. Her hair hadn't been washed. She hugged Dad, then me. We were too stunned to say anything.

Berenbaum followed her in, sat Kayla in his own chair, and stood leaning against a bookcase. "Go ahead, Kayla."

She blotted tears from her eyes before starting to say what she had to say. "I'm so sorry to have worried everyone." Her voice sounded distant, as if she were reciting a speech someone else had written for her.

"We'd like to take you home with us, Kayla," Dad said, as soothingly as he could. "You need your parents, you need your brother."

"They're taking good care of me here." That came out with a bit more conviction, but still uncertain.

I wondered whether she wanted us to argue her out of her belief she was being well taken care of. I wanted to shout that she looked like shit, to hold a mirror up to her face and force her to look into it. I felt that, in this Kayla, I was meeting a total stranger, a ghost of the sister I loved, someone who reminded me of her but was utterly different. The sister I loved was a distant memory.

"Kayla, they've sheltered you, but we're your family. Come home with us," I implored.

She ignored me and leaned forward to get a closer look at Dad. Then, she said matter-of-factly, "There's blood on your face."

Dad stared back at her without flinching. Had he expected her accusation? He understood hallucinations and wasn't going to protest that his face was clean.

"Then come back with us and help me wash it off. Will you?"

She turned to Berenbaum. "Should I?"

"As you wish, Kayla. You're always welcome to come back here if you need to, as I've told you many times. As a Jew, you're always welcome. But certainly you're free to go or come as you wish."

"May I come back for *Shabbat* services, then?"

"Always."

"And to learn more Torah?"

"Always."

"May I come back and live here if I need to?"

"The house of *Hashem* will be a refuge for you if you need refuge. My wife, Sarah, the other women, will continue to love and support you. All you need to do is ask."

Kayla sighed deeply. "OK, Dad. Let's go home and try to wash off that blood."

CHAPTER 110

We left Berenbaum after borrowing his phone to call the police and explain that Kayla had been found. I'm sure he thought he was doing the right thing by hiding Kayla, but she was still a minor, and a rabbi's primary duty should've been to let her parents know where she was.

Kayla, wearing her borrowed clothes, was quiet on the way home. I had no idea where her gown had ended up. I sat up front in the cab, but could see Dad holding Kayla's hand in the back. Kayla just looked out the window. It had gotten dark.

When we got home, Mom was awake, sitting at the kitchen table, smoking. She glanced at us, but said nothing. You could see the tremors in her hand holding the cigarette. Did she even remember that Kayla had been lost to us for two days? I had no idea. Kayla walked into the kitchen as if she hadn't been gone for months, said a perfunctory hello to Mom, and announced she was going to bed.

"Kayla, do you want to talk first about what's happened?"

"No, Dad. You wouldn't understand, and anyway you can't be my shrink because you're my Dad, right?"

"Will you come with me tomorrow to see Dr. Lack?"

"Mom's shrink? Do you think that's a good idea? "

"Try to talk to him. If he thinks he can help you, if you feel he'll help you, we'll stick with him, but if not, we'll find someone else. Deal?"

She shrugged her shoulders, looking too tired to argue. I hoped irrationally that one good night's sleep was all she needed. I'd used up any feeling for prayer at *Chabad*. I was back to just wishing for the things I wanted.

"Did you see the fire?" Kayla spun around to stare at Mom.

"What?"

"I told your father and Max about the fire this afternoon."

"There was no fire, M ..." Dad shot me a look, and I left my sentence unfinished.

Kayla looked at us in amazement, as if Mom seeing a fire that wasn't really there was the strangest thing she'd ever heard. I thought how odd it was the two women in our family had grown so ill with remarkably similar diseases at the same time. Mom's DNA had lodged in Kayla's genes. Or maybe it wasn't DNA at all, maybe something else, maybe just being in the house with the three of us. Whatever the cause, Kayla's paranoia didn't prevent her from understanding that her mother, too, had advancing mental illness.

"We saw the fire, Adel," Dad said in his most comforting, believing voice. "It's out now. You needn't be afraid. Let me give you your evening medicine."

With Dad humoring Mom the way he'd humored Kayla about the blood on his face, I couldn't help but wondering how he could seem so calm in the middle of multiple crises. But, of course, he'd been through an awful lot himself. He was no ordinary father and husband; he'd been forged, as it were, in a cauldron.

"Good night." Kayla, forgetting to wash Dad's face, disappeared into her room.

CHAPTER 111

Kayla did see Dr. Lack the next day, and he sent her to a private psychiatric facility in Westchester County, one of the best, Dad said. Albright House, as I recall. A nondescript name. It's been a long time since I had to remember it. She agreed to Mom and Dad signing her in, after first making us promise to tell Berenbaum where she was and how she'd be out soon to attend services at the *Chabad.*

Mom quieted down around that time, with yet new medicines kicking in. The relative peace gave me a chance to get back to serious study for my exams, but my heart wasn't in it. The idea kept nagging me that more bad stuff was about to happen. I tried to talk to Dad, but he put me off, which darkened my spirits. He seemed preoccupied, unable to work. I wanted desperately to talk to Kayla, but under the rules of Albright House she wasn't allowed to have phone or in-person contact with anyone for her first week. With Dad not wanting to talk, with Mom being Mom, with Kayla out of reach, I was at a loss. After finals, I could do nothing but spend my extra hours at the Fordham library reading about paranoia, *Chabad,* famous violin/piano duos, and anything else that might help me understand.

When the embargo on visits ended, we drove up to see her. Visits were limited to fifteen minutes, and we could talk to her only one at a time. I didn't see the point of these rules, but Dad assured me the psychiatrists knew what they were doing. It was important not to overwhelm the patient. Family contacts were critical to Kayla's well-being, we were told, but too much, too soon, might push Kayla again toward the psychotic end of the spectrum.

Dad suggested Mom visit first. "A mother's love is always the most comforting," he remarked, and no one disagreed. Accordingly, Mom went in first, spent about ten minutes, and emerged humming.

"How did she seem to you, Adel?"

"She's a mental case, too, just like me. Fly like a butterfly, sting like a bee."

"She'll get better. You both will. Did she talk?"

"Just a bit. The little shit."

"About what?" I asked.

"She was sorry to cause trouble."

"Nothing more?"

"We didn't talk much. We just looked at each other. Then she smiled, so I did too. Then she gave me a hug. I gave her one back. Dull as a tack. That's it."

"Great, good start. Max, you want to go next?"

"I'd rather go last, Dad, if you don't mind."

"Sure."

So Dad went in. One of the aides had to knock on the door after fifteen minutes to tell him his time was up. When he emerged, he looked at us and shook his head. "Nothing. She won't open up to me, other than to say she's comfortable for right now, feels she needs to stay here longer, and wants to know if I can have the management bring in a better piano for her to practice on. The one they have downstairs in the rec room is horrible, she says. Way out of tune. Wants me to thank Rabbi Berenbaum again and make a donation to *Chabad*."

"Well, at least she's playing," Mom observed. "Isn't that a good sign, Nicky?"

"Maybe. But she also complained her hands shook so much, she was exhausted after a half hour. That's not the Kayla we know."

Then it was my turn. Kayla was sitting on a chair and motioned me to sit near her on her bed.

"You're the one I wanted to see most, Max."

"It's been very strange with you up here and our not even being able to talk to you, Squirt."

"You haven't called me that in years." I was surprised myself that her old nickname just popped out, but she seemed to have liked my using it.

"Well, I always think of you as a squirt anyway," I responded with an attempt at a smile.

"What did I do to our family, Max? Mom's in hell and I think the stress I've created has pushed her down. And Dad looks shaken too. I've screwed things up for everyone, haven't I?" She reached inside her shirt and pulled out the Star of David necklace.

"Don't get down on yourself. People get sick. You're no more responsible for that than you'd be if you came down with the flu."

"But I did things ..."

"Only the sickness ..."

"I hid from you. I knew that was wrong, but ..."

"Don't trouble ..."

"I was so embarrassed. So many people helped me, August, Herr Lindorf, and I couldn't hold it together. I tried so hard, I really did. I hid away from everyone, at first because I was afraid of ... that horrible man killing me, but then, after ... after." She was struggling.

"You don't have to talk about it, Squirt."

"After that horrible night, the last concert, I knew he was going to kill me, and I had to hide from him, but I also hid from all of you because I was ashamed."

"You don't need to be ashamed, ever." I pulled her out of her chair, made her sit next to me on the bed, and put my arms around her. After a second, she extricated herself and returned to her chair. The energy in the room seemed to grow with her movement. "There's something I didn't tell Mom and Dad, but if I'm right, they'll find out soon enough anyway. I'll tell you if you swear not to say anything to them."

"All right."

"I think I'm pregnant."

I couldn't look her in the face. She said it, not as one might expect a sixteen-year-old girl to bemoan a calamity in her life, but as someone might expect a happily married woman to congratulate herself on long-sought fertility.

"Pregnant." I felt stupid and didn't know what else to say.

"Yes. I'm pretty sure. That's another reason I wanted to stay there at the *Chabad* as long as I did. I felt so vulnerable until I made it inside and then ..." Her voice drifted away, and she never finished. Instead, she tucked the Star of David back under her shirt and looked at the ceiling, absorbed by something I couldn't see.

My time was up.

CHAPTER 112

"What did she say?" I naturally wanted to tell Dad what I'd heard, but I'd given my word to Kayla.

"Nothing I can talk about. Don't ask me."

"Look, your sister has a serious illness. She can't help herself, and secrecy won't help either. You owe it to us to tell us everything."

"No. What I owe is to be Kayla's faithful big brother." I wanted the conversation to end and wanted to get back to Manhattan as soon as possible. I wanted to confront August. No, not exactly right. At that moment, having been so caught off guard by Kayla's announcement, I wanted to kill August. If he'd been there, I'd have found a way, maybe by picking up a chair and smashing it over his head until nothing was left but splatter on the floor. Fortunately, August wasn't there. On the trip back into town, it occurred to me that perhaps a miracle would erase this embryo. Perhaps it was even part of her paranoia to fear that something was living within her. By the time we got to our apartment, I'd calmed down. Brash action made no sense.

I asked Mom and Dad to sit with me for a minute. I wanted to tell them something about why Kayla had hidden from us.

"She was embarrassed?"

"That's what she said, Dad."

"Did she see the fire, too? Was she running away from a fire?"

"No, Mom. She would've told me if she had."

"Oh, because now she's a nut case, just like me, I thought maybe she'd see the same things. It's horrible to be a nut case. I asked God once why he made me like that, and he didn't have a good answer. He wanted to ask *me* what it felt like. You'd think God would know what it felt like to be crazy."

After a few more minutes of inane conversation, Dad convinced Mom she ought to take a nap. In truth, she looked miserable, as bad as Kayla had looked when we found her at *Chabad.* Her skin had a dark grey pallor. For maybe the hundredth time, I wished I'd been born into a plain vanilla family.

I was befuddled about what to do next. Just sit tight until one of Kayla's doctors revealed to Dad and Mom that their daughter was pregnant? Sneak a pregnancy test to Kayla and have her find out there and then? Since she was taking antipsychotics, didn't the doctors need to know if she was pregnant? They surely should've asked her if she'd been sexually active. Or maybe they'd checked her physically? They should have, but maybe they'd been careless. If Kayla was pregnant – and I fervently wished she was not – and went on to deliver a baby, would the baby be malformed? Would the baby turn out crazy too? I even fretted about whether Kayla could continue as a concert pianist if she had a baby to take care of, forgetting the larger problem was whether someone with psychotic paranoia could ever be a professional anything. Half of me still wanted to go down to Bellington and have it out with August, but a confrontation would be useless without first knowing more. The other half wanted to forget everything, change my name, move to a distant city, start over.

I sat at the Steinway, but of course I hadn't practiced in ages. I played a few measures of the Chopin Nocturne in B-Flat Minor, one that I had performed at a recital in Sr. Cantelli's house when I was ten. I played for about half a minute, until I forgot the notes and everything came out jumbled. I gave up. The piano had become my enemy too.

CHAPTER 113

She's been trying to tell Nicky about the messages she hears, as crystal clear as a bell rung on a cold bright winter morning. He doesn't listen. Or he listens, but he pretends not to understand. She tries to tell him that more bad things are coming. He doesn't want to see it. He wants to see her now only as a problem to be solved. She's a burden to him and to the rest of the family.

She's been trying to tell Max too. He smiles, hugs her, and returns to reading the newspaper. He's busy with the crossword puzzle. He's studying the sports pages, wondering about what off-season trades the Mets might make. He disappears into his room.

She needs to make them see that Kayla has changed forever. Adel could see it immediately in the looney bin where they parked Kayla. A mother can sense that the daughter she knew is no longer there. The little girl is entirely gone, and a strange woman sits in her place. Adel wonders who this strange woman might be, what demands she might make.

She doesn't feel well. The pains in her chest, a twinge now and then, discomfort her, and occasionally she feels a sharp jab. There's been so much stress. Maybe it will all pass. But it bothers her that no one will actually consider her seriously anymore, that no one will accept her as full human being whose thoughts and hopes and worries are important. What did she do to deserve this?

CHAPTER 114

Two weeks later, the other shoe dropped.

The day before Kayla was to come home, the call came from Dr. Lack to Dad. The doctors had known for a few days, but had held off telling us about her pregnancy as they tried to prepare Kayla for whatever reaction they thought we'd have. Hours before we left to pick her up, we sat in our living room to talk it through.

"Does August know?"

"I don't think so, Max, unless she snuck off to an unguarded phone. They try as hard as they can to limit contacts to family."

"Is she sick?" asked Mom. "You remember, Nicky, I barfed a lot when I was pregnant."

"Dr. Lack hasn't said anything about pregnancy symptoms. He's concerned about how we'll treat Kayla."

"Why shouldn't we treat her the same as always?"

"We should, he says. But he's afraid that, as hard as we try, we'll show resentment against her."

"Resent?"

"It's like this, Mom. We might resent her if we believe she screwed up her life, because we put so much of our own energies into helping her career, and because, now, well ...." Then I stopped, actually not sure what Dr. Lack thought might happen.

"That's right, Max," Dad said. "Her mental status is shaky at best. Pregnancy makes it harder to control. They haven't been able to alter her medications, and Dr. Lack fears she could revert to full-blown psychosis if we're not careful. He wants us to make sure we give her only our support, not recriminations. And we also need to be aware of the risk that her baby will have some kind of defect."

"She's going to go through with it, Dad?"

"According to Dr. Lack, without doubt. Her doctors raised the issue of termination, and Kayla was adamant. She'll have the baby or die trying, she said."

"What do we do?" I asked.

No one had an answer until Mom said, minutes later, "Pray, I say. All day. God might still let things work out."

CHAPTER 115

We picked up a haggard-looking Kayla. She had a slight tremor of the lips.

"You know I'm going to have a b-b-baby." Kayla's voice was defiant and proud. She expected we'd try to talk her out of going through with her pregnancy, and she intended to set a marker at once that the subject of abortion should not be raised.

"We know." Dad was speaking on behalf of all of us.

"Well, if you're going to tell me not to have m-my b-baby, I'm not going to l-l-listen."

"We're not going to tell you that. But, as your father, I'd like to know how you plan to care for a child. August doesn't even know he's going to be a father, does he?"

"He doesn't. They wouldn't let me use the telephone. But as soon as I get home, I'm going to c-call him."

"What do you expect him to do?" Dad used his patient-talking voice.

"What do you mean?"

"Is he going to be responsible? Be there for you throughout the pregnancy and beyond? Pay for doctors? Support his child? Be a presence in his child's life."

"I n-never thought about that."

"It's time to start."

I wanted to scream. Everything I hoped for Kayla's career was down the toilet. I wanted there to be yelling and recriminations. I wanted to berate August and Kayla for being so careless about birth control. I wanted to shake Kayla by the shoulders and demand to know why she'd thrown away such a promising career, by taking up with August in the first place, by letting him knock her up, by losing her mind. Instead, I forced myself to use Dad's steady tone.

"Kayla, what can I do to help you? Do you want me to talk to August?"

"Certainly not!"

"Well, will you still practice? Will you still like me to walk with you down to the school?"

"I d-don't know. I haven't thought about piano very m-m-much. Practice was very hard for me this past month, with the sh-shakes. With the sh-shitty piano they never replaced. I d-don't see school in my future. And, I'm having a b-baby. D-damn. I c-can't t-t-talk."

"It's the Mellaril, Kayla. One of the side effects. Sometimes it wears off after a while."

"D-damn, Dad, I know it's the meds."

The rest of the ride back into the city was uneventful, with Dad talking about calling friends and helping Kayla find a good obstetrician and about various hospitals for delivery, boring details to me. Just before we turned into our street, Kayla reminded us about the new direction her life was taking.

"B-b-by the way, it's F-Friday, and I plan to go to *Chabad* tomorrow for services. I need to see Rabbi Berenbaum and tell him about my having a b-baby. And I want see Sarah and the other women."

"You're not going to go into hiding again, are you?"

"No, Dad. Max, would you c-come with me, please? Just to k-k-keep me company?"

"Sure." I had no desire to spend a minute in a synagogue or any other house of worship, but I longed to spend more time with Kayla and would've set sail with her in a leaky rowboat on Sheepshead Bay if she asked.

"Mom, can I light *Shabbat* candles tonight?"

"Well, I guess. The apartment's a mess."

"You w-won't laugh at me?

"No, we won't," I said.

"What are you making for dinner, Mom?"

"Nothing. I haven't been cooking."

"I'll pull something together," Dad said quickly.

"You will?

"Happy to do it."

"Thanks."

"Vegetarian."

"Duh."

CHAPTER 116

I don't think I've ever been more uncomfortable in my life than that Saturday morning I attended *Chabad* services with Kayla. I'd been a stranger for years to any kind of Jewish worship, I considered religion a fairy-tale, and I felt as different from the other people there – fellow Jews or not – as could be imagined. During the service, I sat in a back row, self-conscious. Some men – all dressed in black suits, white shirts, and wearing wide-brimmed black hats – tried to welcome me, wishing me "*Shabbat shalom*," peaceful Sabbath, but I could barely utter a civil reply, and attempts at conversation stopped. I didn't know the tunes they sang, didn't care if I knew them or not, and couldn't feel their happiness. It seemed they had drunk from the same vat of Kool-Aid, a Jonestown disaster waiting to happen in the heart of the city. From where I sat, I couldn't see the women's balcony and had no idea how Kayla was getting along.

After the service, people milled about, men and their wives reuniting after being separated during prayer, chatting for a minute with friends before returning to their homes. Where the hell was Kayla? I wanted to get out of there. Before Kayla showed up, however, Berenbaum recognized me.

"*Shabbat shalom*! Max, right? Kayla's brother? I saw Kayla in the balcony."

"Yes, Rabbi. *Shabbat shalom*."

"I hope you're thinking of joining us here at *Chabad*. You know you're always welcome."

"No. You know, I told you, I'm not religious. No disrespect. I just walked with Kayla to keep her company. She wanted to talk to you."

"I heard Kayla was hospitalized. She's better now? Praised be to *Hashem* if she is." As if on cue, Kayla appeared, smiling. I didn't have to answer his question.

"*Shabbat shalom*, Rabbi."

"*Shabbat shalom*, Kayla. I'm so happy to see you again."

"Yes. May we g-go into your office to speak for a few minutes? Max, this won't t-t-take long."

Her look told me that I was to stay away. Berenbaum said goodbyes to congregants, then led Kayla away. I had nothing to do but wait and accept the stares of men and women who saw me – uncomfortably dressed in a grey suit – as out of place. The crowd dwindled until I was alone in the lobby. A few minutes stretched into more than thirty before Kayla and Berenbaum emerged.

"Sorry it took so long," said Kayla. "Turns out there was more to talk about than I'd thought." Kayla's stuttering, so prominent the day before, was fading. I wondered whether that was a sign of her getting acclimated to her drugs or of being less anxious. Either way, the hope arose withing me for a short second that she could continue with the piano.

"Max, tell your folks we here at *Chabad* would like to help Kayla, if we can."

"Help her how?"

"The Almighty will see to it."

CHAPTER 117

"So, what must I do to be *ba'alat t'shuva* when I'm pregnant?"

Rabbi Berenbaum pours water from a plastic bottle into paper cups, and he hands one to Kayla. "No coffee today, because it's *Shabbat*," he says, smiling.

"Of course." She takes a refreshing sip. She hadn't realized how thirsty she was.

"So you ask an excellent question. You should study Torah with Sarah and the other women here. I lead the discussions, Wednesday evenings, right after *ma-ariv*. Give more *tz'dekah*. Light the *Shabbat* candles in your home, if your parents will allow it."

"I did last night. They'd probably let me continue, but I don't think I want to keep living at home."

"Why not? Your family loves you."

"They do. Too much, maybe. But just walking through the apartment makes me sad, particularly when I look at the piano. When I see the music wallpaper in my room. When I look at my mom, I resent her for passing along her genes. When I look at any of them, I'm ashamed – yes, I know, it's not my fault I got sick – but still I feel how disappointed they are, what they gave up to help me. Even though they're careful not to chastise me for getting pregnant, I can't help but feel their disapproval."

He thinks for a moment, looking at her. She's unable to meet his gaze and stares at her feet for a few seconds. "There's more you're worried about, though, isn't there?"

Then she looks at him, her eyes moist. "Well, yes. I suppose. You say light candles, but my family doesn't observe *Shabbat*. What does it mean for me to light *Shabbat* candles, even though the rest of my family will make phone calls or write or watch television in the presence of the candlelight? And, if I'm going to be *ba'alat t'shuva*, how do I avoid hearing the radio and television? How do I avoid those sounds from penetrating into my thoughts? Lock myself in my room?"

"Again, you ask good questions. They show your seriousness, how much you want to focus as you start this new chapter in your life."

"I've always been able to focus on what I wanted."

"Your music, of course."

"And now that music is gone ..."

"Performing as you did may be gone, Kayla, but music doesn't have to be."

"And now that my piano career is gone ... Tell me then. What must I do to embrace a new life as *ba'alat t'shuva* if I'm surrounded in my home by nonbelievers?"

He pauses again to ponder; a long minute elapses until he continues. "I wouldn't give this advice to just anyone, but, in your case ... I have to say I agree with your instinct that you need to leave your family's apartment."

"I was hoping you'd say that. I thought you might."

"Our ancestors often experienced what you feel about your family as well. Our father, Avram, later named Abraham, had to leave his family after he heard *Hashem*'s voice. *Lech l'cha, Hashem* ordered. Leave your father's house."

"And where shall I go when I leave?"

"That's your choice, but let me invite you to stay with us throughout your pregnancy, in the room upstairs. And you may stay for a while after your baby comes. Use your pregnancy as the time during which you transition to becoming a fully observant Jewish woman. Now that we're talking about your family, I see you can do that best if you live with us. But don't cut yourself off from the people who've nurtured you this far. That would be a terrible mistake. *K'bed et avicha v'et amicha.* Honor your father and your mother."

"So I might live a long life. I've been reading Exodus."

"Correct. *Sh'mot* in Hebrew. Your parents will continue to love and help you, Kayla. You need them in the long run, and you can't stay here forever. After a time, you may be more confident in your relation to Judaism and be able to move back with them. We'll see how things are a year from now, say."

She listens to the sounds from the hallway, hearing nothing. The last congregants had long ago left. She knows that Max is waiting for her, and he'll have to wait a bit longer. There's a bit more she needs right now.

"What else does Judaism require of me during the pregnancy? So that my baby and I will be healthy and able to embrace the love of *Hashem*?"

"You'll use the ritual bath, the *mikvah*, during your ninth month. Sarah will explain this to you and help you through it. That and *tz'dekah* and study will prepare you. Now, if you'll forgive me, Sarah is waiting for me a home. Is there more?"

"Yes. You should know that the baby's going to be black. His father is Haitian. Will that make a difference here?"

Rabbi Berenbaum smiles. "Of course not. Jews come in all colors. But does it bother you that the baby will be black?"

"No. I'll love him as much, maybe even more than if he was white."

"Him?"

"Let's just suppose that I know for sure what sex my baby will be."

"You probably do. So the baby will be a boy. What particular hopes do you have for him? How do you want him to grow up?"

"Everything that I'll try to learn now for myself, that I'll turn my heart to completely, I'll try to give to him as well."

The rabbi seems satisfied with her answer. "*Hashem* knows your son already, Kayla."

"How's that possible?"

"*Hashem* has created him. Let me show you the proof in our Scriptures." Rabbi Berenbaum picks up a volume from the side of his desk, flips through a few pages, and reads to her. "*Lo nichad atzmi mi-meka, asher useyti vaseyter, gamli ra-u enecha, al sifr'cha gamlu y'katevu.*"

"Which means ...?"

"This is Psalm 139, King David addressing *Hashem*. King David says, 'My essence wasn't hidden from You when You formed it; rather, You saw my essence, *Hashem*, with Your own eyes, as it was written in Your book.'

What this means is that, if you know you're having a son and that he'll follow your teachings, it's because *Hashem* has written it thus. It is *Hashem*'s story to tell."

Kayla nods her head, pleased with and comforted by the lesson. She will make plans to leave home and move to the *Chabad*, but will otherwise stay as close as she can to her family. She'll honor her father and her mother. And Max, of course, although the Bible doesn't seem to require that explicitly. And she'll need to read Psalm 139 herself and learn the Hebrew so she can read all the Psalms.

Hashem as a writer of souls. *Hashem*'s story to tell. Very good. The idea reminds her of things her mom used to say about God the Creator writing a story, but they no longer sound crazy to Kayla. Her mom was onto something.

CHAPTER 118

She lies in bed, and something gnaws at her mind, a memory fighting its way to the surface, and with the memory a dark and unquenchable rage. She tries to beat back this vision, but the more she resists the clearer it comes into focus. Soon, she relives the event, against her will. Why does she recall now, of all times?

She sees herself entering Kayla's room, and just enough light from the street has seeped around the edge of the blinds to show where Tina lies on the floor. She has fallen next to Kayla's bed, and Adel picks her up.

Kayla's breathing is regular and easy.

In the kitchen now, Adel pulls hard on one foot, needing to punish Tina for bad behavior, and as she does so she hears her own mother's voice loud and grating in her head. But the hard plastic resists Adel's efforts and clings to its original form. Her rage explodes. She opens a kitchen drawer holding their scissors, hammer, screwdrivers, and other tools. She places Tina's leg over the side of the open drawer and forces the drawer closed with all the strength in her body. When she opens it again, Tina's leg is mangled. That will serve Tina right for being an ugly slob. Next, Adel opens a large pair of pliers, grasps Tina's face between its jaws, and squeezes for all she's worth. Button eyes pop out on to the floor, and what was once smooth is torn and gouged. That will teach her to walk alone in Prospect Park. Then the sharp knife. It goes into Tina's plastic belly more readily than Adel would have imagined. That will stop her from being such a cunt.

It doesn't take more than a minute to shred Tina's dress with the kitchen scissors. A whore shouldn't wear nice clothes.

She places what's left of Tina just inside the door of Kayla's room and returns to her own bed. The frenzy passed, she falls asleep and forgets what she's done.

CHAPTER 119

We walked back to our apartment mostly in silence. At one street, Kayla almost stepped out into the path of a speeding car trying to make the light, and I grabbed her hand to hold her back. She smiled and thanked me, then let me continue to hold her hand for another block until she gently pulled it away. I did not want to let go. I felt in a much larger sense Kayla was pulling away, had already pulled away, and I didn't understand how that could've happened.

When we got back, I asked if we could talk. Mom and Dad were out somewhere, so we had the place to ourselves. We sat in our living room, the Steinway lurking as the only witness.

"Okay, Max, what is it you want to talk about? My piano career that's ending, the new life growing inside me, the *Chabad*, or my doll, which I know you destroyed?"

At first, I couldn't believe my ears. She thought I was the one who hurt Tina, when I was just as shocked as Kayla to see her mutilated doll. I assumed she accused me now because she was disturbed, and I had to fight to keep my voice calm. "I didn't do anything to Tina, Kayla. I don't know who did, but it wasn't me. Please believe me."

"I don't know. The way you stared and stared that morning, watching me cry. I'll never forget."

"I was perplexed. Yes, I was watching, staring maybe is the right word, and I was trying to figure out what happened. Did you think I was gloating?"

"Maybe. I know too that once before you'd gone into my room, hadn't you? I mean, without me there?"

I turned red. "Yes, a very long time ago. Twice, in fact. I'm so sorry. I knew it was wrong and stopped. But, I was ... how did you know?"

"I could always tell when my things were put away wrong, Mom moving things around when she tried to clean. But she never bothered with my little diary. It had to be you. And I could sense your guilt, too."

"Why didn't you say anything to me, then?"

"And what? Scold you? My big brother? I didn't want to start a fight. I worshiped you, Max. I wanted to be just like you. I wanted to play the piano because you did. I just hoped you'd stop invading my privacy, and you did."

"Can you forgive me?"

"Of course. I forgave you then. I forgive you now. But later, when Tina ... you know ... it made me think back. You swear you didn't do it?"

"I didn't touch her."

"All right. I'll believe you, although ..."

"Although?"

"I hate to think who did."

"Yeah, either Mom or Dad, and that's even worse." We looked at each other in silent contemplation of the truth. We both understood then, without needing to say anything, the evil-doer had to have been Mom.

"So tell me what you want to talk about."

"What I can do to be the brother you deserve."

"Be there for me, but don't try to change me. Accept me for who I am, and who I'm becoming."

"And who are you becoming, Kayla?"

"I won't be a concert pianist any more. I can see that the drugs I need make me too shaky. And I couldn't possibly focus on practice as I'd need to. So, you have to accept the end of my performing career."

"Maybe, in time, there'll be better meds that don't have the same ..."

"Max. Listen to me, please, for once. Just listen. I know what I can do and what I can't do. It's the fear, as well. The audience watching me on the stage will always be there, looking at me, and I can't take it anymore. Whatever it was that set me off that night – well, even before then – won't disappear."

"I'm so sorry."

"More important is that I'm becoming a mother. This baby will be everything to me. I love him already. This baby will be my life from now on. You'll have to accept him as part of me."

"Him?"

"Don't ask me how I know. I just do. So, I need your support for my motherhood, if you will. If you want to truly know me down the road, that's what I need. If you want to shelter me when I need sheltering, I need you to support me now."

"And August?"

"I love him, but I love this baby more. And now that it's clear I can't perform with August ... well, I'm getting ready to say goodbye to him. Sure, he'll always be my son's father, but my life is heading in a different direction. August and I weren't meant for a life together."

"But ..."

"Max, there's one thing I will insist upon. You must not be angry with me for what I've done. Getting pregnant. You don't have that right. Do you understand?"

It would take me time to understand, but all the same I agreed with her on the spot. It would take me time to let the anger slowly seep out of me, but I knew I had to let it go. "Yes. You have my word."

She smiled for the first time during this conversation. I said the right thing. "Now, the last thing about who I'm becoming has to do with *Chabad*. This will be the most difficult thing for you, but hear me out, please."

"Go ahead."

"There's a concept of *baal'at t-shuva* I'm learning about. I discussed it briefly with Rabbi Berenbaum just now. It means a woman who's returning to Judaism. I want to be that woman."

"You've always been Jewish."

"What I mean is Jewish observance, Jewish on the inside, fully, completely, deeply Jewish. You know, when we were kids, and Mom and Dad had us walking to synagogue on *Shabbat*, you hated it, and Mom and Dad hated it, and why they kept it up for years I'll never know. But, you see, for me it was different. It meant something magical for me, but I was too young to grasp it, and then our home life wasn't terribly Jewish. And it all got swept away by the piano and what I could accomplish in music."

"I'm listening."

"I don't know what drew me to *Chabad* at first, but it rekindled a thirst I felt as a child, the feeling there's much more to my life than just me or even my music. It's the feeling I'm part of something so large it exceeds the universe. It's to be in league with the Creator. It's so much more important than what happens in a concert hall. I know I can't convince you about *Hashem*. I wouldn't try to, because believing has to come from within. For me, over the last few months, turning my life in this direction has become an obvious choice."

She got up from her chair, sat at the piano, and played the same Chopin Mazurka she performed as her encore at the Town Hall debut. I listened, transfixed. Drugs or not, she could still play. At least in our apartment, where she felt safe. When she finished, she turned toward me and asked, "Is any of this making sense?"

"You're returning to our Jewish roots because you need a refuge from the demons chasing you and from the pressure of being a concert pianist. Is that close?"

She laughed, not offended by the way I'd phrased things. "Well, not exactly. But, you know, Jewish roots have a lot to do with it. I think often about Dad's sisters. I wonder what kind of life they might have led if they hadn't been lost in the Holocaust."

"So in part it's because of Ada and Kal Covo?" Of course, Kayla didn't know then what we would learn seven years later.

"No, that's not it either. Or maybe it is. But at *Chabad*, especially during the couple of days when I was hiding, I felt that there is a way forward for me with my life. I intend to become as observant as I can be."

"Someone else, the *rebbe*, will make the rules for you, is what you're saying. You're giving up a large measure of your freedom to think and be rational." I hated myself as soon as I said all that and expected her to take issue, be offended, but was wrong again, as I'd been wrong so many times.

She smiled, came over to hug me, and said, "Yes, in large part that's right. You're starting to understand. I think giving up that so-called freedom is a small price to pay for happiness, don't you?"

CHAPTER 120

With Kayla having more or less moved out of the apartment – and it no longer being necessary to follow her around the country as she performed – there's suddenly a large void that's opened in Nicky's life. The void is accentuated by Max's decreasing presence in the household.

Max is self-sufficient, back hard at his studies, starting to date a girl from Bellington no less, and doesn't need much of Nicky's time. Nicky almost has to beg Max to go with him to the Knicks playoff game against the Nets, but finally Max and Cathy, the new girlfriend, find a way to accept the invitation. The game should be fun. It isn't much fun for Nicky, though. Max and Cathy spend the entire time talking to each other, paying no attention to the Knick's victory. They are completely oblivious to the forty points poured in by Bernard King. They're almost oblivious to Nicky's presence. For reasons he can't put his finger on, Cathy reminds Nicky of Kayla.

And Adel is jittery, as always, but she hasn't been seeing a burning building across the street for a while, hasn't been rhyming as much, and more frequently walks in the park to see the birds. There have been no more excursions to Brooklyn. Maybe the latest round of new drugs is working. She still cooks, but usually just for herself and Nicky. She still smokes. She still drinks chamomile tea. She still talks about Jackie Robinson, but now also talks about the unborn baby, whom she's named

Jackie in honor of her hero. Adel doesn't realize that it's not her call to make, but Kayla happily acquiesces.

So Nicky returns to his practice with a passion he hasn't achieved for years. His patients benefit. But guilt – which lies just below consciousness – plagues him constantly. He represses a desire to confess, about what he can't say, and to whom he can't possibly imagine.

CHAPTER 121

That's most of the story. I hope you haven't skipped anything, assuming I've actually sent this to you. I think I will.

Of course, Mom had everything to do with naming the baby. As soon as Kayla told everyone she was sure was carrying a boy, Mom referred to the unborn child as Jackie. Kayla might have chosen otherwise if left to her own resources, but that was one way in which she still wanted to please Mom.

As I should've expected, Rabbi Berenbaum offered to Kayla move into the *Chabad* on a full-time basis during her pregnancy and stay there as well for a few months after the baby arrived. The *Chabad* congregants, under his wife's supervision, would look after Kayla and, when the time came, her baby too. And that's what happened. Berenbaum gave Kayla a room at the *Chabad*, converting an unused classroom to a little bedroom with a cot and a second-hand crib. When Kayla delivered Jackie, your cousin, they both had a place to stay and many friends who helped care for them for the first few months of Jackie's life.

We wondered what Kayla would do then, when *Chabad* decided that it was time for Kayla and Jackie to move out. We knew she'd return to our home, but we worried about how a mentally ill woman, barely seventeen, someone who might fly into hysterics at a passing shadow, would take care of an infant on her own. Somehow, we all pitched in and managed. I learned how to change diapers. And we accepted Kayla's becoming *baal'at t-shuva* – her term for someone returning to observant Judaism. No. We did more than accept. We supported. As I'm sure you've been reminded by your mother, Kayla has stayed strongly observant ever since.

August dropped Kayla and Jackie immediately. He was too damn busy to have anything to do with his son or with the girl whom he claimed to have loved. Well, maybe it didn't help when I found him again outside Bellington one day not long after Kayla decided to keep his baby and knocked him down hard on the pavement. Fortunately for him, he didn't break any fingers and just had some skin scraped off an elbow. He wouldn't fight me, and, once he was down, I didn't feel like kicking him although I was in a position to put my shoe through his skull. I just told him again he was a fucking asshole and walked away.

Even though I'd roughed him up, August didn't at the time seem to hold it against Kayla. He sent money to Dad for a while to help with Kayla's expenses, but his support stopped quickly after a year. Kayla didn't want to pursue him and didn't feel Jackie needed him as a father figure. She just would say, "August gave me everything I wanted. There he is." And she'd point to Jackie. Then the asshole showed up again, trying to get custody. Out of spite, I think. What a horrible mess, for Jackie and for the entire family, but that's a whole other story. We almost lost Jackie, but I'll give you the details, if you want them, in person. Too much and too anguished for this letter. So, to finish with August, I followed his career for a while – probably wanting to see him fail – but then got bored. He's still performing, has gone through a bunch of accompanists. He's reputed to be difficult to work with, and, when you read his bio on-line, there's no mention of Kayla and no indication he has a son. Just as well.

I'm sorry you kids never got to know your grandmother before she died. I can't say that her heart attack took anyone by surprise, what with her continued smoking and diabetes from the drugs we had to keep her on. But making it to age fifty-three with schizophrenia is pretty good. My mom outlived her life expectancy. She managed a family and, for the longest time, took good care of us. Dad was devastated when she passed on, and for months we could hear him saying her name softly, as if talking to her in her grave.

As for me, just try to imagine how hard it is when the woman you marry falls in love with someone else and disappears with your one-year-old twins to the other side of the country. Your mother and I married too young for sure.

So now you know what you need to know, and I'll bring this to a close. You're finally coming to spend several weeks with me this June, and everyone here eagerly awaits your arrival. One tiny logistical issue: My house in New Jersey has four bedrooms. I have one, Kayla has one, and Jackie has one. You guys will have to share the fourth.

Love, Dad.

EPILOGUE

West Caldwell, New Jersey, June 1999

He shuts off the light in his office and listens. In the early morning hours, their house is quiet. His sister and nephew and his two young teenage children sleep in the three nearby bedrooms. Joseph has naturally elected to use a sleeping bag on the floor rather than share a double bed with his sister.

Max finds his favorite CD and sets it playing through his computer. He listens to the music through headphones. It would not do to let the music be heard anywhere else in the house and disturb the peace of the night. He knows every nuance of Kayla's performance on this CD. He knows that the first selection, Chopin's C Minor Nocturne, will start in *sotto voce* but *crescendo* in its mid-section with frenetic octaves before retreating into near nothingness at its end. The music floods through every cell of his body, lifting him higher and higher. He feels his body craving more, but the Nocturne ends too soon. Chopin's B-Flat Minor Sonata is next. He immerses himself in Kayla's rendering, ready to be swept away.

He knows that no other artist but Kayla could have touched him so deeply.

ACKNOWLEDGEMENTS

The Music Stalker has been in various stages of development since at least 2014. It would be impossible to remember everyone who, at one time or another, looked at a draft and commented. I thank them all profoundly from the depths of my heart. And yet, a few people stand out.

First, I thank Fred Leebron and my fellow participants in the 2014 Tinker Mountain Writer's Conference novel workshop, where twenty pages of the first draft benefited from the light of close, honest scrutiny. Their encouraging comments helped keep this project alive.

Second, I thank Gary Glass, a fellow workshop participant at the 2015 Colgate Writer's Conference, for his review of a later draft of the entire manuscript. I carefully reviewed Gary's thoughtful criticisms before moving forward.

Third, I thank Don Greenfield, a music teacher, who reviewed a very late draft. Don spotted numerous errors, which I was embarrassed to have made and happy to correct.

Fourth, I thank *The Raven's Perch*, which published an earlier version of Chapter 13 as "In the Eye of the Storm" in its October 14, 2018 edition.

Finally, I thank my very patient, loving, and understanding family, without which there would be no point in writing

ABOUT THE AUTHOR

Following a 40-year career as a trial attorney in Washington, DC., Bruce J. Berger turned fulltime to writing, earned a M.F.A. in Creative Writing from American University, and now teaches there. His first novel, *The Flight of the Veil*, is a sequel to *The Music Stalker* and achieved critical success, winning a Bronze Award in General Fiction from Illumination Christian Book Awards. *Kirkus Reviews* called *The Flight of the Veil* "A well-crafted tale about trauma and miracles. Get it." He has also published more than 50 stories and poems in a wide variety of literary journals.

NOTE FROM THE AUTHOR

Word-of-mouth is crucial for any author to succeed. If you enjoyed *The Music Stalker*, please leave a review online—anywhere you are able. Even if it's just a sentence or two. It would make all the difference and would be very much appreciated.

Thanks!
Bruce J. Berger

CPSIA information can be obtained
at www.ICGtesting.com
Printed in the USA
BVHW071059060821
612958BV00001B/2